STREET TALK-1

HOW TO SPEAK & UNDERSTAND AMERICAN SLANG

STREET TALK-1

HOW TO SPEAK & UNDERSTAND
AMERICAN SLANG

DAVID BURKE

OPTIMA BOOKS
Berkeley, California

Front Cover Illustration: Paul Jermann
Back Cover Illustration: Dave Jeno
Inside Illustrations: Shawn Murphy

Optima Books
2820 Eighth Street
Berkeley, California 94710

ISBN 1-879440-00-8
Library of Congress Catalog Card Number 92-149368

Printed in the United States of America
Seventh Printing 2000

This book is dedicated to my little niece Tessa who's totally…
rad, unreal, mind-blowing, drop-dead gorgeous, out of this world,
a ten, a fox, a killer chick, a stunner, a knock-out, a total babe!

preface

Recently, I went to the movies with a French friend of mine named Pascale, who had been studying English for ten years. While we were waiting in line, Pascale's co-worker, Steve, approached him and said,

"Hey, Pascale! What's up?"

To me, this was a completely normal question and I was waiting to hear how he was going to reply. Instead, he looked confused, paused a moment, then cautiously stepped back and looked up. Amused, I rephrased the question for him to make things a little clearer. But Steve didn't stop there and kept right on firing away unmercifully,

*"I couldn't **get over** how **what's-'er-face** got all **bent outta shape** yesterday and **read me the riot act** jus' 'cause I **showed up** a few minutes late ta work. **Man, gimme a break! Betcha** never saw anyone get **so ticked off** 'n **freak out** like that b'fore, huh?"*

Pascale was obviously stunned and didn't know whether to answer "yes," "no," or to give Steve the correct time. After all his years of English study, there were two things he had never learned: *how* we speak–colloquialisms; and *what* we speak–slang.

Colloquialisms cover the extensive array of contractions, pronunciations, and common usage characteristic of all native speakers of American-English. For example, any student of English would undoubtedly understand the following phrase:

"I am going to get upset if he does not quit what he is doing and stop bothering me!"

However, it is more likely to be pronounced like this:

I'm gonna ged upsed if 'e duz'n quit what 'e's doin' 'n stop botherin' me!

Slang encompasses "secret" words and idioms that are consistently used in books, magazines, television, movies, songs, American homes, etc. and generally are reserved only for native speakers. The example above demonstrates how this phase would be spoken by a native; but a native speaker would most likely use slang words in place of the conventional words:

*I am going to **freak out** if he does not **knock it off** and stop **bugging** me!"*

And now, after adding the colloquial contractions, here is our final result:

*I'm gonna **freak oud** if 'e duz'n **knock id off** 'n stop **buggin'** me!*

For the non-native speaker, learning the information in **STREET TALK -1** will equal years of living in America and eliminate the usual time it takes to absorb the intricacies of slang and colloquialisms.

For the American, you're in for a treat as we explore the evolution and variations of some of the most common hilarious expressions and slang terms handed down to us through the years.

STREET TALK -1 is a self-teaching guide divided into five parts:

- **DIALOGUE**

  Twenty to thirty new American expressions and terms (indicated in boldface) are presented as they may be heard in an actual conversation. A translation of the dialogue in standard English is always given on the opposite page followed by an important phonetic version of the dialogue as it would actually be spoken by an American. This page will prove vital to any non-native since, as previously demonstrated, Americans tend to rely heavily on contractions and shortcuts in pronunciation.

- **VOCABULARY**

  This section spotlights all of the slang words and expressions that were used in the dialogue and offers more examples of usage, synonyms, antonyms, and special notes.

- **PRACTICE THE VOCABULARY**

  These word games include all of the new terms and idioms previously learned and will help you to test yourself on your comprehension. (The pages providing the answers to all the drills are indicated at the beginning of this section.)

- **A CLOSER LOOK**

  This section offers the reader a unique look at common words used in slang expressions pertaining to a specific category such as *Body Parts, Proper Names, Numbers, Colors, etc.* A short drill is then presented in preparation for the final section.

- **JUST FOR FUN**

  Here, the reader is offered an entertaining monologue containing many of the words from the same category as previously introduced. This section will surely prove to be hilarious for any native-speaker since it demonstrates the unlimited creativity of our own language.

If you have always prided yourself on being fluent in English, you will undoubtedly be surprised and amused to encounter a whole new world of phrases usually hidden away in the American-English language and usually reserved only for the native speaker…*until now!*

David Burke
Author

NOTE

Slang falls into two very separate categories: suitable and proper as well as obscene and vulgar. In order to be truly fluent in any language, these two groups *must* be learned. **STREET TALK -1** focuses primarily on slang which is very acceptable and commonly used by everyone, and will only explore vulgarisms as far as translating some popular euphemisms created from vulgar expressions.

For a close look at the extremely popular yet forbidden language of obscenities and vulgarisms, refer to: **BLEEP!** - *A Guide to Popular American Obscenities* by David Burke. (See the coupon on the back page for details.)

acknowledgments

I can't thank my family enough for putting up with my incessant questions and brain-picking, my nonstop enthusiasm, and my constant note-taking at the dinner table every time someone says something in slang.

A truly heartfelt and special thanks goes to my best friend, confidant, and shoulder who has always been the driving force behind my perseverance and excitement in everything I do; my mother.

I am very grateful to three of my favorite people on the planet, Janet Graul, Susan Graul and Debbie Wright for making the copy-editing phase of the book such a pleasure.

I owe a special debt of gratitude to Ellen Ross of B. Dalton Booksellers who tolerated my constant phone calls for advice.

legend

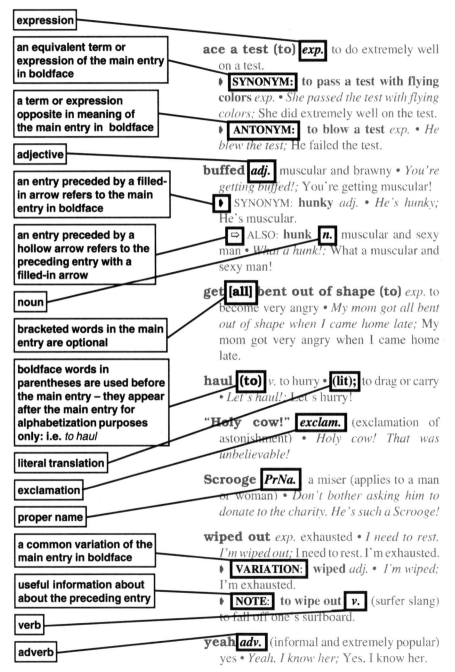

expression

an equivalent term or expression of the main entry in boldface

a term or expression opposite in meaning of the main entry in boldface

adjective

an entry preceded by a filled-in arrow refers to the main entry in boldface

an entry preceded by a hollow arrow refers to the preceding entry with a filled-in arrow

noun

bracketed words in the main entry are optional

boldface words in parentheses are used before the main entry – they appear after the main entry for alphabetization purposes only: i.e. *to haul*

literal translation

exclamation

proper name

a common variation of the main entry in boldface

useful information about about the preceding entry

verb

adverb

ace a test (to) *exp.* to do extremely well on a test.
 ‣ **SYNONYM:** to pass a test with flying colors *exp.* • *She passed the test with flying colors;* She did extremely well on the test.
 ‣ **ANTONYM:** to blow a test *exp.* • *He blew the test;* He failed the test.

buffed *adj.* muscular and brawny • *You're getting buffed!;* You're getting muscular!
 ‣ SYNONYM: **hunky** *adj.* • *He's hunky;* He's muscular.
 ⇨ ALSO: **hunk** *n.* muscular and sexy man • *What a hunk!;* What a muscular and sexy man!

get [all] bent out of shape (to) *exp.* to become very angry • *My mom got all bent out of shape when I came home late;* My mom got very angry when I came home late.

haul (to) *v.* to hurry • **(lit);** to drag or carry • *Let's haul!;* Let's hurry!

"Holy cow!" *exclam.* (exclamation of astonishment) • *Holy cow! That was unbelievable!*

Scrooge *PrNa.* a miser (applies to a man or woman) • *Don't bother asking him to donate to the charity. He's such a Scrooge!*

wiped out *exp.* exhausted • *I need to rest. I'm wiped out;* I need to rest. I'm exhausted.
 ‣ **VARIATION:** wiped *adj.* • *I'm wiped;* I'm exhausted.
 ‣ **NOTE:** to wipe out *v.* (surfer slang) to fall off one's surfboard.

yeah *adv.* (informal and extremely popular) yes • *Yeah, I know her;* Yes, I know her.

contents

At School

Dialogue In Slang

At School...

*Anne joins Peggy, who seems totally **out of it**.*

Anne:	You seem really **ticked off. What's up**?
Peggy:	Just **get out of my face**, would you?!
Anne:	**Chill out! What's eating you**, anyway?
Peggy:	Sorry. It's just that I think I **blew** the **final** and now my parents are going to get all **bent out of shape**. I **like** totally **drew a blank** on everything!
Anne:	Well, now you're really going to **freak out** when I tell you who **aced** it... **what's-her-face**... the one who always **kisses up** to the teacher.
Peggy:	Jennifer Davies? **Give me a break**! I can't **stand** her. She's such a **dweeb**! How could she possibly **ace** it when she keeps **cutting** class all the time?
Anne:	She's the **teacher's pet**, that's why. Besides, he's so **laid back** he lets her **get away with it**. She just really **rubs me the wrong way**. And you know what? I think she's got the **hots** for him, too.
Peggy:	**Get out of here**!
Anne:	I'm **dead serious**. Yesterday, before class starts, she walks up to Mr. Edward's desk and **goes**, 'Good morning, Jim.'
Peggy:	Oh, **gag me**! She's totally **gross**!

Translation of dialogue in standard English

At School...

*Anne joins Peggy, who seems to be **in a daze**.*

Anne: You seem really **angry. What's the matter**?

Peggy: Just **leave me alone**, alright?!

Anne: **Relax! What's the matter with you**, anyway?

Peggy: Sorry. It's just that I think I **failed** the **final examination** and now my parents are going to get all **upset**. I, **uh, couldn't think of any of the answers**!

Anne: Well, now you're really going to be **mad** when I tell you who got **100% on** it... **I forgot her name**... the one who always **flatters** the teacher.

Peggy: Jennifer Davies? **You're kidding**! I don't **like** her! She's such a **moron**! How could she possibly get **100% on** it when she's **absent from** class all the time?

Anne: She's the **teacher's favorite student**, that's why. Besides, he's so **casual** he **permits her to do it**. There's just **something about her I don't like**. And you know what? I think she **really likes** him, too.

Peggy: **You've got to be joking**!

Anne: I'm **very serious**. Yesterday, before class starts, she walks up to Mr. Edward's desk and **says**, 'Good morning, Jim.'

Peggy: Oh, **that makes me sick**! She's totally **disgusting**!

Dialogue in slang as it would be heard

At School...

*Anne joins Peggy, who seems todally **oud of it***.

Anne: You seem really **tict off. What's up?**

Peggy: Jus' **ged oudda my face**, would ja?!

Anne: **Chill out! What's eatin' you**, anyway?

Peggy: Sorry. It's jus' thad I think I **blew** the **final'**n now my parents'r gonna ged all **ben' oudda shape**. I **like** todally **drew a blank** on ev'rything!

Anne: Well, now yer really gonna **freak out** when I tell ya who **aced** it... **what's-'er face**... the one who always **kisses up** ta the teacher.

Peggy: Jennifer Davies? **Gimme a break!** I can't **stand** 'er. She's such a **dweeb!** How could she possibly ace it when she keeps **cudding** class all the time?

Anne: She's the **teacher's pet**, that's why. Besides, he's so **laid back** 'e lets 'er **ged away with it**. She jus' really **rubs me the wrong way**. And ya know what? I think she's got the **hots** fer 'im, too.

Peggy: **Ged oudda here!**

Anne: I'm **dead serious**. Yesterday, before class starts, she walks up ta Mr. Edwards desk'n **goes**, 'Good morning, Jim.'

Peggy: Oh, **gag me!** She's todally **gross!**

Vocabulary

ace a test (to) *exp.* to do extremely well on a test.
⧫ SYNONYM: **to pass a test with flying colors** *exp.* • *She passed the test with flying colors;* She did extremely well on the test.
⧫ ANTONYM: **to blow a test** *exp.* • *He blew the test;* He failed the test.

blow something (to) *exp.* **1.** to fail at something • *I blew the interview;* I failed the interview • **2.** to make a big mistake • *I totally forgot my doctor's appointment. I really blew it;* I totally forgot my doctor's appointment. I really made a mistake.
⧫ SYNONYM: **to goof up something** *exp.* **1.** to make a big mistake • *I forgot to pick her up at the airport! I really goofed up;* I forgot to pick her up at the airport! I really made a mistake • **2.** to hurt oneself • *I goofed up my leg skiing;* I hurt my leg skiing.

chill out (to) *exp.* to calm down.
⧫ NOTE: This expression is commonly shortened to *"Chill!"* On the East Coast, a common variation of this expression is *"to take a chill pill."*
⧫ SYNONYM: **to mellow out** *exp.* • *Don't be so upset about it! Mellow out!;* Don't be so upset about it! Calm down!
⧫ ANTONYM: See - **freak out (to).**

cut class (to) *exp.* to be absent from class without permission.
⧫ SYNONYM (1): **to ditch (a) class** *exp.* • *I'm going to ditch (my) class today;* I'm not going to attend (my) class today.
⧫ SYNONYM (2): **to play hooky** *exp.* • *That's the second time this week he's played hooky;* That's the second time this week he hasn't attended class.
⇨ NOTE: This expression is rarely, if ever, used by younger people. It is much more common among older generations.

dead serious (to be) *exp.* to be extremely serious.
⧫ NOTE: The adjective *"dead"* is commonly used to mean "extremely," "absolutely," or "directly" in the following expressions only:

dead ahead; directly ahead.	*dead right;* absolutely correct.
dead drunk; extremely drunk.	*dead set;* completely decided.
dead last; absolutely last.	*dead tired;* extremely tired.
dead on; absolutely correct.	*dead wrong;* absolutely wrong.

This usage of *dead* would be incorrect in other expressions. For example: *dead happy, dead hungry, dead angry, etc.* are all incorrect expressions.

draw a blank (to) *exp.* to forget suddenly.

◆ SYNONYM: **to blank [out]** *v.* • *I can't believe how I blanked [out] on her name!;* I can't believe how I suddenly forgot her name!

◆ ANTONYM: **to get it** *exp.* **1.** to remember suddenly • *I don't remember the answer. Let me think... I got it!;* I don't remember the answer. Let me think... I suddenly remember! • **2.** to get a sudden idea • *I wonder what we should do today. I got it!;* I wonder what we should do today. I've got an idea! • **3.** to understand • *Now I get it;* Now I understand.

dweeb *n.* moron, simpleton.

◆ NOTE: This is an extremely common noun used mainly by young people.

◆ SYNONYM: **geek** *adj.* • *What a geek!;* What an idiot!

eat (to) *v.* to upset, to anger • *What's eating you today?;* What's upsetting you today?

◆ VARIATION: **to eat up** *exp.* **1.** to upset • *Seeing how unfairly she's being treated just eats me up;* Seeing how unfairly she is being treated really upsets me. • **2.** to enjoy • *He's eating up all the praise he's getting;* He's enjoying the praise he's getting.

final *n.* This is a very popular abbreviation for *"final examination"* which can also be contracted to *"final exam."*

freak out (to) *exp.* **1.** to lose control of one's emotional state, to become very upset and irrational • **2.** to lose grasp of reality temporarily due to drugs.

◆ NOTE: This is an extremely popular expression used by younger people. This expression is also commonly heard in its abbreviated form *"to freak."* • *If he doesn't arrive in five minutes, I'm going to freak;* If he doesn't arrive in five minutes, I'm going to be very upset.

◆ SYNONYM: **to flip out** *exp.* • *If he doesn't arrive in five minutes, I'm going to flip out;* If he doesn't arrive in five minutes, I'm going to be very upset.

⇨ NOTE: This may also be used in reference to drugs.

◆ ANTONYM (1): **to keep one's cool** *exp.* to stay calm, composed • *My mom kept her cool when I told her I destroyed the car;* My mom stayed calm when I told her I destroyed the car.

◆ ANTONYM (2): See - **chill out (to).**

"Gag me!" *exp.* "That makes me sick!"

◆ NOTE: This is a common expression used mainly by younger people, especially teenagers, to signify great displeasure. This expression is considered "valley talk" as it was called in a popular song in the late 1980's called "Valley Girls." The same song also introduced the now out-dated expression, *"Gag me with a spoon!";* That makes me sick! The expression *"Gag me with a spoon!"* is still occasionally heard, but only in jest.

▶ SYNONYM: **"Gross me out!"** *exp.* • *Susan and Bob are going together?! Gross me out!;* Susan and Bob are dating?! That makes me sick!

get [all] bent out of shape (to) *exp.* to become very angry • *My mom got all bent out of shape when I came home late;* My mom got very angry when I came home late.

▶ SYNONYM: **to fly off the handle** *exp.* • *My dad flew off the handle when I wrecked the car;* My dad got really angry when I wrecked the car.

get away with something (to) *exp.* to succeed at doing something dishonest • *He got away with cheating on the test;* He succeeded at cheating on the test.

▶ NOTE: **to get away with murder** *exp.* (very popular) to succeed at being dishonest • *He got away with cheating on the test?! He gets away with murder!* He succeeded at cheating on the test?! He never gets caught!

▶ SYNONYM: **to pull something off** *exp.* to succeed at doing something very difficult but not necessarily dishonest • *"He actually aced the test?" "Yes! He really pulled it off!";* "He actually passed the test?" "Yes! He really succeeded!" • *He pulled off a bank job;* He succeeded at robbing a bank.

▶ ANTONYM: **to get busted** *exp.* to get caught doing something dishonest • *The teacher finally saw him cheating on the test. I knew he'd get busted sooner or later;* The teacher finally saw him cheating on the test. I knew he'd get caught sooner or later.

"Get out of here!" *exp.* 1. "You're kidding!" • 2. "Absolutely not!" • *Is that your girlfriend?" "Get outta here!";* "Is that your girlfriend?" "Absolutely not!"

▶ NOTE (1): This expression, commonly seen as *"Get outta here"* [pronounced: *Ged oudda here*], may be used upon hearing bad news as well as good news • *"I just heard that John's dog got killed." "Get outta here!";* "I just heard that John's dog got killed." "You're kidding! (That's awful!)" • *"I just aced the test!" "Get outta here!";* "I just passed the test!" "You're kidding! (That's terrific!)"

▶ NOTE (2): A common variation of this expression is simply, *"Get out!"* which is also used upon hearing bad news as well as good news. On occasion, you may even hear the expression playfully lenthened to *"Get outta town!"*

▶ SYNONYM: **"No way!"** *exp.* 1. (in surprise and excitement) *"I won a trip to Europe!" "No way!";* "I won a trip to Europe!" "You're kidding!" • 2. (in disbelief) *"I won a trip to Europe!" "No way!";* "I won a trip to Europe!" "I don't believe you!" • 3. (to emphasize "no") *"Do you like her?" "No way!";* "Do you like her?" "Absolutely not!"

⇨ NOTE (1): The difference between **1.** and **2.** depends on the delivery of the speaker)

⇨ NOTE (2): Although the opposite would certainly be logical, the expression, *"Yes way!"* is not really correct, although on occasion you may actually hear it as a witty response to *"No way!"*

⇨ NOTE (3): The most common response to *"No way!"* used by teenagers has recently become *"Way!"*

get out of someone's face (to) *exp.* to leave someone alone • *Get outta my face! I'm busy!;* Leave me alone! I'm busy!

♦ SYNONYM: **to get lost** *exp.* • *Get lost!;* Leave me alone!

♦ ANTONYM: **to hang [out] with someone** *exp.* to spend time with someone (and do nothing in particular) • *I'm going to hang [out] with Debbie today;* I'm going to spend time with Debbie today.

⇨ NOTE (1): A common shortened version of this expression is *"to hang with someone."*

⇨ NOTE (2): The expression *"to hang (out)"* is commonly used to mean, "to do nothing in particular" • *Why don't you go without me? I'm just going to stay here and hang (out) today;* Why don't you go without me? I'm just going to stay here and do nothing in particular.

give someone a break (to) *exp.* **1.** This popular expression is commonly used to indicate annoyance and disbelief. It could best be translated as, "You're kidding!" The expression, *"Give me a break,"* commonly pronounced, *"Gimme a break,"* is very similar to the expression *"Get outta here!"* The significant difference is that *"Get outta here!"* may be used to indicate excitement as well as disbelief, as previously demonstrated. However, *"Gimme a break!"* is *only* used to indicate disbelief. Therefore, if someone were to give you a piece of good news and you were to respond by saying, *"Gimme a break,"* this would indicate that you did not believe a word he/she was saying. **2.** to do someone a favor • *Please, gimme a break and let me take the test again;* Please, do me a favor and let me take the test again • **3.** to give someone an opportunity for success • *I gave him his first big break at becoming an actor;* I gave him his first big opportunity at becoming an actor • **4.** to be merciful with someone • *Since this is your first offense, I'm going to give you a break;* Since this is your first offense, I'm going to be merciful with you.

go (to) *v.* to say • *So, I told the policeman that my speedometer was broken and he goes, 'Gimme a break!';* So, I told the policeman that my speedometer was broken and he says, 'I don't believe a word you're saying!'

♦ NOTE (1): This usage of the verb *"to go"* is extremely common among younger people. You'll probably encounter it within your first few hours in America!

♦ NOTE (2): Although not as popular, you may occasionally hear this term used in the past tense • *So, I told the policeman that my speedometer was broken and he went, 'Gimme a break!';* So, I told the policeman that my speedometer was broken and he said, 'I don't believe a word you're saying!'

♦ NOTE (3): In colloquial American English, it is very common to use the present tense to indicate an event that took place in the past as demonstrated in the dialogue: *Yesterday, before class starts, she walks up to Mr. Edward's desk and goes, 'Good Morning, Jim;'* Yesterday, before class started, she walked up to Mr. Edward's desk and said, 'Good Morning, Jim.'

♦ SYNONYM (1): **to be all** *exp.* • *So, I go up to her and tell her how great she looks since she's lost all that weight and she's all, 'Stop teasing me!';* So, I go up to her and tell her how great she looks since she's lost all that weight and she says, 'Stop teasing me!

⇨ NOTE: This is extremely popular among the younger generations only.

♦ SYNONYM (2): **to be like** *exp.* • *I said hello to her yesterday and she's like, 'Leave me alone!';* I said hello to her yesterday and she said, 'Leave me alone!'

⇨ NOTE (1): This is extremely popular among the younger generations only.

⇨ NOTE (2): These two expressions *"to be all"* and *"to be like,"* are commonly combined: *I walked up to her and she's all like, 'Get outta here!"* • *I walked up to her and she's like all, 'Get outta here!"*

gross (to be) *adj.* to be disgusting • *I'm not eating that! It looks gross!;* I'm not eating that! It looks disgusting!

♦ NOTE: This was created from the adjective "grotesque."

hots for someone (to have the) *exp.* to be interested sexually in someone.

♦ SYNONYM: **to be turned on by someone** *exp.*

⇨ NOTE: It is rare to hear this expression used as *"I'm turned on by her."* It is much more common to hear *"She turns me on."*

⇨ ALSO (1): *Math really turns me on;* I really like math. • *Math is a real turn on/off!;* Math is really exciting/unappealing!

⇨ ALSO (2): *She's a real turn on/off!;* She's very sexy/unappealing!

♦ ALSO: **to be hot** *exp.* to be good looking and sexy • *He's hot!;* He's sexy!

kiss up to someone (to) *exp.* to flatter someone in order to obtain something.

♦ SYNONYM: **to butter someone up** *exp.* • *Stop trying to butter him up!;* Stop trying to flatter him!

♦ ANTONYM: **to put someone down** *exp.* to criticize someone • *Why do you always put me down?;* Why do you always criticize me?

laid back *exp.* calm.

◗ SYNONYM: **easygoing** *adj.* • *She's very easygoing;* She's very calm about everything.

◗ ALSO: **to take it easy** *exp.* **1.** to relax • *I'm going to take it easy all day at the beach;* I'm going to relax all day at the beach • **2.** to calm down • *Don't get so upset! Take it easy!;* Don't get so upset! Calm down! • **3.** to be gentle or careful • *Take it easy driving around those curves!;* Be careful driving around those curves!

◗ ANTONYM: **uptight** *adj.* tense • *She's always so uptight;* She's always so tense.

like *exp.* This is an extremely popular expression used by younger people. It could best be translated as, "how should I put this…" or "uh…" • *He's like really weird;* He's, uh… really weird.

out of it (to be) *exp.* to be in a daze.

◗ SYNONYM: **to be spaced out** *exp.* • *You look really spaced out;* You look really dazed.

◗ ANTONYM: **to have it together** *exp.* to have control of one's emotions • *I think I've got it together now;* I think I'm in control of my emotions now.

◗ ALSO: **to pull it together** *exp.* **1.** to regain control of one's emotions • *After her scare, she needs some time to pull together before she can go back on stage;* After her scare, she needs some time to regain control of her emotions before she can go back on stage. • **2.** to get ready • *I was just asked to make a presentation at work tomorrow, but I don't don't think I'll have time to pull it together;* I was just asked to make a presentation at work tomorrow, but I don't think I'll have time to get ready.

rub the wrong way (to) *exp.* to irritate.

◗ SYNONYM: **to get on someone's nerves** *exp.* • *She gets on my nerves;* She irritates me.

◗ ANTONYM: **to sweep off one's feet** *exp.* to charm someone • *He swept us all off our feet;* He charmed us all.

◗ NOTE: This expression comes from rubbing an animal in the opposite direction of his coat causing him to bristle.

teacher's pet *exp.* the teacher's favorite student • *She never gets in trouble for not doing her homework because she's the teacher's pet;* She never gets in trouble for not doing her homework because she's the teacher's favorite.

ticked [off] (to be) *exp.* (extremely popular) to be angry.

◗ SYNONYM: **to be pissed [off]** *exp.* (extremely popular).

⇨ NOTE: Although having absolutely nothing to do with urinating, some people consider this expression to be vulgar since it comes from the slang verb *"to piss"* meaning "to urinate," a most definitely vulgar expression. The expression *"to be pissed off"* is commonly heard in an abbreviated form: *"to be P.O.'d"* • *She looks really P.O.'d about something!;* She looks really angry about something!

▸ SEE: A Closer Look (2): *Commonly Used Initials,* p. 24.

unable to stand someone or something (to be) *exp.* to be unable to tolerate someone or something • *I just can't stand it anymore!;* I just can't tolerate it anymore!

▸ SYNONYM: **to be unable to handle someone or something** *exp.* • *I can't handle doing homework anymore;* I can't tolerate doing homework anymore.

▸ ANTONYM: **to take someone or something** *exp. I can usually only take her for an hour;* I can usually only tolerate her for an hour.

what's-her-face *exp.* [pronounced: *what's-'er-face*] This expression is commonly used as a replacement for a woman's name when the speaker can not remember it.

▸ SYNONYM: **what's-her-name** *exp.* [pronounced: *what's-'er-name*]

▸ NOTE: The common replacement for a man's name is *"what's-his-face"* [pronounced: *what's-'is-face*] or *"what's-his-name"* [pronounced: *what's-'is-name*] whereas for an object, it would be *"what-cha-macallit"* ("what you may call it") i.e. *Give me that what-cha-macallit;* Give me that thing.

"What's eating you?" *exp.* "What's the matter with you?"

▸ SYNONYM: **"What's with you?"** *exp.*

"What's up?" *exp.* "What's happening?"

▸ SYNONYM: **"What's new?"** *exp.*

▸ NOTE: The expression *"What's up?"* is very casual and is therefore only used with good friends. It would not be considered good form to use this expression when speaking with someone with whom you have strictly a business relationship. Of course, if he/she has become a friend through your dealings, it would certainly be acceptable. Although the expression *"What's new?"* is also very casual, it does not have the same degree of familiarity as does, *"What's up?"* and may be used when addressing just about anyone except perhaps dignitaries, royalty, etc. In this case, it is usually a good idea to avoid using slang entirely, being an informal style of communication. Once again, *you* must be the judge in determining whether or not using slang is appropriate in a given situation.

Practice The Vocabulary

(Answers to Lesson 1, p. 227)

A. Underline the appropriate word that best completes the phrase.

1. Hi, Tom. What's (**up, down, over**)?

2. I don't like her. She's totally (**great, gross, greedy**)!

3. Just get outta my (**head, neck, face**)! I'm busy.

4. (**Freeze, Heat, Chill**) out! You're sure in a bad mood!

5. I think Nancy is (**chopping, cutting, dicing**) class again today.

6. I think I (**blew, inhaled, exhaled**) the test.

7. Hey, look! There's what's-'er-(**neck, arm, face**)!

8. You look really pissed (**off, in, up**).

9. Nothing bothers him. He's very laid (**back, forward, sideways**).

10. I don't like her. She really (**hits, massages, rubs**) me the wrong way.

11. I'm (**alive, sick, dead**) serious.

12. I think she's got the (**hots, warms, colds**) for him.

B. Replace the word(s) in parentheses with the slang synonym from the right column.

1. You seem really *(angry)* _____ .

2. What's *(the matter with)* _____ you?

3. She's totally *(disgusting)* _____ .

4. She's the teacher's *(favorite)* _____ .

5. What's *(happening)* _____ ?

6. I *(passed)* _____ the test!

7. Stop *(flattering)* _____ him.

8. She walked up to him and *(said)* _____ , 'Hi, Jim.'

9. Oh, *(that makes me sick)* _____ .

10. I can't *(tolerate)* _____ her.

A. **aced**

B. **ticked off**

C. **gag me**

D. **up**

E. **eating**

F. **went**

G. **pet**

H. **kissing up to**

I. **gross**

J. **stand**

C. Match the columns.

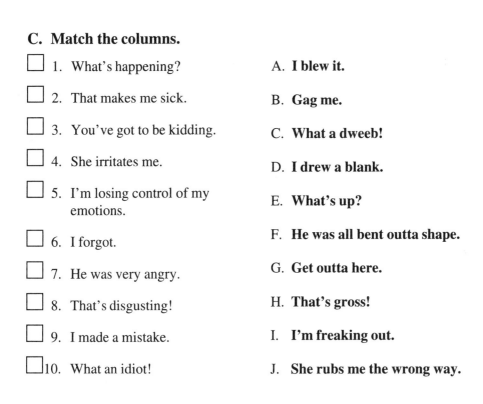

☐ 1. What's happening?

☐ 2. That makes me sick.

☐ 3. You've got to be kidding.

☐ 4. She irritates me.

☐ 5. I'm losing control of my emotions.

☐ 6. I forgot.

☐ 7. He was very angry.

☐ 8. That's disgusting!

☐ 9. I made a mistake.

☐ 10. What an idiot!

A. **I blew it.**

B. **Gag me.**

C. **What a dweeb!**

D. **I drew a blank.**

E. **What's up?**

F. **He was all bent outta shape.**

G. **Get outta here.**

H. **That's gross!**

I. **I'm freaking out.**

J. **She rubs me the wrong way.**

A CLOSER LOOK (1):
Commonly Used Contractions

One of the biggest complaints I hear from foreign students who come to America is that it always seems easier to speak than to understand. The main reason for this is the common use of contractions, which not only makes a series of words unrecognizable to the unsuspecting listener, but also speeds up the language, thereby adding to the burden of comprehension.

The following is a compilation of extremely common contractions which are all very popular and used by everyone! You will find these spelled out phonetically since they are usually only heard. However, some actually do appear routinely in novels, magazines, comic books, and other written works as well. These terms will be marked with an asterisk (*) in the following list.

Make sure you have a good grasp of these since they *will* be used consistently throughout this book because of their widespread popularity.

Standard	Common Contraction
and	*'n*
are	*'r*
are you	*ya*
because	*'cause (*)*
can	*c'n*
come	*c'm*
could have could not have	*could 'a* *couldn 'a*
did you	*didja* or *'dja*
does she	*dushi*
don't know	*dunno (*)*
for	*fer*
give me	*gimme (*)*

Example	Notes
Do you know Nancy*'n* David?	
My parents*'r* on vacation.	
Ya going to the movie? Where *ya* going?	*are you* is contracted only when followed by one or more words. Therefore, it would be incorrect to contract, *How are you?* to *How ya* unless it were followed by one or more words such as: *How ya doing?*
I don't like her *'cause* she's mean.	
I *c'n* be there in one hour.	
C'm over to our house around 9:00.	This contraction does not apply if *come* falls at the end of the sentence.
You *could 'a* hurt yourself! He *couldn 'a* done it.	This also applies to the following: should have = *should 'a* shouldn't have = *shouldn 'a* would have = *would 'a* wouldn't have = *wouldn 'a*
How *didja* do it? How *'dja* do it?	When followed by a word begining with the letter "e," or "a" *'dja* is commonly contracted to *'dj'*: Did you eat yet = **'dj'eat yet?** Did you ask her = **'dj'ask 'er?**
Dushi speak English?	
I *dunno* where you live.	
He works *fer* his father.	This also applies to the following: forgive = **fergive** • forget = **ferget**
Gimme that!	

Standard	Common Contraction
going to	***gonna (*)*** (when followed by a consonant) ***gonnu*** (when followed by a vowel)
goodbye	***g'bye***
got to	***gotta (*)*** (When followed by a consonant - pronounced: *godda*) ***gottu*** (When followed by a vowel - pronounced: *goddu*)
had better	***better***
have to	***hafta***
he	**'e**
he/she has	***he/she 'as***
her	**'er**
him	***'im***
his	**'is**
how did you	***how'dya*** or ***how'dja***

Example	Notes
I'm *gonna* give him a present. I'm *gonnu* invite her to the party.	When followed by a vowel, "going to" is commonly contracted to *gonnu,* although *gonna* is also acceptable. • SEE: got to = *gotta* or *gottu.*
I'll talk to you tomorrow. **G'bye**!	This also applies to the following: good night = **g'night**
I *gotta* give him a present I *gottu* invite her to my party.	When followed by a vowel, "got to" is commonly contracted to *gottu,* although *gotta* is also acceptable.
You *better* leave right now.	
I *hafta* go home immediately.	ALSO: (S)he *hasta/hadda*
Who is*'e*?	This does not apply if *he* begins a sentence.
He *'as* a house at the beach.	
This is *'er* house.	This does not apply if *her* begins a sentence.
I like *'im* a lot	
What's *'is* name?	This does not apply if *his* begins a sentence.
How'dya/How'dja make that?	

Standard	Common Contraction
how do you	**how'dy'a**
how does	*how's*
in front of	*in fronna*
–ing	*–in' (*)*
is that	*izat*
just	*jus'*
leave me	*lee'me*
let me	*lem'me (*)*
of	*a* or *o' (*)*
old	*ol' (*)*
or	*'r*
out of	*outta (*)* (prounounced: *oudda*)

Example	Notes
How'dy'a do it?	When pronounced as two syllables, *how'dya,* the tense changes from present to past. Although subtle, this difference is easily detected by any native-born American. *How'dya do it?* = How did you do it? *How'dy'a do it?* = How do you do it?
How's she feel today?	
He parked *in fronna* the house.	
I'm *goin'* to the store.	
Izat your new car?	ALSO: *Zat your new car?*
Jus' get it later.	
Lee'me alone!	
Lem'me have it.	
He's sort*a* strange It's made *o'* wood	Although you will occasionally see the conjunction *of* contracted to *o',* it is pronounced like *a.* Therefore, *It's made o' wood* would be pronounced, *It's made a wood.*
There's the *ol'* church.	
Do you like ice cream*'r* candy?	As you may have noticed, *'r* is a contraction not only of *are* but of *or* as well. The connotation depends on the context: **I c'n invite Tom'r Peggy.** = I can invite Tom or Peggy. **Tom'n Peggy'r invited.** = Tom and Peggy are invited.
Get *outta* here!	Pronounced: *Ged oudda here!*

Standard	Common Contraction
probably	*prob'ly (*)*
should not have	*shouldn'a*
some	*s'm*
sure	*sher*
them	*'m / 'em (*)*
to	*ta*
want to	*wanna (*)* (when followed by a consonant *or* vowel) *wannu* (when followed by a vowel only)
what	*wud*
what are you	*wachya* or *wacha*

Example	Notes
He'll *prob'ly* come for dinner.	
You *shouldn'a* done that.	
Want *s'm* breakfast?	
Sher, I like chocolate!	A common expression indicating agreement is *For sure!* Pronounced: *Fer sher!*
I like*'m* a lot. / I like *'em* a lot.	
I don't know what *ta* do now.	NOTE (1): This applies to any word that begins with the combination "to" and whose accent does not fall on the first syllable: *today, tomorrow, tobacco, etc.* pronounced: *ta*day, *ta*morrow, *ta*bacco. NOTE (2): When preceded by a word which ends with an "r" or "o" sound, *to* is commonly pronounced *da:* I dunno where *da* go now.
I *wanna* go outside. I *wanna* eat something. I *wannu* avoid the subject.	*Wanna* may be used either before a consonant or a vowel, whereas *wannu* may only be used before a vowel. It would sound strange to the ear to use *wannu* before a consonant such as *I wannu go.*
Wud if we went to the movies?	"What" is pronounced *whad* only when followed by a vowel.
Wachya/Wacha doin'?	This contraction can only occur it if is followed immediately by one or more words. It cannot stand alone: *What are you? Crazy?* It would be incorrect so say: *Wacha? Crazy?*

Standard	**Common Contraction**
what did you	*wudidya* or *wudjya* or *wudja*
what do you	*what cha* or *what chya* or *wuddy'a*
what does	*what's (*)*
what is the	*what's a*
would not have	*wudn'a*
you	*ya (*)* *ja* (common pronunciation when preceded by the letter "d") *y'* (common contraction when followed by a vowel)
why did you	*whyd'ya* or *whydja*
why do you	*why'dy'a*

Example	Notes
Wudidya/Wudjya/ Wudja buy?	
What cha/What chya/ Wuddy'a doing?	When *wuddya* is pronounced as two syllables, *wud'dya,* it becomes past tense. When pronounced as three syllables, *wud'dy'a,* it changes to present tense. This subtle difference is easily detected by any native-born American.
What's he do for a living?	Although a common colloquial contraction for "what does," *what's* is traditionally a contraction for "what is."
What's a matter?	ALSO: *Wassa matta? (*)*
I *wudn'a* done that if I were you.	
How are *ya*? Would *ja* like some ice cream? Did *ja* see that? If *y'ever* need me, just call. Did *y'ever* see the movie?	
Why'dya/Why'dja tell him to leave?	
Why'dy'a work so hard?	When *whydya* is pronounced as two syllables, *why'dya,* it becomes past tense. When pronounced as three syllables, *why'dy'a,* it changes to present tense. This subtle difference is easily detected by any native-born American.

Practice Commonly Used Contractions

(Answers, p. 228)

A. In the following paragraph, write the contraction (or common pronunciation) of the word(s) in italics.

I *just* _____ heard that Nancy *and* _____ Dominic *are* _____

going to _____ have a baby! *Is that* _____ great *or* ____ what?!

Nancy said that Dominic was calm about it. How *can he* _____

be so relaxed?! He *has* _____ a lot *of* _____ control, that's *for* _____

sure _____ ! *What* _____ if she gives birth *to* ____ twins? I *don't know*

_____ what they'd do! They'd *probably* _____ move

out of _____ that house. Maybe they'll *let me* _____ help

them _____ find something in my neighborhood.

A CLOSER LOOK (2):
Commonly Used Initials

Oddly enough, initials make up a large part of American speech and are in constant use. In fact, some initials have almost completely replaced the word(s) that they represent. For example: **T.V.** *(television),* **V.C.R.** *(video cassette recorder),* **A.S.A.P.** *(as soon as possible),* and many others are just a few samples.

The following list should be learned *A.S.A.P.* since they are all extremely popular and are bound to be encountered within a very short time.

-A-

A.A. • Alcoholics Anonymous.

A.A.A. • (referred to as: *"Triple A"*) Automobile Association of America.

A.B.C. • This is a very popular television network; American Broadcasting Corporation.

A.C/D.C. • Alternating current - direct current.
♦ NOTE: This term is also humorous for "bisexual."

A.I.D.S. • Acquired Immune Deficiency Syndrome.

A.M. • Ante meridiem (morning).

A.O.K. • Absolutely.
♦ NOTE: This is used as a stronger form of *"O.K."*

A.P.B. • All points bulletin (police).

A.S.A.P. • As soon as possible.

A.W.O.L. • (army term) Absent without leave.

-B-

B.A. • Bachelor of Arts degree.

B.L.T. • Bacon lettuce and tomato sandwich.

B.O. • Body odor.

B.S. • **1.** This is a common euphemism for the expletive *"Bullshit!"* meaning "Nonsense!" • **2.** Bachelor of Science degree.

B.Y.O.B. • Bring your own bottle.
♦ NOTE: This is a common expression applied to a party at which each person brings his/her own alcoholic beverage to drink.

-C-

C.B. • Citizen band radio.

C.B.S. • This is a popular television network; Columbia Broadcasting System.

C.D. • **1.** Compact disc • **2.** Certificate of Deposit.

C.E.O. • Chief Executive Officer.

C.H.P. • California Highway Patrol.

C.I.A. • Central Intelligence Agency.

C.N.N. • (television) Cable News Network.

C.P.A. • Certified Public Accountant.

C.P.R. • Cardiopulmonary resuscitation.

C.R.T. • Cathode-ray tube • This refers to a computer terminal.

-D-

3-D • Three dimensional.

D.A. • District Attorney.

D.C. • District of Columbia • This refers to Washington, D.C.

D.J. • Disk jockey.

D.O.A. • Dead on arrival.

D.Q. • (sports term) Disqualified

D.T.'s • Delirium tremors • withdrawal symptoms from alcohol addiction.

D.U.I. • (traffic citation) Driving under the influence.

D.W.I. • (traffic citation) Driving while intoxicated.

-E-

E.R. • Emergency room.

E.S.P. • Extra sensory perception.

E.S.P.N. • Entertainment Sports Network.

-F-

F.B.I. • Federal Bureau of Investigation.

F.C.C. • Federal Communications Commission.

F.D.R. • Franklin Delano Roosevelt.

F.M. • (radio) Frequency modulation.

F.Y.I. • For your information.

-G-

G.I. • **1.** Gastrointestinal • **2.** Government Issue.

G.Q. • Gentleman's Quarterly magazine.
 ‣ NOTE: This is a common adjective to describe a man who is very handsome and stylish like the models in G.Q. magazine • *He's very G.Q.;* He's very handsome.

-I-

I. • Interstate highway • *I-5;* Interstate 5.

I.D. • Identification.

I.E. • (Latin) Id est (meaning: *"that is"*).

I.O.U. • I owe you.
 ‣ NOTE: This is a piece of paper that one gives after borrowing money to insure reimbursement.

I.Q. • Intelligence quotient.

I.U.D. • Intrauterine device.

I.V. • Intravenous.

-J-

J.F.K. • John F. Kennedy.

J.V. • Junior varsity.

-K-

K.I.A. • Killed in action (said of a soldier).

K.O. • (boxing term) Knock out.

K.P. • (army term) Kitchen police.

-L-

L.A. • Los Angeles.

L.A.X. • Los Angeles Airport.

L.C.D. • Liquid crystal display.

L.P. • Long-playing recording.

-M-

M.A. • Master of Arts degree.

M.C. • Master of ceremonies.

M.D. • Medical doctor.

M.I.A. • Missing in action (said of a soldier).

M.P. • Mounted police / Military police.

M.S. • Master of Science degree.

-N-

N.F.L. • National Football League.

N.H.L. • National Hockey League.

N.B.A. • National Basketball Association.

-O-

OB-GYN • Obstetrician-Gynecologist.

O.D. • Overdose.

O.J. • Orange juice.

O.K. • All right (used as an affirmation; also *"okay"*).

O.R. • Operating room.

O.T. • Overtime.
  ♦ NOTE: *to put in some O.T. at work;* to do some overtime at work.

-P-

P.B.&J. • Peanut butter and jelly sandwich.

P.C. • Personal computer.
  ♦ NOTE: This has actually become the accepted term when referring to a personal computer.

P.D.Q. • Pretty damn quick (immediately).

P.E. • Physical Education.
  ♦ ALSO: **Phys. Ed.**

P.I. • Private investigator.

P.J.s • Pajamas.

P.M. • Post meridiem (evening).

P.M.S. • Pre-menstrual syndrome.

P.O. • Post office.

P.O.'d. • Pissed off.
  ♦ NOTE: This is slang for "angry."

P.O.W. • Prisoner of war.

P.S. • Postscript.
  ♦ NOTE: This is added to the end of a correspondence when the writer decides to add a closing remark. If an additional remark is to be added, the initials *"P.P.S."* are added.

P.U. • This is a play-on-words of sorts since *"Pew!"* is an interjection used to signify an unpleasant odor. However, when *"Pew!"* is said slowly, it sounds like *"P.U!"*

-R-

R. & B. • (music) Rhythm and blues.

R. & R. • **1.** Rest and relaxation • **2.** Rock and roll.

R.I.P. • Rest in peace.
‣ NOTE: It is common to see these initials on tombstones.

R.N. • Registered nurse.

R.P.M. • Revolutions per minute.

R.S.V.P. • Répondez s'il-vous-plaît.
‣ NOTE: These initials are common at the close of an invitation requesting a response of attendance.

R.V. • Recreational vehicle.

-S-

S.O.B. • This is a popular euphemism for *"son of a bitch."*

S.O.S. • (nautical term) Save our ship.
NOTE: This is also used as a general distress call.

S.T.D. • Sexually transmitted disease.

-T-

T.A. • Teaching assistant.

T.B. • Tuberculosis.

T.D. • (football) Touchdown.

T.G.I.F. • Thank God it's Friday.

T.K.O. • (boxing term) Technical knock out.

T.L.C. • Tender loving care.

T.N.T. • (high explosive) Trinitrotoluene.

T.P. • Toilet paper.

T.V. • Television.

-U-

U. • University.

U.F.O. • Unidentified flying object.

U.H.F. • Ultra high frequency.

U.K. • United Kingdom.

U.P.S. • United Parcel Service.

U.S. • United States.

U.S. of A. • United States of America.

U.S.A. • United States of America.

-V-

V.A. • Veteran's Administration.

V.C.R. • Video cassette recorder.

V.D. • Venereal disease.

V.H.F. • Very high frequency.

V.I.P. • Very important person.

V.P. • Vice president.

V.W. • Volkswagen.

-W-

W.W.I • World War 1.

W.W.II • World War 2.

Practice Using Commonly Used Initials

(Answers, p. 228)

A. Replace the blank with the appropriate initial.

V.P.	**T.A.**	**T.P.**
I.D.	**M.C.**	**B.O.**
D.J.	**C.D.**	**L.A.**
P.J.s	**O.T.**	**U.F.O.**

1. I have to put in some _____ at work tonight.

2. Be on your best behavior at work today. The _____ is coming!

3. I couldn't prove my age because I forgot my _____ .

4. This show is going to be great. I wonder who the _____ is tonight.

5. Look up in the sky! Is that a _____ ?

6. I need to go to the store and pick up some _____ for the bathroom.

7. He smells terrible. What _____ !

8. She's the _____ in our English class.

9. I've lived in _____ all my life.

10. It's time to go to bed. Go put on your _____ .

11. Come listen to this radio program. The _____ is really great!

12. Is that the song from your new _____ ?

Just For Fun...

The following paragraph is an entertaining way to demonstrate the many popular initials that are heard spoken by members of *any* age group. Note that the following initials are extremely popular and common to all native Americans.

"Get a **B.L.T.** and an **O.J.** for the **V.P. A.S.A.P.**, **O.K**? Then go pick up the **T.V.** and **V.C.R.** and go borrow the **P.C.** from your father's **C.P.A.** and the **C.D.** from your friend the **D.J.**, the one with **B.O. P.U**! If you can't fit it all in your **V.W.**, then use my **R.V.** but don't touch the **C.B.**. I got really **P.O.'d** at the last guy who drove my car 'cause he was wearing nothing but **P.J.s** then got a **D.U.I.** from the **C.H.P.** and ended up in the **E.R.** in a hospital in **L.A.** hooked up to an **I.V.** and that's no **B.S**!"

Translation:

"Get a **bacon, lettuce and tomato sandwich** and an **orange juice** for the **vice president as soon as possible, okay**? Then go pick up the **television** and **video-cassette recorder** and go borrow the **personal computer** from your father's **certified public accountant** and the **compact disc player** from your friend the **disc jockey**, the one with **body odor. P.U**! If you can't fit it all in your **Volkswagon**, then use my **recreational vehicle** but don't touch the **citizen band radio**. I got really **pissed off** at the last guy who drove my car 'cause he was wearing nothing but **pajamas** then got a citation for **driving under the influence** from the **California Highway Patrol** and ended up in the **emergency room** in a hospital in **Los Angeles** hooked up to an **intravenous** and that's no **bullshit**!"

NOTE: The following lessons will contain many of the common contractions that were just presented. Be sure that you are familiar with these before moving on!

At the Party

Dialogue in slang

At the Party...

Bob and David arrive at Stephanie's party.

David: I thought this was supposed to be a big **bash**!

Bob: Oh, it will be. Stephanie said it's gonna be huge. We're just early, that's all. So, what do ya think of her house?

David: This **place** is really **cool**. Stephanie's **old man** must be **loaded**. Hey, look! There's that Donna **chick**. **Man**, can she **strut her stuff**! Don't ya think she's a **turn on**?

Bob: **No way**! Have you **lost it**? She may have a great **bod**, but as for her face, **we're talkin' butt ugly**. **Get real**! **Come on**, let's go **scarf out** on some **chow** before it's gone.

David: What is this **stuff**?

Bob: **Beats me**. Looks like something beige. Just **go for it**.

David: **Yuck**! Make me **heave**! Hey, **dude**… this party's a **drag**. I dunno about you, but I'm makin' a **bee line** for the door. **I'm history**!

Translation of dialogue in standard English

At the Party...

Bob and David arrive at Stephanie's party.

David: I thought this was supposed to be a big **party**!

Bob: Oh, it will be. Stephanie said it's going to be huge. We're just early, that's all. So, what do you think of her house?

David: This **house** is really **nice**. Stephanie's **father** must be **rich**. Hey, look! There's that **girl**, Donna! **Let me tell you**, she's a **real show-off**! Don't you think she's **sexy**?

Bob: **Absolutely not**! Are you **crazy**? She may have a great **body**, but as for her face, **it's really ugly**. **Be rational**! **Come along with me**, let's go **eat** some **food** before it's gone.

David: What is this **unidentifiable substance**?

Bob: **I don't know**. It looks like something beige. Just **be courageous**.

David: **How unpleasant**! This makes me **sick**! Hey, **friend**... this party is a **bore**. I don't know about you, but I'm **heading directly** for the door. **I'm leaving**!

Dialogue in slang as it would be heard

At the Party...

Bob'n David arrive at Stephanie's pardy.

David: I thought this was supposed ta be a big **bash**!

Bob: Oh, it will be. Stephanie said it's gonna be huge. We're just early, that's all. So, wad'dy'a think of 'er house?

David: This **place**'s really **cool**. Stephanie's **ol' man** mus' be **loaded**. Hey, look! There's that Donna **chick**. **Man**, c'n she **strut 'er stuff**! Doncha think she's a **turn on**?

Bob: **No way**! Have you **lost it**? She may have a great **bod**, bud as fer her face, **we're talkin' budd ugly**. **Get real**! **C'm'on**, let's go **scarf oud** on s'm **chow** before it's gone.

David: Whad is this **stuff**?

Bob: **Beats me**. Looks like something beige. Jus' **go fer it**.

David: **Yuck**! Make me **heave**! Hey, **dude**… this pardy's a **drag**. I dunno about you, bud I'm makin' a **bee line** fer the door. **I'm history**!

Vocabulary

bash *n.* party • *Great bash!;* Great party!

♦ NOTE: An extremely common expression meaning "to give a party" is "to throw a party (*bash, shindig, etc.*) • *I'm throwing a big bash for my parents;* I'm throwing a big party for my parents.

♦ SYNONYM: **shindig** *n.* This term originally referred to a raucous party in which men would begin fighting and kicking, digging each other in the shin with the toe of their boots. It is now used in jest to indicate a large, noisy, and fun party which may or may not have dancing • *Tonight, we're throwing a big shindig at my house;* Tonight, we're having a big party at my house.

"Beats me!" *exp.* "I don't know!"

♦ SYNONYM: **"Ya got me!"** *exp.* • *"How old do ya think she is?" "Ya got me!;"* "How old do you think she is?" "I don't know!"

bee line for (to make a) *exp.* to go quickly and directly to • *As soon as I get home, I'm makin' a bee line fer the bathroom;* As soon as I get home, I'm going straight to the bathroom.

bod *n.* body • *Look at that hot bod!;* Look at that hot body!

♦ NOTE: This is a popular abbreviation for "body," especially among younger people.

butt ugly (to be) *exp.* to be extremely ugly • *He's butt ugly!;* He's really ugly!

♦ ANTONYM: **to be hot looking** *exp.* to be very good looking and sexy • *He's really hot lookin'!;* He's really good looking!

chick *n.* girl.

♦ NOTE: This is an extremely popular synonym for "girl" although considered to be somewhat disrespectful.

♦ SYNONYM: **broad** *n.* • *Look at that broad over there!;* Look at that woman over there!

⇨ NOTE: The term *"broad,"* which is derogatory, is more common among the older generations, whereas *"chick"* is more popular with younger groups. Occasionally in old movies, especially gangster films, you may hear the word *"tomato"* used to mean, "girl." However, since most of the gangster films took place on the East Coast where the inhabitants have a particular accent, *"tomato"* is oftentimes heard pronounced, *ta-may-da.*

♦ ANTONYM: See **dude.**

chow *n.* food • *Great chow!;* Great food!
> ◗ SYNONYM: **grub** *n.*
> ◗ NOTE: These terms are extremely casual and considered somewhat unrefined. They should not be used in high society or at formal dinners.

"Come on" [pronounced and commonly seen in print as *"c'mon"*] **1.** "Let's go" *exp.* • *It's time to leave. C'mon;* It's time to leave. Let's go • **2.** "Hurry!" *exclam.* • *C'mon! We're gonna be late!;* Hurry! We're going to be late! • **3.** "You're kidding!" *exclam.* • *She got married after knowing him for only a week? C'mon!;* She got married after knowing him for only a week? You're kidding! • **4.** "Be optimistic" • *C'mon. Everything's gonna be fine;* Be optimistic. Everything is going to be fine.

cool *adj.* **1.** (for an event) pleasurable, enjoyable • *My vacation was really cool;* My vacation was really enjoyable • **2.** (for an object) appealing, terrific • *Your house is really cool;* Your house is really terrific. • **3.** (for a person) nice, "one of us" • *Your mom's really cool;* Your mom is really nice. *You c'n talk freely in fronna my mom. She's cool;* You can talk freely in front of my mom. She's one of us. • **4.** upstanding • *What you did for her was really cool;* What you did for her was really upstanding.
> ◗ ANTONYM: **uncool (to be)** *adj.*
> ◗ NOTE: These two terms are extremely popular with the younger generations.

drag (to be a) *n.* to be a bore.
> ◗ SYNONYM: **to be the pits** *exp.* • *This party's the pits;* This party's boring.
> ◗ ANTONYM: **to be rad** *adj.* This abbreviation of the adjective "radical" is popular among the younger generations: *This party's rad!;* This party is great!

dude *n.* man, in general.
> ◗ NOTE: The noun *"dude"* is very popular and shows a great deal of familiarity. This term is usually used by the younger generations. In fact, teenagers now use *"dude"* when referring to teenage girls. It is actually common to hear a teenager say, "Hey, dudes!" when addressing a group of young women.
> ◗ SYNONYM: **guy** *n.*
> ⇨ NOTE (1): This noun is extremely popular and used by all generations and shows no lack of respect whatsoever. It is simply a casual way of saying "man."
> ⇨ NOTE (2): In addition, *"you guys"* is frequently used on the West Coast when referring to a group of men, women, or both. It could best be translated as "everyone." Therefore, it is very common and correct to use it when addressing a group of women: *Hey, you guys! What's up?;* Hi, everyone!

What's happening? In the South, *"ya'll,"* a contraction of *"you all,"* is used in place of *"you guys."*

get real (to) *exp.* to be serious, to become realistic • *When is she gonna get real and find a job?;* What is she going to become realistic and get a job?
 ‣ SYNONYM: **to get a life** *exp.* • *Get a life!;* Get serious!
 ⇨ NOTE: Over the last few years, this expression has become extremely popular.

go for it (to) *exp.* to be courageous and do something • *Don't worry and just go for it!;* Be courageous and just do it!

heave (to) *v.* to vomit profusely.
 ‣ SYNONYM: **to throw one's guts up** *exp.* • *I'm gonna throw my guts up if I eat that;* I'm going to vomit profusely if I eat that.
 ‣ ANTONYM: **to dry heave** *exp.* to go through the motions of vomiting without regurgitating.

history (to be) *exp.* to leave, to no longer exist (in a location, in one's estimation, in life) • **1.** (in a location) *It's already 1:00? I'm history!;* It's already 1:00? I'm gone! • **2.** (in one's estimation) *He cheated me again! I swear, that friend's history!;* He cheated me again! I swear, he's no longer my friend! • **3.** (in life) *You wrecked your dad's car? You're history!;* You wrecked your dad's car? You're going to get killed!
 ‣ SYNONYM: **to be outta here** *exp.* • *I'm outta here!;* I'm leaving!

loaded (to be) *adj.* **1.** to be rich • *I didn't know he was loaded;* I didn't know he was rich • **2.** to be drunk (or on drugs) • *That guy's really loaded;* That man is really drunk.
 ‣ NOTE: The difference between connotations simply depends on the context.

lose it (to) *exp.* **1.** to throw up • **2.** to go crazy • *If he doesn't stop it, I'm gonna lose it;* If he doesn't stop it, I'm going to go crazy.

"Man!" *exclam.* "Wow!"
 ‣ NOTE: The exclamation *"Man!"* can certainly be used among girls since it is only a term of surprise and does not indicate any of the persons involved in the conversation.
 ‣ SYNONYM: **"Boy!"** *exclam.*

"No way!" *exclam.* "Absolutely not!"
 ‣ ALSO: **No way, José!** *exp.* • SEE: *Street Talk II - Rhyming Slang.*

old man *exp.* (disrespectful) **1.** father • **2.** boyfriend • **3.** husband.
 ‣ ANTONYM: **old lady** *exp.* (derogatory) **1.** mother • **2.** girlfriend • **3.** wife.

place *n.* home • *Welcome to our place!;* Welcome to our home?
> ‣ SYNONYM: **pad** *n.* Although no longer used, this word became extremely popular in the 60's when it was introduced by musicians. You may still hear it used in old movies, television shows, or in jest.

scarf out (to) *exp.* to eat a lot.
> ‣ NOTE: On the West Coast, the expression *"to scarf"* or *"to scarf out"* is extremely popular. If you visit any young people in California, for example, you'll probably hear it within the first few hours. Although this expression has great popularity on the West Coast, in the East it is not well known at all. Therefore, when visiting New York, for example, the expressions you are more likely to hear are *"to pig out"* or *"to pork out."* These expressions are equally popular on the West Coast.
> ‣ SYNONYM (1): **to pig out** *exp.* • *I feel sick because I pigged out on pie today;* I feel sick because I ate a lot of pie today.
> ‣ SYNONYM (2): **to pork out** *exp.* to eat a lot • *We're really gonna pork out tonight!;* We're really going to eat a lot tonight!

strut one's stuff (to) *exp.* to show off one's body.
> ‣ SYNONYM: **to let it all hang out** *exp.* to wear skimpy clothing in order to show off one's body • *She lets it all hang out;* She shows off her body.

stuff *n.* **1.** junk • *How can you expect me to eat this stuff?;* How can you expect me to eat this junk? • **2.** merchandise in general • *Look at all this great stuff!;* Look at all this great merchandise! • **3.** possessions • *Don't touch that! That's my stuff!;* Don't touch that! Those are my possessions! • **4.** actions (of a person) • *Can you believe the stuff he did to me?;* Can you believe the things he did to me? • **5.** nonsense • *She actually believed that stuff he told her;* She actually believed that nonsense he told her.

turn on (to be a) *exp.* (said of someone or something) to be sexually exciting.
> ‣ ALSO: **to turn on** *exp.* to excite sexually • *He turns me on;* He excites me.

"We're talkin'... *exp.* "I mean…"
> ‣ NOTE: This expression is used to add emphasis to a statement by modifying the adjective or phrase that follows: *She's weird! We're talkin', from another planet!*; She's weird! I mean, from another planet! Since this expression must begin a sentence, it would be incorrect to say, *"She's we're talkin' weird!"* Also, notice that in this expression, the abbreviated form of *"talking"* is always used.

"Yuck!" *exclam.* used to signify great displeasure.
> ‣ SYNONYM: **Ew!** *exclam.* • *Ew! What is this stuff?*
> ‣ NOTE: **Pew!** *exclam.* used to signify displeasure upon smelling a foul odor.

Practice The Vocabulary

(Answers to Lesson 2, p. 228)

A. Underline the synonym.

1. **bash:**   a. home   b. party

2. **chow:**   a. food   b. house

3. **to scarf out:**   a. to sleep   b. to eat

4. **to be loaded:**   a. to be tired   b. to be rich

5. **"Get real!":**   a. "Get serious!"   b. "Stop that!"

6. **to be a turn on:**   a. to be energetic   b. to be sexy

7. **"Beats me!":**   a. "I don't know!"   b. "I'm leaving!"

8. **dude:**   a. woman   b. man

9. **to make a bee line:** a. to go directly toward   b. to stop

10. **"I'm history":**   a. "I'm sick"   b. "I'm leaving"

B. Rewrite the following phrases replacing the italicized word(s) with the appropriate slang synonym(s) from the right column.

1. I thought this was supposed to be a big *party*.   A. **old man**

   _____

2. Just *be courageous*.

   _____   B. **a turn on**

3. What is this *substance*?

   _____   C. **bash**

4. Don't you think she's *sexy*?   D. **scarf out**

    _____

5. I'm *going straight* for the door.   E. **stuff**

    _____

6. Let's go *eat*.   F. **making a bee line**

    _____

7. This *food* is great!

    _____   G. **go for it**

8. Stephanie's *father* is really nice.

    _____   H. **loaded**

9. I heard your brother is *rich*.

    _____   I. **history**

10. I'm *leaving*.

    _____   J. **chow**

C. Complete the phrases by choosing the appropriate word(s) from the list below.

place	strut	chick
way	yuck	heave
bee line	real	lost
man	we're talkin'	go

1. She's unusual. _____ , weird!

2. Don't be nervous about it. Just _____ for it!

3. You live here? You have a really nice _____ .

4. Look at her _____ her stuff.

5. That _____ is your sister?

6. You actually like him? Get _____ !

7. That's disgusting! Make me _____ !

8. Can I afford to buy that car? No _____ !

9. What are you talking about? Have you _____ it?

10. Where's she going? She just made a _____ for the door.

11. _____ ! This tastes terrible!

12. _____ , is she ever strange!

A CLOSER LOOK:
Fruits and Vegetables Used in Slang

There's no doubt about it; slang is truly limitless. Many common idiomatic expressions have actually been created using the names of insects, animals, people, clothing, etc.

A popular category which has yielded some very colorful and amusing expressions is "fruits and vegetables":

Apple

apple of one's eye (to be the) *exp.* to be one's favorite • *She's the apple of her father's eye;* She's her father's favorite.

Big Apple (the) *exp.* New York • *I live in the Big Apple;* I live in New York.

compare apples and oranges (to) *exp.* to compare two things that simply cannot be compared • *That's ridiculous. Now you're comparing apples and oranges;* That's ridiculous. Now you're comparing two things that simply cannot be compared.

"How do you like them apples?" *exp.* "What do you think of *that?*"
  ♦ NOTE: This expression is said upon retaliation of an offensive act.

Banana

bananas (to be) *exp.* to be crazy • *That guy's bananas!;* That guy's crazy!
 ◗ NOTE: **to go bananas** *exp.* **1.** to become crazy • *I'm so bored I'm going bananas;* I'm so bored I'm going crazy • **2.** to become wild with anger • *She went bananas when she found him cheating;* She became wild with anger when she found him cheating.

play second banana (to) *exp.* to be second choice • *I always play second banana to her;* I'm always second choice to her.

top banana *exp.* main boss • *He's (the) top banana in this company;* He's the main boss in this company.

Bean

bean brain *exp.* idiot • *He's such a bean brain;* He's such an idiot.
 ◗ NOTE: This expression insinuates that the person's brain is no bigger than a bean.

beans about something (not to know) *exp.* not to know anything about something • *I don't know beans about computers;* I don't know anything about computers.

 ◗ NOTE: This expression only works in the negative form. The expression *"to know beans about something"* does not exist.

Bean Town *exp.* Boston, Massachusetts.
 ◗ NOTE: Boston is known for its specialty of baked beans.

Beet

beet red (to be) *exp.* to be extremely red from blushing, embarrassment, etc. • *She was so embarrassed she turned beet red;* She was so embarrassed she turned extremely red.

Cabbage

cabbage *n.* money.
 ◗ NOTE: Although no longer in popular usage, this term is occasionally heard in old movies or used in jest.

Carrot

carrot in front of someone (to dangle a) *exp.* to tempt someone with an unobtainable offer • *The boss told me if I perform well on the job, we'll talk about a salary increase next year. But I think he's just dangling a carrot in front of me;* The boss told me if I perform well on the job, we'll talk about a salary increase next year. But I think he's just tempting me with an unobtainable offer.

Cauliflower

cauliflower ears *exp.* swollen ears usually resulting from a boxing match • *That boxer has cauliflower ears;* That boxer has swollen ears.

Cherry

bowl of cherries (to be a) *exp.* to be wonderful • *Life isn't always a bowl of cherries;* Life isn't always wonderful.

Corn

"For corn sake!" *exclam.* "Oh, my goodness!"
‣ NOTE: This expression, although rather outdated, is still used by the older generations.

corn *n.* melodrama, overemotional drama • *What a bunch of corn!;* What a bunch of melodrama!
‣ ALSO: **corny** *adj.* melodramatic • *The movie was so corny!;* The movie was so melodramatic!

cornball *adj.* ridiculous • *Where did you buy that cornball hat?;* Where did you buy that ridiculous hat?

Cucumber

cool as a cucumber (to be) *exp.* to be calm and composed • *Although he's guilty of the crime, he sure is cool as a cucumber;* Although he's guilty of the crime, he sure is calm and composed.

Fruit

fruit *n.* (derogatory) homosexual • *I think that guy's a fruit;* I think that guy's a homosexual.
‣ NOTE (1): **fruity** *adj.* (derogatory) said of an effeminate homosexual male.
‣ NOTE (2): The term *"fruit"* is extremely derogatory. The accepted term among the homosexual community is *"gay."*

fruitcake *n.* an insane person • *What a fruitcake!;* What a lunatic!
‣ NOTE: The adjective *"nutty,"* literally meaning "full of nuts" is commonly used to mean "crazy." Therefore, don't be surprised if you hear the popular play-on-words: *to be nuttier than a fruitcake;* to be extremely crazy.

Grapes

grapevine (through the) *exp.* coming from an unofficial source, oftentimes a rumor • *I heard it through the grapevine;* I heard it from an unofficial source.

sour grapes *exp.* devaluing something one can not have due to jealousy • *I don't care that I didn't win the car. I wouldn't want a Jaguar anyway. It's too hard to get parts and service. I suppose that's just sour grapes;* I don't care that I didn't win the car. I wouldn't want a Jaguar anyway. It's too hard to get parts and service. I suppose I'm just devaluing it because I didn't win.

Lemon

lemon *n.* worthless merchandise, junk • *That car is a real lemon;* That car is real junk.

Lettuce

lettuce *n.* money.
  ◆ NOTE: Although no longer in popular usage, it is occasionally heard in old movies or used in jest.

Orange

compare apples and oranges (to) *exp.* SEE: *Apple.*

Pea

like two peas in a pod (to be) *exp.* to be identical • *Jan and Johanna are like two peas in a pod;* Jan and Johanna are identical.

pea brain *n.* stupid person • *He's such a pea brain;* He's such a stupid person.
  ◆ NOTE: This expression insinuates that the person's brain is no bigger than a pea.

Peach

a real peach (to be) *exp.* terrific, really nice (said of a person but primarily used sarcastically) • *She's a real peach!;* She's really unpleasant!

peach of a... (to be a) *exp.* to be a great... • *She's a peach of a teacher;* She's a great teacher.
  ◆ NOTE: Although this expression is outdated, it is occasionally heard in old movies or used in jest.

peachy (to be) *exp.* to be terrific • *That's really peachy!;* That's really great!
  ◆ NOTE: Although this expression is outdated, it is occasionally heard in old movies or used in jest.
  ◆ ALSO: **peachy keen** *exp.* terrific.

♦ NOTE: This expression is also outdated although occasionally heard in old movies or used in jest.

Pickle

pickle *n.* predicament • *I really got myself into a pickle this time;* I really got myself into a predicament this time.

Potato

couch potato (to be a) *exp.* to laze habitually on the couch • *He's such a couch potato;* He's does nothing but lie on the couch all the time.

hot potato *exp.* anything that is considered to be potentially dangerous or volatile • *This situation is a real hot potato;* This situation is volatile.

small potatoes *exp.* unimportant • *That's small potatoes compared to the real problem;* That's unimportant compared to the real problem.

Prune

wrinkled as a prune (to be) *exp.* to be very wrinkled •

He's wrinkled as a prune; He's very wrinkled.
♦ ALSO: **prune face** *exp.* wrinkled face (which looks like a prune).

Pumpkin

pumpkin *exp.* (term of endearment) sweetheart, honey • *Hi, pumpkin;* Hi, sweetheart.
♦ NOTE: As a term of endearment, *"pumpkin"* is commonly heard pronounced: *pung-kin.*

Sprout

sprout *n.* short, young person • *He may be a sprout right now, but give him a few more years;* He may be a short person right now, but give him a few more years.
♦ ALSO: **to sprout up** *exp.* to grow suddenly.

Tomato

tomato *n.* (derogatory) girl.
♦ NOTE: Although *"tomato"* is outdated, it is occasionally heard in old movies or used in jest.

Practice the Use of Fruits and Vegetables in Slang

(Answers, p. 229)

A. **Fill in the blanks from the list below with the fruit or vegetable that best completes the phrase.**

apple	bananas	beans
cherries	grapes	cucumber
lemon	pea	pickle
potato	banana	peach

1. He's not smart at all. He's a real _____ brain.

2. I don't know _____ about fixing a car.

3. She's the _____ of her father's eye.

4. He's cool as a _____ .

5. She was so rude to us. I'm telling you, she's a real _____ .

6. Life isn't always a bowl of _____ .

7. Don't be so angry. You know it's just sour _____ .

8. What a predicament! I've never been in such a _____ !

9. He doesn't do anything all day. He's a real couch _____ .

10. He's top _____ around here.

11. This car's a real _____ .

12. She went _____ when I told her the news.

Just For Fun

Now that you're fluent in the use of fruits and vegetables in slang, see if you understand the following paragraph.

"Why can't I go instead of her? I know it's just **sour GRAPES** but she doesn't know **BEANS** about the **Big APPLE** like I do! For **CORN** sake, I'm tired of playing second **BANANA** to that **PEA-brain**. Oh, she's a real **PEACH** of an employee. I'm usually cool as a **CUCUMBER** about things and I know it's just small **POTATOES**, but if you don't let me go, I'm quitting and then you'll really be in a **PICKLE**. How do you like them **APPLES**?!"

Translation:

"Why can't I go instead of her? I know it's just that I'm **upset because I didn't get my way** but she knows **nothing** about **New York** like I do! **Darn**, I'm tired of being **second choice** to that **idiot**. Oh, she's a **great** employee. I'm usually **really calm** about things and I know it's **insignificant**, but if you don't let me go, I'm quitting and then you'll really be in a **predicament**. How do you like **that**?!"

At the Movies

Dialogue in slang

At the Movies...

*Chris and Lisa are seated in the movie theater
waiting for Steve to arrive.*

Chris: I wonder what's **keeping** Steve?

Lisa: Oh, I forgot to tell you. He's not gonna **show up**. He called just
before we **took off**.

Chris: What kind of **line** did he **hand** you this time?

Lisa: Something about his car **dying** again.

Chris: What a **bunch** of **noise**. He doesn't even have a car. He **gets
around** everywhere by bike. I don't know what he's trying **to
pull**. The **guy's** a total **flake**.

Lisa: **You said it**. That's the **last straw**. The guy **lies like a rug**. I
dunno why we've **put up** with him for this long. I'm telling
you, if I **run into** him tomorrow, I'm **reading him the riot
act**. This time, he **blew it big time**. Man, I'm gonna have **a
field day** with him.

Chris: Try not to **lose your cool** too much. One thing's for sure.
It'll be a cold day in hell before we invite him to the movies
again. **By the way**, do you even know what this movie's about?

Lisa: All I know is that the critics **panned** it. They all said the star
kept **blowing his lines**. But you can always **count on** one
thing…if a critic thinks a movie's a **bomb**, it'll be a **smash
hit**.

Translation of dialogue in standard English

At the Movies...

*Chris and Lisa are seated in the movie theater
waiting for Steve to arrive.*

Chris:	I wonder what's **detaining** Steve?
Lisa:	Oh, I forgot to tell you. He's not going to **arrive**. He called just before we **left**.
Chris:	What kind of **excuse** did he **give** you this time?
Lisa:	Something about his car **becoming inoperable** again.
Chris:	What **a lot** of **nonsense**. He doesn't even have a car. He **commutes** everywhere by bike. I don't know what he's trying **to succeed at doing**. The **man** is totally **unreliable**.
Lisa:	**I agree**. That's **all I can tolerate**. The man **always lies**. I don't know why we've **tolerated** him for this long. I'm telling you, if I **inadvertently encounter** him tomorrow, I'm **reprimanding him**. This time, he **made a big mistake**. Man, I'm going to have **a great time** yelling at him.
Chris:	Try not to **lose your temper** too much. One thing is certain. **We'll never** invite him to the movies again. **Incidentally**, do you even know what this movie's about?
Lisa:	All I know is that the critics **criticized it harshly**. They all said the star kept **making mistakes saying his lines**. But you can always **depend on** one thing… if a critic thinks a movie is a **bad production**, it'll be a **huge success**.

53

Dialogue in slang as it would be heard

At the Movies...

Chris'n Lisa'r seaded in the movie theader
waiding fer Steve to arrive.

Chris:	I wonder what's **keeping** Steve?
Lisa:	Oh, I fergot ta tell ya. He's not gonna **show up**. He called jus' before we **took off**.
Chris:	What kinda **line** did'e **hand** ja this time?
Lisa:	Something about 'is car **dying** again.
Chris:	What a **buncha noise**. He doesn't even have a car. He **gets around** everywhere by bike. I dunno what 'e's trying **ta pull**. The **guy's** a todal **flake**.
Lisa:	**You said it.** That's the **las' straw**. The guy **lies like a rug**. I dunno why we've **pud up** with 'im fer this long. I'm telling you, if I **run inta** him tamorrow, I'm **reading 'im the riod act**. This time 'e **blew it big time**. Man, I'm gonna have **a field day** with 'im.
Chris:	Try not ta **lose yer cool** too much. One thing's fer sure. Id'll be **a cold day 'n hell** before we invite 'im ta the movies again. **By the way**, do you even know what this movie's about?
Lisa:	All I know is that the critics **panned** it. They all said the star kept **blowing 'is lines**. But you c'n always **count on** one thing... if a critic thinks a movie's a **bomb**, id'll be a **smash hit**.

Vocabulary

blow it big time (to) *exp.* to make a terrible mistake • *This time, I blew it big time;* This time, I made a terrible mistake.

◖ NOTE: The expression *"to blow it,"* means "to make a mistake" and the expression *"big time"* means, "greatly." *"To blow it big time"* is actually a common expression created out of two popular idioms • *She yelled at me big time;* She really yelled at me. The expression *"big time"* is also commonly used to mean: **1.** renowned • *He's a big time painter;* He's a well known painter • *He's big time;* He's famous. • **2.** on a large scale • *This isn't just a little play he's doing. This is big time!;* This isn't just a little play he's doing. This is the highest he can go in his profession!

blow one's lines (to) *exp.* to make a mistake while speaking one's lines from a script • *He kept blowing his lines tonight;* He kept making mistakes while speaking his lines tonight.

◖ SYNONYM: **to flub one's lines** *exp.* • *She keeps flubbing her lines;* She keeps making mistakes while speaking her lines.

◖ NOTE: These two expressions are very common in the industries of theatre, television, and movies.

bomb *n.* bad production (theater, television, movies, etc.) • *The show was a real bomb;* The show was really bad.

◖ SYNONYM: **turkey** *n.* • *That show was a real turkey;* That show was really bad.

◖ ANTONYM: SEE - **smash.**

◖ ALSO: **to bomb** *v.* to fail • *The movie really bombed;* The movie really failed • *I really bombed on my test;* I really failed my test.

bunch (a) *n.* a lot • *She has a bunch of kids;* She has a lot of children • *Thanks a bunch!;* Thanks a lot!

◖ ALSO: **a whole bunch** *exp.* a large amount • *She has a whole bunch of kids;* She really has many children • *I drank a whole bunch of coffee last night;* I really drank a lot of coffee last night.

◖ SYNONYM: **pile** *n.* • *She has a pile of children;* She has many children.

by the way *exp.* incidentally • *By the way, your father is very nice;* Incidentally, your father is very nice.

◖ NOTE: Occasionally, you may even hear a variation of this expression, *"by the by,"* which is considered pretentious and therefore is used mainly in jest or when making fun of the very rich. It is certainly common in movies when the focus is on high society.

cold day in hell (a) *exp.* never • *It'll be a cold day in hell before I see her again;* I'll never see her again.
♦ SYNONYM: **when donkeys fly** *exp.* • *"Don't you want to date him?" "When donkeys fly!";* "Don't you want to date him?" "Never!"

count on (to) *exp.* to depend on (someone or something) • *I was counting on getting that money;* I was depending on getting that money • *I'm counting on you;* I'm depending on you.

die (to) *v.* to become inoperable • (lit); to expire, to pass away • *The washing machine just died;* The washing machine just became inoperable.
♦ ALSO: **to up and die** *exp.* to become suddenly inoperable • (lit); to expire suddenly • *He just up and died!;* He just died suddenly! • *My car just up and died!;* My car just become suddenly inoperable!
♦ SYNONYM: **to conk out** *exp.* **1.** to be inoperable • *My car conked out in the middle of the street;* My car became inoperable in the middle of the street. • **2.** to fall asleep • *He was so tired when he came home that he just conked out on the sofa;* He was so tired when he came home that he just fell asleep on the sofa.
⇨ ALSO: **to be conked out** *exp.* to be exhausted • *I'm gonna go to bed. I'm conked out;* I'm going to go to bed. I'm exhausted.

field day *exp.* a great time; complete self-indulgence • *At the pastry shop, I had a field day!;* At the pastry shop, I indulged myself! • *When I saw her in the market, I finally told her what I think of her. I had a field day!;* When I saw her in the market, I finally told her what I think of her. I indulged myself!

flake *n.* an unreliable person • *Don't count on him picking you up at the airport on time. He's a real flake;* Don't count on him picking you up at the airport on time. He's really unreliable.
♦ ALSO: **flakey** *adj.* unreliable • *You can't depend on him. He's too flakey;* You can't depend on him. He's too unreliable.

get around (to) *exp.* **1.** to commute • *He gets around by bicycle;* He commutes by bicycle. • **2.** to go from one sexual partner to the other • *She really gets around;* She really goes from one sexual partner to the other. •

3. to avoid • *How are we gonna get around the problem?;* How are we going to avoid the problem?

guy *n.* man (in general) • *Do you know that guy?;* Do you know that man?
   ♦ NOTE: This is extremely popular and used by everyone.
   ♦ SYNONYM: **fellow** *n.* [commonly pronounced: *fella*] • *We just hired that fellow over there;* We just hired that man over there.
      ⇨ NOTE: This is popular among the older generations only.

hand someone something (to) *exp.* to give someone something • *He handed me his car keys;* He gave me his car keys.
   ♦ ALSO: **to hand over** *exp.* to give or relinquish • *He handed over his car keys to me;* He relinquished his car keys to me.

keep someone (to) *exp.* to detain someone •*What's keeping him?;* What's detaining him? • *She kept him after school;* She detained him after school.
   ♦ SYNONYM: **to hold someone up** *exp.* **1.** to detain someone • *What's holding her up?;* What's detaining her? • *She held me up for an hour;* She detained me for an hour. • **2.** to rob someone • *There's the man who held up that old woman!;* There's the man who robbed that old woman!

last straw *exp.* the final act that one can tolerate • *He used my car again without asking me?! That's the last straw!;* He used my car again without asking me?! That's the final incident that I can tolerate!
   ♦ ALSO: **the straw that broke the camel's back** *exp.* This expression conjures up an image of pieces of straw, being placed on a camel's back until it can support no more • *When I found out that she didn't invite me to the party, that was the straw that broke the camel's back;* When I found out that she didn't invite me to the party, that was all I could tolerate.
   ♦ SYNONYM: **"That did it!"** *exp.* • *That did it! I'm leaving!;* That's all I can tolerate! I'm leaving!

lie like a rug (to) *exp.* to tell enormous lies.
   ♦ NOTE: This expression is a play-on-words since the verb *"to lie"* means "to tell untruths" as well as "to span, cover, or stretch out" as does a rug.

line *n.* **1.** an excuse • *You actually believed that line?;* You actually believed that excuse? • **2.** an overused statement used to allure • *While I was sitting at the bar, this guy comes up to me and says, 'Hi. Didn't we meet somewhere before?' I can't believe he used that old line on me!;* While I was sitting at the bar, this guy comes up to me and says, 'Hi. Didn't we meet somewhere before?' I can't believe he used that old overused statement on me!

lose one's cool (to) *exp.* to lose one's temper • *I know I shouldn't have yelled at her but I just lost my cool;* I know I shouldn't have yelled at her but I just lost my temper.

‣ SYNONYM (1): **to blow up** *exp.* *She blew up when I told her I lost her book;* She lost her temper when I told her I lost her book.

‣ SYNONYM (2): **to fly off the handle** *exp.* • *I know I shouldn't have flown off the handle like that;* I know I shouldn't have lost my temper like that.

‣ ALSO: **to lose it** *exp.* to lose one's temper • *I know I shouldn't have yelled at her but I just lost it;* I know I shouldn't have yelled at her but I just lost my temper.

⇨ NOTE: Used in this connotation, it is understood that *"it"* replaces "one's temper."

noise *n.* nonsense • *Don't gimme that noise!;* Don't give me that nonsense!

‣ SYNONYM: **baloney** *n.* • *What he told you was nothing but baloney;* What he told you was nothing but nonsense.

pan (to) *v.* to criticize brutally an element of the arts (such as a play, a movie, an actor, etc.) • *The critics panned the play;* The critics brutally criticized the play.

‣ SYNONYM: **to rake over the coals** *exp.* • *The critics really raked them over the coals;* The critics really criticized them unmercifully.

‣ NOTE: This expression may be used in reference to that which is outside the arts as well.

pull something (to) *exp.* to succeed at doing something dishonest • *What's he trying to pull this time?;* What dishonest thing is he trying to do this time?

‣ SYNONYM: **to get away with something** *exp.* • *What's he trying to get away with this time?;* What dishonest thing is he trying to do this time?

put up with (to) *exp.* to tolerate (someone or something) • *I'm not putting up with this anymore;* I'm not tolerating this anymore.

‣ SYNONYM (1): **to stick it out** *exp.* *Our house guest will be leaving in just two days. Try and stick it out a little longer;* Our house guest will be leaving in just two days. Try and tolerate it a little longer.

‣ SYNONYM (2): **to take something** *exp.* • *I'm not taking this anymore;* I'm not tolerating this anymore.

⇨ NOTE: **I'm mad as hell and I'm not going to take it anymore!** *exp.*

This expression became extremely popular in the 1980's when it was heard in the movie called "Network."

read someone the riot act (to) *exp.* to reprimand someone • *She really read me the riot act;* She really reprimanded me.

‣ SYNONYM: **to lay into someone** *exp.* • *I heard your mother really laid into you!;* I heard your mother really reprimanded you!

run into someone (to) *exp.* to encounter someone unintentionally • *Can you believe it? I ran into him in Paris!;* Can you believe it? I encountered him unintentionally in Paris!

‣ SYNONYM: **to bump into someone** *exp.* • *You'll never guess who I bumped into today!;* You'll never guess who I encountered inadvertently today!

show up (to) *exp.* to arrive • *He finally showed up at 10:00;* He finally arrived at 10:00.

‣ NOTE: **no-show** *n.* one who fails to arrive • *Where's Tom? It looks like he's a no-show;* Where's Tom? It looks like he's not coming.

‣ SYNONYM: **to turn up** *exp.* • *He finally turned up about 8:00;* He finally arrived at 8:00.

smash hit *exp.* a tremendous success • *The movie was a smash hit;* The movie was a tremendous success.

‣ ANTONYM: See - **bomb.**

‣ ALSO: *The movie was a smash;* The movie was a huge success • *The movie was a hit;* The movie was a success.

‣ NOTE: *hit* = success; *smash* = big success; *smash hit* = huge success.

take off (to) *exp.* to leave • *We'd better take off now if we don't want to be late;* We'd better leave now if we don't want to be late.

‣ NOTE: This expression literally refers to the departure of an aircraft but is commonly used colloquially when referring to the departure of a person.

‣ SYNONYM: **to split** *v.* • *We'd better split if we don't want to be late;* We'd better leave if we don't want to be late.

"You said it!" *exclam.* "I agree!"

‣ SYNONYM: **"You got it!"** *exclam.*

Practice The Vocabulary

(Answers to Lesson 3, p. 229)

A. Complete the phrases by choosing the appropriate words from the list below.

keeping	bunch	show up
took off	smash hit	riot act
big time	hand	field day
get around	put up	cool

1. That belongs to me. _____ me that right now!

2. When you talk to your boss, try not to lose your _____ .

3. Where's Janet? I wonder what's _____ her?

4. Tomorrow, I'm visiting a chocolate factory with my sister. We're going to have a _____ !

5. I can't believe you did that! This time you blew it _____ .

6. Steve already left? I wonder why he _____ so early.

7. I'm so mad at him. The next time I see him, I'm reading him the

   _____ .

8. The movie was great! I know it's gonna be a _____ !

9. The teacher gave us a _____ of homework tonight.

10. I can't believe you've _____ with his insults this long.

11. Ever since my car broke, I _____ by bicycle.

12. I wonder what time John is going to _____ .

B. Match the two columns.

☐ 1. You won't believe the excuse he gave me this time.

☐ 2. I agree!

☐ 3. You can depend on me.

☐ 4. We'd better leave.

☐ 5. That's a lot of nonsense.

☐ 6. The movie was really bad.

☐ 7. I didn't think you were going to arrive.

☐ 8. She scolded me.

☐ 9. Incidentally, what are you doing tomorrow?

☐ 10. I inadvertently encountered Chris today.

☐ 11. The man's not dependable.

☐ 12. I can't tolerate it anymore!

A. **The movie was a real bomb.**

B. **By the way, what are you doing tomorrow?**

C. **We'd better take off.**

D. **The guy's a total flake.**

E. **You said it!**

F. **She read me the riot act.**

G. **I ran into Chris today.**

H. **You can count on me.**

I. **That's a bunch of noise.**

J. **That's the last straw!**

K. **You won't believe the line he handed me this time.**

L. **I didn't think you were going to show up.**

C. Underline the word that best completes each phrase.

1. It'll be a (**cool, cold, warm**) day in hell before we invite him to the movies again.

2. What kind of (**circle, square, line**) did he (**foot, hand, arm**) you this time?

3. I don't think he's gonna show (**up, down, in**).

4. The actor kept (**coughing, sneezing, blowing**) his lines.

5. When the critics see the play, you can be sure they'll (**pan, skillet, casserole**) it.

6. We'd better take (**in, out, off**) if we don't wanna be late.

7. He lies like a (**rat, rug, rake**).

8. You can't (**sing, count, talk**) on him. He's a (**flake, flock, fling**).

9. I don't know what you're trying to (**push, shove, pull**).

10. That's the (**first, last, second**) straw! I can't tolerate it any more!

11. I'm (**reading, singing, reciting**) him the riot act!

12. I'm so mad at him. When I see him at the party tomorrow, I'm gonna have a field (**night, week, day**).

A CLOSER LOOK:
Body Parts Used in Slang

As seen in the opening dialogue, an expression was introduced using the verb, "hand": *What kind of line did he **hand** you this time?*

But has slang created even more expressions in which body parts are used? *Make no bones about it!*

Arm

cost an arm and a leg (to) *exp.* to be extremely expensive • *The car cost him an arm and a leg;* The car cost him a lot of money.

one's right arm *exp.* one's valuable partner • *He's my right arm;* He's my valuable partner.

strong-arm someone (to) *exp.* to force someone to do something • *He was strong-armed into doing it;* He was forced into doing it.

twist one's arm (to) *exp.* to force someone to do something • *No one's twisting your arm to do it!;* No one's forcing you to do it!

walk arm in arm (to) *exp.* to walk while holding each other's arm • *They always walk arm in arm down the street;* They always walk holding each other's arm down the street.

Back

get off one's back (to) *exp.* to stop pestering someone • *Get off my back!;* Stop bothering me!

get one's back up (to) *exp.* to make one irritated and angry • *I don't like her. She always gets my back up;* I don't like her. She makes me irritated and angry.
♦ NOTE: This expression is borrowed from the animal kingdom since it is generally used when describing an angry cat.

give the shirt off one's back (to) *exp.* to give all one can • *He'll give the shirt off his back for his friends;* He'll do anything for his friends.

roll off one's back (to) *exp.* not to affect someone • *She insulted me, but I just let it roll off my back;* She insulted me, but I just didn't let it affect me.

turn one's back (to) *exp.* to reject • *He turned his back on me when I needed him;* He rejected me when I needed him.

"You scratch my back, I'll scratch yours" *exp.* You do me a favor, I'll do you a favor • *This time, I'll give you the work for free. You scratch my back, I'll scratch yours;* This time, I'll give you the work for free. You do me a favor, I'll do you a favor.

Bone

bare bone essentials *exp.* necessities (i.e. food, toiletries, etc.) • *We'd better go to the market because we're down to the bare bone essentials;* We'd better go to the market because we're left with only the necessities.
♦ ALSO: **to get down to the bare bone essentials** *exp.* to discuss the most important issues • *Let's get down to the bare bone essentials;* Let's discuss the most important issues.

bone to pick with someone (to have a) *exp.* to have a subject of disagreement, a conflict • *I have a bone to pick with you;* I have a concern to discuss with you.

bone up (to) *exp.* to study or practice • *I need to bone up on my English;* I need to study my English.

bone-breaking *adj.* exceedingly hard work • *This work is bone-breaking!;* This work is terribly hard!

bonehead *n.* a stupid person •
He's a real bonehead; He's
really stupid.

boney *adj.* (or *bony*) so thin that
one's bones show • *She's so
boney;* She's so thin.

lazy bones *exp.* an extremely
lazy person • *Wake up, lazy
bones!;* Wake up, lazy
person!

**no bones about something (to
make)** *exp.* absolutely, un-
questionably, straightforward
• *He made no bones about
telling her to leave;* He was
straightforward about telling
her to leave.

**nothing but skin and bones (to
be)** *exp.* to be extremely thin
• *He's nothing but skin and
bones;* He's extremely thin.

Brain

bean-brain (to be a) *exp.* to be
stupid • *He's a real
bean-brain;* He's really
stupid.

birdbrain *n.* one who is stupid
and irresponsible, whose
brain is no bigger than that of
a bird • *She's such a
birdbrain!;* She's so stupid
and irresponsible!

brainy *adj.* to be very
intelligent • *She's very
brainy;* She's very smart.

pick someone's brain (to) *exp.*
to question someone
carefully in order to further
one's own knowledge • *Since
you're an expert, would you
mind if I pick your brain for
an hour?;* Since you're an
expert, would you mind if I
question you carefully for an
hour?

rack one's brain(s) (to) *exp.* to
strain to remember
something or find a solution
to a problem • *I racked my
brains for an hour but
couldn't remember her
name!;* I strained for an hour
but couldn't remember her
name! • *I racked my brain(s)
trying to find a solution;* I
strained to find a solution.

scatterbrain *n.* one who is
eccentric and flighty • *He's
such a scatterbrain!;* He's so
flighty!
  ♦ ALSO: **to be scatterbrained**
adj. to be eccentric and
flighty • *She's so
scatterbrained!;* She's so
flighty!

Cheek

cheeky (to be) *exp.* to be
disrespectful • *Stop being so
cheeky!;* Stop being so
disrespectful!

tongue in cheek *exp.*
sarcastically • *She said it*

tongue in cheek; She said it sarcastically.

turn the other cheek (to) *exp.* to accept without argument or resistance • *His mother turned the other cheek when he took the cookie;* His mother pretended not to notice when he took the cookie.

Chest

off one's chest (to get something) *exp.* to expose one's burdening feelings to someone • *I need to talk to you and get this off my chest;* I need to talk to you so I can feel better.

Ear

all ears (to be) *exp.* to listen intently • *What happened? I'm all ears;* What happened? I'm listening intently.

bend someone's ear (to) *exp.* to talk to someone incessantly • *He bent my ear for an entire hour;* He talked to me incessantly for an entire hour.

blow it out one's ear (to) *exp.* a contemptuous response to someone's annoying remark • *"My father's a lot smarter than yours!" "Go blow it out your ear!";* "My father's a lot smarter than yours!" "That's nonsense!"*

chew someone's ear off (to) *exp.* to talk to someone incessantly • *He can really chew your ear off;* He can really talk incessantly.

dog-eared *exp.* (said of paper) tattered • *The pages of this book are all dog-eared;* The pages of this book are all tattered.

ear for music (to have an) *exp.* to have an aptitude for music • *He has an ear for music;* He has an aptitude for music.

earful *n.* an excessive amount of verbal input • *I heard an earful of gossip today;* I heard a lot of gossip today.

earmarks *n.pl.* attributes • *He has all the earmarks of being a thief;* He has all the attributes of being a thief.

fall on deaf ears (to) *exp.* to talk to someone who is not listening • *Stop explaining. It's all falling on deaf ears;* Stop explaining. It's all being said to someone who's not listening.

good ear *exp.* an aptitude for distinguishing sounds (such as music, languages, etc.) • *He's able to learn a new language by living in a* *country for only a month. He must have a good ear (for languages);* He's able to learn a new language by living in a country for only a month. He must have an aptitude for distinguishing sounds.

keep one's ear to the ground (to) *exp.* to pay attention to everything one hears • *Keep your ear to the ground;* Pay attention to everything you hear.

perk up one's ears (to) *exp.* to catch one's attention • *It perked up my ears when I heard him mention my name;* It caught my attention when I heard him mention my name.

play by ear (to) *exp.* to be able to play a song on an instrument simply by having heard it previously • *She doesn't read music at all. She plays everything by ear;* She doesn't read music at all. She plays everything simply by having heard it before.
♦ NOTE: The expression *"to play by ear"* is commonly used outside the music world as well to mean, "to improvise" • *Maybe we can have dinner together next week. Let's just play it by ear;* Maybe we can have dinner together next week. Let's just improvise.

put a bug in someone's ear (to) *exp.* to warn someone • *I think the boss is going to be laying off the employees who aren't working hard enough. I just want to put a bug in your ear;* I think the boss is going to be laying off the employees who aren't working hard enough. I just want to warn you.

talk someone's ear off (to) *exp.* to irritate someone by talking too much • *She talked my ear off for a whole hour;* She irritated me by talking for a whole hour.

Elbow

elbow grease *exp.* hard work • *The stain will come off. It just takes some elbow grease;* The stain will come off. It just takes some hard work.

elbow one's way (to) *exp.* to make one's way through a crowd by pushing with one's elbow • *I had to elbow my way through the crowd;* I had to make my way through the crowd by pushing with my elbow.

elbow room (to give someone) *exp.* to give someone space • *I can hardly move. Give me some elbow room;* I can hardly move. Give me some space.

rub elbows with someone (to) *exp.* to socialize with someone • *When I went to Hollywood, I rubbed elbows with all the movie stars;* When I went to Hollywood, I socialized with all the movie stars.

Eye

an eye for an eye *exp.* punishment equal to the harm which was done • "You did something harmful to me, now I'm entitled to do something harmful equally harmful to you."

bedroom eyes (to have) *exp.* to have sexy eyes • *He has such bedroom eyes;* He has such sexy eyes.

eye-catcher *exp.* attractive person or thing • *She's a real eye-catcher;* She's very attractive.

eye for something (an) *exp.* good taste • *He has an eye for art;* He has good taste in art.

eye someone (to) *exp.* to scrutinize someone with great interest • *When I first met her, she eyed me up and down;* When I first met her, she scrutinized me with great interest.

eyesore *n.* something that is offensive to look at • *That painting is an eyesore;* That painting is offensive to look at.

eyes bigger than one's stomach (to have) *exp.* to be less hungry than one thought • *I think I ordered too much food. I guess my eyes are bigger than my stomach;* I think I ordered too much food. I guess I'm less hungry than I thought.

four-eyes *n.* condescending term for one who wears glasses • *Hey, four-eyes!;* Hey, you with the glasses!

give one's eyetooth for something (to) *exp.* to risk anything in order to obtain something • *I'd give my eyetooth to look like her;* I'd risk anything to look like her. ♦ NOTE: The *"eyetooth"* is the upper canine.

give someone a black eye (to) *exp.* to bruise someone's eye by hitting it • *Where did you get that black eye?;* Where did you bruise that eye?

goo-goo eyes at someone (to make) *exp.* to look at someone longingly and romantically • *I hate talking with her because she keeps making goo-goo eyes at me!;* I hate talking with her because she keeps looking at me longingly and romantically!

green-eyed monster *exp.* jealousy • *That's the green-eyed monster talking;* That jealousy talking.

in a pig's eye *exp.* nonsense • *"She told me she speaks ten languages." "In a pig's eye!";* "She told me she speaks ten languages." "That's nonsense!"

keep an eye on someone (to) *exp.* to watch over someone • *I have to stay here and keep an eye on my little brother;* I have to stay here and watch over my little brother.

keep one's eyes peeled (to) *exp.* to stay alert • *Keep your eyes peeled;* Stay alert.

see eye-to-eye (to) *exp.* to be in agreement with someone • *We always see eye to eye;* We're always in agreement.

shuteye *n.* sleep • *I need to get some shuteye;* I need to get some sleep.

Finger

finger-pointing *exp.* passing of blame • *There's been a lot of finger-pointing throughout this case;* There's been a lot

of blame-passing throughout this case.

lift a finger (not to) *exp.* not to do anything • *He never lifts a finger;* He never does anything.

one's finger on something (to put) *exp.* to discover the truth • *I think you just put your finger on it;* I think you just discovered the truth.

someone the finger (to give) *exp.* to make an obscene gesture at someone by showing one's middle finger • *When he drove past me, he gave me the finger;* When he drove past me, he made an obscene gesture.

wrapped around one's little finger (to be) *exp.* to be controlled by someone • *He'll do anything I want. I have him wrapped around my little finger;* He'll do anything I want. I have him under control.

Foot

back on one's feet (to get) *exp.* to reestablish oneself after a failure • *After he lost his job, it took him a while to get back on his feet;* After he lost his job, it took him a while to reestablish himself.

cold feet (to get) *exp.* to lose one's courage at the last moment • *Just when I was about to ask him for a raise, I got cold feet;* Just when I was about to ask him for a raise, I suddenly lost my courage.

footloose (to be) *exp.* to be able to do anything one desires in one's life without any restrictions • *Now that he's divorced, he's footloose;* Now that he's divorced, he can do anything he wants in his life without restrictions.
♦ VARIATION: **to be footloose and fancy-free** *exp.*

foot the bill (to) *exp.* to pay the bill • *I didn't have to pay anything. He said he would foot the entire bill;* I didn't have to pay anything. He said he would pay the entire bill.

footsie (to play) *exp.* to flirt by rubbing someone's feet with one's own feet • *She kept playing footsie with me under the table;* She kept rubbing my feet under the table with her own feet.

get a foot in the door (to) *exp.* to take the first step in attaining a goal • *You didn't get the job yet, but at least it's a foot in the door;* You didn't get the job yet, but at least it's the first step.

get one's feet wet (to) *exp.* to become familiar with a situation • *I don't really know what my job entails. I'm still getting my feet wet;* I don't really know what my job entails. I'm still becoming familiar with it.

hotfoot it (to) *exp.* to hurry • *The movie starts in five minutes! We'd better hotfoot it over to the theater!;* The movie starts in five minutes! We'd better hurry to the theater!
♦ NOTE: This expression is from the early 1900's but is still occasionally used in fun. It conjures up an image of someone whose feet are hot due to moving very fast.

lead foot *n.* to have a tendency to drive fast as if his/her foot were as heavy as lead on the accelerator • *I don't like driving with him. He has a real lead foot;* I don't like driving with him. He drives too fast.

one foot in the grave *exp.* close to death • *The poor man has one foot in the grave;* The poor man is close to death.

one's foot down (to put) *exp.* to forbid • *I have to put my foot down on that;* I have to forbid that.

pussy-foot around (to) *exp.* to be indirect and cautious • *Stop pussy-footing around. What do you want?;* Stop being indirect and cautious. What do you want?

quick on one's feet *exp.* able to arrive at ideas quickly • *He's always been quick on his feet;* He has always been able to arrive at ideas quickly.

stand on one's own two feet (to) *exp.* to be self-reliant • *She has to learn to stand on her own two feet;* She has to learn to be self-reliant.

swept off one's feet (to be) *exp.* to be seduced • *He swept her off her feet as soon as they met;* He seduced her as soon as they met.

throw oneself at someone's feet (to) *exp.* to succumb to someone completely • *He threw himself at her feet;* He completely succumbed to her.

under one's feet (to get) *exp.* to get in someone's way • *She always gets under my feet;* She always gets in my way.
‣ ALSO: **to get underfoot** *exp.* • She always gets underfoot; She always gets in my way.

wrong foot (to get off on the) *exp.* to begin a friendship badly • *We got off on the wrong foot, but now we're friends;* We began badly, but now we're friends.

Gums

flap one's gums (to) *exp.* to talk nonsense • *Stop flapping your gums!;* Stop talking nonsense!

Guts

bust a gut (to) *exp.* to laugh hard • *He busted a gut laughing;* He laughed hard.

gut (to get a) *exp.* to get a big belly • *You're starting to get a gut;* You're starting to get a big belly.

gut reaction *n.* initial and instinctive response • *My gut reaction to him wasn't good;* My initial reaction to him wasn't good.

guts to do something (not to have the) *exp.* not to have the courage to do something • *He doesn't have the guts to be a policeman;* He doesn't have the courage to be a policeman.
‣ ALSO: **to have guts** *exp. I respect you. You have guts;* I respect you. You have courage.

gutsy (to be) *exp.* to be courageous • *She's very gutsy;* She's very courageous.

hate someone's guts (to) *exp.* to despise someone • *I hate her guts!;* I despise her!

spill one's guts (to) *exp.* to disclose one's innermost feelings • *She spilled her guts to me;* She disclosed her innermost feelings to me.

throw one's guts up (to) *exp.* to vomit • *I threw my guts up after drinking those two beers;* I vomited after drinking those two beers. ♦ VARIATION: **to throw up one's guts** *exp.*

Hair

hair-raising *adj.* frightening • *What a hair-raising story!;* What a frightening story!

hairy *adj.* frightening • *That must have been hairy!;* That must have been frightening!

let one's hair down (to) *exp.* to relax and abandon all pretense • *She finally let her hair down in front of us;* She finally relaxed and abandoned all pretense in front of us.

someone's hair (to get in) *exp.* to annoy • *My little brother keeps getting in my hair;* My little brother keeps annoying me.

Hand

at hand (to be) *exp.* pressing, important • *What's the issue at hand?;* What's the pressing issue?

give someone a hand (to) *exp.* **1.** to help • *Can you give me a hand with this?;* Can you help me with this? • **2.** to applaud • *That was a great performance! Let's give him a hand!;* That was a great performance! Let's applaud him!

hand (to) *exp.* to give • *Hand it to me right now!;* Give it to me right now! ♦ ALSO: **to hand over** *exp.* to give • *Hand it over!;* Give it to me!

hand it to someone (to) *exp.* (said in admiration of someone) • *I've got to hand it to you!;* I really admire you!

handout *exp.* offering, charity • *Although he doesn't have any money, he refuses to accept handouts;* Although he doesn't have any money, he refuses to accept charitable donations.

hands down *exp.* **1.** without exception • *I think it's the best movie hands down;* I think it's the best movie without exception • **2.** unanimously • *He won the* *election hands down;* He won unanimously.

know something like the back of one's hand (to) *exp.* to know something extremely well • *I know this city like the back of my hand;* I know this city extremely well.

live hand-to-mouth (to) *exp.* to live day to day on little money • *Since I only have a temporary job, I have to live hand to mouth;* Since I only have a temporary job, I have to live day to day on little money.

old hand at something (an) *exp.* a seasoned expert at something • *I'm an old hand at fixing cars;* I'm a seasoned expert at fixing cars.

on hand *exp.* readily available • *Do you have a screwdriver on hand?;* Do you have a screwdriver available?

out of hand *exp.* out of control • *Things really got out of hand when the police arrived;* Things really got out of control when the police arrived.

right-hand man *exp.* valuable partner • *He's my right-hand man;* He's my valuable partner.

second-hand *adj.* used • *I bought it second-hand;* I

bought it used.

‣ ALSO: **to hear something second-hand** *exp.* to hear something indirectly • *I heard about the accident second-hand;* I heard about the accident indirectly.

short-handed *exp.* low on personnel • *We were short-handed at work today;* We were low on personnel at work today.

the right hand doesn't know what the left is doing *exp.* to be unaware of the actions of an associate • *One of the vice presidents of the company told me to buy the stock and the other told me not to! Obviously, the right hand doesn't know what the left is doing;* One of the vice presidents of the company told me to buy the stock and the other told me not to! Obviously, they're unaware of each other's actions.

try one's hand at something (to) *exp.* to test one's ability at something • *Tomorrow I'm going to try my hand at golf;* Tomorrow I'm going to test my ability at golf.

Head

airhead *n.* one who is irresponsible and flighty • *I wouldn't trust her. She's a* *real airhead;* I wouldn't trust her. She's really irresponsible and flighty.

big head (to have a) *exp.* to be conceited • *His head has gotten big ever since he became a movie star;* He has become conceited ever since he became a movie star.

bite one's head off (to) *exp.* to attack someone verbally • *I criticized her dress and she bit my head off;* I criticized her dress and she attacked me verbally.

head out (to) *exp.* to depart • *Let's head out around 8:00 in the morning;* Let's leave around 8:00 in the morning.

head over heels for someone *exp.* madly in love with someone • *I'm head over heels for my teacher;* I'm madly in love with my teacher.

head trip (to be on a) *exp.* **1.** to be living in an imaginary world, dreaming • *She's on a real head trip. She thinks she's the smartest person in class;* She's living in an imaginary world. She thinks she's the smartest person in class. • **2.** to be conceited • *Get off your head trip!;* Stop acting conceited!

headstrong *exp.* stubborn • *He's always so headstrong;* He's always so stubborn.

"Heads are going to roll" *exp.* "People are going to get in trouble" • *The boss just called them into his office. I think heads are gonna roll;* The boss just called them into his office. I think people are going to get in trouble.

"Heads up!" *exp.* "Look up because there's an object flying toward you!"

headway (to make) *exp.* to make progress • *You're starting to make headway with your French!;* You're starting to make progress with your French!

hit the nail on the head (to) *exp.* to be exactly right • *You hit the nail on head!;* You're exactly right!

hole in one's head (to have a) *exp.* to be crazy • *I think you've got a hole in your head;* I think you're crazy.

hole in the head (to need someone or something like a) *exp.* to have absolutely no need for someone or something • *I need that like a hole in the head;* I have absolutely no need for that.

hothead *n.* a quick-tempered person • *He's such a hothead;* He has such a quick temper.

off the top of one's head *exp.* a coarse estimate, without calculation • *I can't be specific, but off the top of my head, I'd say he'll be arriving in about five minutes;* I can't be specific, but I'd estimate he'll be arriving in about five minutes.

over one's head *exp.* beyond one's comprehension • *I think you just went over his head;* I think you just went beyond his comprehension.

sorehead *n.* grumbler or complainer • *Don't be such a sorehead;* Don't be such a complainer.
‣ NOTE: This is usually said to someone who is grumbling after having lost a game or competition.

swelled head (to have a) *exp.* to be conceited • *I don't like being around her. She has such a swelled head!;* I don't like being around her. She's so conceited!

use one's head (to) *exp.* to use one's intelligence • *Everything he does is stupid. He never uses his head;* Everything he does is stupid. He never uses his intelligence.

Heart

eat one's heart out (to) *exp.* to be envious • *She's going to eat her heart out when she sees me with Tom;* She's going to die of envy when she sees me with Tom.

have a heart (to) *exp.* to have compassion • *The teacher gave us homework to do over the weekend. She doesn't have a heart;* The teacher gave us homework to do over the weekend. She doesn't have compassion.

heart of something (to get to the) *exp.* to get to the core of something • *Let's get to the heart of the problem;* Let's get to the core of the problem.

heart go out to someone (to have one's) *exp.* to feel compassion for someone • *My heart goes out to her;* I feel compassion for her.

heart to do something (not to have the) *exp.* not to be able to do something due to compassion • *I don't have the heart to tell him that his dog died;* I'm too compassionate to tell him that his dog died.

heart-to-heart *n.* a serious discussion • *I need to have a heart-to-heart with my son;* I need to have a serious discussion with my son.

heartache *n.* anguish • *Every time he came home late, he caused me heartache;* Every time he came home late, he caused me anguish.

Heel

Achilles' heel *exp.* vulnerable area • *If you want her to like you, just talk about animals. That's her Achilles' heel;* If you want her to like you, just talk about animals. That's her vulnerable area.

cool one's heels (to) *exp.* to wait • *I cooled my heels for a whole hour before she finally arrived;* I waited for a whole hour before she finally arrived.

drag one's heels (to) *exp.* to delay • *Quit dragging your heels and hurry!;* Quit delaying and hurry!

head over heels for someone *exp.* madly in love with someone • *We're head over heels for my sister's husband;* We're in love with my sister's husband.

"Heel!" *interj.* command given to a dog to walk next to its master's heel • *Heel!;* Walk directly next to me! • *I just taught my dog to heel;* I just taught my dog to walk

directly next to me (and not to run ahead).

heel *exp.* contemptible person • *I hurt her feelings. I feel like such a heel;* I hurt her feelings. I feel like such a contemptible person.

kick up one's heels (to) *exp.* to frolic • *I can't wait to go on vacation. I need to kick up my heels!;* I can't wait to go on vacation. I need to play!

walk on one's heels (to) *exp.* to walk too closely to someone • *Stop walking on my heels!;* Stop walking so closely to me!

Hip

shoot from the hip (to) *exp.* to act or respond impulsively • *He never thinks before he speaks. He just shoots from the hip;* He never thinks before he speaks. He just responds impulsively.

Knuckle

knuckle down (to) *exp.* to get serious and stop playing • *We've got to knuckle down and clean this house;* We've got to get serious and clean this house.

knuckle sandwich (to give someone a) *exp.* to hit

someone with the fist • *How would you like a knuckle sandwich?!;* How would you like to be hit with my fist?!

knuckle under (to) *exp.* to surrender • *He finally knuckled under because the pressure was simply too much;* He finally surrendered because the pressure was simply too much.

knuckle-head *n.* fool • *You knuckle-head!;* You fool!
♦ NOTE: This is a very mild and somewhat amusing insult.

Leg

hollow leg (to have a) *exp.* (said of someone with a huge appetite) • *I don't know how he can eat so much. He must have a hollow leg;* I don't know how he can eat so much. He must be storing the food in a hollow leg.

leg it (to) *exp.* to walk • *Let's leg it to work today;* Let's walk to work today.

leg to stand on (not to have a) *exp.* not to have any justification for something • *He'll never win the court case. He doesn't have a leg to stand on;* He'll never win the court case. He doesn't have any justification.

pay an arm and a leg (to) *exp.* to pay a lot of money • *That couch cost an arm and a leg;* That couch cost a lot of money.

pull someone's leg (to) *exp.* to tell someone lies (usually in jest) • *Stop pulling my leg!;* Stop teasing me!

shake a leg (to) *exp.* to hurry • *We'd better shake a leg if we don't want to be late;* We'd better hurry if we don't want to be late.

stretch one's legs (to) *exp.* to move around after having been motionless for a long period • *I'm going outside to stretch my legs;* I'm going outside to move around.

Lip

button one's lip (to) *exp.* to stop talking • *Button your lip!;* Stop talking!

fat lip *exp.* a swollen lip from getting punched in the mouth • *Stop teasing me or I'll give you a fat lip!;* Stop teasing me or I'll punch you in the mouth.

keep a stiff upper lip (to) *exp.* to keep one's emotions under control • *Don't worry. Just keep a stiff upper lip;* Don't worry. Just control yourself.

lip *exp.* disrespectful talk • *I don't want any more lip out of you!;* I don't want any more disrespectful talk from you!

pay someone lip service (to) *exp.* to downgrade the importance of something; that which comes from the mouth and not the heart • *What I'm saying is true. I'm not just paying you lip service;* What I'm saying is true. I'm talking from my heart.

"Read my lips" *exp.* an insulting statement, maligning the listener's ability to comprehend • *"Watch me closely and I'll repeat."*

Liver

lily-livered (to be) *exp.* to be cowardly • *I've never met anyone so lily-livered;* I've never met anyone so cowardly.

chopped liver (to be) *exp.* to be insignificant • *He always ignores me. What am I? Chopped liver?;* He always ignores me. What am I? Insignificant?

Mouth

bad-mouth someone (to) *exp.* to spread unfavorable rumors about someone • *I don't like her. She always bad-mouths me;* I don't like her. She always spreads unfavorable rumors about me.

big-mouth *n.* a talker • *Don't tell her anything. She's got a big mouth;* Don't tell her anything. She's a gossiper.

blabbermouth *n.* a talker; a gossiper • *Don't tell him any secrets. He's a real blabbermouth;* Don't tell him any secrets. He's a real gossiper.

down in the mouth *exp.* depressed • *You look down in the mouth. What's wrong?;* You look depressed. What's wrong?

live hand-to-mouth (to) *exp.* to live day to day on little money • *Since I only have a temporary job, I have to live hand to mouth;* Since I only have a temporary job, I have to live day to day on little money.

mouth *n.* language • *I don't like your mouth!;* I don't like the kind of language you're using!

mouth off (to) *exp.* to be disrespectful and insolent • *You should have heard him mouth off to the teacher;* You should have heard him be disrespectful to the teacher.

run off at the mouth (to) *exp.* to talk nonstop • *Stop running off at the mouth!;* Stop talking so much!

shoot off one's mouth (to) *exp.* to say whatever comes to one's mind • *Think a little before you go shooting off your mouth!;* Think a little before you say whatever comes to your mind.

Neck

neck (to) *v.* to kiss and caress • *I saw them necking in the park;* I saw them kissing in the park.

neck of the woods (to be in someone's) *exp.* to be in someone's vicinity • *I was in your neck of the woods and thought I'd come by and visit;* I was in your vicinity and thought I'd come by and visit.

neck-and-neck (to be) *exp.* to be even in a competition • *The two runners are neck-and-neck;* The two runners are even.

pain in the neck (to be a) *exp.* to be annoying • *He's such a pain in the neck;* He's so annoying.

redneck *exp.* bigot, prejudiced • *He's a real redneck;* He's a real bigot.

stick one's neck out for someone (to) *exp.* to risk a lot for someone • *I stuck my neck out for him;* I risked a lot for him.

wring someone's neck (to) *exp.* to strangle someone • *If I catch him, I'm gonna wring his neck!;* If I catch him, I'm going to strangle him!

Nerve

get on someone's nerves (to) *exp.* to annoy someone • *You're getting on my nerves!;* You're annoying me!

hit a nerve (to) *exp.* to bring up a sensitive issue • *I think you just hit a nerve with him;* I think you just brought up a sensitive issue with him.

nerve *exp.* audacity • *You have some nerve!;* You have some audacity!

nerves on edge (to have one's) *exp.* to be overwrought • *I think I need a drink. My nerves are on edge;* I think I need a drink. I'm over- wrought.

nervy (to be) *exp.* to have audacity • *She's really nervy;* She has a lot of audacity.

Nose

as plain as the nose on one's face *exp.* very obvious • *It's as plain as the nose on your face;* It's very obvious.

hard-nosed *exp.* stubborn • *You're always so hard-nosed!;* You're always so stubborn.

keep one's nose to the grindstone (to) *exp.* to work diligently • *If you keep your nose to the grindstone, you'll succeed;* If you keep working diligently, you'll succeed.

"It's no skin off my nose" *exp.* "It's of no concern to me" • *Whether she comes to my party or not, it's no skin off my nose.*

nose dive (to take a) *exp.* to fail suddenly • *His health took a nose dive;* His health failed suddenly.
♦ NOTE: This expression is said of airplanes that suddenly lose power and fall quickly and suddenly to the ground.

nose for something (to have a) *exp.* to have a knack for finding something • *She has a nose for finding bargains;* She has a knack for finding bargains.

nose out (to) *exp.* to slightly defeat • *He nosed him out of the competition;* He defeated him in the competition.
♦ VARIATION: **to win by a nose** *exp.*

nose out of joint (to get one's) *exp.* to become offended • *Now, don't get your nose out of joint;* Now, don't get offended.

nosey *adj.* curious • *She so nosey!;* She's so intrusive!

one's nose in the air (to have) *exp.* to be snobbish, conceited, vain • *She never talks to me. She always has her nose in the air;* She never talks to me. She's always so snobbish.

pay through the nose (to) *exp.* to pay a lot of money • *I had to pay through the nose to get that dress;* I had to pay a lot of money to get that dress.

poke one's nose in someone's business (to) *exp.* to meddle in someone's business • *He came over to poke his nose in my business;* He came over to meddle in my business.

right under one's nose (to be) *exp.* to be obvious • *The answer is right under your nose;* The answer is obvious.

turn one's nose up at someone or something (to) *exp.* to reject someone or something • *She turned up her nose at* *the dinner;* She refused to eat the dinner.

Palm

eating out of the palm of one's hand (to have someone) *exp.* to have total control over someone • *I know he'll sign the contract. I have him eating out of the palm of my hand;* I know he'll sign the contract. I have total control over him.

in the palm of one's hand (to have someone) *exp.* to have total control over someone • *I know he'll sign the contract. I have him in the palm of my hand;* I know he'll sign the contract. I have total control over him.

palm off something on someone (to) *exp.* to rid oneself of something undesirable by giving it to someone • *My brother palmed off his old bicycle on me;* My brother rid himself of his old unwanted bicycle.

Shoulder

cold shoulder (to give someone the) *exp.* not to speak to someone, to snub • *He's giving me the cold shoulder;* He's not speaking to me.

rest on one's shoulders (to) *exp.* to depend on someone • *The job rests on your shoulders now;* The job depends on you now.

speak straight from the shoulder (to) *exp.* to speak directly and straightforwardly • *I spoke straight from the shoulder and told him I didn't like the way he treated me yesterday;* I spoke directly and straightforwardly and told him I didn't like the way he treated me yesterday.

Spine

spineless *adj.* cowardly • *He was really angry at his boss but was afraid to tell him. Sometimes he's so spineless!;* He was really angry at his boss but was afraid to tell him. Sometimes he's so cowardly!

Stomach

one's eyes bigger than one's stomach (to have) *exp.* to be less hungry than one thought. ♦ SEE: *Eyes*

unable to stomach someone or something *exp.* unable to tolerate someone or something • *I can't stomach her;* I can't tolerate her.

Throat

jump down one's throat (to) *exp.* to attack someone verbally • *I gave her a suggestion and she jumped down my throat;* I gave her a suggestion and she attacked me verbally.

Thumb

all thumbs *exp.* clumsy • *I could never be a surgeon. I'm all thumbs;* I could never be a surgeon. I'm clumsy.

rule of thumb *exp.* informal procedure or convention • *It's a rule of thumb to water plants in the morning before the temperature gets too high;* It's an informal procedure to water plants in the morning before the temperature gets too high.

thumb a ride (to) *exp.* to hitchhike • *Since we ran out of gas, we were forced to thumb a ride into the city;* Since we ran out of gas, we were forced to hitchhike into the city.

thumbs up *exp.* approval • *He gave me a thumbs up on the project;* He approved the project.
‣ ANTONYM: **thumbs down** *exp.* disapproval.

under one's thumb *exp.* under one's control • *He'll do anything I ask. I have him under my thumb;* He'll do anything I ask. I have him under my control.

Toe

on one's toes *exp.* alert • *There could be trouble, so be on your toes;* There could be trouble, so be alert.

tip toe around someone (to) *exp.* to be cautious around someone • *She's so unpredictable that you have to tip toe around her;* She's so unpredictable that you have to be cautious around her.

toe the line (to) *exp.* to behave properly • *If he doesn't toe the line, fire him!;* If he doesn't behave properly, fire him!

toe-to-toe (to go) *exp.* to fight • *They're going toe-to-toe again!;* They're fighting again!

Tongue

hold one's tongue (to) *exp.* to stop talking • *Hold your tongue! You've said enough already;* Stop talking! You've said enough already.

speak a tongue (to) *exp.* to speak a language • *How many tongues does she speak?* How many languages does she speak?

"The cat's got your tongue?" *exp.* "You have nothing to say?"

tongue-tied (to be) *exp.* to be speechless or unable to speak coherently • *Whenever I talk in front of an audience, I get tongue-tied;* Whenever I talk in front of an audience, I become speechless.

Tooth

by the skin of one's teeth *exp.* barely • *I passed the test by the skin of my teeth;* I barely passed the test.

fight tooth and nail (to) *exp.* to fight violently • *I fought tooth and nail to stop the county from condemning the library;* I fought hard to stop the county from condemning the library.

long in the tooth (to be) *exp.* to be old • *Our dog is getting long in the tooth;* Our dog is getting old.

one's teeth chatter (to have) *exp.* to shiver • *I'm so cold my teeth are chattering;* I'm so cold I'm shivering.

set one's teeth on edge (to) *exp.* to make one shudder • *That high pitched sound sets my teeth on edge;* That high pitched sound makes me shudder.

sweet tooth *exp.* a passion for confections • *I've never met anyone with such a sweet tooth;* I've never met anyone who enjoys confections so much.

Practice Using Body Parts in Slang

(Answers, p. 230)

A. **Complete the following expressions by choosing the correct body part from the list below. NOTE: Not all of the words are used.**

arm	finger	knuckle	spine
back	foot	leg	stomach
bone	gums	lip	throat
brain	guts	liver	thumb
butt	hair	mouth	toe
cheek	hand	neck	tongue
ear	head	nerve	tooth
elbow	heart	nose	
eye	heel	shoulder	

1. That car must have cost you an _____ and a leg.

2. I'm scared. I just don't have the _____ to do it.

3. I love chocolate! I guess I have a sweet _____ .

4. Don't _____ in! It doesn't concern you.

5. She talked my _____ off for an entire hour.

6. She actually invited herself to the party! What _____ !

7. I've got a _____ to pick with him.

8. She jumped down my _____ for no reason at all.

9. Don't listen to him. He's just flapping his _____ .

10. Since we don't have enough money for a taxi, I supposed we'd better _____ a ride.

11. When you went to Hollywood, did you rub _____ with any movie stars?

12. Order anything you want from the menu. I'm going to _____ the bill.

Just For Fun...

Test yourself on the expressions that you just learned!

"I know she likes to **spill her GUTS** and **chew off your EAR** nonstop but you just have **to keep a stiff upper LIP** and **put your FOOT down** or else just **turn the other CHEEK** and stop getting all **up in ARMS.** I know it's hard to **let it roll off your BACK** but if you can't **STOMACH** her, you'd better **have a HEART-to-HEART** which is better than just **giving her the cold SHOULDER** or **jumping down her THROAT.** I've got a **BONE to pick** with her too and I keep **racking my BRAINS** on how to talk to her without **biting her HEAD off** but I always get **cold FEET.** Oh, did you hear her **MOUTH off** yesterday about how she **KNUCKLED under** and bought a new car that she **fell HEAD over HEELS** for? If you ask me, I think she **paid through the NOSE!**"

Translation:

"I know she likes to **tell you everything she's thinking** and **talk to you nonstop** but you have **to be strong** and **be insistent** or else just **relax and ignore it** and stop getting all **upset.** I know it's hard to **ignore it** but if you can't **tolerate** her, you'd better have an **intimate discussion** which is better than **not talking to her anymore** or **attacking her verbally.** I've got a **problem to discuss** with her too and I keep trying to **determine** how to talk to her without **yelling,** but I always get **nervous.** Oh, did you hear her **brag** yesterday about how she **succumbed** and bought a new car that she **fell in love** with? If you ask me, she **paid too much money!**"

At the Mall

Dialogue in slang

At the Mall...

Debbie and Alicia are out shopping.

Debbie: Oh, **brother**! **Get a load** of that **number** she's wearing. I wouldn't be **caught dead** in that. What a **scream**!

Alicia: I forgot you always **get a kick** out of **trashing** everyone in the mall. I think that's the only reason you **drag** me here.

Debbie: Okay, okay, I'll behave. Let's go **hit** the stores but I can only **window shop** 'cause I'm **broke**... unless you let me **sponge** a few **bucks** off you.

Alicia: Sure, what do I care? I'm **rolling in it**!

Debbie: Great, then let's **shop till we drop**!

Alicia: **Gee**, look at the blouse in that window. It's **drop-dead gorgeous**! I've got to have it. **Holy cow**! 200 **bucks**? **Talk about** a **rip-off**! Like I'm really going to **fork out** that kind of **dough** for a blouse.

Debbie: **Hold it down**! Let's just **get going**. This **joint**'s a little **too rich for my blood**.

Alicia: That really **bugs** me. That thing **had my name on it**. Come on, I want to go **drown my sorrows** in a vat of ice cream.

Debbie: **Now you're talkin'**!

Translation of dialogue in standard English

At the Mall...

Debbie and Alicia are out shopping.

Debbie: Oh, **wow**! **Just look at** that **outfit** she's wearing. I would **never** wear that. How **funny**!

Alicia: I forgot you always **enjoy criticizing** everyone in the mall. I think that's the only reason you **force** me to come here.

Debbie: Okay, okay, I'll behave. Let's go **into** the stores, but I can only **browse** because I **don't have any money**... unless you let me **borrow** a few **dollars** from you.

Alicia: Sure, what do I care? I'm **rich**!

Debbie: Great, then let's **shop until we're exhausted**!

Alicia: **Well**, look at the blouse in that window. It's really **gorgeous**! I've got to have it. **Wow**! 200 **dollars**? **That sure is thievery**! It's absurd to think that I'm really going to **spend** that kind of **money** for a blouse.

Debbie: **Don't talk so loud**! Let's just **leave**. This **place** is a litte **too expensive**.

Alicia: That really **upsets** me. That thing **was perfectly suited to me**. Come on, I want to go **cheer up by eating** a vat of ice cream.

Debbie: **That's a good idea**!

Dialogue in slang as it would be heard

At the Mall...

Debbie 'n Alicia 'r out shopping.

Debbie: Oh, **brother**! **Ged a load a** that **number** she's wearing. I wouldn' be **caught dead**'n that. Whad a **scream**!

Alicia: I fergot you always **ged a kick** outta **trashing** everyone in the mall. I think that's the only reason you **drag** me here.

Debbie: Okay, okay, I'll behave. Let's go **hit** the stores bud I c'n only **window shop** '**cause** I'm **broke**... unless you let me **sponge** a few **bucks** off ya.

Alicia: Sher, whad do I care? I'm **rolling in it!**

Debbie: Great, then let's **shop till we drop**!

Alicia: **Gee**, look at the blouse in that window. It's **drop-dead gorgeous**! I've gotta have it. **Holy cow**! 200 **bucks**? **Talk aboud** a **rip off**! Like I'm really gonna **fork out** that kind 'a **dough** fer a blouse.

Debbie: **Hold it down**! **Let's jus' get going**. This **joint's** a liddle **too rich fer my blood**.

Alicia: That really **bugs** me. That thing **had my name on it**. C'mon, I wanna go **drown my sorrows** in a vad of ice cream.

Debbie: Now **yer talkin'**!

Vocabulary

broke *exp.* destitute • *I can't afford that. I'm broke;* I can't afford that. I'm destitute.
> ALSO (1): **stone/flat broke** *exp.* completely destitute • *I'm stone/flat broke;* I'm completely destitute.
> ALSO (2): **busted** *adj.* (variation of *"broke"*) destitute.
> SYNONYM: **down and out** *exp.* • *The poor man is really down and out;* The poor man is really destitute.

"Brother!" *exclam.* (said in contempt) • *Oh, brother! How could she wear that?;* I can't believe it! How could she wear that?
> NOTE: Used as an exclamation, *"brother"* can certainly be used among women.
> SYNONYM: **"Come on!"** *exclam.* • *Come on! How could she wear that?;* I can't believe it! How could she wear that?

buck *n.* dollar • *Can you lend me five bucks?;* Can you lend me five dollars?

bug (to) *v.* to annoy • *That really bugs me!;* That really annoys me!
> SYNONYM: **to burn one up** *exp.* • *He really burns me up!;* He really makes me mad!

caught dead (not to be) *exp.* not to want to be seen in a certain condition • *I wouldn't be caught dead wearing that hat;* I would never want to be seen wearing that hat.

dough *n.* money • *How much dough have you got?;* How much money do you have?
> NOTE: This old term is mainly heard in old movies or in jest.

drag someone somewhere (to) *exp.* to bring someone somewhere against his/her will • *I had to drag him to the party;* I had to bring him to the party against his will.

drop-dead gorgeous *exp.* very beautiful • *She's drop-dead gorgeous;* She's very beautiful.
> SYNONYM: **a knock-out** *exp.* • *She's a knock-out;* She's beautiful.

drown one's sorrows (to) *exp.* to cheer one up (usually by drinking) • *Let's go drown our sorrows;* Let's go cheer ourselves up by having a few drinks.

fork out (to) *exp.* to pay • *How much money did you have to fork out to buy that car?;* How much money did you have to pay to buy that car?
  ‣ SYNONYM: **to cough up** *exp.* • *I had to cough up $100 for my car repair;* I had to pay $100 for my car repair.

"Gee!" *exclam.* (exclamation of surprise or wonder, a euphemism for "Jesus")
  • *Gee, I wonder how he did that!*
  ‣ SYNONYM: **"Wow!"** *exclam.* • *Wow, I wonder how he did that!*

get a kick (to) *exp.* to enjoy very much • *I get a kick out of your sister;* I enjoy your sister very much.
  ‣ SYNONYM: **to get a charge** *exp.* • *I get a charge out of going to the beach;* I really enjoy going to the beach.

get going (to) *exp.* to leave • *Let's get going;* Let's leave.
  ‣ SYNONYM: **to split** *exp.* • *Let's split;* Let's leave.

have one's name on something (to) *exp.* to be perfectly suited to someone • *That shirt has my name on it;* That shirt is perfectly suited to me.
  ‣ SYNONYM: **to fit to a T** *exp.* • *That dress fits me to a T;* That dress fits me perfectly.

hit the stores (to) *exp.* to enter the stores • *Let's go hit the stores;* Let's go to the stores.

hold it down (to) *exp.* to be quiet • *Hold it down when you go to the library;* Be quiet when you go to the library.
  ‣ SYNONYM: **to pipe down** *exp.* • *Pipe down!;* Be quiet!

"Holy cow!" *exclam.* (exclamation of astonishment) • *Holy cow! That was unbelievable!*
  ‣ SYNONYM: **"Holy Toledo!"** *exp. Holy Toledo! That was unbelievable!*

joint *n.* **1.** place (in general) • *This is a nice joint;* This is a nice place. • **2.** a marijuana cigarette.
  ‣ SYNONYM: **spot** *n.* • *This is a nice spot;* This is a nice place.

load (to get a) *exp.* to observe • *Get a load of that beautiful house!;* Observe that beautiful house!
  ‣ SYNONYM: **to check out** *exp.* • *Check out that car!;* Observe that car!

"Now you're talkin' " *exp.* "Now you're being sensible."
  ‣ NOTE: In this expression, the verb *"talking"* is usually heard in its abbreviated form *"talkin'."*
  ‣ SYNONYM: **"I'm with you"** *exp.*

number *exp.* **1.** outfit • *What do you think of the new number I just bought?;* What do you think of the new outfit I just bought? • **2.** a very attractive person • *She's quite a number!;* She's very pretty!

rip-off *n.* thievery • *You were charged $400 for a pair of pants? What a rip-off!;* You were charged $400 for a pair of pants? What thievery!
♦ ALSO: **rip-off** *v.* to cheat someone of money • *You were charged $400 for a pair of pants? You were ripped off!;* You were charged $400 for a pair of pants? You were cheated!
♦ SYNONYM: **highway robbery** *exp.* • *I'm not paying that much money for that! That's highway robbery!;* I'm not paying that much money for that! That's thievery!

rolling in it *exp.* rich • *You have a beautiful house! You must be rolling in it!;* You have a beautiful house! You must be rich!
♦ NOTE: In this expression, *"it"* represents "money."
♦ SYNONYM: **to have money to burn** *exp.* • *She has money to burn;* She's rich.

scream (to be a) *exp.* to be hilarious • *That movie was a scream!;* That movie was hilarious!
♦ SYNONYM: **to be a hoot** *exp.* • *Your mother's a real hoot;* Your mother's really funny.

shop till one drops (to) *exp.* to shop until one has no more energy left • *Let's shop till we drop!;* Let's shop till we don't have any more energy!

sponge off someone (to) *exp.* to borrow money from someone • *He always sponges off me;* He always borrows money from me.
♦ SYNONYM: **to hit someone up** *exp.* to ask to borrow money from someone • *He hit me up for $200;* He asked me if he could borrow $200.

"Talk about a(n)..." *exclam.* "That was a real..." • *Talk about a funny movie!;* That was a real funny movie! • *Talk about an idiot!;* That person is a real idiot!

too rich for my blood *exp.* expensive • *This restaurant is too rich for my blood;* This restaurant is too expensive for me.
♦ SYNONYM: **pricey** *adj.* • *That's very pricey;* That's very expensive.

trash someone (to) *exp.* **1.** to criticize someone unmercifully • *I didn't come here to have you trash me!;* I didn't come here to have you criticize me so unmercifully! • **2.** to destroy something • *My brother borrowed my car and trashed it;* My brother borrowed my car and destroyed it.

✦ SYNONYM: **to rake someone over the coals** *exp.* • *His mother raked him over the coals;* His mother criticized him unmercifully.

window-shop (to) *exp.* to look in store windows without making any purchases • *Since I don't have any money, I can only window-shop;* Since I don't have any money, I can only look in the store windows without making any purchases.

Practice The Vocabulary

(Answers to Lesson 4, p. 230)

A. Underline the definition of the expression in boldface:

1. **to get a load of something:**
    a. to arrive   b. to observe   c. to leave

2. **to be rolling in it:**
    a. to be tired   b. to be energetic   c. to be rich

3. **to bug someone:**
    a. to annoy someone   b. to hit someone   c. to hug someone

4. **rip off:**
    a. outfit   b. thievery   c. funny

5. **to trash someone:**
    a. to criticize someone   b. to like someone   c. to hit someone

6. **to get a kick out of something:**
    a. to enjoy   b. to dislike   c. to become sick

7. **to sponge:**
    a. to lend   b. to steal   c. to borrow

8. **to get going:**
    a. to laugh   b. to arrive   c. to leave

9. **"What a scream!":**
    a. "What a difficulty"   b. "How funny!"   c. "How strange!"

10. **to be broke:**
    a. to be destitute   b. to be funny   c. to be rich

11. **to fork out:**
    a. to spend   b. to criticize   c. to eat

12. **joint:**
    a. money   b. place   c. car

B. Fill in the blank with the word that best completes the phrase.

1. Get a _____ of that dress she's wearing.
    a. **toad**   b. **load**   c. **road**

2. I want to go _____ my sorrows.
    a. **drown**   b. **crown**   c. **brown**

3. Let's shop till we _____ .
    a. **drop**   b. **stop**   c. **crop**

4. Since I don't have a lot of money, I can only _____ shop.
    a. **door**   b. **chimney**   c. **window**

5. I get a _____ out of that comedian.
    a. **hit**   b. **kick**   c. **punch**

6. Do you have a few _____ I could borrow?
    a. **bucks**   b. **sponges**   c. **windows**

7. Why do you want to _____ me to that stupid party?
    a. **brag**   b. **rag**   c. **drag**

8. I would never _____ out that kind of money on a dress.
    a. **fork**   b. **spoon**   c. **knife**

9. That's a lot of _____ to spend on a car!
    a. **pastry**   b. **dough**   c. **cake**

10. You spent $100 on that? What a _____ off!
    a. **tear**   b. **break**   c. **rip**

11. That dress is beautiful! It has my _____ on it.
    a. **name**   b. **fame**   c. **lame**

12. This restaurant is too rich for my _____ .
    a. **flood**   b. **water**   c. **blood**

C. Match the two columns.

☐ 1. Let's go attack the stores.

☐ 2. That sure is thievery!

☐ 3. Now that's a good idea.

☐ 4. Be quiet.

☐ 5. What do you think of this little outfit?

☐ 6. What a scream!

☐ 7. That's absolutely beautiful.

☐ 8. Let's leave.

☐ 9. I'd never want to be seen wearing that.

☐ 10. She really criticized me.

☐ 11. I'm going to cheer myself up by drinking.

☐ 12. He's rich.

A. **I wouldn't be caught dead wearing that.**

B. **Hold it down.**

C. **How funny!**

D. **He's rolling in it.**

E. **That's drop-dead gorgeous.**

F. **She really trashed me.**

G. **Talk about a rip-off!**

H. **What do you think of this little number?**

I. **Let's get going.**

J. **Now you're talkin'.**

K. **I'm going to drown my sorrows.**

L. **Let's go hit the stores.**

A CLOSER LOOK:
Food Used in Slang

Since eating certainly comes up in conversation on a daily basis, it was only a matter of time before terms concerning food would become part of the slang repertoire. The following list demonstrates this imaginative usage.

Bacon

to bring home the bacon *exp.* to earn a living • *We both bring home the bacon;* We both earn a living.

Beef

beef something up (to) *exp.* to improve something • *We have to beef up this script;* [or] *This script needs beefing up;* We have to improve this script.

beef *exp.* **1.** a quarrel • *I heard you had a beef with your teacher today;* I heard you had a quarrel with your teacher today. • **2.** a complaint • *I'm calling that store to register a beef;* I'm calling that store to register a complaint. • **3.** substance • *Your concept is weak. Where's the beef?;* Your concept is weak. Where's the substance?

beefy *adj.* big and muscular • *That football player is so beefy!;* That football player is so big and muscular.

Bite

bite on someone (to put the) *exp.* to ask for a loan • *Mark just put the bite on me;* Mark just asked me for a loan.

bite one's head off (to) *exp.* to verbally attack someone • *Why do you always bite my head off?;* Why do you always verbally attack me?

bite one's tongue (to) *exp.* to keep from saying anything • *I'm so angry at her but I promise to bite my tongue;* I'm so angry at her but I promise to keep from saying anything.

bite the bullet (to) *exp.* to do something unpleasant yet necessary • *You simply have to bite the bullet and do it;* You simply have to do it no matter how unpleasant it is.

bite the dust (to) *exp.* (usually used figuratively) to die or be killed • *We almost bit the dust skiing down that slope!;* We practically died skiing down that slope!

Bread

best thing since sliced bread (the) *exp.* the very best, fantastic • *This word processor is the best thing since sliced bread!;* This word processor is fantastic!

bread *n.* money • *How much bread have you got?;* How much money do you have?
♦ NOTE: This old term is used in old movies or in jest.

bread winner *n.* the member of the family who supports the family monitarily • *She's the bread winner of the family;* She's the one who supports the family.

Bun

bun in the oven (to have a) *exp.* (humorous) to be pregnant • *I hear you have a bun in the oven!;* I hear you're pregnant!

buns *exp.* buttocks • *He's got great buns from jogging;* He's got real muscular, round buttocks from jogging.

freeze one's buns off (to) *exp.* to be extremely cold • *We froze our buns off this winter;* We were extremely cold this winter.
♦ NOTE: The noun *"buns"* is a common slang synonym for "buttocks."

Cake

cakewalk *exp.* extremely easy • *This is going to be a cakewalk;* This is going to be extremely easy.

piece of cake *exp.* easy • *The exam was a piece of cake!;* That exam was easy!

Cheese

big cheese *exp.* boss • *He's the big cheese here;* He's the boss here.

cheese it (to) *v.* to leave quickly, to flee • *Cheese it! The cops!;* Let's leave quickly! The police!
♦ NOTE: This is considered gangster language and is only heard in movies, on television, or in jest.

cheesecake *n.* suggestive photographs • *Did you see these photos? Talk about cheesecake!;* Did you see those photos? Talk about suggestive!

cheesy *adj.* cheap and lacking in taste • *Don't wear that shirt. It looks cheesy;* Don't wear that shirt. It looks cheap and lacking in taste.

cut the cheese (to) *exp.* to pass gas • *Who cut the cheese?* Who passed gas?

Chew

chew someone out (to) *exp.* to scold someone • *He really chewed me out!;* He really scolded me.

chew the fat (to) *exp.* to converse in a leisurely fashion • *We sat in the park and chewed the fat for a while;* We sat in the park and conversed for a while.

Clam

clam *n.* dollar • *He stole fifty clams from me!;* He stole fifty dollars from me!
♦ NOTE: This term is rarely used, yet occasionally is heard in old movies or in jest.

clam up (to) *exp.* to stop talking • *We tried to get him to confess but he just clammed up;* We tried to get him to confess but he just stopped talking.

happy as a clam *exp.* extremely happy • *The little boy was happy as a clam swimming in the pool;* The little boy was extremely happy swimming in the pool.

Coffee

wake up and smell the coffee (to) *exp.* to become aware • *You trusted him? Wake up and smell the coffee!;* You trusted him? Become aware!

Cook

cook something up (to) *exp.* to prepare or devise something • *What trouble are you cooking up?* What trouble are you preparing?

cook with gas (to) *exp.* to perform extremely well • *Now you're cookin' with gas!;* Now you're performing well!

cooking on all four burners (not to be) *exp.* not to have all of one's faculties • *That guy's not cooking on all four burners;* That guy doesn't have all his faculties.

goose cooked (to have one's) *exp.* to be in big trouble • *If my mother sees us, our goose is gonna be cooked;* If my mother sees us, we're going to be in big trouble.

"What's cookin'?" *exp.* • "What's happening?"
♦ NOTE: In this expression, the verb *"cooking"* is commonly heard in its contracted form *"cookin'."*

Cookie

caught with one's hand in the cookie jar (to be) *exp.* to be caught in the act • *I'm telling* *you that she stole it! I caught her with her hand in the cookie jar;* I'm telling you that she stole it! I caught her in the act.

smart cookie (to be a) *exp.* to be smart and clever • *My mother's a smart cookie;* My mother's smart and clever.

"That's the way the cookie crumbles" *exp.* "That's just how things are" • *It's too bad you lost the contest but that's the way the cookie crumbles;* It's too bad you lost the contest but that's just how things are.
▶ VARIATION: **"That's how the cookie crumbles"** *exp.*

toss one's cookies (to) *exp.* to vomit • *The last time I went on a boat, I tossed my cookies;* The last time I went on a boat, I vomited.

tough cookie *exp.* strict • *He's one tough cookie;* He's very strict.

Cracker

crackers *adj.* (British) crazy • *Living all alone on the desert island made him go crackers;* Living all alone on the desert island made him go crazy.

Dough

dough *n.* money • *How much dough have you got?;* How much money do you have?
▶ NOTE: This term is only used in old movies or in jest.

Eat

eat high off the hog (to) *exp.* to eat expensive foods • *I ate at Nancy's house last night. They really eat high off the hog;* I ate at Nancy's house last night. They really eat expensive foods.

eat it (to) *exp.* • **1.** to crash • *I almost ate it skiing!;* I almost crashed skiing! • **2.** to fail • *I really ate it on the test;* I really failed the test.

eat one up (to) *exp.* **1.** to irritate one greatly • *That really eats me up;* That really irritates me • **2.** to sadden one greatly • *That's really eating me up;* That's really making me sad.
▶ NOTE: The difference between **1.** and **2.** depends on the connotation.

eat one's words (to) *exp.* to retract what one said • *I'm going to make him eat his words;* I'm going to make him retract what he said.

Enchilada

big enchilada *exp.* boss • *He's the big enchilada;* He's the boss.

whole enchilada (the) *exp.* the entire matter • *...And that ended our vacation. That's the whole enchilada;* ...And that ended our vacation. That's the entire story.

Feed

chicken feed *exp.* a trifle, small amount • *That's chicken feed;* That's a trifle.

feed one's face (to) *exp.* to eat • *Let's go feed our faces;* Let's go eat.

put on the feed bag (to) *exp.* to eat • *Let's go put on the feed bag;* Let's go eat.

spoon-feed someone (to) *exp.* to explain something slowly to someone • *He's so slow. You have to spoon-feed everything to him;* He's so slow. You have to explain everything to him slowly.

Fish

different kettle of fish *exp.* another issue • *That's a different kettle of fish;* That's another story.

fine kettle of fish *exp.* a predicament • *That's a fine kettle of fish!;* That's a real predicament!

fishy *adj.* peculiar • *Something's fishy around here;* Something's peculiar around here.

Fruitcake

nutty as a fruitcake (to be) *exp.* to be crazy • *That guy's nuttier than a fruitcake;* That guy's crazy.
‣ VARIATION: **to be nuttier than a fruitcake** *exp.*
‣ NOTE: These two expressions are a play on words. The expression *"to be nutty"* means "to be silly and nonsensical" and it is also common knowledge that a fruitcake is filled with nuts. Hence, *"to be nutty as a fruitcake"* or *"to be nuttier than a fruitcake."*

Fudge

"Fudge!" *exp.* • *"Darn it!"*

fudge around with something (to) *exp.* to fumble around with something • *Stop fudging around with the television!;* Stop fumbling around with the television!

fudge it (to) *exp.* **1.** to blunder • *I fudged my work;* I blundered on my work. • **2.** to improvise • *I wasn't* *sure how to do the job so I just fudged it;* I wasn't sure how to do the job so I just improvised.

Gravy

gravy (to be) *exp.* said of additional money that one earns beyond what is expected • *Once we break even, the rest will be gravy;* Once we break even, the rest will be additional income.

gravy train *exp.* a job that yields a high return for little effort • *He'll never leave his job. It's a real gravy train;* He'll never leave his job. It yields a high return for little effort.

Ham

ham (to be a) *exp.* a performer who overacts • *What a ham!;* What an overacting performer!
♦ VARIATION: **to be a ham bone** *exp.*

ham it up (to) *exp.* to overact • *He's really hamming it up;* He's really overacting.

Hotcake

sell like hotcakes (to) *exp.* to sell well • *His books are selling like hotcakes;* His books are selling well.

Mustard

cut the mustard (to) *exp.* to succeed at a job • *The boss fired him because he couldn't cut the mustard;* The boss fired him because he couldn't do his job.

Noodle

limp as a noodle *exp.* totally droopy • *When I got out of the jacuzzi, I was limp as a noodle;* When I got out of the jacuzzi, I was totally droopy.

noodle *n.* head or brains • *You know the answer. Just use your noodle!;* You know the answer. Just use your brains!

noodle around (to) *exp.* to idle or play around • *We're just noodling around;* We're just playing around.

noodlehead *n.* stupid person • *What a noodlehead!;* What a stupid person!

off one's noodle *exp.* crazy • *You're off your noodle!;* You're crazy!

wet noodle *exp.* a hindrance when it comes to having fun • *I don't want to invite him. He's a wet noodle;* I don't want to invite him. He hinders everyone else's fun.

Pie

easy as pie *exp.* extremely easy • *You can do it. It's easy as pie;* You can do it. It's very easy.

sweetie-pie *n.* term of endearment • *Hi, sweetie-pie;* Hi, darling.

Sandwich

knuckle sandwich *exp.* (a) fist in the face • *If you don't stop bothering me, I'm gonna give you a knuckle sandwich!;* If you don't stop bothering me, I'm going to hit you in the face with my fist!

sandwiched *adj.* trapped between • *I got sandwiched between the doors of the elevator;* I got trapped between the doors of the elevator.

Stew

in a stew *exp.* **1.** upset • *Don't get yourself in such a stew about it;* Don't get so upset about it. • **2.** in a dilemma • *I don't know what to do. I'm in a real stew;* I don't know what to do. I'm in a real dilemma.

Sugar

sugar *n.* term of endearment • *How are you, sugar?;* How are you, darling?

sugar-coat something (to) *exp.* to make something seem less unpleasant than it really is • *She tries to sugar-coat her unreasonable demands so they're harder to refuse;* She tries to make her demands seem attractive so they're harder to refuse.

sugar daddy *exp.* man who provides money to the one he keeps • *That must be her sugar daddy;* That must be the man who keeps her.

sweet as sugar *exp.* very lovable • *She's sweet as sugar;* He's very lovable.

Practice Food Terms Used in Slang

(Answers, p. 231)

A. Circle the word that best completes the phrase.

1. In our family, my mother brings home the (**cake, bacon, coffee**).

2. You actually trusted him? Wake up and smell the (**bacon, cake, coffee**).

3. He bit the (**clam, cookie, dust**) driving around the curve so fast.

4. So, that's the whole (**enchilada, fruitcake, cookie**).

5. He got fired because he couldn't cut the (**catsup, mayonnaise, mustard**).

6. If you don't stop it, I'm gonna give you a knuckle (**fudge, sandwich, cookie**).

7. Don't get yourself into such a (**stew, fruitcake, mustard**).

8. I don't like that actor. I think he's a (**bacon, cake, ham**).

9. It's easy as (**mustard, pie, cake**).

10. Well, this is a fine kettle of (**fish, pie, cake**).

11. Did Julie put the (**bite, fudge, cookie**) on you for a loan, too?

12. Don't (**salt, sugar, pepper**)-coat it. Just ask for what you want.

13. He never wants to do anything with us. I swear he's such a wet (**fruitcake, sandwich, noodle**).

14. Teaching her anything takes so long. You have to (**spoon, fork, ladle**)-feed everything to her.

15. You can't trick him. He's a real smart (**cake, noodle, cookie**).

Just For Fun...

The following paragraph contains some popular expressions which were created using terms pertaining to food. If you've studied the material in the previous section, you should have no trouble understanding the monologue on the next page. It should be *"easy as pie!"*

"You're not going to believe what's **COOKING** around here. John just got fired. Even though his job is **a piece of CAKE**, he just can't seem **to cut the MUSTARD** and keeps **FUDGING** his work. The boss was so mad when he caught him just **NOODLING around** and **CHEWING the FAT** on the job again, I thought he was going **to give him a knuckle SANDWICH**. After all, he is the **big CHEESE** around here and a real **tough COOKIE**. I just don't know how John is going to be able to make that kind of **DOUGH** and **bring home the BACON** now and you know his wife **has a BUN in the oven**! You just don't act like that in front of the boss. He'd better **wake up and smell the COFFEE** or he's really going to **EAT** it. Sometimes I just don't think he's **COOKING on all FOUR BURNERS**. Well, there it is... **the whole ENCHILADA**."

Translation:

"You're not going to believe what's **happening** around here. John just got fired. Even though his job is **easy**, he just can't seem **to succeed** at his job and keeps **making mistakes** at his work. The boss was so mad when he caught him being **idle** and **chatting** on the job again, I thought he was going **to punch him in the face**. After all, he is the **boss** around here and very **strict**. I just don't know how John is going to be able to make that kind of **money** and **make a living** now and you know his wife is **pregnant**! You just don't act like that in front of the boss. He'd better become **aware** or he's really going to **fail**. Sometimes I just don't think he **has all of his faculties**. Well, there it is... **the whole story**."

The New Car

Dialogue in slang

The New Car...

Richard is showing Paul his new car.

Paul: This is a nice **set of wheels**. How much did the dealer **soak** you for this?

Richard: A **pile**. I'll probably have to **moonlight** for the rest of my life, but **so what**, it'll be worth it. It sure **beats** the **clunker** I had before. Come on, **hop in**. Let's **take a spin**. You're not gonna believe how this **sucker** can **haul**.

Paul: Okay then, **punch it**! **Whoa**! This thing can really **burn rubber**.

Richard: And it **corners like it's on rails**. **Check out** what happens when I **nail the brakes**. It can **stop on a dime**.

Paul: **Jeez**, just watch out for **cops** or you're gonna end up in the **slammer**. You know that **lead foot** of yours.

Richard: **Yeah**, I know. I went through my last set of **skins**, in **no time flat**. I even had three **blowouts** in two weeks.

Paul: Now watch... you've only had your car for a day and some guy'll probably **run a light** and **total** it!

Richard: **Knock it off**, would you? What are you trying to do? **Jinx** it?

Translation of dialogue in standard English

The New Car...

Richard is showing Paul his new car.

Paul:	This is a nice **car**. How much did the dealer **charge** you for this?
Richard:	**A lot**. I'll probably have to **work nights** for the rest of my life, but **that's all right**, it'll be worth it. It sure **is better than** the **old car** I had before. Come on, **get in**. Let's **take a drive**. You're not going to believe how this **car** can **move**.
Paul:	Okay then, **let's go fast**! **Wow**! This thing can really **accelerate fast**.
Richard:	And it **goes around corners smoothly**. **Observe** what happens when I **put on the brakes suddenly**. It can **stop quickly**.
Paul:	**Hey**, just watch out for **policemen** or you're going to end up in **jail**. You know you **tend to go fast**.
Richard:	**Yes**, I know. I went through my last set of **tires fast**. I even had three **flat tires** in two weeks.
Paul:	Now watch… you've only had your car for a day and some guy'll probably **go through a red light** and **destroy** it!
Richard:	**Stop that**, would you? What are you trying to do? **Curse** it?

Dialogue in slang as it would be heard

The New Car...

Richard is showing Paul 'is new car.

Paul: This is a nice **seta wheels**. How much did the dealer **soak ya** fer this?

Richard: A **pile**. I'll prob'ly have ta **moonlight** fer the resta my life, but **so what**, id'll be worth it. It sher **beats** the **clunker** I had before. C'mon, **hop in**. Let's **take a spin**. Yer not gonna believe how this **sucker** c'n **haul**.

Paul: Okay then, **punch it**! **Whoa**! This thing c'n really **burn rubber**.

Richard: And it **corners** like it's on **rails**. **Check out** what happens when I **nail the brakes**. It c'n **stop on a dime**.

Paul: **Jeez**, jus' watch out fer **cops** or yer gonna end up'n the **slammer**. Ya know that **lead foot** a yours.

Richard: **Yeah**, I know. I went through my last **sed a skins**, in **no time flat**. I even had three **blowouts** in two weeks.

Paul: Now watch... you've only had yer car fer a day 'n some guy'll prob'ly **run a light** 'n **todal** it!

Richard: **Knock id off**, would ja? What'r ya tryin' ta do? **Jinx** it?

Vocabulary

beat something (to) *exp.* to surpass, to outshine • *Your new house sure does beat that other one;* Your new house sure does surpass that other one.
 ♦ ANTONYM: **not to hold a candle to someone or something** *exp.* not to be as good as someone or something • *Your new house doesn't hold a candle to your other one;* Your new house isn't as good as your other one.
 ♦ ALSO: **to beat one** *exp.* not to know • *Beats me!;* I don't know!

blowout *n.* **1.** a flat tire • *I had a blowout on the way home;* I got a flat tire on the way home [or] *My tire blew out on the way home;* • **2.** to have a feast • *We had a real blowout at my mom's house last night;* We had such a feast at my mom's house last night.

burn rubber (to) *exp.* to accelerate quickly (and leave a skid mark) • *We'd better burn rubber or we're gonna be late;* We'd better leave quickly or we're going to be late.
 ♦ SYNONYM: **to peel out** *exp.* • *This car can really peel out!;* This car can really accelerate quickly!
 ♦ SEE: **to punch it.**

check out (to) *exp.* to observe (someone or something) • *Check her out!;* Examine her!
 ♦ SYNONYM: **to get a load of someone or something** *exp.* • *Get a load o' him. Have you ever seen such an ugly shirt?;* Observe him. Have you ever seen such an ugly shirt?

clunker *n.* an old and broken-down car • *You actually bought that clunker?;* You actually bought that old broken-down car?
 ♦ NOTE: The noun *"clunker"* may also be used to indicate any inferior piece of machinery • *That washing machine is a real clunker;* That washing machine is really inferior.
 ♦ SYNONYM: **jalopy** *n.*
 ⇨ NOTE: Although the term *"jalopy"* comes from the 1920's, it is still occasionally heard in jest and in old movies. It is used to mean both "an old and battered car" as well as "car" in general: 1. *Is that your new jalopy?;* Is that your new car? • **2.** *You spent $1,000 on that jalopy?;* You spent $1,000 on that old car? The difference in connotation between **1.** & **2.** depends on the context and delivery of the speaker.

cop *n.* police officer (very popular) • *Don't drive so fast. There's a cop behind you;* Don't drive so fast. There's a policeman behind you.
  ♦ NOTE: In old gangster movies, you will undoubtedly hear the term *"copper"* which is simply a variation of the noun *"cop." * When used by a civilian, the term *"cop"* is considered to be disrespectful (although some police officers actually use this term when referring to others in their own profession), and the term *"copper"* is simply derogatory.
  ♦ SYNONYM (1): **pig** *n.* • The derogatory term *"pig"* was extremely popular during the 1960's, and is still occasionally heard, especially in movies of the period.
  ♦ SYNONYM (2): **C.H.P.** *exp.* • This is an extremely popular acronym for the California Highway Patrol (Officer) • *You'd better stop. There's a C.H.P. behind you;* You'd better stop. There's a California Highway Patrol Officer behind you.

corner like it's on rails (to) *exp.* said of a car that can go around curves smoothly • *This baby corners like it's on rails;* This car goes around corners like it's on rails.
  ♦ NOTE: The term *"baby"* is commonly used to refer to any exceptional merchandise: (*e.g.,* when taking about a refrigerator) *This baby really keeps things cold!*
  ♦ SEE: **sucker.**

haul (to) *v.* to hurry • (lit); to drag or carry • *We only have five minutes to get there. Let's haul!;* We only have five minutes to get there. Let's hurry!
  ♦ NOTE: Another variation of *"to haul"* is *"to haul butt."* In this expression, the noun *butt* can certainly be replaced with any number of slang synonyms, i.e. *buns, ass (vulgar), etc.*

hop in (to) *exp.* (very popular) to enter • (lit); to enter by jumping on one foot • *If you want a ride to school, hop in!;* If you want a ride to school, enter!
  ♦ VARIATION: **to hop on in** *exp.* • *If you want a ride to school, hop on in!*
  ⇨ NOTE: If the preposition *"in"* is omitted from this expression (*"to hop on"*), it takes on the meaning of *"to mount"* • *Want to ride my bike? Hop on!;* Want to ride my bike? Climb up!

in no time flat *exp.* immediately • *The police arrived in no time flat;* The police arrived immediately.
  ♦ SYNONYM: **in a jiffy** *exp.* • *I'll be there in a jiffy;* I'll be there immediately.

Jeez! *exclam.* (or **Geez!**) This exclamation of surprise is actually a euphemism for *"Jesus Christ!"* • *Jeez! I can't believe he did that!*
‣ SYNONYM: **Man!** *exclam.* • *Man! I can't believe he did that!*

jinx someone or something (to) • **1.** *v.* to curse someone or something• *If you talk about it too much, you may jinx it;* If you talk about it too much, you may curse it. • **2.** *n.* that which causes bad luck • *Every time I'm with her, something terrible happens. I think she's a curse;* Every time I'm with her, something terrible happens. I think she causes bad luck.
‣ SYNONYM: **to put a whammy on something or someone** *exp.* • *The witch put a whammy on him;* The witch put a curse on him.

knock it off (to) *exp.* to stop • *Could you please knock it off? Your drums are driving me crazy!;* Could you please stop it? Your drums are driving me crazy!
‣ SYNONYM: **to hold it** *exp.* • *Could you hold it for a moment?;* Could you stop that for a moment?
⇨ ALSO: **to hold it down** *exp.* to be quieter • *Hold it down in there!;* Be quieter in there!

lead foot (to have a) *exp.* to have a tendency to drive fast • *I hate driving with him. He has such a lead foot;* I hate driving with him. He has such a tendency to drive fast.
‣ NOTE: This conjures up an image of someone with such a heavy foot, that the accelerator is always pressed down to the floor.

moonlight (to) *v.* to work a second job (traditionally in the evenings • *She has to moonlight because she doesn't make enough money for rent;* She has to work a second job because she doesn't make enough money for rent.

nail the brakes *exp.* to apply the brakes suddenly • *If I hadn't nailed the brakes at that very moment, I would have been in a fender-bender;* If I hadn't applied the brakes at that very moment, I would have been in an accident.
‣ NOTE: The term *"fender-bender"* is popularly used to mean a "minor accident."

pile (a) *n.* a lot • *He gave me a pile of excuses;* He gave me a lot of excuses.
‣ SYNONYM: **a mess** *n.* • (lit); disorder • *The teacher gave us a mess of homework;* The teacher gave us a lot of homework.

punch it (to) *exp.* to accelerate quickly, to push the accelerator down to the floor in one quick motion • *If she sees us, we're gonna be in trouble! Punch* *it!;* If she sees us, we're going to be in trouble! Push the accelerator down to the floor!

♦ SYNONYM: **to put the pedal to the metal** *exp.* • (lit); to put the pedal (accelerator) to the floor.

run a [red] light (to) *exp.* to go through a red light • *I got a ticket for running a [red] light;* I got a ticket for going through a [red] light.

set of skins *exp.* set of tires • *My first set of skins only lasted six months;* My first set of tires only lasted six months.

set of wheels *exp.* car • *Nice set of wheels!;* Nice car!

♦ ALSO: **wheels** *n.* • Nice wheels!; Nice car!

♦ NOTE: Cars are commonly referred to by their abbreviated names. Examples are given in the following list:

Alpha Romeo =	*Alpha*	Mercury =	*Merc*	
BMW =	*Beemer*	Oldsmobile =	*Olds*	
Cadillac =	*Caddy*	Recreational Vehicle =	*RV*	
Chevrolet =	*Chevy*	Rolls Royce =	*Rolls*	
Corvette =	*Vet*	Thunderbird =	*T-Bird*	
Jaguar =	*Jag*	Volkswagen =	*VW / V-dub /*	
Limousine =	*Limo / Stretch*		*Beetle / Bug*	
Mercedes Benz =	*Benz*			

slammer (to throw someone in the) *n.* to put someone in jail • *They threw him in the slammer for robbery;* They threw him in jail for robbery.

♦ NOTE: Although the noun *"slammer"* was considered jive talk in the 1930's, it is still used in jest and occasionally heard in old movies.

♦ SYNONYM (1): **to put someone away** *exp.* • *They put him away for five years;* They put him in jail for five years.

♦ SYNONYM (2): **to lock someone up (and throw away the key)** *exp.* • *They should have locked him up (and thrown away the key) years ago;* They should have put him (permanently) in jail years ago.

♦ SYNONYM (3): **to send someone up the river** *exp.* *They sent him up the river;* They put him in jail.

⇨ NOTE: Although this expression was created in the mid 1800's, it is still occasionally heard used in jest as well as in old movies.

"So what!" *exclam.* This is an exclamation of indifference • *He didn't like the gift I gave him? So what!;* He didn't like the gift I gave him? I don't care!

♦ SYNONYM: **"Big deal!"** *exclam.* • *Big deal if she's always late!;* I don't care if she's always late!

soak (to) *v.* to overcharge • *They really soak you at that restaurant;* They really overcharge at that restaurant.
  ‣ SYNONYM: **to take someone** *exp.* • **1.** to overcharge • *How much did they take you for?;* How much did they cheat you out of? • **2.** to con • *The swindler took him for all his money;* The swindler conned him out of all his money.

stop on a dime (to) *exp.* to stop suddenly • *It's a good thing I was able to stop on a dime when the little girl jumped in front of my car;* It's a good thing I was able to stop suddenly when the little girl jumped in front of my car.

sucker *n.* **1.** a general term for any object or person • *What a beautiful necklace! This sucker must have cost a fortune!* • *He's been training for years. That sucker can really box!* • **2. an extremely gullible person** • *You believed everything she told you? What a sucker!;* You believed everything she told you? What a gullible person you are!
  ‣ SYNONYM: **baby** *n.* • *This baby must have cost a fortune!*

take a spin (to) *exp.* to take a short excursion in a car • (lit); to take a twirl (around the block, the neighborhood, etc.) • *Want to take a spin in my new car? Hop in!;* Want to take a quick excursion in my car? Come in!
  ‣ NOTE: It is extremely common to use the verbs *"to hop"* and *"to jump"* literally meaning "to leap or bound," when referring to entering a car.

total (to) *v.* to destroy completely • *His car was totalled in the accident;* His car was completely destroyed in the accident.
  ‣ SYNONYM: **to trash** *v.* **1.** to destroy completely • (lit); to reduce something to a state ready for the trash • *She trashed her new bicycle;* She ruined her new bicycle • **2.** to criticize unmercifully • *I can't believe how she trashed him!;* I can't believe how she criticized him so severely!

"Whoa!" *exclam.* exclamation of surprise and amazement • *You passed the test? Whoa!*

yeah *adv.* (informal and extremely popular) yes • *Yeah, I know her;* Yes, I know her.
  ‣ SYNONYM: **yep/yup/uh,huh** *adv.* (informal) • *"Are you coming right back?" "Yep/Yup/Uh,huh";* "Are you coming right back?" "Yes."

Practice The Vocabulary

[Answers to Lesson 5, p. 231]

A. **Complete the sentences by filling in the blanks with the appropriate word from the list below.**

wheels	pile	knock
flat	run	dime
clunker	jinx	soak
spin	haul	totaled

1. What a beautiful car! How much did they _____ you for it?

2. You're really bothering me! _____ it off!

3. The movie starts in ten minutes, but if we hurry, we could get there in no time _____ .

4. We'd better _____ or we're gonna be late.

5. Would you like to take a _____ in my new car?

6. I'll let you borrow my car as long as you promise not to _____ any lights.

7. Is this your new car? Nice set of _____ !

8. Luckily my car can stop on a _____ or I would've crashed into that other car.

9. I'm begining to think he's a real _____ . Every time he's near me, something terrible happens.

10. You actually bought that old _____ ? I've never seen a car in such awful condition.

11. I spent a _____ of money eating at that restaurant.

12. I heard you just _____ you car! Were you hurt?!

B. Underline the word(s) that best complete(s) the phrase.

1. How much did the dealer (**rinse, soak, wash**) you for this?

2. He just (**completed, finished, totaled**) his car today.

3. I'm tired because I work during the day and (**moonlight, daylight, twilight**) at night.

4. You'd better drive fast if you don't want to be late. (**Kill, Slap, Punch**) it!

5. Check (**in, over, out**) that girl over there!

6. If I hadn't (**nailed, hammered, wrenched**) the brakes in time, I would have crashed.

7. You sure do have a (**wooden, steel, lead**) foot. You always drive so fast.

8. As soon as the light turns green, watch me burn (**wood, rubber, paper**).

9. Watch out for (**wheels, clunkers, cops**). You don't want to get a ticket.

10. Did you hear about the burglar who's been terrorizing the city? He finally ended up in the (**slammer, sucker, spin**).

11. It may take me a year to pay off my trip to Europe, but so (**why, when, what**)? It'll be worth it.

12. Your new bicycle is great. It sure (**beats, hits, punches**) your old one.

13. Your car rides so smoothly. It corners like it's on (**wheels, rails, skins**).

14. If you want a ride, (**punch, check, hop**) in!

**C. Choose the appropriate slang synonym of the italicized word(s).
Write the corresponding letter of the correct answer in the box.**

☐ 1. This is a nice *car*.

☐ 2. This car can stop *quickly*.

☐ 3. She talks so much when she drives
      that I get scared she's going to *go
      through* a light.

☐ 4. Her car was *ruined* in the accident.

☐ 5. *Yes*, he really is talented.

☐ 6. What are you trying to do? *Curse* it?

☐ 7. We're late. *Hurry!*

☐ 8. She ended up in *jail*.

☐ 9. *Stop it!*

☐ 10. He's a *policeman*.

A. **Knock it off**

B. **run**

C. **Yeah**

D. **Jinx**

E. **the slammer**

F. **on a dime**

G. **set of wheels**

H. **Punch it**

I. **cop**

J. **totaled**

A CLOSER LOOK:
Car and On-the-road Slang

Since the majority of Americans own cars, the following list includes some
very popular terms that are heard frequently. If you're planning on driving
into any gas station in America, this list could prove invaluable.

blow a tire (to) *exp.* to get a flat
tire • *I blew a tire right in the
middle of the intersection;* I got
a flat tire right in the middle of
the intersection.

blow the doors off (to) *exp.*
(figurative) to pass a car at such
a speed that the resulting
suction rips the doors off the
other car • *My car can blow the
doors off yours;* My car can go
a lot faster than yours.

blowout *n.* a ruptured tire • *Oh,
no! I think I just got another
blowout;* Oh, no! I think I just
got another flat tire.

broadside (to) *v.* to hit the side of
another car with the front of
one's own car • *The driver next
to me fell asleep and broadsided
me!;* The driver next to me fell
asleep and hit the side of my car
with the front of his car.
♦ SEE: **to sideswipe.**

brodey (to do a) *exp.* to spin a car 180 degrees • *Since the road was so slippery, when I applied the brakes hard, I did a brodey;* Since the road was so slippery, when I applied the brakes hard, the car spun around 180 degrees.

bumper-to-bumper *exp.* said of heavy traffic • *The traffic was bumper-to-bumper all the way home;* The traffic was extremely heavy all the way home.

burn rubber (to) *exp.* to accelerate so quickly as so leave a skid mark • *Every time he accelerates, he likes to burn rubber;* Every time he accelerates, he likes to leave so quickly that he leaves a skid mark.

conk out (to) *exp.* to fail to operate • *My car conked out in the middle of the desert;* My car failed to operate in the middle of the desert.

cop *n.* (very popular) police officer • *Don't drive so fast. There's a cop behind you;* Don't drive so fast. There's a policeman behind you.
♦ NOTE: In old gangster movies, you will undoubtedly hear the term *"copper"* which is simply a variation of the noun *"cop."* When used by a civilian, the term *"cop"* is considered to be disrespectful (although some police officers actually use this word when referring to others in their own profession), and the term *"copper"* is simply derogatory.
♦ NOTE: The term *"copper"* comes from the large copper buttons that were worn on the original police uniforms.

dash *n.* popular abbreviation of "dashboard."

deuce coupe *n.* car that seats only two people.

eat one's dust (to) *exp.* to be left behind by a fast moving car • *You're gonna eat my dust!;* You're going to be left behind by my fast car!

fender bender *n.* an insignificant traffic accident which causes little damage • *Don't worry, I'm fine. It was just a little fender bender;* Don't worry, I'm fine. It was just a little insignificant traffic accident.

"Fill 'er up!" *exp.* popular expression meaning, "Fill up the tank with gas!"
♦ NOTE: Although English generally has no masculine or feminine nouns as do the Romance languages, occasionally one may indeed surface. In the expression *"Fill 'er up,"* "'er" (a contraction of

"her") represents "car, boat, ship, airplane, etc." It is not uncommon to hear the pronoun *she* used when referring to a car: *What a car! She's a beauty!;* What a car! It's a beauty!

flat *n.* a popular abbreviation of: *a flat tire • Sorry I'm late. I got a flat on the way here;* Sorry I'm late. I got a flat tire on the way here.

flat-foot *n.* (from the 1960's) police officer • *There's a flat-foot behind you;* There's a police officer behind you.
♦ NOTE: Although outdated, this term is especially heard in old gangster movies and occasionally in jest.

floor it (to) *exp.* to push the accelerator all the way to the floor • *There they are! Floor it!;* There they are! Push the accelerator all the way to the floor!

four-wheeler *n.* any size truck with four-wheel drive • *I just bought myself a four wheeler;* I just bought myself a truck with four-wheel drive.

fuzz *n.* (very popular in the 1960's) police officer • *It's the fuzz!;* It's the police!
♦ NOTE: This term has been outdated since the 1960's but has recently reappeared in the

term *"fuzz-buster."*
♦ SEE: **fuzz-buster.**

fuzz-buster *n.* a device which is attached inside the car and used to detect a police officer's radar. This gives the driver ample time to slow down to the speed limit, thus avoiding a traffic citation • (lit); police-exterminator.
♦ NOTE: Another variation of *"to haul"* is *"to haul butt."* In this expression, the noun *butt* can certainly be replaced with any number of slang synonyms, i.e. *buns, ass (vulgar), etc.*

head-on *adj.* an abbreviation of *"head-on collision."*
♦ ALSO: **to hit head-on** *exp.* to hit another car traveling in the opposite direction • *I just barely avoided hitting him head-on!;* I just barely avoided hitting the car traveling in the opposite direction!

high rider *n.* vehicle that rides high off the ground.
♦ SEE: **low rider.**

hop up (to) *exp.* to improve the performance of the engine.
♦ SEE: **to soup up**

jalopy *n.* old and dilapidated car • *You actually paid money for that jalopy?;* You actually paid money for that old car?

jam on the brakes (to) *exp.* to apply the brakes in one quick motion • *I had to jam on the brakes in order to avoid the accident;* I had to apply the brakes in one quick motion in order to avoid the accident.

jaywalk (to) *exp.* to walk across the street from a prohibited point to another thereby obstructing traffic • *The police are very strict about jay-walking;* The police are very strict about walking across the street from a prohibited point to another.
♦ NOTE: **jaywalker** *n.* one who jaywalks.

jump-start (to) *exp.* to start one's car battery off someone else's battery • *My battery died but luckily we were able to start the car by jump-starting it;* My battery died but luckily we were able to start the car off someone else's battery.
♦ NOTE: The expression *"to jump a car"* is a common abbreviation of *"to jump start a car"; I need to get my car jumped.*

lay scratch (to) *exp.* to accelerate so quickly as to leave a skid mark • *He always lays scratch when he accelerates;* He always leaves a skid mark when he accelerates.
♦ NOTE: This expression is

primarily used by the younger generation.

leave in the dust (to) *exp.* to pass someone quickly in a car (leaving a cloud of dust behind) • *We sure left them in the dust;* We sure passed them quickly.

lemon *n.* an unreliable car • *You really bought a lemon!;* You really bought an inferior car!
♦ NOTE: This term can be used for any inferior appliance as well: *This washing machine doesn't work. What a lemon!;* This washing machine doesn't work. What an inferior appliance!

light it up (to) *exp.* (popular expression among car aficionados) to start the engine.

loaded *adj.* said of a car which is sold with many extras such as radio, air conditioning, power windows, etc. • *The car only costs $9,000 fully loaded!;* The car only costs $9,000 including all the extras!

low rider *n.* one who drives a car which rides low to the ground.
♦ SEE: **high rider.**

nail it (to) *exp.* to apply either the brakes or accelerator with force • *I had to nail the brakes to avoid the accident;* I had to apply the brakes with force in order to avoid the accident.

ociffer *n.* (very popular in the 1960's yet very derogatory) police officer • *Hey, ociffer!*
♦ SYNONYM: **pig** *n.* (popularized in the 1960's).

peel out (to) *exp.* to accelerate quickly • *When they saw us coming, they peeled out;* When they saw us coming, they accelerated quickly.

pileup *n.* an accident involving a number of cars • *Let's avoid that street. I heard there was just a pileup there;* Let's avoid that street. I heard there was just an accident involving a number of cars there.

pop the clutch (to) *exp.* to release the clutch quickly causing the car to lurch forward • *I don't like sticks because I keep popping the clutch;* I don't like cars with manual transmission because I keep causing the car to lurch forward.
♦ NOTE: The noun *"stick"* is a popular abbreviation for "a car with a stick shift," whereas *"automatic"* is an abbreviation of *"automatic transmission"* • *Is your car stick or automatic?;* Is your car a stick shift or automatic transmission?

punch it (to) *exp.* to accelerate quickly • *As soon as the light turns green, punch it!* As soon as the light turns green, accelerate quickly!

put it in high gear (to) *exp.* to move into high speed • *Put it in high gear or we're gonna be late!;* Move into high speed or we're going to be late.
♦ NOTE: This expression refers not only to cars, but to people as well • *You're not dressed yet? Put it in high gear!;* You're not dressed yet? Move into high speed!

put the pedal to the metal (to) *exp.* to push the accelerator all the way to the metal floor of the car • *We have to be there in five minutes! Put the pedal to the metal!;* We have to be there in five minutes! Push the accelerator all the way to the floor!
♦ NOTE: This expression is part of the large world of rhyming slang. In the United States, the word "metal" is pronounced *"medal,"* rhyming with *"pedal."*
♦ SEE: *Street Talk II - Rhyming Slang.*

rattletrap *n.* old and dilapidated car (which rattles when driven) • *What a rattletrap!* What a dilapidated car!

rear-ender *n.* an accident involving one car hitting another from behind • *I got into a rear-ender on the way to work;* I got into an accident involving one car hitting another from behind on the way to work.

rev up (to) *exp.* to push the accelerator while the car is in neutral as a way to warm up the engine • *Rev up your engine;* Warm up your engine.
◗ NOTE: This expression may be applied to people as well • *I'm all revved up. Let's start the contest;* I'm all warmed up. Let's start the contest.

set of wheels *exp.* car • *Nice set of wheels!;* Nice car!

sideswipe (to) *v.* to scrape the side of another car with the side of one's own car • *The driver next to me fell asleep and sideswiped me!;* The driver next to me fell asleep and scraped the side of my car with the side of his car!

soup up an engine (to) *exp.* to increase the power and performance of an engine • *I souped up my engine for the race;* I increased the power and performance of my engine for the race.
◗ SEE: **to hop up.**

spare tire *n.* paunch • *He was always so athletic! I can't believe he's developed such a big spare tire!;* He was always so athletic! I can't believe he's developed such a big paunch!

spin doughnuts (to) *exp.* to pull the steering wheel to one side forcing the vehicle to spin around in circles.

strip a car (to) *exp.* to steal parts of a car • *My car got stripped!* Parts of my car have been stolen!
◗ ALSO: **a stripped car** *exp.* a car that has no extras such as radio, air conditioning, power windows, etc. • *The car sells for $14,000 stripped;* The car sells for $14,000 with no extras.
• SEE: **loaded**

tail (to) *v.* to drive closely behind another car • *I hate when people tail me!;* I hate when people drive closely behind me!
◗ NOTE: This is a popular abbreviation of "to tailgate."

tank up (to) *exp.* **1.** to fill up the gas tank with fuel. • **2.** to drink alcohol • *They really tanked up last night;* They really drank last night.

wheel *n.* popular abbreviation of "steering wheel" • *Take the wheel...I'm think I'm gonna faint!;* Take the steering wheel...I think I'm going to faint!

♦ ALSO: **to spin one's wheels** *exp.* to put forth a fruitless effort • *If you don't discuss your plan with the boss before you start, you're just going to end up spinning your wheels; If you don't discuss your plan with the boss before you start, you're just* going to end up working fruitlessly.

wheelie *n.* a maneuver in which a vehicle is temporarily running on the back two of its four wheels (or one wheel if a bicycle or motorcycle).

♦ NOTE: A popular expression is *to pop a wheelie; to do a wheelie.*

Practice Car Slang

(Answers, p. 232)

A. Choose the letter of the term that goes with the expression.

1. I think we just got a _____ . Maybe we ran over a nail.
   a. **flat**   b. **float**   c. **fly**

2. My car's really fast. I bet my car could _____ the doors off his.
   a. **rain**   b. **exhale**   c. **blow**

3. The traffic was bumper to _____ .
   a. **tire**   b. **trunk**   c. **bumper**

4. I put my drink on the _____ and it fell off and spilled all over me when I accelerated.
   a. **dash**   b. **disc**   c. **dish**

5. My car just conked _____ right in the middle of the street.
   a. **in**   b. **up**   c. **out**

6. Be careful not to drive over the speed limit or you may get stopped by a _____ .
   a. **cow**   b. **cop**   c. **cap**

7. _____ it! They're gaining on us!
   a. **Floor**   b. **Ceiling**   c. **Wall**

8. We need to gas _____ before we leave.
   a. **in**   b. **up**   c. **down**

9. My battery just died. We'd better try and _____ start the car.
   a. **jump**   b. **skip**   c. **hop**

10. The car included all the extras. I bought it fully _____ .
   a. **emptied**   b. **filled**   c. **loaded**

11. My car broke down again. What a _____ !
   a. **grapefruit**   b. **lemon**   c. **tangerine**

12. You'd better take the _____ . I'm starting to feel faint.
   a. **clutch**   b. **tire**   c. **wheel**

Just For Fun...

Once you've mastered the following paragraph, you'll certainly be ready to have a discussion with any car enthusiast.

"That was close! If I hadn't **jammed on the brakes,** I would have gotten into a **fender-bender** when I **blew a tire** on my **four wheeler**. Once I finally fixed it, my car **conked out** and I had to **jump-start it**. What a **lemon**! I was running late and had **to put the pedal to the metal**. Man, did I ever **burn rubber** when I **peeled out**. My **set of wheels** can really **haul** 'cause the engine's been **souped up**. The guy behind me really **ate my dust**. You should have seen me **blow the doors off him**!"

Translation:

"That was close! If I hadn't **quickly applied the brakes,** I would have gotten into a **little accident** when I **got a flat tire** on my **four wheel drive truck**. Once I finally fixed it, my car **broke down** and I had **to start it by pushing the car and releasing the clutch suddenly**. What **an inferior car**! I was running late and had **to drive fast**. Man, did I ever **make a skid mark** when I **accelerated so fast**. My car can really **move fast** 'cause the engine's **performance has been increased**. The guy behind me really was **covered in smoke from my car when I accelerated**. You should have seen me **pass** him!"

At the Gym

Dialogue in slang

At the Gym...

Kim and Liz just got out of an aerobics class.

Liz: Isn't he the best instructor? I think he's so **hot**. For a guy who's that **buffed**, he can really **get down**. **Wow**! I really feel **revved**, don't you?

Kim: **So help me**, I'm gonna **get you** for this.

Liz: **What's with you**? Didn't you think it was fun?!

Kim: Oh, yeah! I **had a blast**! I love **sweating like a pig** with a bunch of **lardos** with **pot bellies** who all **reek to high heaven**. Sorry, I'm just not into this health **kick**.

Liz: Oh, **get off it**. It wasn't such a **killer** class. **Guy**, don't be such a **wuss**. You just have to **get into it**. Like they say, **no pain, no gain**.

Kim: I'm **wiped out**. I think I'll just let myself **go to hell in a handbasket**, thank you.

Liz: Look, next time get yourself some **comfy** shoes and you'll be **rarin' to go**. You're gonna come back again with me, aren't you?

Kim: **When hell freezes over**. I'm just not **cut out** for jumping up and down for an hour to music that makes my teeth vibrate. But **thanks** for inviting me.

Liz: Come on. You'll feel better after we **hit the showers**.

Kim: Like I'm really going to **strip down** and show this body **in the raw** in front of total strangers. Have you **flipped**?

Translation of dialogue in standard English

At the Gym...

Kim and Liz just got out of an aerobics class.

Liz: Isn't he the best instructor? I think he's so **sexy**. For a guy who's that **muscular**, he can really **be unrestrained and wild**. **I can't believe this**! I really feel **energized**, don't you?

Kim: **I swear**, I'm going to **kill you** for this.

Liz: **What's wrong**? Didn't you think it was fun?!

Kim: Oh, yes! **I had a great time**! I love **sweating profusely** with a bunch of **fat people** with **big stomachs** who all **smell bad**. Sorry, I'm just not interested in this health **fad**.

Liz: Oh, **stop talking nonsense**. It wasn't such a **difficult** class. **I can't believe it**, don't be such a **weakling**. You just have to **immerse yourself in it**. Like they say, **without suffering, there's no growth**.

Kim: I'm **exhausted**. I think I'll just let myself **deteriorate severely**, thank you.

Liz: Look, next time get yourself some **comfortable** shoes and you'll be **invigorated and ready for action**. You are going to come back again with me, aren't you?

Kim: **Never**. I'm just not **inherently capable** of jumping up and down for an hour to music that makes my teeth vibrate. But **thank you** for inviting me

Liz: Come on. You'll feel better after we **go to** the showers.

Kim: It's crazy if you think that I'm not going to **undress** and show this body **naked** in front of total strangers. Have you gone **crazy**?

Dialogue in slang as it would be heard

At the Gym...

Kim and Liz just got out of an aerobics class.

Liz: Isn't 'e the best instructor? I think e's so **hot**. Fer a guy ooz's that **buft**, he c'n really **get down**. **Wow**! I really feel **revved**, don't you?

Kim: **So help me**, I'm gonna **get cha** fer this.

Liz: **What's with you**? Didn't cha think it was fun?!

Kim: Oh, yeah! **I had a blast**! I love **sweading like a pig** with a buncha **lardos** with **pot bellies** who all **reek ta high heaven**. Sorry, I'm jus' nod inta this health **kick**.

Liz: Oh, **ged off it**. It wasn't such a **killer** class. **Guy**, don't be such a **wuss**. Ya jus' hafta **ged into it**. Like they say, **no pain, no gain**.

Kim: I'm **wypt out**. I think I'll jus' let myself **go da hell in a han'basket**, thank you.

Liz: Look, next time get ch'erself some **comfy** shoes 'n you'll be **rarin' ta go**. You're gonna come back again with me, aren't cha?

Kim: **When hell freezes over**. I'm jus' not **cud out** fer jumpin' up 'n down fer an hour ta music that makes my teeth vibrate. But **thanks** fer inviding me.

Liz: C'm'on. You'll feel bedder after we **hit the showers**.

Kim: Like I'm really gonna **strip down** 'n show this body 'n **the raw** 'n fronna todal strangers. Have you **flipt**?

Vocabulary

blast *n.* a wonderful time • *We had a blast at his party!;* We had a wonderful time at his party!

  ♦ SYNONYM: **ball** *n.* • *I'm going to have a ball on vacation!;* I'm going to have a wonderful time on vacation!

buffed *adj.* muscular and brawny • *You're really getting buffed!;* You're really getting muscular!

  ♦ SYNONYM: **hunky** *adj.* • *He's hunky;* He's muscular.

    ⇨ ALSO: **hunk** *n.* muscular and sexy man • *What a hunk!;* What a muscular and sexy man!

comfy *adj.* popular abbreviation of the adjective "comfortable" • *This couch is really comfy;* This couch is really comfortable.

cut out for something *exp.* inherently capable of something • *I'm not cut out to be a teacher;* I'm not capable of being a teacher.

  ♦ NOTE: This figurative expression refers to a mold from which one is cut determining one's abilities or disabilities from birth.

flip (to) *v.* **1.** to go crazy • *Sometimes I think you've flipped!;* Sometimes I think you've gone crazy! • **2.** to go crazy with excitement • *I flipped when I saw her perform;* I went crazy with excitement when I saw her perform.

get down (to) *exp.* to let oneself be unrestrained and wild • *When she dances, she really gets down!;* When she dances, she really lets herself be unrestrained and wild!

  ♦ SYNONYM: **to let it all hang out** *exp.* • *There's no need to get embarrassed. Just let it all hang out!;* There's no need to get embarrassed. Just let yourself be unrestrained and wild!

get into something (to) *exp.* to immerse oneself in something • *I don't like dancing. I just can't get into it;* I don't like dancing. I just can't immerse myself in it.

  ♦ ALSO: **to get into it** *exp.* to get into the mood • *I'm sorry but I just can't get into it;* I'm sorry but I just can't get into the mood. • *I'm not into talking about it right now;* I'm not in the mood to talk about it right now.

get off it (to) *exp.* **1.** to stop talking nonsense • *Oh, get off it! You don't really have a twin!;* Oh, stop talking nonsense! You don't really have a twin! • **2.** to change the subject • *Get off it! You've been talking about the same thing for* *an hour!;* Change the subject! You've been talking about the same thing for an hour!

❱ SYNONYM: **to get out of here** *exp.* • *Get outta here! I don't believe you!;* Stop talking nonsense! I don't believe you!

⇨ NOTE: In this expression, it is very common to contract "out of" to become *"outta."*

get someone (to) *exp.* to seize (and punish) someone • *I'm going to get him for stealing my homework!;* I'm going to kill him for stealing my homework!

"Guy!" *exclam.* exclamation denoting surprise or disbelief • *Guy! I can't believe he did that to you!*

❱ NOTE: Although *"Guy!"* is literally a slang term for "Man!" it may be used in a conversation when speaking with women as well. *"Man!"* may also be used as an exclamation, a common synonym for *"Guy!"*

hell in a handbasket/handbag (to go to) *exp.* to deteriorate severely • *She's really gone to hell in a handbasket/handbag;* She's really deteriorated severely.

hit the showers (to) *exp.* to go to the shower facility of a gymnasium • *Time to hit the showers!;* Time to go to the showers!

❱ NOTE: The verb *"to hit"* is popularly used in gyms when referring to taking a shower. However, it is also commonly used when going to other locations as well, i.e. bar, town, beach, etc. • *Let's go hit the bars tonight;* Let's go to the bars tonight.

hot *adj.* sexy • *He's really hot!;* He's really sexy!

in the raw *exp.* naked • *He walks around his house in the raw;* He walks around his house naked.

❱ SYNONYM: **in the buff** *exp. There's a man standing outside in the buff!;* There's a man standing outside naked!

⇨ ALSO **buffo** *adj.* • *She walks around her house buffo;* She walks around her house naked.

kick *n.* **1.** fad or craze • *How long has he been on this exercise kick?;* How long has he been into this exercise fad? • **2.** enjoyment • *I got a kick out of that film;* I really enjoyed that film. • **3.** *pl.* fun • *We sneaked into the theatre just for kicks;* We snuck into the theatre just for fun.

killer *adj.* **1.** that which is very difficult • *What a killer assignment!;* What a difficult assignment! • **2.** exceptional, extraordinary • *That's a killer dress!;* That's a beautiful dress!

lardo *n.* (derogatory) fat person • *If you don't stop eating all that chocolate, you're gonna turn into a lardo;* If you don't stop eating all that chocolate, you're going to become a fat person.

    ▸ SYNONYM (1): **oinker** *n.* (humorous yet derogatory) one who eats like a pig.

      ⇨ NOTE: This slang term comes from the sound a pig makes, *"oink!"*

    ▸ SYNONYM (2): **fatso / fatty** *n.* (humorous yet derogatory) • *What a fatso! / What a fatty!*

"No pain no gain" *exp.* "Without suffering, there is no (physical) growth."

    ▸ NOTE: This expression was originally developed by bodybuilders and is still very popular at any gym. It is also occasionally heard when referring to emotional growth: *I know it hurts to tell him, but 'no pain no gain.';* I know it hurts to tell him, but 'without suffering, there is no (emotional) growth.'

pot belly *exp.* a fat stomach (which is round like a pot) • *If I ever get a pot belly, I'm gonna kill myself!;* If I ever get a fat stomach, I'm going to kill myself!

    ▸ ALSO: **pot** *n.* a common abbreviation of *"pot belly"* • *Did you notice that Jeff is starting to get a pot?;* Did you notice that Jeff is starting to get a fat stomach?

rarin' to go *exp.* invigorated and ready for action • *After that long nap, I'm rarin' to go!;* After that long nap, I'm invigorated and ready for action!

    ▸ NOTE: In this expression, *"rarin'"*, the contracted form of *"raring"* is always used. Otherwise, this expression would actually sound unnatural.

reek (to) *exp.* to stink • *That cheese reeks!;* That cheese stinks!

    ▸ ALSO: **to reek to high heaven** *exp.* to stink intensely • That rotten egg reeks to high heaven!; That rotten egg stinks unbelievably!

revved *adj.* primed and ready • *After that workout, I'm revved!;* After that workout, I'm primed and ready!

    ▸ ALSO: **revved up** *exp.* • *After that lecture, I'm really revved up;* After that lecture, I'm really primed and ready.

      ⇨ NOTE: This adjective is traditionally used to refer to a car that has been warmed up and ready to drive.

    ▸ SYNONYM: **charged up** *exp.* • *If you're all charged up, let's go on a hike;* If you're all primed and ready, let's go on a hike.

      ⇨ NOTE: Traditionally, this expression is used when referring to a battery.

"So help me..." *exp.* "I swear" • *So help me, if he bothers me again, I'll kill him!;* I swear, if he bothers me again, I'll kill him!

strip down (to) *exp.* to undress • *She stripped down to nothing!;* She undressed until she was wearing nothing!

♦ ALSO (1): **to strip** *v.* • *When I got my physical examination, the doctor made me strip;* When I got my physical examination, the doctor made me undress.

♦ ALSO (2): **stripper** *n.* man or woman who performs in a nightclub while undressing and dancing • *She's a stripper?!;* She's a performer who undresses in a nightclub?

♦ ALSO (3): **striptease** *n.* sexually provocative performance of one or more people who undress while dancing • *She does striptease at night;* She does sexually provocative performances of undressing and dancing at night.

♦ ALSO (4): **strip joint** *n.* night club that features striptease acts.

sweat like a pig (to) *exp.* to perspire profusely • *I sweat like a pig when I work out;* • I perspire profusely when I work out.

"What's with you?" *exp.* (very popular) "What's bothering you?"

♦ SYNONYM: **"What's eating you?"** *exp.*

"When hell freezes over" *exp.* "Absolutely never" • *"When do you suppose he'll graduate from college?" "When hell freezes over";* "When do you suppose he'll graduate from college?" "Absolutely never!"

wiped out *exp.* exhausted • *I need to rest. I'm wiped out;* I need to rest. I'm exhausted.

♦ VARIATION: **wiped** *adj.* • *I'm going to bed. I'm wiped;* I'm going to bed. I'm exhausted.

♦ SYNONYM: **to be pooped** *exp.* • *I'm pooped!;* I'm exhausted.

⇨ NOTE: Occasionally, you may hear the outdated expression *"to be too pooped to pop"* used *only* in jest.

♦ NOTE: **to wipe out** *v.* (surfer slang) to fall off one's surfboard.

"Wow!" *exclam.* exclamation denoting surprise or disbelief • *Wow! That's a beautiful car!*

♦ SYNONYM: **"Geez! (or "Jeez!")** *exclam.* • *Geez! What an idiot!*

⇨ NOTE: *"Geez!"* is a euphemism for *"Jesus Christ!"*

wuss *n.* weakling • *Don't be such a wuss. Just ask him for a raise!;* Don't be such a coward. Just ask him for a raise!

♦ ALSO: **wussy** *adj.* cowardly, spineless • *I've never seen anyone so wussy before;* I've never seen anyone so spineless before.

thanks *exp.* a very common abbreviation of *"thank you."*

♦ NOTE: This abbreviation should only be used in an informal setting since it implies familiarity and comfort between the speakers.

Practice The Vocabulary

[Answers to Lesson 6, p. 232]

A. Complete the sentences by choosing the appropriate word(s) from the list below. Make all necessary changes.

comfy	revved	wow
get off it	hit	strip down
raw	flipped	cut
high heaven	get	hot

1. In a nudist colony, the first thing you do is to _____ .

2. Oh, _____ ! All you do is complain.

3. Even if it takes the rest of my life, I'm going to _____ you for this!

4. It reeks to _____ in this gym!

5. We're leaving on vacation in just a few minutes. I'm so _____ !

6. He's so sexy. That's what I call one _____ guy.

7. _____ ! Did you see that? It was fantastic!

8. Ah, this chair is so _____ .

9. I'm exhausted after a day with these children. I'm just not _____ out to be a teacher.

10. You yelled at your new boss? Have you _____ ?

11. After that workout, I can't wait to _____ the showers.

12. At the nude beach, I bet I saw a thousand people in the _____ .

B. Underline the word(s) in parentheses that best complete(s) the sentence.

1. Look at that girl over there! Don't you think she's (**hot, hat, heat**)?

2. He must have been working out for a long time. Look how (**flipped, revved, buffed**) he is.

3. So (**hurt, help, heal**) me, I'm going to kill him if I ever see him again.

4. Did you notice that Steven is starting to get a big (**pot, pan, bowl**) belly?

5. She's really starting to let herself go to hell in a (**sock, pot belly, handbasket**).

6. After having a good night's sleep, I'm (**rarin' to go, in the raw, buffed**) this morning.

7. Can you believe how hot it is today? I'm sweating like a (**squirrel, cow, pig**).

8. I'm so sore after this workout. But like they say, "No pain, no (**plane, gain, brains**).

9. You don't think the exercise class was easy? Don't be such a (**wish, wash, wuss**).

10. –Would you ever like to go parachuting? –When (**hell, heaven, purgatory**) freezes over!

11. You look real angry about something. What's (**against, from, with**) you?

12. I'm bored in this dance class. I just can't get (**out from, down under, into**) it.

C. Match the columns.

☐ 1. It smells terrible.

☐ 2. She lets herself be unrestrained and wild on the dance floor.

☐ 3. I had a wonderful time.

☐ 4. He always walks around naked.

☐ 5. I think he's become crazy.

☐ 6. That fat person never stops eating.

☐ 7. She's into a new health craze.

☐ 8. What a difficult class!

☐ 9. I'm not inherently capable of this kind of work.

☐ 10. Are your new shoes comfortable?

☐ 11. He's really deteriorating.

☐ 12. Stop talking nonsense.

A. **I think he's flipped.**

B. **Get off it.**

C. **I had a blast.**

D. **What a killer class!**

E. **He always walks around in the raw.**

F. **Are your new shoes comfy?**

G. **That lardo never stops eating.**

H. **It reeks to high heaven.**

I. **I'm not cut out for this kind of work.**

J. **She's into a new health kick.**

K. **He's going to hell in a handbasket.**

L. **She gets down on the dance floor.**

A CLOSER LOOK:
Clothing Used in Slang

Interestingly, clothing has yielded many colorful slang expressions that are commonly heard in any conversation. Even an American who reads this list would undoubtedly be surprised to find so many common expressions featuring names of different parts of clothing, yet would have to agree that these are indeed found in popular usage.

Belt

belt *n.* swallow or gulp of an alcoholic beverage • *I think he took a couple belts before work;* I think he took a couple swallows of alcohol before work.

belt someone (to) *exp.* to hit someone (usually with the fist) • *He insulted her so she just hauled off and belted him!;* He insulted her so she just launched an attack and hit him!
◆ NOTE: The expression *"to haul off,"* meaning "to launch an attack," is extremely popular when used before an act of violence.

hit someone below the belt (to) *exp.* to commit a contemptible or unfair act • *Can you believe that she stole my client from me? That sure was hitting me below the belt;* Can you believe that she stole my client from me? That sure was a contemptible act.

Bonnet

bee in one's bonnet (to have a) *exp.* to be in a bad mood • *He sure has a bee in his bonnet!;* He's sure in a bad mood!

Boot

boot up (to) *exp.* to start up a computer • *We have a lot of work to do. Let's boot up the computer;* We have a lot of work to do. Let's start up the computer.
◆ NOTE: This expression is commonly shorten to *"to boot"* • *The computer is ready for you. I just booted it;* The computer is ready for you. I just started it.

boot camp *n.* Naval and Marine Corps training center • *He spent a year in boot camp;* He spent a year at the Naval and Marine Corps training center.

boot someone (to) *exp.* to eject someone • *He booted me out of his office;* He ejected me from his office.

bootleg (to) *v.* to make or sell illegal whisky • *I caught him bootlegging again;* I caught him selling illegal whisky again.

give someone the boot (to) *exp.* to fire someone from office • *After ten years of service, they gave me the boot;* After ten years of service, they fired me.

shake in one's boots (to) *exp.* to shake with fear • *When I saw the ghost, I started shaking in my boots!;* When I saw the ghost, I started shaking with fear!

"You bet your boots!" *exp.*
"Certainly!" • *"Did you pass
your driving test?" "You bet
your boots!";* "Did you pass
your driving test?" "Certainly!"

Collar

blue collar worker *exp.* one
who does manual work, i.e.
construction worker,
mechanic, etc.

hot under the collar *exp.*
irritable and angry • *What's
wrong with her? She seems
hot under the collar;* What's
wrong with her? She seems
angry.

Cuff

cuffs *n.pl.* common
abbreviation for "handcuffs"
• *Slap the cuffs on him;* Put
the handcuffs on him.

off the cuff *exp.*
extemporaneous, unrehearsed
• *He says the funniest things
right off the cuff;* He says the
funniest things
extemporaneously.

Gloves

**lay a glove on someone (not
to)** *exp.* not to touch
someone • *Don't you lay a
glove on him!;* Don't you
touch him!

wear kid gloves (to) *exp.* to be
very gentle and delicate (with
someone) • *If you're going to*

*criticize her children, you'd
better wear kid gloves;* If
you're going to criticize her
children, you'd better be very
gentle.

Hat

"Hang onto your hat!" *exp.*
"Get ready to hear
something astounding" •
*You're not going to believe
what I have to tell you.
Hang onto your hat!;*
You're not going to believe
what I have to tell you. Get
ready to hear something
astounding!

**hat off to someone (to have
one's)** *exp.* to respect
someone • *My hat's off to
your father. I certainly
could never do the kind of
work he does;* I really
respect your father. I
certainly could never do the
kind of work he does.

keep it under one's hat (to)
exp. to keep a secret • *I think
she's pregnant! Just make
sure to keep it under your
hat;* I think she's pregnant!
Just make sure you keep it a
secret.

old hat *exp.* **1.** outdated • *That
style of dance is old hat;* That
style of dance is outdated. •
2. familiar • *Do I know how
to repair a transmission?
That's old hat!;* Do I know

how to repair a transmission? I'm very familiar with that!

wear more than one hat (to) *exp.* to have more than one responsibility or position (at work, in an organization, etc.) • *He wears many hats at work;* He has many different responsibilities at work.

Heel

heel (to be a) *exp.* to be a contemptible person • *I didn't mean to hurt her feelings. I feel like such a heel;* I didn't mean to hurt her feelings. I feel like such a contemptible person.

Pants

ants in one's pants (to have) *exp.* to be squirmy and restless • *Would you stop fidgeting! You always have ants in your pants!;* Would you stop fidgeting! You're always so restless!

caught with one's pants down (to be) *exp.* to be caught unprepared • *He really caught me with my pants down;* He really caught me unprepared.

charm the pants off someone (to) *exp.* to be irresistibly charming • *He charms the pants off people;* He's irresistibly charming.

fly by the seat of one's pants (to) *exp.* to improvise • *I have no idea how to do this but I'm just gonna fly by the seat of my pants;* I have no idea how to do this but I'm just going to improvise.

smarty pants *exp.* an intellectual who shows off • *She always yells out the answers in class. What a smarty pants;* She always yells out the answers in class. What a showoff.

sue someone's pants off (to) *exp.* to sue someone for all the money he/she has (including his/her last piece of clothing) • *I'm going to sue your pants off!;* I'm going to sue you for all the money you have!

wear the pants in the family (to) *exp.* to be the head of the family • *It's obvious who wears the pants in that family;* It's obvious who is the head of that family.

Shirt

give someone the shirt off one's back (to) *exp.* to be extremely generous (to the point where one would give away one's last piece of clothing) • *He'd give you the shirt off his back;* He's extremely generous.

keep one's shirt on (to) *exp.* to be patient • *Keep your shirt on!;* Be patient!

lose one's shirt (to) *exp.* to lose everything that one owns (for example, due to a financial endeavor that failed) • *He lost his shirt when he went gambling;* He lost everything he owned when he went gambling.

stuffed shirt *exp.* pretentious and uptight • *He's a real stuffed shirt;* He's really pretentious and uptight.

Shoes

"If the shoe fits, wear it" *exp.* an affirmation of one's character trait • *"You really think I'd cheat her?" "If the shoe fits, wear it!";* "You really think I'd cheat her?" "I certainly do!"
♦ NOTE: This expression is commonly shortened to *"If the shoe fits!"*

goody two-shoes *exp.* an ostentatiously virtuous person • *She's a goody two-shoes;* She's an ostentatiously virtuous person.

in one's shoes *exp.* in one's situation • *If I were in your shoes, I'd fire him;* If I were you, I'd fire him.

Sleeve

up one's sleeve (to have something) *exp.* to have a secret plan • *I have a feeling she has something up her sleeve;* I have a feeling she has a secret plan.

wear one's heart on one's sleeve (to) *v.* to be extremely compassionate • *She wears her heart on her sleeve;* She's very compassionate.

Sock

beat the socks off someone (to) *exp.* to beat thoroughly • *I won! I beat the socks off the others!;* I won! I beat the others thoroughly!

put a sock in it (to) *exp.* to shut one's mouth • *Oh, put a sock in it!;* Oh, shut up!

Wig

wig out (to) *exp.* to lose control of one's emotional state, to become extremely upset and irrational • *You should have seen the teacher wig out!;* You should have seen the teacher lose control of her emotional state!

Practice Using Clothing in Slang

(Answers, p. 233)

A. Choose the letter of the appropriate response.

1. **to boot someone out**:
    a. to eject someone
    b. to hit someone

2. **to belt someone**:
    a. to chase someone
    b. to hit someone

3. **to have a bee in one's bonnet**:
    a. to be in a good mood
    b. to be in a bad mood

4. **to shake in one's boots**:
    a. to laugh hard
    b. to be afraid

5. **to wear kid gloves**:
    a. to be very gentle and delicate
    b. to be stern

6. **to be old hat**:
    a. to be out-dated
    b. to be in a bad mood

7. **to be a heel**:
    a. to be intelligent
    b. to be contemptible

8. **to fly by the seat of one's pants**:
    a. to be well prepared
    b. to improvise

9. **to be a stuffed shirt**:
    a. to be pretentious
    b. to be afraid

10. **to put a sock in it**:
    a. to eject someone
    b. to shut one's mouth

Just For Fun...

If you have trouble understanding the next monologue, *keep your shirt on!* Just go back and review the list on the previous pages and try again.

"I just met the new employee today. Have you noticed that he always looks like he **has something up his SLEEVE**? And he seems to be a real **stuffed SHIRT** that you have **to wear kid GLOVES** around 'cause he's always **hot under the COLLAR** about something. Well, **if I were in his SHOES**, I'd **make sure to charm the PANTS off** the boss or he might **get the BOOT** his first day! I tell you this right now, if he starts mouthing off at me, I'll either tell him **to put a SOCK in it** or **BELT** him!"

Translation:

"I just met the new employee today. Have you noticed that he always looks like he is **planning something secretly**? And he seems to be a real **pretentious person** that you have to **treat gently** 'cause he's always **angry** about something. Well, **if I were him**, I'd **really make sure to charm** the boss or he might get **fired** his first day! I tell you this right now, if he starts mouthing off at me, I'll either tell him to **shut his mouth** or **hit** him!"

The House Guest

Dialogue in slang

The House Guest...

Jim is telling Cecily about his house guest.

Cecily: **Hey**, Jim. **What's going on**? You look like a **basket case**!

Jim: **You can say *that* again**. Susan's brother **dropped in** from out of town, so I offered to **put him up** for a few days. He's **driving me up a wall**. For one thing, he's **eating me out of house and home**. He **stays up till all hours of the night** watching the **tube**, then **raids the fridge** before he **turns in**. The guy's a **bottomless pit**. You should see the way he **puts it away**. He even **belches** after he eats.

Cecily: How gross. I can't **handle** people like that. Does he at least **give you a hand** around the house?

Jim: He **doesn't lift a finger**! I **bend over backwards** cleaning up all day and he **sleeps in** until noon. Oh, and **check this out**... then he gets on the **horn** with his friends and invites them over.

Cecily: Man, what a **freeloader**. You better do something quick or he'll never **hit the road**. After all, he's **got it made in the shade** here.

Jim: You think he might stay even longer?!

Cecily: Now, don't go **falling apart**. If you're that **fed up**, just **kick him out**... but do it with **kid gloves**. I know! Tell him a **white lie** like you're getting the house fumigated!

Jim: That wouldn't be a lie!

Translation of dialogue in standard English

The House Guest...

Jim is telling Cecily about his house guest.

Cecily: **Hello**, Jim. **What's happening**? You look **overwrought**!

Jim: **That's very true**. Susan's brother **arrived without notice** from out of town, so I offered to **lodge him** for a few days. He's **really bothering me**. For one thing, he's **eating everything in our house nonstop**. He **remains awake until early in the morning** watching **television**, then **eats everything out of the refrigerator** before he **goes to bed**. The guy's **got an insatiable appetite**. You should see the way he **eats voraciously**. He even **burps** after he eats.

Cecily: How gross. I can't **tolerate** people like that. Does he at least **offer you assistance** around the house?

Jim: He **doesn't do anything**! I **strive vigorously** cleaning up all day and he **sleeps late** until noon. Oh, and **listen to this**... then he gets on the **telephone** with his friends and invites them over.

Cecily: Man, he really **imposes upon your generosity**. You had better do something quick or he'll never **leave**. After all, he's **got an easy time of it** here.

Jim: You think he might stay even longer?!

Cecily: Now, don't go **losing control** of your emotions. If **you've tolerated all you can**, just **eject him**... but do it **delicately**. I know! Tell him a **harmless lie** like you're getting the house fumigated!

Jim: That wouldn't be a lie!

145

Dialogue in slang as it would be heard

The House Guest...

Jim is telling Cecily about his house guest.

Cecily: **Hey**, Jim. **What's goin' on**? You look like a **basket case**!

Jim: **You c'n say** *thad* **again**. Susan's brother **dropt in** from outta town, so I offered ta **put 'im up** fer a few days. He's **drivin' me up a wall**. Fer one thing, he's **eading me outta house'n home**. He **stays up till all hours'a the night** watching the **tube** then **raids the fridge** before 'e **turns in**. The guy's a **bottomless pit**. You should see the way he **puts id away**. He even **belches** after 'e eats.

Cecily: How gross. I can't **handle** people like that. Does 'e at least **give you a hand** aroun' the house?

Jim: He **doesn't lift a finger**! I **bend over backwards** cleaning up all day and he **sleeps in** until noon. Oh, and **check this out**... then 'e gets on the **horn** with 'is friends 'n invites 'em over.

Cecily: Man, whad a **freeloader**. Ya better do something quick 'r he'll never **hit the road**. After all, he's **god it made in the shade** here.

Jim: Ya think 'e might stay even longer?!

Cecily: Now, don't go **falling apart**. If y'r that **fed up**, jus' **kick 'im out**... but do it with **kid gloves**. I know! Tell 'im a **white** lie like y'r gedding the house fumigated!

Jim: That wouldn't be a lie!

Vocabulary

basket case *exp.* overwrought • *When she found out that her in-laws were going to stay for a week, she was a basket case;* When she found out that her in-laws were going to stay for a week, she was overwrought.
 ♦ SYNONYM: **to freak out** *exp.* • *When she was told that her car was destroyed, she freaked out!;* When she was told that her car was destroyed, she was overwrought.

belch (to) *v.* to burp in a loud and crude manner • *He belched at the dinner table!;* He burped crudely at the dinner table!

bend over backwards (to) *exp.* to strive vigorously • *I bent over backwards to prepare everything for the party;* I strived vigorously to prepare everything for the party.

bottomless pit *exp.* a person with an insatiable appetite • *I can't believe how much you can eat. You really are a bottomless pit!;* I can't believe how much you can eat. You really have an insatiable appetite!
 ♦ SYNONYM: **to have a hollow leg** *exp.*
  ⇨ NOTE: This expression conjures up an image of someone's food going right past the stomach and into a hollow leg. • *She eats so much she must have a hollow leg.*

check someone or something out (to) *exp.* to observe or examine someone or something • *Check out what happens when I add water to the flour;* Observe what happens when I add water to the flour.
 ♦ SYNONYM: **to get a load of someone or something** *exp.* • *Get a load of what happens when I attach these two wires together;* Observe what happens when I attach these two wires together.

drive someone up a wall (to) *exp.* to annoy someone greatly • *He's starting to drive me up a wall!;* He's starting to annoy me immensely!

drop in (to) *exp.* to arrive without notice • *He didn't even call. He just dropped in;* He didn't even call. He just arrived without notice.

eat someone out of house and home (to) *exp.* to eat constantly in someone else's house • *I don't know what I'll do if he stays here any longer! He's eating us out of house and home!;* I don't know what I'll do if he stays here any longer! He keeps eating everything we have!

fall apart (to) *exp.* to lose control of one's emotions • *When she learned of her father's death, she fell apart;* When she learned of her father's death, she lost control of her emotions.

  ‣ SYNONYM: **to lose it** *exp.* • to lose control of one's emotions • *I think she's starting to lose it;* I think she's starting to lose control of her emotions.

fed up (to be) *exp.* to have tolerated all one can • *I'm fed up with this work!;* I've tolerated all I can with this work!

  ‣ SYNONYM: **to have had it up to here** *exp.* • *I've had it up to here!;* I tolerated all I can!

    ⇨ NOTE: This expression is commonly used in conjunction with a hand gesture where the speaker indicates a line over the head symbolizing that he/she is overfilled with intolerable acts.

freeloader *n.* one who imposes upon another's kindness or hospitality without sharing the cost or responsibility involved • *My uncle has been staying with us for three weeks and has never offered to pay for anything. What a freeloader!;* My uncle has been staying with us for three weeks and has never offered to pay for anything. He's the kind of person who imposes upon the generosity of others with no intention of reciprocation.

give/lend someone a hand (to) *exp.* to offer someone assistance • *Can I give/lend you a hand with that?;* Can I offer you assistance with that?

handle someone or something (to be unable to) *exp.* to be unable to tolerate someone or something • *I can't handle babysitting my little brother;* I can't tolerate babysitting my little brother.

  ‣ ALSO: **to handle someone or something** *exp.* to be capable of managing someone or something • *I just got a new big job. I'll have a lot of responsibilities but I know I can handle it;* I just got a new job. I'll have a lot of responsibilities but I know I'm capable of managing it.

  ‣ SYNONYM: **to be unable to take someone or something** *exp.* • *I can't take this anymore!;* I can't tolerate this anymore!

hey • **1.** *exp.* hello, hi • *Hey, Steve!;* Hi, Steve! • **2.** *exclam.* used to indicate a sudden thought or idea • *Hey, I've got an idea! I know how we can do this!* • **3.** *exclam.* used to attract someone's attention • *Hey, Kirk! Wait for me!* • *Hey, be careful! You almost went through the red light!*

hit the road (to) *exp.* to leave • *It's getting late. I'd better hit the road;* It's getting late. I'd better leave. • *Hit the road!;* Leave!

  ‣ SYNONYM (1): **to beat it** *exp.* • *Beat it!;* Leave!

  ‣ SYNONYM (2): **to scram** *exp.* • *Scram!;* Leave!

horn *n.* telephone (since the shape of a horn resembles that of the receiver of a telephone) • *Get on the horn and call the restaurant for reservations;* Get on the phone and call the restaurant for reservations.
◗ NOTE: *"phone"* is a commonly used abbreviation of "telephone."

kick someone out (to) *exp.* to eject someone • *The manager kicked the children out of the theater for being noisy;* The manager ejected the children from the theater for being noisy.
◗ SYNONYM: **to boot someone out** *exp.*
◗ NOTE: These two expressions are used figuratively although they are occasionally seen depicted literally in cartoons and comic strips.

kid gloves (to use/wear) *exp.* to be delicate and tactful • *She's very sensitive about this issue. You have to handle her with kid gloves;* She's very sensitive about this issue. You have to be delicate and tactful with her.

lift a finger (not to) *exp.* not to be helpful, to be lazy • *I do all the work and he doesn't ever lift a finger!;* I do all the work and he is never helpful!
◗ NOTE: It would be incorrect to use this expression in the positive sense: *to lift a finger.*
◗ SYNONYM: **not to do dirt** *exp.* • *He doesn't do dirt around here!;* He doesn't offer any help around here!

made in the shade (to have it) *exp.* to have an easy time of something • *This test isn't long! Once I answer the questions in this difficult section, I should have it made in the shade;* This test isn't long! Once I answer the questions in this difficult section, I should have an easy time of it.
◗ NOTE: For an extensive list of more rhyming slang, see *Street Talk II.*

put someone up (to) *exp.* to lodge someone • *Can you put me up for the night?;* Can you lodge me for the night?
◗ NOTE: **to put someone up to something** *exp.* to convince someone to do something • *He put me up to it!;* He convinced me to do it!

put it away (to) *exp.* • (lit); to put something in its place • to eat voraciously • *He can really put it away!;* He can really eat voraciously!
◗ NOTE: In this expression, *"it"* refers to "food.".
◗ SYNONYM: **to scarf it up** *exp.* • *Did you see how he can scarf it up?;* Did you see how he can eat voraciously?

raid the fridge (to) *exp.* to attack the food in the refrigerator • *Last night, I got so hungry in the middle of the night that I raided the fridge;* Last night, I got so hungry in the middle of the night that I ate everything out of the refrigerator.
◗ NOTE: The noun *"fridge"* is a popular abbreviation of "refrigerator."

sleep in (to) *exp.* to sleep past a usual wake-up time • *He slept in till 9:00;* He slept past his usual wake-up time till 9:00.

‣ SYNONYM: **to sleep the morning away** *exp.* to waste an entire morning by sleeping • *Wake up! You don't want to sleep the morning away!;* Wake up! You don't want to waste an entire morning by sleeping!

stay up till all hours of the night (to) *exp.* to remain awake until early in the morning • *I'm exhausted! Last night, I stayed up till all hours of the night;* I'm exhausted! Last night, I stayed awake until early in the morning.

‣ NOTE: The term *"till"* is a popular abbreviation of "until."

‣ SYNONYM: **to pull an all-nighter** *exp.* to stay awake all night (extremely popular among students) • *I pulled an all-nighter in order to study for the test today;* I stayed awake all night in order to study for the test today.

take off *exp.* to leave (said of airplanes) • *We'd better take off or we're gonna be late;* We'd better leave or we're going to be late.

‣ SYNONYM: **to beat it** *exp.* • *You'd better beat it before she comes back!;* You'd better leave before she comes back.

tube *n.* television • *All he does is sit watching the tube all day;* All he does is sit watching the television all day.

‣ NOTE: The noun *"tube"* actually refers to the "picture tube" but is popularly used to refer to the television set itself.

‣ SYNONYM: **boob tube** *exp.*

⇨ NOTE: The noun *"boob"* is a slang term for "idiot" since it is said that those who sit endlessly in front of the television set will become mindless.

turn in (to) *exp.* to go to bed • *It's getting late. I think I'll turn in;* It's getting late. I think I'll go to bed.

‣ SYNONYM: **to hit the hay** *exp.* • *It's time to hit the hay!;* It's time to go to bed!

"What's going on?" *exp.* "What's happening?"

‣ SYNONYM: **"What's up?"** *exp.*

white lie *exp.* harmless untruth used to avoid confrontation • *I didn't feel like going into work today, so I told the boss I was sick. It was just a little white lie;* I didn't feel like going into work today so I told the boss I was sick. It was just a little harmless untruth.

"You can say *that* again!" *exclam.* "That's very true!"

‣ NOTE: In this expression, it is important to stress the word *"that."*

‣ SYNONYM: **"I'll say!"** *exp.*

⇨ NOTE: In this expression, it is important to stress the contraction *"I'll."*

Practice The Vocabulary

(Answers to Lesson 7, p. 233)

A. Replace the word(s) in italics with the slang equivalent from the right column.

1. I *tried vigorously* _____ to make this a good party.

2. What's *happening* _____ ?

3. He's *annoying me* _____ .

4. Can I *help you* _____ with that?

5. He *doesn't do anything* _____ all day.

6. *Examine* _____ what happens when I walk up to her and say hello.

7. I have to *leave* _____ .

8. If you don't want to go, tell him a *little insignificant* _____ lie like you're sick or something.

9. Get on the *telephone* _____ and call Susan immediately.

10. Why don't you just *eject him from* _____ your house?

11. She's really *losing control of her emotions* _____ .

12. I can't *tolerate* _____ people like that.

A. **hit the road**

B. **handle**

C. **doesn't lift a finger**

D. **white**

E. **horn**

F. **falling apart**

G. **going on**

H. **check out**

I. **driving me up a wall**

J. **bent over backwards**

K. **kick him out of**

L. **give you a hand**

B. Fill in the blank with the appropriate letter.

1. What's wrong? You look like a _____ case!
   a. **pot**   b. **basket**   c. **pan**

2. I can't _____ her.
   a. **sit**   b. **lie**   c. **stand**

3. He has a huge appetite. He's eating us out of house and _____ .
   a. **apartment**   b. **mansion**   c. **home**

4. Can you _____ for a few days?
   a. **put me up**   b. **put me off**   c. **put me on**

5. I bent over _____ trying to get this house clean.
   a. **backwards**   b. **forward**   c. **sideways**

6. She _____ apart when she learned of his death.
   a. **lifted**   b. **fell**   c. **fed up**

7. I told him a _____ lie.
   a. **black**   b. **red**   c. **white**

8. What an appetite! Did you see how he put it _____ ?
   a. **away**   b. **out**   c. **over**

9. There's a great show on the _____ in about five minutes.
   a. **handle**   b. **tube**   c. **fridge**

10. Can you give me a _____ with this?
    a. **hand**   b. **foot**   c. **leg**

11. I have to _____ the road or I'm going to be late.
    a. **punch**   b. **slap**   c. **hit**

12. I have a house guest who just dropped _____ from out of town.
    a. **out**   b. **in**   c. **up**

C. Underline the correct definition of the slang term(s) in boldface.

1. **to fall apart**:
   a. to lose control of one's emotions   b. to laugh

2. **to be a bottomless pit**:
   a. to be in a bad mood   b. to have an insatiable appetite

3. **to check something out**:
   a. to examine something   b. to leave

4. **to drive someone up a wall**:
   a. to fall in love with someone   b. to annoy someone

5. **"You can say *that* again!"**:
   a. "That's very true!"   b. "You're crazy!"

6. **to drop in**:
   a. to fall   b. arrive without notice

7. **to have it made in the shade**:
   a. to have an easy time of something   b. to be in a bad mood

8. **to be fed up**:
   a. to have tolerated all one can   b. to be exhausted

9. **to turn in**:
   a. to go to bed   b. to leave quickly

10. **horn**:
    a. little insignificant lie   b. telephone

11. **to put someone up**:
    a. to tolerate someone   b. to lodge someone

12. **to put it away**:
    a. to eat voraciously   b. to cry

A CLOSER LOOK:
Colors Used in Slang

Colors make up a large part of the slang pool and provide us with an array of imaginative adjectives and expressions. Any foreigner is bound to hear at least one of the following expressions within his/her first few days in America.

Black

black as coal *exp.* extremely dark or evil • *Her heart is black as coal;* Her heart is extremely evil.

black as the night *exp.* extremely dark • *My bedroom is always black as the night;* My bedroom is always very dark.

black out (to) *exp.* to faint • *High elevations tend to make me black out;* High elevations tend to make me faint.
♦ ALSO: **black out** *n.* an interruption in electric power causing the lights to go out • *The electricity went off and caused a black out;* The electricity went off and caused total darkness.

blackball someone (to) *exp.* to prevent someone from being hired or accepted to a specific group • *He can't find work because he was blackballed;* He can't find work because he's being prevented from being hired.
♦ SYNONYM: SEE - **blacklist someone (to).**

blacklist someone (to) *exp.* to prevent someone from being hired or accepted to a specific group • *He can't find work because he was blacklisted;* He can't find work because he's being prevented from being hired.
♦ NOTE: This expression comes from the McCarthy period when those who were thought to be communists or communist sympathizers were put on a "blacklist" and targeted for discrimination.
♦ SYNONYM: SEE - **blackball someone (to).**

give someone a black eye (to) *exp.* to hit someone in the eye causing the surrounding area to become bruised • *I made a comment about his girl friend and he gave me a black eye!;* I made a comment about his girlfriend and he hit me in the eye!

in the black *exp.* financially sound (said of a business) • *This year, we're in the black;* This year, we're financially sound.

♦ NOTE: Ledger sheets show positive numbers in black ink and negative numbers in red.

♦ SEE: **in the red.**

little black book *exp.* a "secret" little book containing names and phone numbers of important individuals usually for dating • *How much money will you give me for my little black book?;* How much money will you give me for my little book of important names and phone numbers?

Blue

"What in blue blazes!?" *exclam.* exclamation of surprise and annoyance • *What in blue blazes is going on here?!*

blue *adj.* depressed • *I'm feeling sort of blue today;* I'm feeling sort of depressed today.

bluegrass *n.* a type of country music based on the song and dances of the Southern Appalachians. It is usually played at a fast energetic tempo.

blues (the) *n.pl.* **1.** melancholy songs • *I love singing the blues;* I love singing melancholy songs. • **2.** depression • *I've got the blues;* I'm depressed.

out of the blue *exp.* without warning, out of nowhere • *The other driver appeared out of the blue;* The other driver appeared out of nowhere.

♦ VARIATION: **out of the clear blue** *exp.*

swear up a blue streak (to) *exp.* to swear excessively • *She can really swear up a blue streak!;* She can really swear excessively!

talk till one is blue in the face (to) *exp.* to talk while being ignored • *I talked to her till I was blue in the face and she still made the same mistake;* I talked but she ignored me and still made the same mistake.

Gray

gray area *exp.* unclear and uncertain issue • *I'm having trouble answering you because that's a gray area;* I'm having trouble answering you because that's an unclear and uncertain issue.

gray matter *exp.* intelligence, "brains" • *I don't know why he makes such stupid mistakes. I guess he just doesn't have much gray matter;* I don't know why he makes such stupid mistakes. I guess he just doesn't have much intelligence.

Green

green *adj.* novice • *I wouldn't hire him if I were you. He's really green;* I wouldn't hire him if I were you. He's a real novice.

green around the gills (to look) *exp.* to look sick • *What's wrong with you today? You look green around the gills;* What's wrong with you today? You look sick.
♦ NOTE: Originally, this expression applied only to fish which, if green around the gills, were considered inedible because of sickness.

green thumb (to have a) *exp.* to have a talent for gardening and making plants grow • *You have so many plants here. You must really have a green thumb;* You have so many plants here. You must really have a talent for gardening.

green with envy *exp.* exceedingly envious • *When I told her my news, she was absolutely green with envy;* When I told her my news, she was extremely envious.

green-eyed monster *exp.* envy • *I can't believe you would say something like that. You know it's just the green-eyed monster talking;* I can't believe you would say something like that. You know it's just envy talking.

greenbacks *n.pl.* money.
♦ NOTE: This term is outdated yet occasionally heard in old films.

the grass is always greener on the other side *exp.* situations always seem better other than where one is • *I'd like to move to a small town where there are no cars, no pollution and no hassles. But I suppose the grass is always greener on the other side;* I'd like to move to a small town where there are no cars, no pollution and no hassles. But I suppose that situations always seem better other than where one is.
♦ NOTE: This expression is also commonly contracted to *"the grass is always greener."*

Pink

in the pink *exp.* be healthy •
*You look like you're in the
pink today;* You look like
you're healthy today.
▸ NOTE: This expression
conjures up an image of
someone whose cheeks are
rosy and healthy looking
from the sun.

pinko *n.* (derogatory) a person
of liberal or mildly radical
socialist political opinions,
communist sympathizer.
▸ SEE: **Red** *n.*

pinky *n.* one's little finger • *He
always wears a ring on his
pinky;* He always wears a
ring on his little finger.

tickled pink *exp.* thrilled •
*When I heard about your new
job, I was tickled pink;* When
I heard about your new job, I
was thrilled.

Purple

purple heart *exp.* purple ribbon
with a medal given for
someone who sustains an
injury while in combat • *He
received a purple heart in
World War II;* He received a
medal for sustaining injuries
while in combat.

purple passion *exp.* an intense
passion • *I have a purple
passion to become an actor;* I
have an intense passion to
become an actor.

Red

beet red *exp.* very red (like a
beet) • *She turned beet red
from embarrassment;* She
turned as red as a beet from
embarrassment.

**catch someone red-handed
(to)** *exp.* to discover someone
in the process of committing
a dishonest act • *I know he's
guilty. I caught him
red-handed;* I know he's
guilty. I caught him in the
process of committing a
dishonest act.

in the red *exp.* in financial
trouble (said of a business) •
This year, we're in the red;
This year, we're in financial
trouble.
▸ NOTE: Ledger sheets show
positive numbers in black ink
and negative numbers in red.
• SEE: **in the black.**

paint the town red (to) *exp.* to
go partying • *Tonight, we're
going to paint the town red!;*
Tonight, we're going to go
partying!

Red *n.* (derogatory) communist
• *I think he's a Red;* I think
he's a communist.
▸ NOTE: This slang term was

used in an American movie title in the mid-1980's called "Reds" which dealt with communism.

red cent (not to have a) *exp.* not to have a single coin, to be broke • *I can't lend you any money. I don't have a red cent;* I can't lend you any money. I don't have a single coin.
▸ NOTE: It would not be correct usage to use this expression in a positive sense: *to have a red cent.*

red faced *exp.* embarrassed • *Did you see how red faced he was?;* Did you see how embarrassed he was?

red hot *exp.* exceptional • *That team's red hot!;* That team's exceptional!

red tape *exp.* excessive and seemingly unnecessary procedures • *I had to go through a lot of red tape to get a refund;* I had to go through a lot of excessive procedures to get a refund.

red-letter day *exp.* an important occasion • *This is a red-letter day in our community;* This is an important occasion in our community.

redneck *n.* (derogatory) bigot, prejudiced • *His father is a real redneck;* His father is a real bigot.
▸ NOTE: This expression pertains to the rural working class who are said to be intolerant of any race other than white. The term originated because rural people are associated with sunburned necks.

roll out the red carpet for someone (to) *exp.* to give someone first-class treatment • *When the executive committee comes to visit, we have to roll out the red carpet;* When the executive committee comes to visit, we have to give them first-class treatment.
▸ ORIGIN: When celebrities arrive to an event, it is common to roll out an actual red carpet for them to walk on so as to not dirty their shoes on the ground.
▸ ALSO: **to give someone the red-carpet treatment** *exp.* to give someone first-class treatment.

see red (to) *exp.* to be furious • *When I saw her with my old boyfriend, I saw red!;* When I saw her with my old boyfriend, I was furious!

White

white as a ghost *exp.* extremely pale, usually due to fear • *You look white as a ghost!;* You look terribly pale!

white as a sheet *exp.* extremely pale, usually due to fear • *She was white as a sheet!;* She was extremely pale!

white-bread (to be) *adj.* to be very traditional, ordinary, and unadventurous in one's tastes or values • *She'd never have sex before marriage. She's very white-bread;* She'd never have sex before marriage. She has very traditional values.
♦ NOTE: This adjective suggests someone who is very traditional and unadventurous since white bread was considered the typical bread in the homes of most Americans. Within the past twenty years, bread recipes have become more and more daring using innovative ingredients other than traditional flour and water.

white elephant *exp.* a small object of little value that just collects dust in one's home • *You wouldn't believe all the white elephants she has in her house;* You wouldn't believe all the small objects that just collect dust in her house.

white-knuckle *exp.* denotes tension, suspense, fear • *It was a real white-knuckle ride coming here;* It was a real frightening ride coming here.

white lie *exp.* a trivial lie which is used to get someone out of a difficult situation or to spare one's feelings • *I didn't want to go to work today, so I told my boss a white lie;* I didn't want to go to work today so I told my boss a trivial lie.

whites of their eyes (to see the) *exp.* to see someone at close range • *Don't shoot till you see the whites of their eyes;* Don't shoot till you see them at close range.

Yellow

yellow *adj.* cowardly • *You're not going to confront her? What are you, yellow?;* You're not going to confront her? What are you, scared?

Practice Colors in Slang

(Answers, p. 234)

**A. Fill in the blank with the appropriate color from the list below.
Note that some of the colors may be used more than once.**

white	**red**	**pink**
green	**gray**	**blue**
	black	

1. It takes a long time to get a passport because of all the _____ tape.

2. The airplane trip was terrible. It was a real _____-knuckle ride.

3. He's really stupid. I don't think he has much _____ matter.

4. You should have heard how he swore up a _____ streak!

5. Your plants are beautiful! You must really have a _____ thumb.

6. I've never seen you so healthy. You're really in the _____ today.

7. I was tickled _____ to find out about your new job.

8. Our business is going very well. We're still in the _____ .

9. What's the matter? You look sort of _____ today.

10. Can you lend me some money? I haven't got a _____ cent.

Just For Fun...

If you find that you have some difficulty understanding the next paragraph, don't be *blue*. Just go back and review the Inside Info section and try again!

"At first, I was **YELLOW** and probably looked **GREEN around the gills** when I had to tell the boss that the company was **in the RED**, which made him **PURPLE with rage** and start **swearing up a BLUE streak**. But then I realized that I'd made a mistake and that we were actually **in the BLACK**. He was **tickled PINK** and decided to celebrate by **painting the town RED**. I was **GREEN with envy** and sort of feeling **BLUE** since I was dying to go although I didn't have a **RED** cent. Then suddenly he invited me **right out of the BLUE!**"

Translation:

"At first, I was **scared** and probably looked **sick** when I had to tell the boss that the company was having **financial troubles**, which made him **furious** and start to **swear nonstop**. But then I realized that I'd made a mistake and that we were actually **doing well financially**. He was **thrilled** and decided to celebrate by **partying in town**. I was **so envious** and feeling **depressed** since I was dying to go although I didn't have a **single** cent. Then suddenly he invited me **without warning!**"

At Work

Dialogue in slang

At Work...

*Dave and Eric are talking about some of the **goings on** at work.*

Dave: Whatever you're **up to**, you'd better **put it on the back burner**. It looks like we're gonna be doing Mark's job, too. You won't believe **what's up**.

Eric: So, give me the **lowdown**.

Dave: Mark is in with the boss getting **chewed out** for **calling in sick** again. I'm telling you, the guy gets **ripped** just about every night and then can't **make it in** to work the next day. And when he does, he keeps **screwing up**.

Eric: He can't even **cut it** when he's **stone sober**.

Dave: Well, if he doesn't **clean up his act** soon, he's going to get himself **canned**.

Eric: Man, I'm such a **wimp** that if I **downed** as much **booze** as he does, I'd be **barfing my guts up** nonstop.

Dave: I **hear ya'**, not to mention being **zoned** the next day, too. The thing that **gets** me is that when Mark drinks, he **flies off the handle** and starts **mouthing off** at everyone, then doesn't **have a clue** why people are **ticked off** at him the next day.

Translation of dialogue in standard English

At Work...

Dave and Eric are talking about some of the **occurrences** *at work.*

Dave: Whatever you're **doing**, you'd better **postpone it**. It looks like we're going to be doing Mark's job, too. You won't believe **what's happening**.

Eric: So, **inform** me.

Dave: Mark is in with the boss getting **reprimanded** for **not arriving to work again because of sickness**. I'm telling you, the guy gets **totally drunk** just about every night and then can't **arrive to work** the next day. And when he does, he keeps **making mistakes**.

Eric: He's **not even capable** when he's **completely sober**.

Dave: Well, if he doesn't **improve his behavior** soon, he's going to get himself **fired**.

Eric: Man, I'm such a **weakling** that if I **drank** as much **alcohol** as he does, I'd be **throwing up violently** continuously.

Dave: I **agree**, not to mention being **senseless** the next day, too. The thing that **annoys** me is that when Mark drinks, he **gets suddenly angry** and starts **speaking rudely** to everyone, then doesn't have the **slightest idea** why people are **mad** at him the next day.

Dialogue in slang as it would be heard

At Work...

*Dave 'n Eric 'r talking about some o' the **goings on** at work.*

Dave: Wudever **y'r up to**, you'd better **pud it on the back burner**. It looks like we're gonna be doin' Mark's job, too. You won't believe **what's up**.

Eric: So, gimme the **lowdown**.

Dave: Mark is in with the boss **gedding chewed out** fer **calling in sick** again. I'm telling you, the guy gets **ripped** just aboud every night and then can't **make id in** ta work the next day. And when 'e does, he keeps **screwing up**.

Eric: He can' even **cud it** when 'e's stone sober.

Dave: Well, if 'e doesn't **clean up 'is act** soon, he's gonna ged 'imself **canned**.

Eric: Man, I'm such a **wimp** thad if I **downed** as much **booze** as he does, I'd be **barfing my guts up** nonstop.

Dave: I **hear ya**, not ta mention bein' **zoned** the next day, too. The thing that **gets me** is that when Mark drinks, he **flies off the handle** 'n starts **mouthing off** at everyone, then doesn't **have a clue** why people 'r **tick't off** at 'im the next day.

Vocabulary

barf up one's guts (to) *exp.* to vomit violently • *I got the stomach flu and barfed my guts up all night;* I got the stomach flu and vomited violently all night.

booze *n.* alcohol • *His breath always smells of booze;* His breath always smells of alcohol.

call in sick (to) *exp.* to telephone those in charge at work and inform them that one is sick • *Where's Richard today? Did he call in sick again?;* Where's Richard today? Did he call those in charge at work again and inform then that he's sick?

canned (to get) *exp.* to get fired • *Did you hear? Ed just got canned!;* Did you hear? Ed just got fired!
  ♦ SYNONYM: **to get sacked** *exp. You'd better be careful or you're going to get yourself sacked!;* You'd better be careful or you're going to get yourself fired!

chew out (to) *exp.* to reprimand • *My father chewed me out when I took the car without asking;* My father reprimanded me when I took the car without asking.
  ♦ SYNONYM: **to come down on someone** *exp.* • *My mother came down on me because I got home late;* My mother reprimanded me because I came home late.

clean up one's act (to) *exp.* to improve one's behavior • *You'd better clean up your act right now or the boss is gonna fire you!;* You'd better improve your behavior right now or the boss is going to fire you!
  ♦ SYNONYM (1): **to get one's act together** *v.* • **1.** to improve one's behavior • *If you want to join us, you'd better get your act together;* If you want to join us, you'd better improve your behavior. • **2.** to get prepared • *The guests are going to arrive in five minutes! Get your act together!;* The guests are going to arrive in five minutes! Get prepared!
  ♦ SYNONYM (2): **to shape up** *exp.* • *If you don't shape up right now, I'm going to send you to your room!;* If you don't improve your behavior right now, I'm going to send you to your room!

cut it (to) *exp.* to be capable of doing something, to be successful • *I tried to be a teacher for a few years but I just couldn't cut it;* I tried to be a teacher for a few years but I just wasn't capable of doing it.

♦ SYNONYM: **to pull it off** *exp.* • *I tried but I just couldn't pull it off;* I tried but I just couldn't succeed.

down something (to) *exp.* to drink something • *Did you see how much brandy he downed?;* Did you see how much brandy he consumed?

♦ SYNONYM: **to put away** *exp.* • *How can you put away that much alcohol?;* How can you drink that much alcohol?

fly off the handle (to) *exp.* to become suddenly enraged • *When I told my mother about the car accident, she flew off the handle;* When I told my mother about the car accident, she became suddenly enraged.

♦ SYNONYM: **to blow one's top** *exp.* • *She blew her top when I arrived late;* She became suddenly enraged when I arrived late.

get one (to) *exp.* to annoy one • *He really gets me;* He really annoys me.

♦ SYNONYM: **to bug one** *exp.* • *My little sister is bugging me;* My little sister is annoying me.

goings on *exp.* that which is happening • *Have you heard about the goings on between Michelle and Eric?;* Have you heard about that which is happening between Michelle and Eric?

have a clue (not to) *exp.* not to have the slightest idea • *I haven't got a clue why he's so angry at me;* I haven't the slightest idea why he's so angry at me.

♦ SYNONYM: **to be clueless** *exp.* • *I'm clueless!;* I haven't got the slightest idea!

♦ ANTONYM: **to get a clue** *exp.* to become aware and enlightened • *Oh, get a clue! He's lying to you!;* Oh, become aware and enlightened! He's lying to you!

"I hear ya" *exp.* "I agree with you."

♦ NOTE: In this expression, it is common to use *"ya"* which is the common pronunciation of "you."

lowdown *exp.* the whole story • *Give me the lowdown. How did everything go?;* Tell me the whole story. How did everything go?

♦ SYNONYM: **to give someone the dirt** *exp.* • *What happened? Give me the dirt!;* What happened? Bring me up-to-date!

⇨ ALSO: **to dish the dirt** *exp.* to gossip • *There they go dishing the dirt again;* There they go gossiping again.

make it in (to) *exp.* to arrive to a particular destination (usually at home or work) • *What time did you make it in last night?;* What time did you arrive home last night?

♦ SYNONYM: **to roll in** *exp.* to arrive (usually late yet unhurried) • *She finally rolled in about 9:00;* She finally arrived to work about 9:00.

mouth off (to) *exp.* to speak rudely • *Can you believe how her children mouth off to her?;* Can you believe how her children speak so rudely to her? ▸ SYNONYM: **to shoot off one's mouth** *exp.* to speak rudely and somewhat irrationally • *Stop shooting off your mouth. You don't know what you're talking about!;* Stop speaking rudely and irrationally. You don't know what you're talking about!

put something on the back burner (to) *exp.* to postpone something • *You'll have to put your project on the back burner for now. There just isn't enough time to do it;* You'll have to postpone your project for now. There just isn't enough time to do it. ▸ NOTE: This expression comes from the culinary world where the less crucial items to be cooked are placed on the back burner of the stove.

ripped *adj.* extremely drunk • *Don't let him drive home! He's ripped!;* Don't let him drive home! He's totally drunk! ▸ SYNONYM: **plastered** *adj.* • *If I drink just one glass of wine, I get plastered;* If I drink just one glass of wine, I get extremely drunk. ▸ NOTE: **tipsy** *adj.* slightly drunk • *I'm starting to feel tipsy;* I'm starting to feel drunk.

screw up (to) *exp.* to make a mistake, to blunder • *I really screwed up when I forgot to pick up my mom from the airport;* I really blundered when I forgot to pick up my mom from the airport. ▸ ALSO: **screw-up** *n.* one who makes a lot of blunders • *He's such a screw-up!;* He makes so many blunders! ▸ SYNONYM: **to goof up** *exp.* • *I think I goofed up my test;* I think I made a big mistake on my test.

stone sober *exp.* completely sober • *Of course I can drive. I'm stone sober!;* Of course I can drive. I'm thoroughly sober! ▸ SYNONYM: **to be cold sober** *exp.*

ticked off *exp.* angry • *That really ticks me off;* That really makes me angry. ▸ ALSO: **to be ticked** *exp.* to be angry • *I'm really ticked;* I'm really angry.

up to something *exp.* **1.** in the process of doing something • *What are you up to?;* What are you in the process of doing? • **2.** in the process of doing something suspicious • *Hey! What are you up to?!;* Hey! What kind of sneaky thing are you doing? • **3.** to be in the mood • *Are you up to going to the movies?;* Are you in the mood to go to the movies? • **4.** to be healthy enough to do something • *Are you up to walking to the store after your surgery?;* Are you healthy enough to walk to the store after your surgery? ▸ NOTE: The difference in connotation between **1.** and **2.** depends on the inflection and intent of the speaker.

"What's up?" *exp.* "What's happening?"

> ♦ SYNONYM (1): **"What's going down?"** *exp.*
>
> ♦ SYNONYM (2): **"What's shakin'?"** *exp.*
>
> ⇨ NOTE: The contracted form of the verb "shaking" is commonly used in this popular expression.

wimp *n.* weakling • *He'll never take control. He's such a wimp;* He'll never take control. He's such a weakling.

zoned *adj.* dazed and senseless, oblivious • *I'm zoned today because I only got two hours of sleep last night;* I'm oblivious today because I only got two hours of sleep last night.

> ♦ SYNONYM: **out of it** *exp.* • *I feel out of it today;* I feel oblivious today.

Practice The Vocabulary

[Answers to Lesson 8, p. 234]

A. Replace the following italicized word(s) with the appropriate slang synonym(s) from the right column.

1. What are you *doing* _____ today?

    A. **ripped**

2. I *understand* _____ you.

    B. **canned**

3. I got *reprimanded* _____ by the boss today.

    C. **hear**

4. I'm getting *drunk* _____ .

    D. **barfed up his guts**

5. Don't *drink* _____ that so fast.

    E. **chewed out**

6. He *vomited* _____ after drinking so much.

    F. **down**

7. It really *annoys* _____ me how she brags all the time.

    G. **ticked off**

8. I heard he just got *fired* _____ .

    H. **up to**

9. You look *angry* _____ .

    I. **a clue**

10. I don't have *any idea* _____ why she's so angry.

    J. **gets**

B. Match the columns.

☐ 1. You'd better improve your behavior right now!

☐ 2. You won't believe what's happening.

☐ 3. He keeps making mistakes.

☐ 4. Don't be such a weakling.

☐ 5. I just got fired.

☐ 6. We're going to have to postpone the project.

☐ 7. You're drunk!

☐ 8. Has he come to work yet?

☐ 9. What are you so angry about?

☐ 10. Stop speaking rudely!

A. **Don't be such a wimp.**

B. **Stop mouthing off!**

C. **You'd better clean up your act right now!**

D. **He keeps screwing up.**

E. **I just got canned.**

F. **You're ripped!**

G. **We're going to have to put the project on the back burner.**

H. **Has he made it in to work yet?**

I. **What are you so ticked off about?**

J. **You won't believe what's up.**

C. Choose the word(s) in parentheses that best complete(s) the sentence.

1. Hi, Malcolm! What's (**up, down, over**)?

2. He called (**up, down, in**) sick again?

3. That's the fifth mistake you've made in an hour. Why do you keep screwing (**up, down, in**)?

4. This job is too hard for me. I just can't (**slice, chop, cut**) it.

5. How can you drink so much (**lowdown, burner, booze**)?

6. I just can't seem to concentrate. I feel (**canned, chewed out, zoned**).

7. When I told him the news, he (**ran, flew, jumped**) off the handle.

8. You should have heard him (**ear, mouth, head**) off at the boss today.

9. He'd better (**wipe, dirty, clean**) up his act soon if he wants to keep this job.

10. What happened? Give me the (**lowdown, handle, wimp**).

11. You can't lift that? What a (**clue, wimp, burner**)!

12. I'm not drunk. I'm (**rock, bolder, stone**) sober.

A CLOSER LOOK:

Fish, Insects, and Animals Used in Slang

It is absolutely amazing how many expressions can be created out of anything that can fly, crawl, or slither. The following list demonstrates that slang is as creative and limitless as the imagination.

Alligator

"See ya later alligator" *exp.* "See you soon!;
▸ NOTE: Notice that the pronoun "you" has been contracted to *"ya"* which is extremely popular in this expression. It would actually sound strange to say "See you later alligator."

Animal

animal *n.* one who is extremely aggressive sexually • *Be careful. He's an animal!;* Be careful. He's extremely aggressive sexually!

Ant

ants in the pants (to have) *exp.* to be restless • *Do you have ants in your pants or what?;* Are you restless or what?

antsy *adj.* restless • *He's always so antsy;* He's always so restless.

Ape

ape over something or someone (to go) *exp.* to go crazy with excitement for something or someone • *He went ape over the present I gave him;* He went crazy over the gift I gave him.

ape shit over something or someone (to go) *exp.* to go crazy with excitement for something or someone • *He went ape shit over the new car his father gave him;* He went crazy with excitement over the new car his father gave him.

♦ NOTE: This is a vulgar, yet popular, equivalent of: **ape for something or someone (to go)** *exp.*

Ass

ass *n.* (vulgar) **1.** fool • *What an ass!;* What a fool! • **2.** buttocks • *Move your ass!;* Hurry!

jackass *exp.* (vulgar) fool • *Don't be such a jackass!;* Don't be such an fool!

Bat

bats in the belfry (to have) *exp.* to be crazy • *He's got bats in the belfry;* He's crazy. ♦ NOTE (1): **belfry** *n.* bell tower. ♦ NOTE (2): This expression is no longer in popular usage yet still heard on occassion in old movies and in jest.

batty *adj.* crazy • *You're batty!;* You're crazy!

blind as a bat *exp.* very blind • *Without my glasses, I'm blind as a bat;* Without my glasses, I can't see a thing.

Beaver

beaver *n.* (vulgar) vagina.

busy as a beaver *exp.* extremely busy • *She's always busy as a beaver;* She's always extremely busy.

eager beaver *exp.* extremely eager • *Calm down! You're such an eager beaver!;* Calm down! You're so eager!

Bee

bee in one's bonnet (to have a) *exp.* to be in a bad mood • *She sure has a bee in her bonnet today!;* She's sure in a bad mood today!

busy as a bee *exp.* extremely busy • *He never seems to have time to talk. He's always busy as a bee;* He never seems to have time to talk. He's always so busy.

mind one's own bee's wax (to) *exp.* to mind one's own business • *Mind your own bee's wax!;* Mind your own business!

Bird

"A little bird told me" *exp.* "An unnamed source told me." ♦ VARIATION: **"A little birdie told me"**

bird *n.* woman or girl (British) • *Do you know that bird?;* Do you know that girl?

bird legs *exp.* very thin legs • *For a runner, he sure has bird legs;* For a runner, he sure has thin legs.

"Birds of a feather flock together" *exp.* "People who are alike attract each other."

early bird *exp.* a person who gets up early in the morning • *You're such an early bird!;* You get up so early!

eat like a bird (to) *exp.* to have a small appetite • *She eats like a bird;* She eats so little.

for the birds (to be) *exp.* said of anything inferior or of an absurd situation • *This car is for the birds!;* This car doesn't work!

give/flip someone the bird (to) *exp.* to give someone an obscene gesture with the middle finger • *I waved to her from my car and she gave/flipped me the bird!;* I waved to her from my car and she gave me an obscene gesture!

jailbird *n.* prisoner • *He's a jailbird;* He's a prisoner.

"The early bird catches the worm" *exp.* "He who gets up early accomplishes more."

Buck

buck *n.* (extremely popular) dollar • *Can you lend me five bucks?;* Can you lend me five dollars?

buck up (to) *exp.* to cheer up • *Buck up! Things are getting better!;* Cheer up! Things are getting better!

Bug

as snug as a bug in a rug *exp.* extremely comfortable • *"Were you comfortable in your new bed last night?" "I was as snug as a bug in a rug";* "Were you comfortable in your new bed last night?" "I was extremely comfortable."

bug *n.* virus, cold • *My sister can't come to your party 'cause she caught a bug;* My sister can't come to your party because she caught a cold.

bug (to) *v.* to annoy • *Stop bugging me!;* Stop annoying me!

work out all the bugs (to) *exp.* to remedy all the problems • *My new invention is almost ready. I just need a few more hours to work out all the bugs;* My invention is almost ready. I just need a few more hours to remedy all the problems.

Buffalo

buffalo (to) *exp.* to trick • *He buffaloed me!;* He tricked me!

buffaloed *adj.* tricked • *I can't believe how I was buffaloed into buying this!;* I can't believe how I was tricked into buying this!

Bull

bull shit *exp.* (vulgar yet extremely popular) nonsense • *That's a bunch of bull shit;* That's a bunch of nonsense. ♦ NOTE: *"bull"* or *"B.S."* is a common euphemism for *"bull shit."*

bull-headed *exp.* stubborn • *Sometimes you can be so bull-headed!;* Sometimes you can be so stubborn!

cock-and-bull story *exp.* ridiculous and unbelievable story • *Every time I go to his house, his father tells me cock-and-bull stories;* Every time I go to his house, his father tells me ridiculous stories.

take the bull by the horns (to) *exp.* to take the initiative • *You've got to just take the bull by the horns and do it yourself;* You've got to just

take the initiative and do it yourself.

Bunny

dumb bunny *exp.* stupid person • *What a dumb bunny!;* What a stupid person!

ski bunny *exp.* woman or girl who wears the latest fashion when going skiing.

Butterfly

butterflies (to have) *exp.* to be nervous and jittery • *I always get butterflies when I speak in front of large groups;* I always get nervous when I speak in front of large groups.

Camel

straw that broke the camel's back (the) *exp.* the final act that one can tolerate • *She borrowed my dress again without asking?! That's the straw that broke the camel's back!;* She borrowed my dress again without asking?! That's the final act that I can tolerate!

Cat

cat call *exp.* a whistle targeted toward a pretty woman or girl indicating excitement about her beauty • *You should hear the cat calls she* *gets whenever she walks down the street!;* You should hear the whistles she gets whenever she walks down the street!

catnap *n.* a short nap • *I'll meet you at the movies right after I take a little catnap;* I'll meet you at the movies right after I take a little nap.

copycat *n.* one who emulates another person's actions • *Every time I buy something, she buys the same thing. She's such a copycat!;* Every time I buy something, she buys the same thing. She's such an imitator!

"Curiosity killed the cat" *exp.* "Curiosity leads to danger."

pussy cat *exp.* **1.** term of endearment such as *"honey, sweetheart, darling, etc.* • **2.** gentle person • *He's such a pussy cat;* He's such a gentle person.

rain cats and dogs (to) *exp.* to rain heavily • *It's raining cats and dogs outside;* It's raining heavily outside.

scaredy cat (to be a) *exp.* to be a coward • *He's such a scaredy cat;* He's such a coward.
 ♦ VARIATION: **to be a scaredy pants** *exp.*

something the cat dragged in *exp.* said of a person who just enters a room • *Look what the cat dragged in;* Look who just walked in.
 ♦ NOTE: This expression is commonly used in two ways: **1.** when referring to an unpopular person • When this is the case, the expression would not be said loudly enough for the targeted person to hear • **2.** upon the entrance of someone who is well-liked • When this is the case, the expression would be said directly to the person, signifying affection and friendly teasing.

"The cat's got your tongue?" *exp.* "Are you speechless (due to shock, surprise, fear)?"

Chicken/Hen

chicken out (to) *exp.* to lose one's courage • *He chickened out at the last minute;* He lost his courage at the last minute.

chicken shit *exp.* (vulgar yet popular) • **1.** coward • *She's such a chicken shit;* She's such a coward. • **2.** petty, small • *My boss paid me chicken shit wages;* My boss paid me small wages.

count one's chickens before they're hatched (not to) *exp.* not to count on something before it's a reality • *Don't go counting your chickens before they're hatched;* Don't depend on it before it's a reality.

hen-pecked *exp.* said of a man who lets himself be completely dominated by his wife • *He's been hen-pecked for the past 25 years;* He's been dominated by his wife for the past 25 years.

run around like a chicken with its head cut off (to) *exp.* said of one who runs around aimlessly but frantically, getting little or nothing accomplished but makes a big tumult • *At work, he always runs around like a chicken with its head cut off. He needs to get organized;* At work, he always runs around frantically and gets little or nothing accomplished. He needs to get organized.
‣ NOTE: This expression refers to the fact that after cutting off a chicken's head, the body oftentimes continues to run around frantically and aimlessly.

spring chicken *exp.* youthful • *He jogs ten miles a day and*
he's no spring chicken!; He jogs ten miles a day and he's not very youthful!
‣ NOTE: Although the phrase *"He's not a spring chicken"* is certainly correct, a more common construction is *"He's no spring chicken."* This form is an extremely popular contraction of *"not a"* and used for greater emphasis, i.e.: She's not a beauty = *She's no beauty!* / He's not a gentleman = *He's no gentleman! etc.*

Clam

clam *n.* dollar • *I'll lend you 25 clams and that's all!;* I'll lend you 25 dollars and that's all!
‣ NOTE: Although this term is no longer in popular use, it is still occasionally heard in jest and in old gangster films.

clam up (to) *exp.* to keep quiet • *When I asked him if he saw who stole it, he clammed up;* When I asked him if he saw who stole it, he kept quiet.

Cow

cow (to have a) *exp.* to get extremely upset • *When I told my mother that I wouldn't be home until midnight, she had a cow!;* When I told my mother that I wouldn't be home until midnight, she got extremely upset!

♦ NOTE: This expression gained new popularity in the late 1980's due to a popular television show in which the son was known for using this expression. As of the beginning of the 1990's, it is common to see bumper stickers with the expression, *Don't have a cow, man!;* a common phrase used in this show meaning, "Don't get so upset, pal!"

♦ NOTE: Interestingly enough, in South Africa the expression is *"to have a puppy."*

fat cow *exp.* extremely fat • *What a fat cow!;* What a fat person!

"Holy cow!" *exclam.* denoting surprise and amazement • *Holy cow! Look at the size of that car!*

"Till the cows come home!" *exp.* "For a long time!"

Crocodile

"In a while crocodile" *exp.* "See you soon."

Dog

dog *n.* **1.** ugly person • *She's a real dog;* She's really ugly. • **2.** man (in general) • *You clever dog!;* You clever

person! • **3.** failure • *The new movie is a dog;* The new movie is a failure. • **4.** *pl.* feet • *My dogs are aching!;* My feet are aching! • Occasionally you will hear the play-on-words *My dogs are barking!;* My feet are aching!

♦ NOTE: The difference between **1.** and **2.** depends on the context.

dog do(o) *exp.* dog excrement • *Look out! You almost stepped in dog do(o);* Be careful! You almost stepped in dog excrement.

dog-eared *exp.* said of a page whose corners are bent • *When I lent you my book, it was in perfect condition. Now the pages are all dog-eared!;* When I lent you my book, it was in perfect condition. Now the corners of the pages are all bent!

doghouse (in the) *exp.* in trouble with someone • *I'm really in the doghouse now. I forgot my wife's birthday;* I'm really in trouble now. I forgot my wife's birthday.

♦ NOTE: This expression was created because it was said that when a husband would get in trouble with his wife, he was made to spend the night in the doghouse. This expression is now used figuratively between any two people, not necessary just husband and wife.

dog-tired *exp.* exhausted • *I'm going to bed. I'm dog-tired;* I'm going to bed. I'm exhausted.

dog-eat-dog *exp.* said of a situation where only the strong survive • *It's a dog-eat-dog world out there;* Only the strong survive in the world.

hound (to) *v.* to pester • *I have to keep hounding him if I want him to get things done;* I have to keep pestering him if I want him to get things done.

lucky dog *exp.* very lucky individual • *You lucky dog!;* You lucky person!

"My dogs are barking" *exp.* "My feet are hurting."

put on the dog (to) *exp.* to dress up • *I went to a formal dinner so I really put on the dog;* I went to a formal dinner so I really dressed up.
♦ NOTE: Although no longer in frequent use, this expression is still occasionally used by the older generations and in old movies.

rain cats and dogs (to) *exp.* to rain heavily • *It's raining cats and dogs outside;* It's raining heavily outside.

sick as a dog *exp.* extremely ill • *He's sick as a dog;* He's really sick.

sly dog *exp.* cunning and shrewd individual • *You sly dog!;* You cunning person!

top dog (to be) *exp.* to be the head of a company, organization, etc. • *He's top dog around here;* He's the head around here.
♦ NOTE: In the expression *"to be top dog,"* the definite article *the* is customarily dropped. It is not very common to hear *"to be **the** top dog."*

Duck

dead duck *exp.* certain to get into trouble or reprimanded • *If you stay here, you're a dead duck;* If you stay here, you're certain to get into trouble.

sitting duck *exp.* vulnerable to attack • *You're a sitting duck if you stand outside during a tornado;* You're vulnerable to attack if you stand outside during a tornado.

Eagle

bald as an eagle *exp.* very bald
• *He's bald as an eagle;* He's very bald.

eagle eyes *exp.* name given someone who is very alert •
Just call me "eagle eyes!";
Just call me "alert!"

Elephant

have a memory like an elephant (to) *exp.* to have an excellent memory • *She has a memory like an elephant;* She has an excellent memory.
♦ NOTE: This expression refers to the common belief that elephants never forget.

white elephant *exp.* an insignificant object which serves no real purpose other than to catch dust in someone's home • *Did you see the gift she gave me? What should I do with this white elephant?;* Did you see the gift she gave me? What should I do with this object?

Fish

fishy *adj.* suspicious • *That seems fishy to me;* That seems suspicious to me.
♦ ALSO: **to smell something fishy** *exp.* to be suspicious • *I smell something fishy here;* Something seems odd to me.

make fish eyes at someone (to) *exp.* to look at someone with desire • *That guy is making fish eyes at you;* That guy is looking at you with desire.

"That's a different kettle of fish" *exp.* "That's a different story."

"This is a fine kettle of fish!" *exclam.* "This is a terrible situation!"

Fox

fox *n.* a sexy person • *She's a real fox;* She's a real cute person.

foxy *adj.* sexy • *What a foxy mama!;* What a sexy young woman!

sly as a fox (to be) *exp.* to be extremely cunning.

Frog

have a frog in one's throat (to) *exp.* to have a temporarily raspy voice due to something caught in one's throat • *You sound like you have a frog in your throat;* You sound like you have something caught in your throat.

Goat

get someone's goat (to) *exp.* to annoy someone • *He really* *gets my goat;* He really annoys me.

old goat *exp.* a lecherous old man.

put on kid gloves (to) *exp.* to be delicate • *He's very sensitive about this issue. So when you talk to him, make sure to put on kid gloves;* He's very sensitive about this issue. So when you talk to him, make sure you're very delicate.
‣ NOTE: A *"kid"* is a young goat, yet also used in slang to refer to a child.

scapegoat *n.* an object of (unfounded) blame • *I'm always the scapegoat when anything goes wrong;* I'm always the object of unfounded blame.

Goose

goose someone (to) *exp.* to pinch someone on the buttocks • *I was standing in the bus during rush hour and I suddenly got goosed!;* I was standing in the bus during rush hour and I suddenly got pinched on my buttocks! • *He goosed her in public!;* He pinched her buttocks in public!

receive/get goose egg (to) *exp.* to receive/get nothing • *You know what I got for my*

birthday? Goose egg; You know what I got for my birthday? Nothing.
‣ NOTE: This is due to the fact that a goose egg is shaped like a giant zero.

silly goose *exp.* (used affectionately) fool • *You're such a silly goose;* You're such a fool.

wild goose chase *exp.* a pointless search • *How can we possibly find what the boss asked us for? I think we're on a wild goose chase;* How can we possibly find what the boss asked us for? I think we're on a pointless search.

Hog

hog *n.* **1.** an overeater • *Have you ever eaten with him? He's such a hog!;* Have you ever eaten with him? He's such an overeater! • **2.** a greedy person • *I can't believe he took all of it. He's such a hog!;* I can't believe he took all of it. He's so greedy!

hog heaven (to be in) *exp.* to be in euphoria • *This swimming pool is perfect on a hot day. I'm in hog heaven!;* This swimming pool is perfect on a hot day. I'm in ecstasy!

hog something (to) *exp.* to take over something • *She always hogs all the space in our bedroom;* She always takes over all the space in our bedroom.

hogwash *n.* nonsense • *That's a bunch of hogwash;* That's a lot of nonsense.

hoggish *adj.* greedy • *Don't be so hoggish and share with your brother;* Don't be so greedy and share with your brother.

road hog *exp.* a driver who dominates the road • *You'll never be able to pass that driver. He's such a road hog;* You'll never be able to pass that driver. He's dominating the road.

Horse

beat a dead horse (to) *exp.* to do something in vain • *Stop asking him to do you a favor. You're beating a dead horse;* Stop asking him to do you a favor. You're asking him in vain.

charley horse *exp.* a cramp in one's leg • *My mother told me that whenever you get a charley horse, you should get up and walk;* My mother told me that whenever you get a cramp in your leg, you should get up and walk.

from the horse's mouth *exp.* direct from the source • *I'm telling you the truth. I got it right from the horse's mouth;* I'm telling you the truth. I got it right from the source.

horse around (to) *exp.* to prance and joke • *Stop horsing around. We have work to do;* Stop joking. We have work to do.

horse of a different color (a) *exp.* a different issue • *That's a horse of a different color;* That's another issue.

horse's ass *exp.* (vulgar) fool • *He's such a horse's ass;* He's such a fool.

"Horse shit!" *exclam.* (vulgar) "Nonsense!"

"Horsefeathers!" *exclam.* "Nonsense!"

hung like a horse *exp.* said of a man who is sexually well-endowed • *He's hung like a horse!;* He's well-endowed!

on one's high horse *exp.* pretentious • *Get off your high horse!;* Stop acting so pretentious!

Lamb

gentle as a lamb *exp.* extremely kind and tender • *My dog is as gentle as a lamb;* My dog is very kind and tender.

in two shakes of a lamb's tail *exp.* immediately • *I'll be there in two shakes of a lamb's tail;* I'll be there immediately.

Mole

make a mountain out of a molehill (to) *exp.* to turn a trivial issue into a large issue • *Why do you always have to make a mountain out of a molehill?;* Why do you always have to make turmoil out of nothing?

Monkey

grease monkey *exp.* a mechanic • *He's a grease monkey;* He's a mechanic.

make a monkey out of someone (to) *exp.* to make a fool out of someone • *You made a monkey out of her;* You made a fool out of her.

monkey around (to) *exp.* to prance and joke • *Stop monkeying around. We have work to do;* Stop joking. We have work to do.

monkey suit *exp.* tuxedo • *I hate going to weddings and wearing a monkey suit;* I hate going to weddings and wearing a tuxedo.

monkey's uncle (to be a) *exp.* expression of astonishment • *I'll be a monkey's uncle! He built that car all by himself!*

more fun than a barrel of monkeys *exp.* extraordinarily fun • *We had more fun on vacation than a barrel of monkeys ;* We had extraordinary fun on vacation.

throw a monkey wrench into something (to) *exp.* to stop the process of something • *We were about to begin construction on the building but the contractor threw a monkey wrench into the project;* We were about to begin construction on the building but the contractor stopped the process.

Mouse

meek as a mouse *exp.* extremely gentle and harmless • *Don't be afraid of him. He's as meek as a mouse;* Don't be afraid of him. He's extremely gentle and harmless.

mousy *adj.* **1.** shy and reserved • *She's sort of mousy;* She's

rather shy and reserved •
2. drab and grayish • *Her hair
is mousy brown;* Her hair is
grayish-brown.

Owl

night owl *exp.* an individual
who likes to stay up until late
at night • *You're a real night
owl, aren't you?;* You like
staying up late at night, don't
you?

wise owl *exp.* a very knowing
and perceptive individual •
Your father's a real wise owl;
You're father is a very
perceptive man.

Pig

eat like a pig (to) *exp.* to
overeat • *When it comes to
food, she eats like a pig;*
When it comes to food, she
overeats.

"In a pig's eye!" *exclam.*
"Never!" • *"Would you ever
go out with her?" "In a pig's
eye!";* "Would you ever go
out with her?" "Never!"

pig out (to) *exp.* to eat a lot •
*I'm starving! Let's go pig
out;* I'm starving! Let's go
eat a lot.

pigheaded *adj.* stubborn •
You're always so pigheaded!;
You're always so stubborn!

"When pigs fly!" *exp.* "Never!"
• *Marry him?! When pigs
fly!;* Marry him?! Never!

Pigeon

pigeon *n.* **1.** one who is easily
swindled • *Mark is so
gullible. What a pigeon!;*
Mark is so gullible. He's so
easily swindled! • **2.** informant • *The gangster
committed murder when he
discovered his partner was a
pigeon for the police;* The
gangster committed murder
when he discovered his
partner was an informant for
the police.

pigeonhole (to) *v.* to categorize
or group • *Don't pigeonhole
me! There are a lot of other
things I can do besides just
answer phones!;* Don't
categorize me! There are a
lot of other things I can do
besides just answer phones!

stool pigeon *exp.* (especially
common among children) an
informant • *You told her
what happened?! You're a
stool pigeon!;* You told her
what happened?! You're an
informant!

Rabbit

rabbit ears *exp.* antenna • *The
picture on the television isn't
very sharp. I think we need to*

buy some new rabbit ears;
The picture on the television
isn't very sharp. I think we
need to buy a new antenna.

Rat

dirty rat *exp.* a contemptible
person • *You dirty rat!;* You
contemptible person!
‣ NOTE: This is a stronger
version of *"rat."* It is
common to use the adjective
"dirty" in other expressions
as well to mean "despicable
or base." For example: *She's
a dirty liar;* She's a
despicable liar, etc.

rat *n.* a contemptible person •
You rat!; You contemptible
person!

rat fink *exp.* a contemptible
person • *You rat fink!;* You
contemptible person!
‣ NOTE: This expression was
especially popular in the
1960's but is still
occasionally heard in jest.

rat (to) *v.* to report someone to
the authorities • *I can't
believe that my best friend
ratted on me!;* I can't believe
that my best friend reported
me!

rat race *exp.* daily work routine
• *Well, I suppose it's time to
go back into the rat race;*
Well, I suppose it's time to

go back to my daily work
routine.

smell a rat (to) *exp.* to be
suspicious of someone • *I'm
beginning to smell a rat here;*
I'm beginning to become
suspicious of him/her.

**flush/pour one's money down
a rat hole (to)** exp. to invest
one's money in a non-
profitable venture, to throw
away one's money • *If you
invest in his company, you're
flushing/pouring your money
down a rat hole;* If you invest
in his company, you're
throwing away your money.

Skunk

drunk as a skunk *exp.*
extremely intoxicated • *He's
drunk as a skunk!;* He's
really intoxicated!

Snail

slow as a snail *exp.* extremely
slow • *I hate hiking with him.
He's slow as a snail;* I hate
hiking with him. He's so slow.

Snake

**"If it'd been a snake, it
would've bitten you"** *exp.*
said of anything which is in
plain sight • *What do you
mean you couldn't find it? If
it'd been a snake, it would've*

bitten you!; What do you mean you couldn't find it? It was in plain sight!

slippery as a snake (as) *exp.* crafty and shrewd • *I don't trust him. He's slippery as a snake;* I don't trust him. He's crafty.

snake (a real) *exp.* a contemptible person • *He's a real snake;* He's a contemptible person.
♦ VARIATION: **a (real) snake in the grass** *exp.*

snake eyes *exp.* said of a pair of dice each displaying one dot • *Every time I rolled, I got snake eyes;* Every time I threw the dice, they displayed one dot each.
♦ NOTE: The expression *"to roll"* is commonly used in gambling to mean "to throw dice."

Sheep

sheepish *adj.* **1.** embarrassed • *Ever since I scolded her, she's been acting very sheepish with me;* Ever since I scolded her, she's been acting very embarrassed with me • **2.** meek, timid • *She's nice but rather sheepish;* She's nice but rather timid.

Squirrel

squirrelly *adj.* untrustworthy, suspicious • *I'd never go into business with him. He seems squirrelly to me;* I'd never go into business with him. He seems suspicious to me.

Turkey

quit cold turkey (to) *exp.* to relinquish a bad habit instantly • *He quit smoking cold turkey;* He quit smoking instantly.

talk turkey (to) *exp.* to talk frankly • *Okay. Let's talk turkey;* Okay. Let's talk frankly.

turkey *n.* **1.** idiot, fool • *What a turkey!;* What a jerk!
♦ NOTE: The use of the adjective *"jive"* with the noun *"turkey"* is especially common among African-Americans: *You jive turkey!;* You fool! • **2.** failure • *The movie was a real turkey!;* The movie was a real failure!

Whale

whale *n.* fat person • *She's a whale!;* She's fat!

whale of a (a) *exp.* an extraordinary • *He told us a whale of a story;* He told us an extraordinary story.

whale on someone (to) *exp.* to beat someone • *Did you see her whale on her son in the market?;* Did you see her beat her son in the market?

Wolf

hungry as a wolf *exp.* extremely hungry • *I'm hungry as a wolf;* I'm extremely hungry.

wolf *n.* a sexually aggressive person • *Be careful. He's a real wolf!;* Be careful. He's a real sexually aggressive person.

wolf down something (to) *exp.* to eat something in a hurry • *Stop wolfing down your food!;* Stop eating so fast!

Worm

can of worms *exp.* a very complicated and delicate topic • *I really opened up a can of worms when I asked him how his marriage was;* I really opened a complicated and delicate subject when I asked him how his marriage was.

worm *exp.* a contemptible person • *You like him? He's such a worm!;* You like him? He's such a contemptible person!

"The early bird catches the worm" *exp.* "He who gets up early, accomplishes more."

worm out of a situation (to) *exp.* to default on an obligation • *He promised he'd help me but he wormed out of it at the last minute;* He promised he'd help me but he defaulted on his obligation at the last minute.

worm something out of someone (to) *exp.* to coax someone into giving someone something • *I wasn't planning on telling her what happened last night but she wormed it out of me;* I wasn't planning on telling her what happened last night but she coaxed me into giving her information.

Practice Using Fish, Insects & Animals in Slang

(Answers, p. 235)

A. Underline the word that best completes the sentence.

1. Don't have a (**horse, cow, donkey**)! Just relax.
2. You think she's pretty? I think she's a real (**cat, dog, duck**).
3. It's raining (**fish, sheep, cats**) and dogs.
4. He's bald as an (**eagle, elephant, animal**).
5. She gave it to you free? That sounds (**fishy, sheepish, turkey**) to me.
6. He's sexy! What a (**fox, goat, goose**)!
7. I can't stand her. She really gets my (**goose, frog, goat**).
8. I think I was sent on a wild (**frog, cat, goose**) chase.
9. He's never serious. He always (**hogs, horses, dogs**) around.
10. I'm starving. Let's go (**mouse, owl, pig**) out.
11. (**Pigs, Pigeons, Rats**)! I missed the bus.
12. She's drunk as a (**skunk, snail, snake**).

B. From the right column, choose the slang equivalent of the word(s) in italics.

☐ 1. I'm feeling *restless*.   A. **bug**

☐ 2. She went *crazy with excitement*.   B. **antsy**

☐ 3. Wad a *quarrel*.   C. **have a cow**

☐ 4. This situation is *absurd*.   D. **cats and dogs**

☐ 5. You're really starting to *annoy* me!   E. **for the birds**

☐ 6. He *pinched my buttocks!*   F. **goosed me**

☐ 7. You're such *an imitator!*   G. **beef**

☐ 8. It's raining *heavily*.   H. **a copycat**

☐ 9. Why are you so *cowardly?*   I. **chicken**

☐ 10. Don't *get so upset!*   J. **ape**

Just For Fun...

If the following paragraph seems a little intimidating because of all the new terms, *don't have a cow!* Most of these words were just used in the last two exercises.

> "Holy **COW**! This is a **fine kettle of FISH**. It's raining **CATS** and **DOGS**! This weather's **for the BIRDS**. I was planning on leaving **in two shakes of a LAMB's tail**, but this **throws a MONKEY wrench into** my plans. This really **gets my GOAT**. I was going to meet Nancy, who's such a **FOX,** to **PIG out** at a restaurant for lunch and **WOLF down a sandwich** but I'm too **CHICKEN** to drive in this kind of weather with all the **road HOGS** out there. Now we'll probably get into a **BEEF** 'cause she'll **go APE** and say it's **BULL**, then accuse me of being a real **turkey** for trying **to WORM out of** our date, but I'd be a **sitting DUCK** out there in my little **VW BUG. RATS!**"

Translation:

> "**Oh, no**! This is an **awful predicament**. It's raining **heavily**! This weather's **terrible**. I was planning on leaving **immediately**, but this is a **big obstacle** to my plans. This really **annoys me**. I was going to meet Nancy, who's such a **sexy** girl, to **eat** at a restaurant for lunch and **eat a sandwich quickly**, but I'm too **afraid** to drive in this kind of weather with all the **bad drivers** out there. Now we'll probably get into a **quarrel** because she'll **get upset** and say it's **nonsense**, then accuse me of being a real **jerk** for trying **to extricate myself from** our date but I'd be a **perfect target** out there in my little **Volkswagen car. Darn!**"

At the Market

Dialogue in slang

At the Market...

Chellie and Hoodie are **picking up** *some* **odds and ends** *at the market.*

Chellie: I'm **bummed**. The candy section's been **cleaned out**. They're **fresh out** of all the good **stuff**.

Hoodie: Oh, **give it a rest**. You just **stuffed your face** a half hour ago. I swear, you have a **one-track mind**. Here, why don't you buy one of these papers instead. It'll **take your mind off** food.

Chellie: I'm **totally sure**! How can you read those things? They're so stupid. **Lookit**: "Woman **dumps** her husband when she **catches him red-handed** with another woman... from Mars!"

Hoodie: Talk about getting **caught with your pants down**. Well, if you don't buy it, I will.

Chellie: I don't **get it**. You always **rag on** me if I buy one of those. Now you tell me that you actually **fall for** that stuff they print in those **rags**?

Hoodie: No, but I **get a kick out of** reading the articles. **Uh, oh.** Speaking of women from Mars, **look what the cat dragged in**... Angie Stevens. I can't **put my finger on** what's different about her.

Chellie: **Get a clue**, would ya! She's had plastic surgery **in a big way**. Don't you remember that **honker** she used to have?

Hoodie: That's right. Wouldn't you have done the same thing if you looked like her?

Chellie: **Forget that noise**! You've got to be **nuts** to **go under the knife** as many times as she has.

Translation of dialogue in standard English

At the Market...

Chellie and Hoodie are **buying**
various small items *at the market.*

Chellie: I'm **depressed**. The candy section's been **emptied**. They're **completely depleted** of all the good **merchandise**.

Hoodie: Oh, **stop talking nonsense**. You just **ate voraciously** a half hour ago. I swear, you have your **thoughts permanently focused on one topic**. Here, why don't you buy one of these papers instead. It'll **remove your thoughts from** food.

Chellie: That's completely ridiculous! They're so stupid. **Observe**: "Woman **abandons** her husband when she **captures him** in with another woman... from Mars!"

Hoodie: Talk about getting **caught at an inopportune time**. Well, if you don't buy it, I will.

Chellie: I **don't understand it**. You always **harass** me if I buy one of those. Now you tell me that you're actually **tricked into believing** all that nonsense they print in those **absurd magazines**?

Hoodie: No, but I **really enjoy** reading the articles. **Oh, no**. Speaking of women from Mars, look **what annoying person walked in**...Angie Stevens. I can't **determine** what's different about her.

Chellie: **Become aware**, would you! She's had **extensive** plastic surgery. Don't you remember that **huge nose** she used to have?

Hoodie: That's right. Wouldn't you have done the same thing if you looked like her?

Chellie: **There's no possibility**! You've got to be **crazy** to **undergo surgery** as many times as she has.

Dialogue in slang as it would be heard

At the Market...

Chellie and Hoodie'r **picking up** *s'm*
odds'n ends *at the market.*

Chellie: I'm **bummed**. The candy section's been **cleaned out**. They're **fresh outta** all the good **stuff**.

Hoodie: Oh, **give id a rest**. You just **stuffed yer face** a half hour ago. I swear, you have a **one-track mind**. Here, why doncha buy one a these papers instead. Id'll **take yer mind off** food.

Chellie: I'm **todally sher**! They're so stupid. **Lookit:** "Woman **dumps** 'er husband when she **catches 'im red-handed** with another woman… from Mars!"

Hoodie: Talk about gedding **caught with yer pants down**. Well, if you don't buy it, I will.

Chellie: I don' **ged it**. You always **rag on** me if I buy one a those. Now ya tell me that chu actually **fall fer** all that stuff they print in those **rags**?

Hoodie: No, bud I **ged a kick** outta reading the articles. **Uh, oh**. Speaking of women from Mars, **look what the cat dragged in**… Angie Stevens. I can't **put my finger on** what's different about 'er.

Chellie: **Ged a clue**, would ja! She's had plastic surgery **in a big way**. Doncha remember that **honker** she used ta have?

Hoodie: That's right. Wouldn'chu 'ave done the same thing if you looked like her?

Chellie: **Ferget that noise**! You've gotta be **nuts** ta **go under the knife** as many times as she has.

Vocabulary

bummed *adj.* disappointed, depressed • *I couldn't go with my friends to the movies because I got sick. I'm bummed;* I couldn't go with my friends to the movies because I got sick. I'm disappointed.

    ♦ NOTE: This is a contraction of *"bummed out"* which is equally popular.

    ♦ SYNONYM: **down in the dumps** *exp. What's wrong? You look down in the dumps;* What's wrong? You look depressed.

catch someone red-handed (to) *exp.* to capture someone doing something dishonest • *I caught him red-handed stealing the money;* I caught him stealing the money.

caught with one's pants down *exp.* to be caught at an inopportune time or when one is unprepared • *I'm afraid that you caught me with my pants down. I can't answer that until I do some research;* I'm afraid that you've contacted me at an inopportune time. I can't answer that until I do some research.

cleaned out *exp.* emptied (of one's stock, merchandise, or money) • *This is the third store I've been to that's been cleaned out of flour;* This is the third store I've been to that's been emptied of flour.

dump (to) *exp.* to abandon or rid oneself of • *After 20 years, she dumped her husband;* After 20 years, she abandoned her husband.

fall for (to) *exp.* **1.** to be tricked into believing • *You actually fell for all those lies?;* You actually believed all those lies? • **2.** to fall in love • *I fell for her the moment I saw her;* I fell in love with her the moment I saw her.

    ♦ SYNONYM: **taken in (to be)** *exp.* • *I can't believe that you let yourself be taken in by his lies;* I can't believe that you let yourself be tricked into believing his lies.

    ⇨ ALSO: **to be taken** *exp.* to be cheated • *He charged you too much! I'm afraid you were taken!;* He charged you too much! I'm afraid you were cheated!

"Forget that noise!" *exp.* "That's an impossibility!" • *Forget that noise! I'd never do anything like that!;* That's an impossibility! I've never do anything like that!

    ♦ NOTE: In the above expression, it is very common to stress the article

*"that": Forget **that** noise!*
▸ SYNONYM: **"Get real!"** *exp.*

fresh out of something *exp.* **1.** totally depleted of something • *We're fresh out of eggs;* We're totally depleted of eggs. • **2.** to have recently left something (a school, a country, etc.) • *He's fresh out of school;* He's just graduated from school. • *She's fresh out of the military;* She has recently left the military.

get a kick out of something (to) *exp.* to enjoy greatly • *I get a kick out of working;* I really enjoy working.
▸ SYNONYM: **to get a charge out of something** *exp.* • *I get a charge out of flying;* I really enjoy flying.

get a clue (to) *exp.* to become aware • *Get a clue! He's trying to rip you off!;* Become aware! He's trying to cheat you!
▸ SYNONYM: **to wake up and smell the coffee** *exp. Wake up and smell the coffee! He's trying to rip you off!;* Become aware! He's trying to cheat you!

get it (to) *exp.* to understand • *You'd better explain it to me again. I still don't get it;* You'd better explain it to me again. I still don't understand.
▸ SYNONYM: **"Gotcha"** *exp.* "I understand you."
▸ NOTE: This is a popular contraction of *"I got you"* meaning "I understand you."

give it a rest (to) *exp.* **1.** to stop talking nonsense • *Oh, give it a rest! You know that's a lie!;* Oh, stop talking nonsense. You know that's a lie! • **2.** to stop dwelling on something • *Are you going to talk about that again? Can't you just give it a rest?;* Are you going to talk about that again? Can't you just stop dwelling on it?
▸ SYNONYM: **to hang it up** *exp.* • *Hang it up! I'm tired of listening to this!;* Stop talking nonsense! I'm tired of listening to this!

go under the knife (to) *exp.* to undergo surgery • *What time are you going under the knife?;* What time are you having surgery?

honker *n.* large nose • *Jimmy Durante was known for his huge honker;* Jimmy Durante was known for his huge nose.
▸ NOTE: This term originated because early cars had horns which were activated by squeezing a large bulbous rubber balloon called a honker.

in a big way *exp.* severely • *She cheated on her test in a big way;* She cheated extensively on her test.

◆ SYNONYM: **big-time** *exp.* extensive • *She had big-time surgery;* [or] *She had surgery big-time;* She had extensive surgery.

"Look what the cat dragged in!" *exclam.* "Look what annoying person walked in!"
◆ NOTE: This expression is commonly used in two ways: **1.** when referring to an unpopular person • When this is the case, the expression would not be said loudly enough for the targeted person to hear • **2.** upon the entrance of someone who is well-liked • When this is the case, the expression would be said directly to the person, signifying affection and friendly teasing.

"Lookit" *exp.* "Observe" • *Lookit! A rainbow!;* Observe! A rainbow!
◆ NOTE: *"Lookit"* is a popular contraction of "Look at it."

nuts *adj.* to be crazy • *Don't walk outside in the snow dressed in those shorts! What are you, nuts?;* Don't walk outside in the snow dressed in those shorts! Are you crazy?
◆ SYNONYM: **wacked out** *exp.* • *That guy keeps talking to himself. I think he's really wacked out;* That guy keeps talking to himself. I think he's really crazy.

odds and ends *exp.* various insignificant items • *What kind of odds and ends did you buy at the store?;* What kind of various insignificant items did you buy at the store?

one-track mind (to have a) *exp.* to have one's thoughts permanently focused on one topic • *All she ever does is talk about eating. She sure does have a one-track mind;* All she ever does is talk about eating. She sure does have all her thoughts permanently focused on one topic.

pick up (to) *exp.* **1.** to purchase • *Did you pick up some bread at the store for me?;* Did you purchase some bread at the store for me? • **2.** to contract (a sickness) • *I think I picked up a cold from one of the other students;* I think I caught a cold from one of the other students. • **3.** to find someone for a sexual encounter • *He goes to bars just to pick up women;* He goes to bars just to meet women for sexual encounters.

put one's finger on something (to) *exp.* to determine the problem or cause of something • *I think you just put your finger on it. The reason for his depression is boredom;* I think you just determined the problem. The reason for his depression is boredom.
◆ SYNONYM: **to hit the nail on the head** *exp.* • *You hit the nail on the head.*

You should be a detective!; You determined the cause of it. You should be a detective!

rag *n.* magazine or newspaper containing absurd articles and commentaries • *You actually buy those rags?;* You actually buy those ridiculous magazines?

rag on someone (to) *exp.* to harass someone • *Stop ragging on him!;* Stop harassing him!
♦ SYNONYM: **to pick on someone** *exp.* • *Stop picking on me!;* Stop harassing me!

stuff *n.* **1.** merchandise in general • *Look at all this great stuff!;* Look at all this great merchandise! • **2.** possessions • *Don't touch that! That's my stuff!;* Don't touch that! Those are my possessions! • **3.** junk • *How can you expect me to eat this stuff?;* How can you expect me to eat this junk? • **4.** actions (of a person) • *Can you believe the stuff he did to me?;* Can you believe the actions he did to me? • **5.** nonsense • *She actually believed that stuff he told her;* She actually believed that nonsense he told her.
♦ NOTE: You may have noticed that you've already encountered this word in lesson two where it was used to mean "junk." It is important to use it here as well since its definition of "merchandise in general" is also extremely popular.

stuff one's face (to) *exp.* to eat heartily • *We really stuffed our faces at the party;* We really overate at the party.
♦ SYNONYM: **to chow down** *exp.* • *I'm getting hungry. Wanna go chow down?;* I'm getting hungry. Do you want to go eat?

take one's mind off something (to) *exp.* to remove one's thoughts from a certain subject • *Let's go to the movies. It'll take your mind off your troubles;* Let's go to the movies. It'll remove your thoughts from your troubles.

totally sure *exclam.* incredulous • *She got elected president of the school? I'm totally sure!;* She got elected president of the school? I don't believe it!

"Uh, oh!" *exclam.* expression signifying sudden displeasure or panic • *Uh, oh! What did I do with my car keys?*
♦ SYNONYM: **"Yike!"** *exclam.* • *Yike! What was that?!*
⇨ ALSO: **"Yikes!"**

Practice The Vocabulary

(Answers to Lesson 9, p. 235)

A. Complete the sentences by choosing the appropriate word from the list below.

big way	red-handed	fell
fresh	kick	clue
get	rest	honker
nuts	ends	pick

1. I get a _____ out of going to parties!

2. That woman is talking to herself. I think she's _____ .

3. They caught the thief _____ .

4. You actually _____ for that lie she told you?

5. I need to _____ up some vegetables at the market.

6. Her mother yelled at her in a _____ !

7. Get a _____ ! She's only interested in your money.

8. I went to the market but they were _____ out of eggs.

9. I don't _____ it. Why would she want to go out with him?

10. I found some great odds and _____ at the flea market today.

11. Give it a _____ ! Your argument is ridiculous.

12. He'd be handsome if he didn't have such a huge _____ .

B. Underline the correct definition of the word(s) in boldface.

1. **to pick up**:
   a. to purchase   b. to sell

2. **to rag on someone**:
   a. to compliment someone   b. to harass someone

3. **rag**:
   a. absurd movie   b. absurd magazine

4. **in a big way**:
   a. severely   b. mildly

5. **to stuff one's face**:
   a. to overeat   b. to yell at someone

6. **to go under the knife**:
   a. to cook   b. to undergo surgery

7. **to be bummed**:
   a. to be destitute   b. to be depressed

8. **to dump someone**:
   a. to hit someone   b. to abandon someone

9. **to fall for something**:
   a. to be tricked into believing something   b. to drop something

10. **to forget that noise**:
    a. to be an impossibility   b. to be loud

11. **to get a kick out of something**:
    a. to enjoy greatly   b. to destroy

12. **not to get it**:
    a. not to arrive on time   b. not to understand

ranklin T...
732)8/...
www.fran...

ser...
seri...

tle: S...
nderstan...
ate due...

tle: Tow...
ichigan guide...
ate due: 4...

tle: Surviv...
nversations...
ate due: 4...

SK US ABOUT HAPPENINGS@TPL
HE LIBRARY'S NEWSLETTER!

C. Match the columns.

☐ 1. She undergoes surgery today.

☐ 2. I think you just determined the problem.

☐ 3. Let's go do something to remove your thoughts from your troubles.

☐ 4. That's ridiculous!

☐ 5. Observe.

☐ 6. Stop harassing me.

☐ 7. Look what annoying person walked in.

☐ 8. Business was terrific today. We were emptied of our stock in one hour.

☐ 9. She lied to me severely.

☐ 10. They've got great merchandise in this store.

☐ 11. Your thoughts are permanently focused on one topic.

☐ 12. Stop dwelling on that.

☐ 13. You look depressed today.

☐ 14. She abandoned her husband after twenty years of marriage.

A. **Give it a rest.**

B. **Lookit.**

C. **Look what the cat dragged in.**

D. **I'm totally sure!**

E. **You have a one-track mind.**

F. **I think you just put your finger on it.**

G. **Stop ragging on me.**

H. **They've got great stuff in this store.**

I. **Let's go do something to take your mind off your troubles.**

J. **She goes under the knife today.**

K. **Business was terrific today. We were cleaned out in one hour.**

L. **She lied to me in a big way.**

M. **She dumped her husband after twenty years of marriage.**

N. **You look bummed today.**

A CLOSER LOOK:
Proper Names Used in Slang

In the previous chapter, we saw how animals have crept into American slang, providing us with an unlimited supply of colorful expressions. But wait! Have we humans been unfairly neglected? There is only one answer to that question: *No way, José!*

Proper names have given birth to many other imaginative expressions in American slang as demonstrated by the following list.

Betsy

"Heaven's to Betsy!" *exclam.* exclamation denoting surprise, amazement or shock • *Heaven's to Betsy! Look who's here! It's so good to see you again;* • *Heaven's to Betsy! That's our house on fire!*
♦ NOTE: This expression is used by the older generations.

Adam

know someone from Adam (not to) *exp.* to be completely unfamiliar with someone • *I don't know him from Adam;* I am completely unfamiliar with him.

Bertha

big Bertha *exp.* a term given to a fat woman • *Look at that big Bertha over there!;* Look at that fat woman over there!

Bob

"Yes siree, Bob" *exp.* "Absolutely" • *"So, did you pass your test?" "Yes siree Bob!";* "So, did you pass your test?" "Absolutely!"
♦ NOTE: When pronouncing this expression, it is important *not* to pause before the name *"Bob."* This would actually sound incorrect. This expression is pronounced as if *"siree"* and *"Bob"* were one word: *"Yes sireeBob!"*
♦ NOTE: The noun *"siree"* is a slang deformation of the *"sir."*
♦ NOTE: This expression is mainly used by the older generations.

Charley

charley horse *exp.* a painful muscle cramp in one's leg • *"Why are you limping?" "I've got a charley horse in my leg";* "Why are you

limping?" "I've got a painful muscle cramp in my leg."
◆ NOTE: Although this comes from a proper name, *"charlie"* is generally not capitalized in this expression.

Dick

dick *PrNa.* **1.** (vulgar) penis • *I can see his dick through his bathing suit!;* I can see his penis through his bathing suit! • **2.** (vulgar) obnoxious person • *He's such a dick!;* He's so obnoxious!
◆ NOTE: Although this comes from a proper name, when used to mean "penis," *"dick"* is generally not capitalized in this expression.

house dick *exp.* house detective • *That guy over there is the house dick;* That guy over there is the house detective.
◆ NOTE: This expression actually refers to the character Dick Tracy and can be shortened simply to *"Dick": I think that guy's a Dick;* I think that guy's a detective.
◆ NOTE: As seen in the above, the name *"Dick"* has three meanings • **1.** penis • **2.** obnoxious, arrogant person • **3.** detective. The different connotations simply depend on context and the intent of the speaker.

◆ NOTE: Although this comes from a proper name, *"dick"* is generally not capitalized in this expression.

private dick *exp.* private detective • *His father's a private dick;* His father's a private detective.
◆ NOTE: Although this comes from a proper name, *"dick"* is generally not capitalized in this expression.

Tom, Dick and Harry *exp.* each and every man • *You expect me to give money to every Tom, Dick and Harry who approaches me?;* You expect me to give money to each and every man who approaches me?

Fanny

fanny *PrNa.* buttocks, rear end • *Her mother gave her daughter a spanking on her fanny;* Her mother gave her daughter a spanking on her rear end.
◆ NOTE: Although this comes from a proper name, *"fanny"* is generally not capitalized in this expression.

Fritz

on the fritz *exp.* inoperable • *The television is on the fritz;* The television is out of order.

♦ NOTE: Although this comes from a proper name, *"fritz"* is generally not capitalized in this expression.

fritz out (to) *exp.* to cease to operate • *My radio just fritzed out;* My radio just ceased to operate.
♦ NOTE: Although this comes from a proper name, *"fritz"* is generally not capitalized in this expression.

George

"By George!" *exclam.* (British) This is an exclamation denoting surprise • *By George! Isn't that your sister with that man?*
♦ NOTE: This expression is British in origin and used only in jest in America.

Guy

guy *PrNa.* man in general • *Do you know that guy?;* Do you know that man?
♦ NOTE: Although this comes from a proper name, *"guy"* is generally not capitalized in this expression.

Jack

"Hit the road, Jack!" *exclam.* *Leave!;*
♦ VARIATION: *Hit the road!*

jack shit *exp.* (vulgar) nothing • *He doesn't know jack shit about mechanics;* He knows nothing about mechanics.
♦ NOTE (1): Although this expression is vulgar, it is extremely popular.
♦ NOTE (2): A popular euphemism for this expression is simply **"not to know jack"**: *I dunno jack about plumbing;* I don't know a thing about plumbing.

Jack-of-all-trades *exp.* an individual who knows a little about everything • *Bob can fix anything. He's a real Jack-of-all-trades;* Bob can fix anything. He really knows a little about everything.

jack someone around (to) *exp.* to mislead someone • *Car salesmen always jack you around;* Car salesmen always mislead you.
♦ NOTE: Although this comes from a proper name, *"jack"* is generally not capitalized in this expression.

Jackie

"Quicker than you can say 'Jackie Robinson'" *exp.* immediately • *I'll be back quicker than you can say 'Jackie Robinson';* I'll be right back.
♦ NOTE: This expression is no

longer popular although it may be used in old movies, by older generations, or in jest.

Joe

Joe *adj.* the epitome • *Look how he's dressed. He looks like Joe College;* Look how he's dressed. He looks like the epitome of a college man.

Joe Blow *exp.* man in general • *Every Joe Blow thinks he can solve the world's problems;* Every man in general thinks he can solve the world's problems.

Joe Schmoe *exp.* man in general • *Every Joe Schmoe thinks he can be president!;* Every man in general thinks he can be president.

John

john *n.* bathroom, latrine • *He's been in the john for the past hour;* He's been in the bathroom for the past hour.
♦ NOTE (1): This term is considered to be extremely casual and should only be used with family and friends.
♦ NOTE (2): Although this comes from a proper name, *"John"* is generally not capitalized in this expression.

John *n.* prostitute's client • *She just found herself a new John;* She just found herself a new client.

Johnny

Johnny on the spot (to be) *exp.* to be prompt • *He arrived Johnny on the spot;* He arrived promptly.
♦ NOTE: This expression is occasionally used by the older generations only.

Jose

"No way, Jose!;" *exclam.* "That's impossible!"
♦ NOTE: This exclamation is mainly used by the younger generations.

Juan

Don Juan *exp.* a handsome, suave, and romantic man • *Her new boyfriend is a real Don Juan;* Her new boyfriend is really handsome, suave, and romantic.
♦ NOTE: This expression comes from the fictional character *"Don Juan,"* known for his amorous nature.

Louise

"Geez, Louise!" *exclam.* exclamation denoting surprise • *Geez Louise! Why did you spend all your money on that?!*

Micky

slip someone a Micky (to) *exp.* to sneak a drug into someone's drink • *I walked in just in time. She was about to slip him a Micky;* I walked in just in time. She was about to sneak a drug in his drink.

Nick

Saint Nick *pron.* an affectionate term for *"Saint Nicholas"* also known as Santa Claus.

Pat

have something down pat (to) *exp.* to know something perfectly • *I have slang down pat;* I know slang perfectly.
♦ NOTE: Although this comes from a proper name, *"pat"* is generally not capitalized.

Paul

rob Peter to pay Paul (to) *exp.* to do something beneficial at the expense of something else • *She's actually going to sell all of her furniture in order to have enough money to go on her trip. She won't even have enough money for rent! Talk about robbing Peter to pay Paul!;* She's actually going to sell all of her furniture in order to have enough money to go on her trip. She won't even have

enough money for rent! Talk about doing something beneficial at the expense of something else.

Peter

"For Pete's sake!" *exclam.* exclamation denoting astonishment and annoyance *Oh, for Pete's sake! I can't believe you did that!*
♦ NOTE: *"Pete"* is a nickname for "Peter."

"For the love of Pete!" *exclam.* exclamation denoting surprise (from excitement or annoyance) *For the love of Pete! How could she paint something so awful?*
♦ NOTE (1): *Pete* is a nickname for "Peter."
♦ NOTE (2): This expression is used by the older generations only.

peter *n.* (humorous) penis • *That must be a female turtle. I can't see a peter!;* That must be a female turtle. I can't see a penis!
♦ NOTE: Although this comes from a proper name, *"peter"* is generally not capitalized in this expression.

peter out (to) *exp.* to diminish in energy • *I was strong in the beginning of the race but petered out near the end;* I was strong in the beginning of the race but my energy diminished near the end.

♦ NOTE: Although this comes from a proper name, *"peter"* is generally not capitalized in this expression.

Ralph

ralph (to) *v.* to vomit • *I'm so full, I could ralph;* I'm so full I could vomit.

♦ NOTE: This verb is used primarily by the younger generations only.

Randy

randy *adj.* sexually aroused • *My dog is in heat. I've never seen him so randy;* My dog is in heat. I've never seen him so sexually aroused.

Roger

"Roger!" *exp.* "Communication received!"

♦ NOTE: This expression in which the pronoun *"Roger"* signifies "Received," was originally used in the Air Force to signal completion of a conversation between pilot and ground control.

Sam

Uncle Sam *exp.* the United States government • *Uncle Sam takes money out of my paycheck each week;* The United States government takes money out of my paycheck each week.

Scott

scott free (to get off) *exp.* to be totally cleared of all blame • *The thief got off Scott free;* The thief was totally cleared of all blame.

♦ NOTE: Although this comes from a proper name, *"scott"* is generally not capitalized in this expression.

Scrooge

Scrooge *PrNa.* a miser (applies to a man or woman) • *Don't bother asking him to donate to the charity. He's such a Scrooge!;* Don't bother asking him to donate to the charity. He's such a miser!

Susan

Lazy Susan *exp.* a revolving tray used for serving food or condiments • *The waiter put a Lazy Susan on the table which was full of different condiments;* The waiter put a revolving tray on the table which was full of different condiments.

Thomas/Tom

Doubting Thomas *exp.* a skeptical person • *I don't mean to be a doubting Thomas, but I don't believe him;* I don't mean to be skeptical, but I don't believe him.

tomfoolery *exp.* foolishness • *Stop this tomfoolery at once!;* Stop this foolishness at once!

Peeping Tom *exp.* name given to a man who spies in windows • *There's a Peeping Tom outside my window!;* There's a man who's spying in my window!

Willy

willies (to have the) *exp.* to be scared and uneasy • *I have the willies in this house;* I'm scared and uneasy in this house.

willy-nilly *exp.* haphazardly • *Since he was in a hurry, he chose which shirt to wear willy-nilly;* Since he was in a hurry, he chose which shirt to wear haphazardly.

Practice Using Proper Names in Slang

(Answers, p. 236)

A. Choose the proper name that best fits the sentence.

1. Why are you limping? Is it a _____ horse?
   a. **DICK**   b. **STEVE**   c. **CHARLEY**

2. My radio is on the _____ .
   a. **FRITZ**   b. **DON**   c. **JACK**

3. He's know a little about everything. He's a real _____-of-all-trades.
   a. **BOB**   b. **DAVID**   c. **JACK**

4. She's not very pretty. She's sort of a plain _____ .
   a. **DEBBIE**   b. **JAN**   c. **JANE**

5. After drinking all that water, I have to go to the _____ .
   a. **JOHN**   b. **ED**   c. **ERIC**

6. You want me to go with you to the zoo instead of going to school? No way, _____ !
   a. **JOHN** b. **JOSÉ** c. **RENÉE**

7. For _____ sake! I locked my keys in the car!
   a. **PAUL'S** b. **PETE'S** c. **MIKE'S**

8. After she drank it, she fainted. I think someone slipped her a _____ .
   a. **MICKY** b. **PETER** c. **MIKE**

9. I feel sick. I think I'm gonna _____ .
   a. **SAM** b. **SCOTT** c. **RALPH**

10. Uncle _____ takes a lot of money out of my paycheck each week.
    a. **PAUL** b. **STEVE** c. **SAM**

11. I just saw a peeping _____ outside my window!
    a. **TOM** b. **JOHN** c. **ERIC**

12. Walking down this dark alley gives me the _____ .
    a. **HARRYS** b. **WILLIES** c. **STEVES**

Just For Fun...

Here is a short monologue to test yourself on the use of proper names in American slang.

"**No way, JOSÉ**! My car's **on the FRITZ** again. **For PETE'S sake**! With **Uncle SAM** taking so much money from me this year, I won't be able to afford repairs. **Geez LOUISE**! Thinking of spending all that money **gives me the WILLIES** and makes me want **to RALPH**. I don't mean to be a **doubting THOMAS** but I should probably hire a private **DICK** to see if my mechanic is trying **to JACK me around. Yes siree BOB**!"

Translation:

"**That's impossible**! My car's **defective** again. **Oh, no**! With the **government** taking so much money from me this year, I won't be able to afford repairs. **Oh, no**! Thinking of spending all that money **makes me uneasy** and makes me want **to vomit**. I don't mean to be **skeptical** but I should probably hire a private **investigator** to see if my mechanic is trying **to mislead me**. **Absolutely**!"

At the Restaurant

Dialogue in slang

At the Restaurant...

Jeff and Julie are looking for a place to eat.

Jeff: **What do you say** we **stop in** at that **burger joint** over there and **grab a bite**?

Julie: **Fat chance**! If you think I'd ever **set foot** in that **dive** again, you've **got a screw loose**. The last time I ate that **slop**, I almost **lost it**! Besides, the service **stinks** there, too. It was the first time I ever **stiffed a waiter**.

Jeff: Yeah. I had a **sneaking suspicion** it was going be like that **right off the bat**. Not seeing a **living soul** anywhere sort of **tipped me off**. Hey! How about that one over there?

Julie: Oh, **come off it**! That place is too **ritzy** for us. It **costs an arm and a leg**!

Jeff: Don't **have a cow**. It's **on me**.

Julie: In that case, I'm right behind you.

(moments later...)

Julie: I can't wait to **chow down**.

Jeff: Just don't order everything on the menu, okay? I know how much you can **polish off** in one sitting. You're such a **porker**, it's amazing you're not some kind of **blimp**.

Julie: So, **I'm into** food. Listen, I have to run to the **john**. Just order me a deluxe burger but **hold** the **fries**. I want to save room for dessert to **wash it down**!

Translation of dialogue in standard English

At the Restaurant...

Jeff and Julie are looking for a place to eat.

Jeff: **What do think about the idea** of **going into that hamburger restaurant** over there and **get something to eat quickly?**

Julie: **Never!** If you think I'd ever **enter** that **inferior restaurant** willingly again, you're **crazy**. The last time I ate that **mediocre food**, I almost **vomited**! Besides, the service is **terrible** there, too. It was the first time I **didn't leave a tip**.

Jeff: Yes. I had a **feeling** it was going be like that **right from the beginning**. Not seeing a **single person** anywhere **informed me**. Hey! How about that one over there?

Julie: Oh, **stop talking nonsense!** That place is too **lavish** for us. It's **extremely expensive!**

Jeff: Don't **get upset**. I'm **paying**.

Julie: In that case, I'm right behind you.

(moments later...)

Julie: I can't wait to **eat**.

Jeff: Just don't order everything on the menu, okay? I know how much you can **eat** in one sitting. You're such a **pig**, it's amazing you're not some kind of **fat person**.

Julie: So, **I enjoy** food. Listen, I have to run to the **bathroom**. Just order me a deluxe burger but **omit** the **French fries**. I want to save room for dessert to **follow up the meal!**

213

Dialogue in slang as it would be heard

At the Restaurant...

Jeff 'n Julie 'r looking fer a place ta eat.

Jeff: **Wuddya say** we **stop in** at that **burger joint** down the street'n **grab a bite**?

Julie: **Fat chance**! If you think I'd ever **set foot**'n that **dive** again, you've **god a screw loose**. The last time I ate that **slop**, I almost **lost it**! Besides, the service **stinks** there, too. It was the first time I ever **stift a waider**.

Jeff: Yeah. I had a **sneaking suspicion** it was gonna be like that **ride off the bat**. Not seeing a **living soul** anywhere sorta **tipt me off**. Hey! How 'bout that one over there?

Julie: Oh, **come off it**! That place's too **ritzy** fer us. It **costs an arm 'n a leg**!

Jeff: Don't **have a cow**. It's **on me**.

Julie: In that case, I'm right behin' ja.

(moments later...)

Julie: I can't wait ta **chow down**.

Jeff: Just don' order everything on the menu, okay? I know how much you c'n **polish off**'n one sitting. Yer such a **porker**, it's amazing you're not some kinda **blimp**.

Julie: So, **I'm inta** food. Listen, I have ta run ta the **john**. Just order me a deluxe burger but **hold** the **fries**. I wanna save room fer dessert ta **wash it down**!

Vocabulary

blimp *n.* fat person • (lit); dirigible • *She's a real blimp!;* She's really fat!
> ♦ VARIATION: **blimpo** *n.* • *What a blimpo!;* What a fat person!
> ♦ NOTE: Both of these terms are humorous yet derogatory.

burger joint *exp.* restaurant that specializes in hamburgers • *That's the best burger joint in town;* That's the best restaurant for hamburgers in town.

chow down (to) *exp.* to eat • *I'm starving. Let's go chow down;* I'm starving. Let's go eat.
> ♦ ALSO: **chow** *n.* food • *Great chow!;* Great food!

come off it (to) *exp.* to stop talking nonsense • *"Why don't you buy that car over there?" "Come off it! I could never afford that";* "Why don't you buy that car over there?" "Stop talking nonsense! I could never afford that."
> ♦ SYNONYM: **Yeah, right!** *exp.* (sarcastic) • *"Have you thought about traveling abroad on your vacation?" "Yeah, right! I'll never have enough money for that!";* "Have you thought about traveling abroad on your vacation?" "Stop talking nonsense! I'll never have enough money for that!"

cost an arm and a leg (to) *exp.* to be extremely expensive • *That dress cost me an arm and a leg but it was worth it;* That dress was extremely expensive but it was worth it.
> ♦ SYNONYM: **to cost big bucks** *exp.* • *I can't buy that piano. It costs big bucks;* I can't buy that piano. It's extremely expensive.
> ♦ NOTE: *"Buck"* is slang for "dollar."

dive *n.* inferior restaurant • *I can't believe you took her to that dive on your first date!;* I can't believe you took her to that inferior restaurant on your first date!
> ♦ SYNONYM: **greasy spoon** *exp.* • *Every time I eat at that greasy spoon, I get sick;* Every time I eat at that inferior restaurant, I get sick.

"Fat chance" *exp.* "There is no possibility of that" • *"Maybe your father will lend you his new car." "Fat chance!";* "Maybe your father will lend you his new car." "There is no possibility of that!"
> ♦ SYNONYM: **not a chance in hell** *exp.* "Do you think he'll pass the test?" *"Not a chance in hell!";* "Do you think he'll pass the test?" "There is no possibility of that!"

fries *n.* a popular abbreviation of French fries • *I'll have a burger and fries;* I'll have a hamburger and French fries.

grab a bite (to) *exp.* to get something to eat quickly • *Let's grab a bite before the movie;* Let's get something to eat quickly before the movie.
  ◗ SYNONYM: **to eat on the run** *exp.* to eat while en route • *We don't have time to stop and eat. Let's just eat on the run;* We don't have time to stop and eat. Let's just eat en route.
  ◗ NOTE: There is a slight difference between these two expressions: *"to grab a bite"* indicates that the subject has just enough time to stop and eat, whereas the expression *"to eat on the run"* depicts someone who does not have the time to stop and therefore must eat while proceeding to his/her destination. Both expressions are extremely popular.

have a cow (to) *exp.* to become angry and upset • *Don't have a cow, man!;* Don't get so angry and upset, friend!
  ◗ NOTE: This expression has always been popular but has become even more so in the early 1990's due to a popular television cartoon in which the younger son is known for always using this phrase. It is very common to see T-shirts, bumper stickers, etc. bearing this expression.

hold (to) *exp.* to omit • *I'd like a hamburger but hold the mustard;* I'd like a hamburger but omit the mustard.
  ◗ NOTE: This is extremely popular slang when placing a food order.

into (to be) *adj.* **1.** to enjoy (something) • *I'm really into golf;* I enjoy golf • **2.** to be infatuated with (someone) • *You're really into him, aren't you?;* You're really infatuated with him, aren't you?
  ◗ SYNONYM: **to dig** *v.* • *I dig football;* I enjoy football • *I really don't dig him;* I really don't like him.
  ⇨ NOTE: The verb *"to dig"* was especially popular in the 1960's and is occasionally heard today particularly in movies and television shows of the period.

john *n.* toilet • *I have to run to the john;* I have to go to the toilet.
  ◗ NOTE: Here is some interesting trivia that most Americans are not even aware of. Many years ago, John Crapper invented the first flush toilet. His design was referred to as a *"John Crapper"* which was later shortened to *"John"* or *"Crapper."* Oddly enough, the term *"john"* is extremely popular and simply casual slang yet the term *"crapper"* is considered vulgar. This was taken one step further in the expression *"to take a crap"* meaning "to defecate" and is also extremely popular yet vulgar.

living soul *exp.* a person • *There wasn't a living soul in that city;* There was absolutely no one in that city.

lose it (to) *exp.* **1.** to vomit • *I almost lost it at the restaurant when they served snails!;* I almost vomited at the restaurant when they served snails!
‣ NOTE: As learned in lesson one, the expression *"to lose it"* has other slang meanings as well: **2.** to let go suddenly of one's mental faculties • *In the middle of the test, I just lost it;* In the middle of the test, I just forgot everything • **3.** to become very angry • *If he doesn't stop bothering me, I'm gonna lose it;* If he doesn't stop bothering me, I'm going to get very angry.

on someone *exp.* **1.** paid for by someone • *Order anything you want from the menu. It's on my father;* Order anything you want from the menu. My father is paying. • **2.** to harass someone • *You're always on me about something!;* You're always harassing me about something!
‣ SYNONYM: **to pick up the check/tab** *exp.* • *Let me pick up the check/tab this time;* Let me pay the bill this time.

polish off something (to) *exp.* to eat something completely • *He polished off that hamburger in a few minutes;* He ate that complete hamburger in a few minutes.
‣ SYNONYM: **to eat up a storm** *exp.* • *We ate up a storm at the restaurant;* We ate a lot at the restaurant.

porker *n.* **1.** one who eats like a pig • *Did you see him eat? What a porker!;* Did you see him eat? What a pig! • **2.** one who is fat • *She's a real porker!;* She's a real fat pig!
‣ SYNONYM: **oinker** *n.* (humorous yet derogatory) one who eats like a pig.
⇨ NOTE: This slang term comes from the sound a pig makes, *oink!*

right off the bat *exp.* right from the beginning • *I liked her right off the bat;* I liked her right from the beginning.
‣ SYNONYM: **from the get go** *exp.* • *They didn't like each other from the get go;* They didn't like each other right from the beginning.

ritzy *adj.* expensive and lavish • *This is some ritzy hotel here!;* This is an extremely expensive and lavish hotel here!
‣ NOTE: The term *"some"* is commonly used in two ways: **1.** *adv.* extremely • Note that when this expression is used, the article which precedes the adjective is simply replaced by *"some"*: *This is a ritzy hotel = This is some ritzy hotel!* • *This is a nice house = This is some nice house!* **2.** *adj.* impressive • (only when *some* precedes the noun directly) • *This is a very nice house = This is some house!* • *She is a very good student = She is some student!*

screw loose (to have a) *exp.* to be eccentric, to be slightly crazy • *That woman is screaming at an imaginary person. I think she has a screw loose;* That woman is screaming at an imaginary person. I think she's slightly crazy.
‣ NOTE: On occasion, you may hear this expression slightly transposed: *"to have a loose screw,"* although this is not as common as *"to have a screw loose."*
‣ SYNONYM (1): **not to be playing with a full deck** *exp.* • *That woman is talking to her purse. I don't think she's playing with a full deck;* That woman is talking to her purse. I don't think she's totally rational.
⇨ NOTE: This humorous expression is taken from the game world of cards where if the participants are not playing with a full deck, the game will be irregular and unbalanced. When this expression is used in regards to a crazy person, it implies that the individual is not functioning with a full set of brains.
‣ SYNONYM (2): **"The lights are on but nobody's home"** *exp.* (humorous) "The person seems to be awake yet completely lacking in awareness."

slop *n.* inferior food • *How can you expect me to eat this slop?;* How can you expect me to eat this inferior food?
‣ NOTE: The term *"slop"* is traditionally used in reference to "pig feed."
‣ ANTONYM: **goodies** *exp.* food that is pleasing to the eye and the palate • *If I start eating these goodies, I won't be able to stop!;* If I start eating this good food, I won't be able to stop!

sneaking suspicion *exp.* (growing) feeling (about something or someone) • *I have a sneaking suspicion that he was the one who stole the bracelet;* I have a growing feeling that he was the one who stole the bracelet.

set foot in (to) *exp.* **1.** to enter willingly • *I wouldn't set foot in there if you paid me;* I wouldn't enter there willingly if you paid me • **2.** to enter a room by only one footstep • *As soon as I set foot in the room, she started insulting me;* As soon as I entered the room by only one footstep, she started insulting me.

stiff a waiter (to) *exp.* not to leave a tip for a waiter • *That waiter is so unpleasant, I bet he always gets stiffed;* That waiter is so unpleasant, I bet he never gets a tip.

stink (to) *v.* to be extremely unsatisfactory • (lit); to smell badly • *This whole situation stinks!;* This whole situation is extremely unsatisfactory!
‣ SYNONYM (1): **to suck** *v.* • *The service here sucks!;* The service here is extremely unsatisfactory!
‣ SYNONYM (2): **to bite** *v.* • *This situation bites!;* This situation is terrible!

♦ NOTE: When used to mean *"to be extremely unsatisfactory,"* the verbs *"to suck"* and *"to bite"* take on vulgar connotations and should, therefore, be used with discretion. The verb *"to stink,"* however, is not vulgar.

stop in (to) *exp.* to enter for a brief stay • *He stopped in to say hello and lingered for three hours!;* He entered for a brief stay and lingered for three hours!

tip someone off (to) *exp.* to inform someone • *"How did you discover that she was the burglar?" "One of the neighbors tipped me off";* "How did you discover that she was the burglar?" "One of the neighbors informed me."

wash it down (to) *exp.* **1.** to drink in order to make something unpalatable go down easier • *I need some water to wash this hamburger down;* I need some water to make this hamburger go down easier. • **2.** to follow up a meal with either more food or drink • *Let's order dessert to wash it all down;* Let's order dessert to follow up the meal.

"What do you say..." *exp.* "What do you think about the idea of ..." • *What do you say we go to the movies tonight?;* What do you think about the idea of going to the movies tonight?

Practice The Vocabulary

(Answers to Lesson 10, p. 236)

A. Circle the word in parentheses that best completes the sentence.

1. That car costs an arm and a (**foot, leg, head**).

2. Let's go chow (**up, back, down**).

3. He's so fat. What a (**blimp, dive, john**)!

4. You think you'll actually win the contest? (**Thin, Big, Fat**) chance!

5. Relax! Don't have a (**cow, horse, lamb**)!

6. I'd like to order a hamburger but (**hold, take, drop**) the mustard.

7. I love music. I'm really (**into, out of, off of**) it!

8. I feel sick. I think I'm gonna (**find, take, lose**) it.

9. I liked him right off the (**ritzy, living soul, bat**).

10. She eats nonstop. What a (**porker, slop, dive**)!

11. He's crazy. I think he has a (**nail, bolt, screw**) loose.

12. I hate that restaurant. I'm never setting (**arm, leg, foot**) in there again!

B. Match the columns.

☐ 1. I'm starving. Let's go eat the rest of the chocolate cake.

☐ 2. Let's enter their house briefly to say hello.

☐ 3. The service here is extremely unsatisfactory.

☐ 4. Would you like something to drink to follow up your meal?

☐ 5. This waiter is horrible. I'm not leaving a tip!

☐ 6. I don't see anyone at all.

☐ 7. I have a growing feeling that I shouldn't have come here.

☐ 8. What do you think about the idea of going to eat?

☐ 9. What an inferior restaurant!

☐ 10. I can't eat this inferior food.

☐ 11. I was just informed that your friend is lying to you.

☐ 12. This is a great restaurant that specializes in hamburgers.

A. **I can't eat this slop.**

B. **This waiter is horrible. I'm stiffing him!**

C. **I have a sneaking suspicion that I shouldn't have come here.**

D. **Let's stop in at their house to say hello.**

E. **What do you say we go eat?**

F. **The service here stinks.**

G. **Would you like a drink to wash that down?**

H. **I was just tipped off that your friend is lying to you.**

I. **I don't see a living soul.**

J. **I'm starving. Let's go polish off the rest of the chocolate cake.**

K. **This is a great burger joint.**

L. **What a dive!**

C. Complete the following sentences by using the word list below.

blimp	chow	come
dive	fat	cow
fries	hold	into
screw	slop	stiff

1. You expect me to eat that _____ ?

2. The food here is terrible. Let's get out of this _____ .

3. I'd like a hotdog with mustard but _____ the catsup.

4. That waiter is so rude that I'm gonna _____ him.

5. I didn't know you were _____ music. Wanna go to the concert?

6. All you ever do is eat. Do you want to turn into a _____ ?

7. For lunch I had a hamburger and _____ .

8. Oh, _____ off it! That's a lot of nonsense!

9. Relax! Don't have a _____ !

10. Do you want to _____ down at the new restaurant with me?

11. You think the boss is going to give you a raise? _____ chance!

12. He's really strange. I think he has a _____ loose.

A CLOSER LOOK:
Numbers Used in Slang

Another addition to the American repertory of slang is the clever use of numbers, which is demonstrated in the following colorful assortment of expressions.

0 (zero)

zero (to be a) *exp.* to be deficient of any redeeming qualities • *You're dating him? He's such a zero!;* You're dating him? He's totally deficient of any redeeming qualities!

zero in on someone or something (to) *exp.* to come closer to finding someone or something • *In the medical world, they're zeroing in on a cure for the common cold;* In the medical world, they're coming closer to finding a cure for the common cold.

1 (one)

from day one *exp.* right from the start • *He was mean to me from day one;* He was mean to me right from the start.

give someone the once over (to) *exp.* to scrutinize someone • *You should have seen how his brothers and sisters gave me the once over when they met me for the first time;* You should have seen how his brothers and sisters scrutinized me when they met me for the first time.

one-in-a-million *exp.* exceptional • *You're one in a million!;* You're exceptional!

2 (two)

goody two shoes *exp.* an ostentatiously virtuous person • *She's such a good two-shoes;* She's such an ostentatiously virtuous person.

like two peas in a pod *exp.* identical • *Those twins are like two peas in a pod;* Those twins are identical.

3 (three)

get the third degree (to) *exp.* to be interrogated • *As soon as I got home, my mother gave me the third degree;* As soon as I got home, my mother interrogated me.

5 (five)

"Gimme five!" *exp.*
    ♦ NOTE: This expression is an

abbreviation of "Give me five fingers!" It is used as a greeting or a congratulatory gesture in which each person raises his/her hand and slaps it against the other person's hand. This gesture is also called a *"high five"* since the slap occurs as each person's hand is high in the air.

6 (six)

deep six someone (to) *exp.* (gangster jargon) to kill someone • *I want you to go deep six him;* I want you to go kill him.

six of one, half a dozen of the other (to be) *exp.* to amount to the same thing, to make no difference • *You can either meet us before the show for dinner or afterwards for dessert. It's six of one, half a dozen of the other;* You can either meet us before the show for dinner or afterwards for dessert. It makes no difference.

7 (seven)

seventh heaven (in) *exp.* in ecstasy • *It was wonderful being on vacation for a whole month. I was in seventh heaven!;* It was wonderful being on vacation for a whole month. I was in ecstasy!

8 (eight)

behind the eight ball *exp.* in a difficult position • *I want to be honest with the boss, but if I tell him the truth, he may fire me. I feel like I'm behind the eight ball on this one;* I want to be honest with the boss, but if I tell him the truth, he may fire me. I feel like I'm in a difficult position on this one.

9 (nine)

cloud nine (on) *exp.* euphoric • *Ever since she met Tom, she's been on cloud nine;* Ever since she met Tom, she's been euphoric.

dressed to the nines *exp.* extremely fancily dressed • *Last year at her party, everyone was dressed to the nines;* Last year at her party, everyone was extremely fancily dressed.

nine-to-five *exp.* a job that starts at 9:00 a.m. and goes to 5:00 p.m. • *I'm tired of the same old nine-to-five;* I'm tired of the same old job that starts at 9:00 a.m. to 5:00 p.m.

the whole nine yards (to go) *exp.* to go to the limit • *You should have seen how she decorated the house for the party. She went the whole nine yards;* You should have seen how she decorated the house for the party. She went to the limit.

10 (ten)

ten (to be a) *exp.* to be first-rate • *That girl is beautiful. She's a real ten!;* That girl is beautiful. She's really first-rate!

top ten *exp.* the first ten most popular songs • *Her song just made top ten!;* Her song just became one of the ten most popular!

hang ten (to) *exp.* (surfing slang) to surf with all ten toes curled around the front of the surfboard.

22 (twenty-two)

Catch twenty-two *exp.* a no-win situation in which one strategy is hindered by another • *In order to get the job, I need experience. But in order to get experience, I need a job! What a Catch twenty-two!;* In order to get the job, I need experience. But in order to get experience, I need a job! What a no-win situation!
♦ NOTE: This expression comes from a satirical novel by Joseph Heller.

23 (twenty-three)

"Twenty-three skidoo" *exp.* to leave • *Twenty-three skidoo!;* Let's leave!
♦ NOTE: This is an expression that was born around the 1900's and is now only used in jest yet heard occasionally in old movies, cartoons, etc.

40 (forty)

forty winks (to grab) *exp.* to take a nap • *I'm going to grab forty winks before we leave;* I'm going to take a nap before we leave.

top forty *exp.* the first forty most popular songs • *Her song just made top forty!;* Her song just became one of the forty most popular!

45 (forty-five)

forty-five *exp.* an abbreviation for "a small record which turns at forty-five revolutions per minute."

86 (eighty-six)

eighty-six (to) *exp.* **1.** to get rid of • *We had to eighty-six the hors d'oeuvres because they were too expensive;* We had to get rid of the hors d'oeuvres because they were too expensive • **2.** to kill • *They eighty-sixed him;* They killed him.

88 (eighty-eight)

eighty-eight (the) *n.* piano (due to its 88 keys) • *There's my ol' eighty-eight;* There's my trusty piano.
⬩ NOTE: The adjective "old" is commonly abbreviated to *"ol'"* and is used to mean "trusty or faithful."

1,000 (one thousand)

"If I've told you once, I've told you a thousand times" *exp.* "I've repeated to you several times" • *If I've told you once, I've told you a thousand times, he's lying!;* I've repeated to you several times, he's lying!

1,000,000 (one million)

million of them (a) *exp.* a repertory of a million jokes • *I've got a million of 'em!;* I have a repertory of a million jokes!
⬩ NOTE: This expression commonly uses *"'em"* which is the contracted form of "them."

never in a million years *exp.* absolutely never • *I'll never learn how to cook in a million years;* I'll absolutely never learn how to cook.

one-in-a-million *exp.* exceptional • *You're one in a million!;* You're exceptional!

Practice Using Numbers in Slang

(Answers, p. 237)

A. Underline the correct number that goes with the expression.

1. She was nasty from day _____ .
   a. **one**   b. **two**   c. **three**

2. We're starting to _____ in on the problem.
   a. **zero**   b. **one**   c. **two**

3. As soon as I got home, my mother gave me the _____ degree.
   a. **first**   b. **second**   c. **third**

4. I hate my job. It's always the same old nine to _____ .
   a. **four**   b. **five**   c. **six**

5. They're identical, like _____ peas in a pod.
   a. **two**   b. **three**   c. **four**

6. I love this vacation. I'm in _____ heaven!
   a. **sixth**　　　　　　b. **seventh**　　　　　　c. **eighth**

7. Wow! You're really dressed to the _____ !
   a. **sevens**　　　　　　b. **eights**　　　　　　c. **nines**

8. Both choices are going to get me into trouble. What a catch _____ !
   a. **twenty-one**　　　　b. **twenty-two**　　　　c. **twenty-three**

9. I'm exhausted. I'm gonna go get _____ winks.
   a. **twenty**　　　　　　b. **thirty**　　　　　　c. **forty**

10. I really like you. You're _____ in a million.
    a. **one**　　　　　　　b. **two**　　　　　　　c. **three**

Just For Fun...

The following paragraph presents some expressions which contain numbers. Once you're able to understand all of them, why not *go the whole nine yards* and review all of the final monologues in each lesson?

"As soon as I got home, my mother **gave me the THIRD degree** to try and **ZERO in** on what I was doing all night. Well, after my **NINE-to-FIVE**, I **grabbed FORTY winks** then went to a party with Cecily who was dressed **to the NINES**. I was in **SEVENTH heaven** 'cause she's **ONE in a MILLION**. At the party, they didn't have any good **FORTY-FIVES** so I sat down at the piano and played a few songs that were real **top FORTY**. Playing the ol' **EIGHTY-EIGHT** sure **put me on cloud NINE**."

Translation:

"As soon as I got home, my mother **interrogated** me to try and **determine** what I was doing all night. Well, after my **job**, I **took a nap** then went to a party with Cecily who was dressed **elegantly**. I was in **ecstasy** 'cause she's **exceptional**. At the party, they didn't have any good **records** so I sat down at the piano and played a few songs that were **voted the forty most popular**. Playing the ol' **piano** sure **made me euphoric**."

ANSWERS TO LESSONS 1-10

LESSON ONE - *At School*

Practice the Vocabulary

A.
1. up
2. gross
3. face
4. Chill
5. cutting
6. blew
7. face
8. off
9. back
10. rubs
11. dead
12. hots

B.
1. pissed off
2. eating
3. gross
4. pet
5. up
6. aced
7. kissing up to
8. went
9. gag me
10. stand

C.
1. E
2. B
3. G
4. J
5. I
6. D
7. F
8. H
9. A
10. C

A CLOSER LOOK (1):
Practice Commonly Used Contractions

I *just* __jus'__ heard that Nancy *and* __'n__ Dominic *are* __'r__ *going to*

__gonna__ have a baby! *Is that* __Izat__ great *or* __'r__ what?! Nancy

said that Dominic was calm about it. How *can he* __c'n 'e__ be so relaxed?!

He *has* __'as__ a lot *of* __a__ control, that's *for* __fer__ *sure* __sher__ !

What __Whad__ if she gives birth *to* __ta__ twins? I *don't know* __dunno__

what they'd do! They'd *probably* __prob'ly__ move *out of* __outta__ that

house. Maybe they'll *let me* __lem'me__ help *them* __'em__ find

something in my neighborhood.

A CLOSER LOOK (2):
Practice Using Commonly Used Initials

A. 1. O.T.   7. B.O.
   2. V.P.   8. T.A.
   3. I.D.   9. L.A.
   4. M.C.   10. P.J.s
   5. U.F.O.   11. D.J.
   6. T.P.   12. CD

LESSON TWO - *At the Party*

Practice the Vocabulary

A. 1. b   6. b
   2. a   7. a
   3. b   8. b
   4. b   9. a
   5. a   10. b

B. 1. C   6. D
   2. G   7. J
   3. E   8. A
   4. B   9. H
   5. F   10. I

C. 1. We're talkin'   7. heave
   2. go   8. way
   3. place   9. lost
   4. strut   10. bee line
   5. chick   11. Yuck
   6. real   12. Man

A CLOSER LOOK:
Practice the Use of Fruits and Vegetables in Slang

A. 1. pea   7. grapes
   2. beans   8. pickle
   3. apple   9. potato
   4. cucumber   10. banana
   5. peach   11. lemon
   6. cherries   12. bananas

LESSON THREE - *At the Movies*

Practice the Vocabulary

A. 1. Hand   7. riot act
   2. cool   8. smash hit
   3. keeping   9. bunch
   4. field day   10. put up
   5. big time   11. get around
   6. took off   12. show up

B. 1. K   7. L
   2. E   8. F
   3. H   9. B
   4. C   10. G
   5. I   11. D
   6. A   12. J

C. 1. cold   7. rug
   2. line, hand   8. count, flake
   3. up   9. pull
   4. blowing   10. last
   5. pan   11. reading
   6. off   12. day

A CLOSER LOOK:
Practice Using Body Parts in Slang

A. 1. arm   7. bone
   2. guts   8. throat
   3. tooth   9. gums
   4. butt   10. thumb
   5. ear   11. elbows
   6. nerve   12. foot

LESSON FOUR - *At the Mall*

Practice the Vocabulary

A. 1. b   7. c
   2. c   8. c
   3. a   9. b
   4. b   10. a
   5. a   11. a
   6. a   12. b

B. 1. b
   2. a
   3. a
   4. c
   5. b
   6. a
   7. c
   8. a
   9. b
   10. c
   11. a
   12. c

C. 1. L
   2. G
   3. J
   4. B
   5. H
   6. C
   7. E
   8. I
   9. A
   10. F
   11. K
   12. D

A CLOSER LOOK:
Practice Food Terms Used in Slang

A. 1. bacon
   2. coffee
   3. dust
   4. enchilada
   5. mustard
   6. sandwich
   7. stew
   8. ham
   9. pie
   10. fish
   11. bite
   12. sugar
   13. noodle
   14. spoon
   15. cookie

LESSON FIVE - *The New Car*

Practice the Vocabulary

A. 1. soak
   2. Knock
   3. flat
   4. haul
   5. spin
   6. run
   7. wheels
   8. dime
   9. jinx
   10. clunker
   11. pile
   12. totaled

B. 1. soak
   2. totaled
   3. moonlight
   4. Punch
   5. out
   6. nailed
   7. lead
   8. rubber
   9. cops
   10. slammer
   11. what
   12. beats
   13. rails
   14. hop

C. 1. G
   2. F
   3. B
   4. J
   5. C
   6. D
   7. H
   8. E
   9. A
   10. I

A CLOSER LOOK:
Practice Car Slang

A. 1. a
   2. c
   3. c
   4. a
   5. c
   6. b
   7. a
   8. b
   9. a
   10. c
   11. b
   12. c

LESSON SIX - *At the Gym*

Practice the Vocabulary

A. 1. strip down
   2. get off it
   3. get
   4. high heaven
   5. revved
   6. hot
   7. Wow
   8. comfy
   9. cut
   10. flipped
   11. hit
   12. raw

B. 1. hot
2. buffed
3. help
4. pot
5. handbasket
6. rarin' to go
7. pig
8. gain
9. wuss
10. hell
11. with
12. into

C. 1. H
2. L
3. C
4. E
5. A
6. G
7. J
8. D
9. I
10. F
11. K
12. B

A CLOSER LOOK:
Practice Using Clothing in Slang

A. 1. a
2. b
3. b
4. b
5. a
6. a
7. b
8. b
9. a
10. b

LESSON SEVEN - *The House Guest*

Practice the Vocabulary

A. 1. J
2. G
3. I
4. L
5. C
6. H
7. A
8. D
9. E
10. K
11. F
12. B

B. 1. b
   2. c
   3. c
   4. a
   5. a
   6. b

   7. c
   8. a
   9. b
   10. a
   11. c
   12. b

C. 1. a
   2. b
   3. a
   4. b
   5. a
   6. b

   7. a
   8. a
   9. a
   10. b
   11. b
   12. a

A CLOSER LOOK:
Practice Colors in Slang

A. 1. red
   2. white
   3. gray
   4. blue
   5. green

   6. pink
   7. pink
   8. black
   9. blue
   10. red

LESSON EIGHT - *At Work*

Practice the Vocabulary

A. 1. H
   2. C
   3. E
   4. A
   5. F

   6. D
   7. J
   8. B
   9. G
   10. I

B. 1. C
   2. J
   3. D
   4. A
   5. E
   6. G
   7. F
   8. H
   9. I
   10. B

C. 1. up
   2. in
   3. up
   4. cut
   5. booze
   6. zoned
   7. flew
   8. mouth
   9. clean
   10. lowdown
   11. wimp
   12. stone

A CLOSER LOOK:
Practice Using Fish, Insects, and Animals in Slang

A. 1. cow
   2. dog
   3. cats
   4. eagle
   5. fishy
   6. fox
   7. goat
   8. goose
   9. horses
   10. pig
   11. Rats
   12. skunk

B. 1. B
   2. J
   3. G
   4. E
   5. A
   6. F
   7. H
   8. D
   9. I
   10. C

LESSON NINE - *At the Market*

Practice the Vocabulary

A. 1. kick
   2. nuts
   3. red-handed
   4. fell
   5. pick
   6. big way
   7. clue
   8. fresh
   9. get
   10. ends
   11. rest
   12. honker

B. 1. a   7. b
    2. b   8. b
    3. b   9. a
    4. a   10. a
    5. a   11. a
    6. b   12. b

C. 1. J   8. K
    2. F   9. L
    3. I   10. H
    4. D   11. E
    5. B   12. A
    6. G   13. N
    7. C   14. M

A CLOSER LOOK:
Practice Using Proper Names in Slang

A. 1. c   7. b
    2. a   8. a
    3. c   9. c
    4. c   10. c
    5. a   11. a
    6. b   12. b

LESSON TEN - *At the Restaurant*

Practice the Vocabulary

A. 1. leg   7. into
    2. down   8. lose
    3. blimp   9. bat
    4. Fat   10. porker
    5. cow   11. screw
    6. hold   12. foot

B. 1. J
  2. D
  3. F
  4. G
  5. B
  6. I

7. C
8. E
9. L
10. A
11. H
12. K

C. 1. slop
  2. dive
  3. hold
  4. stiff
  5. into
  6. blimp

7. fries
8. come
9. cow
10. chow
11. Fat
12. screw

A CLOSER LOOK:
Practice Using Numbers in Slang

A. 1. a
  2. a
  3. c
  4. b
  5. a

6. b
7. c
8. b
9. c
10. a

glossary

The glossary contains all the slang, idioms, and expressions that were used in the dialogues.

-A-

ace a test (to) *exp.* to do extremely well on a test.
  ♦ SYNONYM: **to pass a test with flying colors** *exp.* • *She passed the test with flying colors;* She did extremely well on the test.
  ♦ ANTONYM: **to blow a test** *exp.* • *He blew the test;* He failed the test.

-B-

barf up one's guts (to) *exp.* to vomit violently • *I got the stomach flu and barfed my guts up all night;* I got the stomach flu and vomited violently all night.

bash *n.* party • *Great bash!;* Great party!
  ♦ NOTE: An extremely common expression meaning "to give a party" is "to throw a party (*bash, shindig, etc.*) • *I'm throwing a big bash for my parents;* I'm throwing a big party for my parents.
  ♦ SYNONYM: **shindig** *n.* This term originally referred to a raucous party in which men would begin fighting and kicking, digging each other in the shin with the toe of their boots. It is now used in jest to indicate a large, noisy, and fun party which may or may not have dancing • *Tonight, we're throwing a big shindig at my house;* Tonight, we're having a big party at my house.

basket case *exp.* overwrought • *When she found out that her in-laws were going to stay for a week, she was a basket case;* When she found out that her in-laws were going to stay for a week, she was overwrought.
  ♦ SYNONYM: **to freak out** *exp.* • *When she was told that her car was destroyed, she freaked out!;* When she was told that her car was destroyed, she was overwrought.

beat something (to) *exp.* to surpass, to outshine • *Your new house sure does beat that other one;* Your new house sure does surpass that other one.
  ♦ ANTONYM: **not to hold a candle to someone or something** *exp.* not to be as good as someone or something • *Your new house doesn't hold a candle to your other one;* Your new house isn't as good as your other one.
  ♦ ALSO: **to beat one** *exp.* not to know • *Beats me!;* I don't know!

"Beats me!" *exp.* "I don't know!"
  ♦ SYNONYM: **"Ya got me!"** *exp.* • *"How old do ya think she is?" "Ya*

got me!;" "How old do you think she is?" "I don't know!"

bee line for (to make a) *exp.* to go quickly and directly to • *As soon as I get home, I'm makin' a bee line fer the bathroom;* As soon as I get home, I'm going straight to the bathroom.

belch (to) *v.* to burp in a loud and crude manner • *He belched at the dinner table!;* He burped crudely at the dinner table!

bend over backwards (to) *exp.* to strive vigorously • *I bent over backwards to prepare everything for the party;* I strived vigorously to prepare everything for the party.

blast *n.* a wonderful time • *We had a blast at his party!;* We had a wonderful time at his party!
♦ SYNONYM: **ball** *n.* • *I'm going to have a ball on vacation!;* I'm going to have a wonderful time on vacation!

blimp *n.* fat person • (lit); dirigible • *She's a real blimp!;* She's really fat!
♦ VARIATION: **blimpo** *n.* • *What a blimpo!;* What a fat person!
♦ NOTE: Both of these terms are humorous yet derogatory.

blow it big time (to) *exp.* to make a terrible mistake • *This time, I blew it big time;* This time, I made a terrible mistake.
♦ NOTE: The expression *"to blow it,"* means "to make a mistake" and the expression *"big time"* means, "greatly." *"To blow it big time"* is actually a common expression created out of two popular idioms • *She yelled at me big time;* She really yelled at me. The expression *"big time"* is also commonly used to mean: **1.** renowned • *He's a big time painter;* He's a well known painter • *He's big time;* He's famous. • **2.** on a large scale • *This isn't just a little play he's doing. This*

is big time!; This isn't just a little play he's doing. This is the highest he can go in his profession!

blow one's lines (to) *exp.* to make a mistake while speaking one's lines from a script • *He kept blowing his lines tonight;* He kept making mistakes while speaking his lines tonight.
♦ SYNONYM: **to flub one's lines** *exp.* • *She keeps flubbing her lines;* She keeps making mistakes while speaking her lines.
♦ NOTE: These two expressions are very common in the industries of theatre, television, and movies.

blow something (to) *exp.* **1.** to fail at something • *I blew the interview;* I failed the interview • **2.** to make a big mistake • *I totally forgot my doctor's appointment. I really blew it;* I totally forgot my doctor's appointment. I really made a mistake.
♦ SYNONYM: **to goof up something** *exp.* **1.** to make a big mistake • *I forgot to pick her up at the airport! I really goofed up;* I forgot to pick her up at the airport! I really made a mistake • **2.** to hurt oneself • *I goofed up my leg skiing;* I hurt my leg skiing.

blowout *n.* **1.** a flat tire • *I had a blowout on the way home;* I got a flat tire on the way home [or] *My tire blew out on the way home;* • **2.** to have a feast • *We had a real blowout at my mom's house last night;* We had such a feast at my mom's house last night.

bod *n.* body • *Look at that hot bod!;* Look at that hot body!
♦ NOTE: This is a popular abbreviation for "body," especially among younger people.

bomb *n.* bad production (theater, television, movies, etc.) • *The show was a real bomb;* The show was really bad.

‣ SYNONYM: **turkey** *n.* • *That show was a real turkey;* That show was really bad.

‣ ANTONYM: SEE - **smash.**

‣ ALSO: **to bomb** *v.* to fail • *The movie really bombed;* The movie really failed • *I really bombed on my test;* I really failed my test.

booze *n.* alcohol • *His breath always smells of booze;* His breath always smells of alcohol.

bottomless pit *exp.* a person with an insatiable appetite • *I can't believe how much you can eat. You really are a bottomless pit!;* I can't believe how much you can eat. You really have an insatiable appetite!

‣ SYNONYM: **to have a hollow leg** *exp.*

⇨ NOTE: This expression conjures up an image of someone's food going right past the stomach and into a hollow leg. • *She eats so much she must have a hollow leg.*

broke *exp.* destitute • *I can't afford that. I'm broke;* I can't afford that. I'm destitute.

‣ ALSO (1): **stone/flat broke** *exp.* completely destitute • *I'm stone/flat broke;* I'm completely destitute.

‣ ALSO (2): **busted** *adj.* (variation of *"broke"*) destitute.

‣ SYNONYM: **down and out** *exp.* • *The poor man is really down and out;* The poor man is really destitute.

"Brother!" *exclam.* (said in contempt) • *Oh, brother! How could she wear that?;* I can't believe it! How could she wear that?

‣ NOTE: Used as an exclamation, *"brother"* can certainly be used among women.

‣ SYNONYM: **"Come on!"** *exclam.* • *Come on! How could she wear that?;* I can't believe it! How could she wear that?

buck *n.* dollar • *Can you lend me five bucks?;* Can you lend me five dollars?

buffed *adj.* muscular and brawny • *You're really getting buffed!;* You're really getting muscular!

‣ SYNONYM: **hunky** *adj.* • *He's hunky;* He's muscular.

⇨ ALSO: **hunk** *n.* muscular and sexy man • *What a hunk!;* What a muscular and sexy man!

bug (to) *v.* to annoy • *That really bugs me!;* That really annoys me!

‣ SYNONYM: **to burn one up** *exp.* • *He really burns me up!;* He really makes me mad!

bummed *adj.* disappointed, depressed • *I couldn't go with my friends to the movies because I got sick. I'm bummed;* I couldn't go with my friends to the movies because I got sick. I'm disappointed.

‣ NOTE: This is a contraction of *"bummed out"* which is equally popular.

‣ SYNONYM: **down in the dumps** *exp. What's wrong? You look down in the dumps;* What's wrong? You look depressed.

bunch (a) *n.* a lot • *She has a bunch of kids;* She has a lot of children • *Thanks a bunch!;* Thanks a lot!

‣ ALSO: **a whole bunch** *exp.* a large amount • *She has a whole bunch of kids;* She really has many children • *I drank a whole bunch of coffee last night;* I really drank a lot of coffee last night.

‣ SYNONYM: **pile** *n.* • *She has a pile of children;* She has many children.

burger joint *exp.* restaurant that specializes in hamburgers • *That's the best burger joint in town;* That's the best restaurant for hamburgers in town.

burn rubber (to) *exp.* to accelerate quickly (and leave a skid mark) • *We'd better burn rubber or we're gonna be late;* We'd better leave quickly or we're going to be late.
▸ SYNONYM: **to peel out** *exp.* • *This car can really peel out!;* This car can really accelerate quickly!
▸ SEE: **to punch it.**

butt ugly (to be) *exp.* to be extremely ugly • *He's butt ugly!;* He's really ugly!
▸ ANTONYM: **to be hot looking** *exp.* to be very good looking and sexy • *He's really hot lookin'!;* He's really good looking!

by the way *exp.* incidentally • *By the way, your father is very nice;* Incidentally, your father is very nice.
▸ NOTE: Occasionally, you may even hear a variation of this expression, *"by the by,"* which is considered pretentious and therefore is used mainly in jest or when making fun of the very rich. It is certainly common in movies when the focus is on high society.

-C-

call in sick (to) *exp.* to telephone those in charge at work and inform them that one is sick • *Where's Richard today? Did he call in sick again?;* Where's Richard today? Did he call those in charge at work again and inform then that he's sick?

canned (to get) *exp.* to get fired • *Did you hear? Ed just got canned!;* Did you hear? Ed just got fired!
▸ SYNONYM: **to get sacked** *exp.* *You'd better be careful or you're going to get yourself sacked!;* You'd better be careful or you're going to get yourself fired!

catch someone red-handed (to) *exp.* to capture someone doing something dishonest • *I caught him red-handed stealing the money;* I caught him stealing the money.

caught dead (not to be) *exp.* not to want to be seen in a certain condition • *I wouldn't be caught dead wearing that hat;* I would never want to be seen wearing that hat.

caught with one's pants down *exp.* to be caught at an inopportune time or when one is unprepared • *I'm afraid that you caught me with my pants down. I can't answer that until I do some research;* I'm afraid that you've contacted me at an inopportune time. I can't answer that until I do some research.

check out (to) *exp.* to observe (someone or something) • *Check her out!;* Examine her!
▸ SYNONYM: **to get a load of someone or something** *exp.* • *Get a load o' him. Have you ever seen such an ugly shirt?;* Observe him. Have you ever seen such an ugly shirt?

check someone or something out (to) *exp.* to observe or examine someone or something • *Check out what happens when I add water to the flour;* Observe what happens when I add water to the flour.
▸ SYNONYM: **to get a load of someone or something** *exp.* • *Get a load of what happens when I attach these two wires together;* Observe what happens when I attach these two wires together.

chew out (to) *exp.* to reprimand • *My father chewed me out when I took the car without asking;* My father reprimanded me when I took the car without asking.
▸ SYNONYM: **to come down on someone** *exp.* • *My mother came*

down on me because I got home late;
My mother reprimanded me because I came home late.

chick *n.* girl.
 ♦ NOTE: This is an extremely popular synonym for "girl" although considered to be somewhat disrespectful.
 ♦ SYNONYM: **broad** *n.* • *Look at that broad over there!;* Look at that woman over there!
   ⇨ NOTE: The term *"broad,"* which is derogatory, is more common among the older generations, whereas *"chick"* is more popular with younger groups. Occasionally in old movies, especially gangster films, you may hear the word *"tomato"* used to mean, "girl." However, since most of the gangster films took place on the East Coast where the inhabitants have a particular accent, *"tomato"* is oftentimes heard pronounced, *ta-may-da.*
 ♦ ANTONYM: See **dude.**

chill out (to) *exp.* to calm down.
 ♦ NOTE: This expression is commonly shortened to *"Chill!"* On the East Coast, a common variation of this expression is *"to take a chill pill."*
 ♦ SYNONYM: **to mellow out** *exp.* • *Don't be so upset about it! Mellow out!;* Don't be so upset about it! Calm down!
 ♦ ANTONYM: See - **freak out (to).**

chow down (to) *exp.* to eat • *I'm starving. Let's go chow down;* I'm starving. Let's go eat.
 ♦ ALSO: **chow** *n.* food • *Great chow!;* Great food!

chow *n.* food • *Great chow!;* Great food!
 ♦ SYNONYM: **grub** *n.*
 ♦ NOTE: These terms are extremely casual and considered somewhat unrefined. They should not be used in high society or at formal dinners.

clean up one's act (to) *exp.* to improve one's behavior • *You'd better clean up your act right now or the boss is gonna fire you!;* You'd better improve your behavior right now or the boss is going to fire you!
 ♦ SYNONYM (1): **to get one's act together** *v.* • **1.** to improve one's behavior • *If you want to join us, you'd better get your act together;* If you want to join us, you'd better improve your behavior. • **2.** to get prepared • *The guests are going to arrive in five minutes! Get your act together!;* The guests are going to arrive in five minutes! Get prepared!
 ♦ SYNONYM (2): **to shape up** *exp.* • *If you don't shape up right now, I'm going to send you to your room!;* If you don't improve your behavior right now, I'm going to send you to your room!

cleaned out *exp.* emptied (of one's stock, merchandise, or money) • *This is the third store I've been to that's been cleaned out of flour;* This is the third store I've been to that's been emptied of flour.

clunker *n.* an old and broken-down car • *You actually bought that clunker?;* You actually bought that old broken-down car?
 ♦ NOTE: The noun *"clunker"* may also be used to indicate any inferior piece of machinery • *That washing machine is a real clunker;* That washing machine is really inferior.
 ♦ SYNONYM: **jalopy** *n.*
   ⇨ NOTE: Although the term *"jalopy"* comes from the 1920's, it is still occasionally heard in jest and in old movies. It is used to mean both "an old and battered car" as well as "car" in general: 1. *Is that your new jalopy?;* Is that your new car? • **2.** *You spent $1,000 on that jalopy?;* You spent $1,000 on that old car? The difference in connotation between **1.**

& **2.** depends on the context and delivery of the speaker.

a cold day in hell *exp.* never • *It'll be a cold day in hell before I see her again;* I'll never see her again.
♦ SYNONYM: **when donkeys fly** *exp.* • *"Don't you want to date him?" "When donkeys fly!";* "Don't you want to date him?" "Never!"

come off it (to) *exp.* to stop talking nonsense • *"Why don't you buy that car over there?" "Come off it! I could never afford that";* "Why don't you buy that car over there?" "Stop talking nonsense! I could never afford that."
♦ SYNONYM: **Yeah, right!** *exp.* (sarcastic) • *"Have you thought about traveling abroad on your vacation?" "Yeah, right! I'll never have enough money for that!";* "Have you thought about traveling abroad on your vacation?" "Stop talking nonsense! I'll never have enough money for that!"

"Come on" [pronounced and commonly seen in print as *"c'mon"*] **1.** "Let's go" *exp.* • *It's time to leave. C'mon;* It's time to leave. Let's go • **2.** "Hurry!" *exclam.* • *C'mon! We're gonna be late!;* Hurry! We're going to be late! • **3.** "You're kidding!" *exclam.* • *She got married after knowing him for only a week? C'mon!;* She got married after knowing him for only a week? You're kidding! • **4.** "Be optimistic" • *C'mon. Everything's gonna be fine;* Be optimistic. Everything is going to be fine.

comfy *adj.* popular abbreviation of the adjective "comfortable" • *This couch is really comfy;* This couch is really comfortable.

cool *adj.* **1.** (for an event) pleasurable, enjoyable • *My vacation was really cool;* My vacation was really enjoyable • **2.** (for an object) appealing, terrific • *Your house is really cool;* Your house is really terrific. • **3.** (for a person) nice, "one of us" • *Your mom's really cool;* Your mom is really nice. *You c'n talk freely in fronna my mom. She's cool;* You can talk freely in front of my mom. She's one of us. • **4.** upstanding • *What you did for her was really cool;* What you did for her was really upstanding.
♦ ANTONYM: **uncool (to be)** *adj.*
♦ NOTE: These two terms are extremely popular with the younger generations.

cop *n.* police officer (very popular) • *Don't drive so fast. There's a cop behind you;* Don't drive so fast. There's a policeman behind you.
♦ NOTE: In old gangster movies, you will undoubtedly hear the term *"copper"* which is simply a variation of the noun *"cop."* When used by a civilian, the term *"cop"* is considered to be disrespectful (although some police officers actually use this term when referring to others in their own profession), and the term *"copper"* is simply derogatory.
♦ SYNONYM (1): **pig** *n.* • The derogatory term *"pig"* was extremely popular during the 1960's, and is still occasionally heard, especially in movies of the period.
♦ SYNONYM (2): **C.H.P.** *exp.* • This is an extremely popular acronym for the California Highway Patrol (Officer) • *You'd better stop. There's a C.H.P. behind you;* You'd better stop. There's a California Highway Patrol Officer behind you.

corner like it's on rails (to) *exp.* said of a car that can go around curves smoothly • *This baby corners like it's on rails;* This car goes around corners like it's on rails.

♦ NOTE: The term *"baby"* is commonly used to refer to any exceptional merchandise: (*e.g.,* when taking about a refrigerator) *This baby really keeps things cold!*
♦ SEE: **sucker.**

cost an arm and a leg (to) *exp.* to be extremely expensive • *That dress cost me an arm and a leg but it was worth it;* That dress was extremely expensive but it was worth it.
♦ SYNONYM: **to cost big bucks** *exp.* • *I can't buy that piano. It costs big bucks;* I can't buy that piano. It's extremely expensive.
♦ NOTE: *"Buck"* is slang for "dollar."

count on (to) *exp.* to depend on (someone or something) • *I was counting on getting that money;* I was depending on getting that money • *I'm counting on you;* I'm depending on you.

cut class (to) *exp.* to be absent from class without permission.
♦ SYNONYM (1): **to ditch (a) class** *exp.* • *I'm going to ditch (my) class today;* I'm not going to attend (my) class today.
♦ SYNONYM (2): **to play hooky** *exp.* • *That's the second time this week he's played hooky;* That's the second time this week he hasn't attended class.
⇨ NOTE: This expression is rarely, if ever, used by younger people. It is much more common among older generations.

cut it (to) *exp.* to be capable of doing something, to be successful • *I tried to be a teacher for a few years but I just couldn't cut it;* I tried to be a teacher for a few years but I just wasn't capable of doing it.
♦ SYNONYM: **to pull it off** *exp.* • *I tried but I just couldn't pull it off;* I tried but I just couldn't succeed.

cut out for something *exp.* inherently capable of something • *I'm not cut out to be a teacher;* I'm not capable of being a teacher.
♦ NOTE: This figurative expression refers to a mold from which one is cut determining one's abilities or disabilities from birth.

-D-

dead serious (to be) *exp.* to be extremely serious.
♦ NOTE: The adjective *"dead"* is commonly used to mean "extremely," "absolutely," or "directly" in the following expressions only: This usage of *dead* would be incorrect in other expressions. For example: *dead happy, dead hungry, dead angry, etc.* are all incorrect expressions.

die (to) *v.* to become inoperable • (lit); to expire, to pass away • *The washing machine just died;* The washing machine just became inoperable.
♦ ALSO: **to up and die** *exp.* to become suddenly inoperable • (lit); to expire suddenly • *He just up and died!;* He just died suddenly! • *My car just up and died!;* My car just become suddenly inoperable!
♦ SYNONYM: **to conk out** *exp.* **1.** to be inoperable • *My car conked out in the middle of the street;* My car became inoperable in the middle of the street. • **2.** to fall asleep • *He was so tired when he came home that he just conked out on the sofa;* He was so tired when he came home that he just fell asleep on the sofa.
⇨ ALSO: **to be conked out** *exp.* to be exhausted • *I'm gonna go to bed. I'm conked out;* I'm going to go to bed. I'm exhausted.

dive *n.* inferior restaurant • *I can't believe you took her to that dive on* *your first date!;* I can't believe you took her to that inferior restaurant on your first date!

▶ SYNONYM: **greasy spoon** *exp.* • *Every time I eat at that greasy spoon, I get sick;* Every time I eat at that inferior restaurant, I get sick.

dough *n.* money • *How much dough have you got?;* How much money do you have?

▶ NOTE: This old term is mainly heard in old movies or in jest.

down something (to) *exp.* to drink something • *Did you see how much brandy he downed?;* Did you see how much brandy he consumed?

▶ SYNONYM: **to put away** *exp.* • *How can you put away that much alcohol?;* How can you drink that much alcohol?

drag (to be a) *n.* to be a bore.

▶ SYNONYM: **to be the pits** *exp.* • *This party's the pits;* This party's boring.

▶ ANTONYM: **to be rad** *adj.* This abbreviation of the adjective "radical" is popular among the younger generations: *This party's rad!;* This party is great!

drag someone somewhere (to) *exp.* to bring someone somewhere against his/her will • *I had to drag him to the party;* I had to bring him to the party against his will.

draw a blank (to) *exp.* to forget suddenly.

▶ SYNONYM: **to blank [out]** *v.* • *I can't believe how I blanked [out] on her name!;* I can't believe how I suddenly forgot her name!

▶ ANTONYM: **to get it** *exp.* **1.** to remember suddenly • *I don't remember the answer. Let me think... I got it!;* I don't remember the answer. Let me think... I suddenly remember! • **2.** to get a sudden idea • *I wonder what we should do today. I got it!;* I

wonder what we should do today. I've got an idea! • **3.** to understand • *Now I get it;* Now I understand.

drive someone up a wall (to) *exp.* to annoy someone greatly • *He's starting to drive me up a wall!;* He's starting to annoy me immensely!

drop in (to) *exp.* to arrive without notice • *He didn't even call. He just dropped in;* He didn't even call. He just arrived without notice.

drop-dead gorgeous *exp.* very beautiful • *She's drop-dead gorgeous;* She's very beautiful.

▶ SYNONYM: **a knock-out** *exp.* • *She's a knock-out;* She's beautiful.

drown one's sorrows (to) *exp.* to cheer one up (usually by drinking) • *Let's go drown our sorrows;* Let's go cheer ourselves up by having a few drinks.

dude *n.* man, in general.

▶ NOTE: The noun *"dude"* is very popular and shows a great deal of familiarity. This term is usually used by the younger generations. In fact, teenagers now use *"dude"* when referring to teenage girls. It is actually common to hear a teenager say, "Hey, dudes!" when addressing a group of young women.

▶ SYNONYM: **guy** *n.*

⇨ NOTE (1): This noun is extremely popular and used by all generations and shows no lack of respect whatsoever. It is simply a casual way of saying "man."

⇨ NOTE (2): In addition, *"you guys"* is frequently used on the West Coast when referring to a group of men, women, or both. It could best be translated as "everyone." Therefore, it is very common and correct to use it when addressing a group of women: *Hey, you guys! What's up?;* Hi, everyone! What's happening? In the

South, *"ya'll,"* a contraction of *"you all,"* is used in place of *"you guys."*

dump (to) *exp.* to abandon or rid oneself of • *After 20 years, she dumped her husband;* After 20 years, she abandoned her husband.

dweeb *n.* moron, simpleton.
♦ NOTE: This is an extremely common noun used mainly by young people.
♦ SYNONYM: **geek** *adj.* • *What a geek!;* What an idiot!

-E-

eat (to) *v.* to upset, to anger • *What's eating you today?;* What's upsetting you today?
♦ VARIATION: **to eat up** *exp.* **1.** to upset • *Seeing how unfairly she's being treated just eats me up;* Seeing how unfairly she is being treated really upsets me. • **2.** to enjoy • *He's eating up all the praise he's getting;* He's enjoying the praise he's getting.

eat someone out of house and home (to) *exp.* to eat constantly in someone else's house • *I don't know what I'll do if he stays here any longer! He's eating us out of house and home!;* I don't know what I'll do if he stays here any longer! He keeps eating everything we have!

-F-

fall apart (to) *exp.* to lose control of one's emotions • *When she learned of her father's death, she fell apart;* When she learned of her father's death, she lost control of her emotions.
♦ SYNONYM: **to lose it** *exp.* • to lose control of one's emotions • *I think she's starting to lose it;* I think she's starting to lose control of her emotions.

fall for (to) *exp.* **1.** to be tricked into believing • *You actually fell for all those lies?;* You actually believed all those lies? • **2.** to fall in love • *I fell for her the moment I saw her;* I fell in love with her the moment I saw her.
♦ SYNONYM: **taken in (to be)** *exp.* • *I can't believe that you let yourself be taken in by his lies;* I can't believe that you let yourself be tricked into believing his lies.
⇨ ALSO: **to be taken** *exp.* to be cheated • *He charged you too much! I'm afraid you were taken!;* He charged you too much! I'm afraid you were cheated!

"Fat chance" *exp.* "There is no possibility of that" • *"Maybe your father will lend you his new car." "Fat chance!";* "Maybe your father will lend you his new car." "There is no possibility of that!"
♦ SYNONYM: **not a chance in hell** *exp.* *"Do you think he'll pass the test?" "Not a chance in hell!";* "Do you think he'll pass the test?" "There is no possibility of that!"

fed up (to be) *exp.* to have tolerated all one can • *I'm fed up with this work!;* I've tolerated all I can with this work!
♦ SYNONYM: **to have had it up to here** *exp.* • *I've had it up to here!;* I tolerated all I can!
⇨ NOTE: This expression is commonly used in conjunction with a hand gesture where the speaker indicates a line over the head symbolizing that he/she is overfilled with intolerable acts.

field day *exp.* a great time; complete self-indulgence • *At the pastry shop, I had a field day!;* At the pastry shop, I indulged myself! • *When I saw her in the market, I finally told her what I think of her. I had a field day!;* When I saw her in the market, I finally told her what I think of her. I indulged myself!

final *n.* This is a very popular abbreviation for *"final examination"* which can also be contracted to *"final exam."*

flake *n.* an unreliable person • *Don't count on him picking you up at the airport on time. He's a real flake;* Don't count on him picking you up at the airport on time. He's really unreliable.
♦ ALSO: **flakey** *adj.* unreliable • *You can't depend on him. He's too flakey;* You can't depend on him. He's too unreliable.

flip (to) *v.* **1.** to go crazy • *Sometimes I think you've flipped!;* Sometimes I think you've gone crazy! • **2.** to go crazy with excitement • *I flipped when I saw her perform;* I went crazy with excitement when I saw her perform.

fly off the handle (to) *exp.* to become suddenly enraged • *When I told my mother about the car accident, she flew off the handle;* When I told my mother about the car accident, she became suddenly enraged.
♦ SYNONYM: **to blow one's top** *exp.* • *She blew her top when I arrived late;* She became suddenly enraged when I arrived late.

"Forget that noise!" *exp.* "That's an impossibility!" • *Forget that noise! I'd never do anything like that!;* That's an impossibility! I've never do anything like that!
♦ NOTE: In the above expression, it is very common to stress the article *"that"*: *Forget **that** noise!*
♦ SYNONYM: **"Get real!"** *exp.*

fork out (to) *exp.* to pay • *How much money did you have to fork out to buy that car?;* How much money did you have to pay to buy that car?
♦ SYNONYM: **to cough up** *exp.* • *I had to cough up $100 for my car repair;* I had to pay $100 for my car repair.

freak out (to) *exp.* **1.** to lose control of one's emotional state, to become very upset and irrational • **2.** to lose grasp of reality temporarily due to drugs.
♦ NOTE: This is an extremely popular expression used by younger people. This expression is also commonly heard in its abbreviated form *"to freak."* • *If he doesn't arrive in five minutes, I'm going to freak;* If he doesn't arrive in five minutes, I'm going to be very upset.
♦ SYNONYM: **to flip out** *exp.* • *If he doesn't arrive in five minutes, I'm going to flip out;* If he doesn't arrive in five minutes, I'm going to be very upset.
⇨ NOTE: This may also be used in reference to drugs.
♦ ANTONYM (1): **to keep one's cool** *exp.* to stay calm, composed • *My mom kept her cool when I told her I destroyed the car;* My mom stayed calm when I told her I destroyed the car.
♦ ANTONYM (2): See - **chill out (to)**.

freeloader *n.* one who imposes upon another's kindness or hospitality without sharing the cost or responsibility involved • *My uncle has been staying with us for three weeks and has never offered to pay for anything. What a freeloader!;* My uncle has been staying with us for three weeks and has never offered to pay for anything. He's the kind of person who imposes upon the generosity of others with no intention of reciprocation.

fresh out of something *exp.* **1.** totally depleted of something • *We're fresh out of eggs;* We're totally depleted of eggs. • **2.** to have recently left something (a school, a country, etc.) • *He's fresh out of school;* He's just graduated from school. • *She's fresh out of the military;* She has recently left the military.

fries *n.* a popular abbreviation of French fries • *I'll have a burger and fries;* I'll have a hamburger and French fries.

-G-

"Gag me!" *exp.* "That makes me sick!" ♦ NOTE: This is a common expression used mainly by younger people, especially teenagers, to signify great displeasure. This expression is considered "valley talk" as it was called in a popular song in the late 1980's called "Valley Girls." The same song also introduced the now out-dated expression, *"Gag me with a spoon!";* That makes me really sick! *"Gag me with a spoon!"* is still occasionally heard, but only in jest. ♦ SYNONYM: **"Gross me out!"** *exp.* • *Susan and Bob are going together?! Gross me out!;* Susan and Bob are dating?! That makes me sick!

"Gee!" *exclam.* (exclamation of surprise or wonder, a euphemism for "Jesus") • *Gee, I wonder how he did that!* ♦ SYNONYM: **"Wow!"** *exclam.* • *Wow, I wonder how he did that!*

get [all] bent out of shape (to) *exp.* to become very angry • *My mom got all bent out of shape when I came home late;* My mom got very angry when I came home late. ♦ SYNONYM: **to fly off the handle** *exp.* • *My dad flew off the handle when I wrecked the car;* My dad got really angry when I wrecked the car.

get a clue (to) *exp.* to become aware • *Get a clue! He's trying to rip you off!;* Become aware! He's trying to cheat you! ♦ SYNONYM: **to wake up and smell the coffee** *exp. Wake up and smell the coffee! He's trying to rip you off!;* Become aware! He's trying to cheat you!

get a kick (to) *exp.* to enjoy very much • *I get a kick out of your sister;* I enjoy your sister very much. ♦ SYNONYM: **to get a charge** *exp.* • *I get a charge out of going to the beach;* I really enjoy going to the beach.

get a kick out of something (to) *exp.* to enjoy greatly • *I get a kick out of working;* I really enjoy working. ♦ SYNONYM: **to get a charge out of something** *exp.* • *I get a charge out of flying;* I really enjoy flying.

get around (to) *exp.* **1.** to commute • *He gets around by bicycle;* He commutes by bicycle. • **2.** to go from one sexual partner to the other • *She really gets around;* She really goes from one sexual partner to the other. • **3.** to avoid • *How are we gonna get around the problem?;* How are we going to avoid the problem?

get away with something (to) *exp.* to succeed at doing something dishonest • *He got away with cheating on the test;* He succeeded at cheating on the test. ♦ NOTE: **to get away with murder** *exp.* (very popular) to succeed at being dishonest • *He got away with cheating on the test?! I swear, he gets away with murder;* He succeeded at cheating on the test?! I swear, he never gets caught. ♦ SYNONYM: **to pull something off** *exp.* to succeed at doing something very difficult but not necessarily dishonest • *"He actually aced the* *test?" "Yes! He really pulled it off!";* "He actually passed the test?" "Yes! He really succeeded!" • *He pulled off a bank job;* He succeeded at robbing a bank.

♦ ANTONYM: **to get busted** *exp.* to get caught doing something dishonest • *The teacher finally saw him cheating on the test. I knew he'd get busted sooner or later;* The teacher finally saw him cheating on the test. I knew he'd get caught sooner or later.

get down (to) *exp.* to let oneself be unrestrained and wild • *When she dances, she really gets down!;* When she dances, she really lets herself be unrestrained and wild!

♦ SYNONYM: **to let it all hang out** *exp.* • *There's no need to get embarrassed. Just let it all hang out!;* There's no need to get embarrassed. Just let yourself be unrestrained and wild!

get going (to) *exp.* to leave • *Let's get going;* Let's leave.

♦ SYNONYM: **to split** *exp.* • *Let's split;* Let's leave.

get into something (to) *exp.* to immerse oneself in something • *I don't like dancing. I just can't get into it;* I don't like dancing. I just can't immerse myself in it.

♦ ALSO: **to get into it** *exp.* to get into the mood • *I'm sorry but I just can't get into it;* I'm sorry but I just can't get into the mood. • *I'm not into talking about it right now;* I'm not in the mood to talk about it right now.

get it (to) *exp.* to understand • *You'd better explain it to me again. I still don't get it;* You'd better explain it to me again. I still don't understand.

♦ SYNONYM: **"Gotcha"** *exp.* "I understand you."

♦ NOTE: This is a popular contraction of *"I got you"* meaning "I understand you."

get off it (to) *exp.* **1.** to stop talking nonsense • *Oh, get off it! You don't really have a twin!;* Oh, stop talking nonsense! You don't really have a twin! • **2.** to change the subject • *Get off it! You've been talking about the same thing for an hour!;* Change the subject! You've been talking about the same thing for an hour!

♦ SYNONYM: **to get out of here** *exp.* • *Get outta here! I don't believe you!;* Stop talking nonsense! I don't believe you!

⇨ NOTE: In this expression, it is very common to contract "out of" to become *"outta."*

get one (to) *exp.* to annoy one • *He really gets me;* He really annoys me.

♦ SYNONYM: **to bug one** *exp.* • *My little sister is bugging me;* My little sister is annoying me.

"Get out of here!" *exp.* **1.** "You're kidding!" • **2.** "Absolutely not!" • *"Is that your girlfriend?" "Get outta here!";* "Is that your girlfriend?" "Absolutely not!"

♦ NOTE (1): This expression, commonly seen as *"Get outta here"* [pronounced: *Ged oudda here*], may be used upon hearing bad news as well as good news • *"I just heard that John's dog got killed." "Get outta here!";* "I just heard that John's dog got killed." "You're kidding! (That's awful!)" • *"I just aced the test!" "Get outta here!";* "I just passed the test!" "You're kidding! (That's terrific!)"

♦ NOTE (2): A common variation of this expression is simply, *"Get out!"* which is also used upon hearing news as well as good news. On occasion, you may even hear the expression playfully lenthened to *"Get outta town!"*

♦ SYNONYM: **"No way!"** *exp.* **1.** (in surprise and excitement) *"I won a trip to Europe!" "No way!";* "I won a trip to Europe!" "You're kidding!" • **2.** (in

disbelief) *"I won a trip to Europe!"*
"No way!"; "I won a trip to Europe!"
"I don't believe you!"• **3.** (to
emphasize "no") *"Do you like her?"*
"No way!"; "Do you like her?"
"Absolutely not!"
⇨ NOTE (1): The difference
between **1.** and **2.** depends on the
delivery of the speaker)
⇨ NOTE (2): Although the opposite
would certainly be logical, the
expression, *"Yes way!"* is not really
correct, although on occasion you
may actually hear it as a witty
response to *"No way!"*
⇨ NOTE (3): The most common
response to *"No way!"* used by
teenagers has recently become
"Way!"

get out of someone's face (to)
exp. to leave someone alone • *Get
outta my face! I'm busy!;* Leave me
alone! I'm busy!
♦ SYNONYM: **to get lost** *exp.* • *Get
lost!;* Leave me alone!
♦ ANTONYM: **to hang [out] with
someone** *exp.* to spend time with
someone (and do nothing in
particular) • *I'm going to hang out
with Debbie today;* I'm going to
spend time with Debbie today.
⇨ NOTE (1): A common shortened
version of this expression is *"to hang
with someone."*
⇨ NOTE (2): The expression *"to
hang [out]"* is commonly used to
mean, "to do nothing in particular" •
*Why don't you go without me? I'm
just going to stay here and hang (out)
today;* Why don't you go without me?
I'm just going to stay here and do
nothing in particular.

get real (to) *exp.* to be serious, to
become realistic • *When is she gonna
get real and find a job?;* What is she
going to become realistic and get a
job?
♦ SYNONYM: **to get a life** *exp.* • *Get a*

life!; Get serious!
⇨ NOTE: Over the last few years,
this expression has become extremely
popular.

get someone (to) *exp.* to seize (and
punish) someone • *I'm going to get
him for stealing my homework!;* I'm
going to kill him for stealing my
homework!

give it a rest (to) *exp.* **1.** to stop
talking nonsense • *Oh, give it a rest!
You know that's a lie!;* Oh, stop
talking nonsense. You know that's a
lie! • **2.** to stop dwelling on something
• *Are you going to talk about that
again? Can't you just give it a rest?;*
Are you going to talk about that
again? Can't you just stop dwelling
on it?
♦ SYNONYM: **to hang it up** *exp.* •
*Hang it up! I'm tired of listening to
this!;* Stop talking nonsense! I'm tired
of listening to this!

give someone a break (to) *exp.* **1.**
This popular expression is commonly
used to indicate annoyance and
disbelief. It could best be translated
as, "You're kidding!" The expression,
"Give me a break," commonly
pronounced, *"Gimme a break,"* is
very similar to the expression *"Get
outta here!"* The significant
difference is that *"Get outta here!"*
may be used to indicate excitement as
well as disbelief, as previously
demonstrated. However, *"Gimme a
break!"* is *only* used to indicate
disbelief. Therefore, if someone were
to give you a piece of good news and
you were to respond by saying,
"Gimme a break," this would
indicate that you did not believe a
word he/she was saying. **2.** to do
someone a favor • *Please, gimme a
break and let me take the test again;*
Please, do me a favor and let me take
the test again • **3.** to give someone an

opportunity for success • *I gave him his first big break at becoming an actor;* I gave him his first big opportunity at becoming an actor • **4.** to be merciful with someone • *Since this is your first offense, I'm going to give you a break;* Since this is your first offense, I'm going to be merciful with you.

give/lend someone a hand (to) *exp.* to offer someone assistance • *Can I give/lend you a hand with that?;* Can I offer you assistance with that?

go (to) *v.* to say • *So, I told the policeman that my speedometer was broken and he goes, 'Gimme a break!';* So, I told the policeman that my speedometer was broken and he says, 'I don't believe a word you're saying!'
▶ NOTE (1): This usage of the verb *"to go"* is extremely common among younger people. You'll probably encounter it within your first few hours in America!
▶ NOTE (2): Although not as popular, you may occasionally hear this term used in the past tense • *So, I told the policeman that my speedometer was broken and he **went**, 'Gimme a break!';* So, I told the policeman that my speedometer was broken and he said, 'I don't believe a word you're saying!'
▶ NOTE (3): In colloquial American English, it is very common to use the present tense to indicate an event that took place in the past as demonstrated in the dialogue: *Yesterday, before class **starts**, she **walks** up to Mr. Edward's desk and **goes**, 'Good Morning, Jim;'* Yesterday, before class started, she walked up to Mr. Edward's desk and said, 'Good Morning, Jim.'
▶ SYNONYM (1): **to be all** *exp.* • *So, I go up to her and tell her how great*

she looks since she's lost all that weight and she's all, 'Stop teasing me!'; So, I go up to her and tell her how great she looks since she's lost all that weight and she says, 'Stop teasing me!'
⇨ NOTE: This is extremely popular among the younger generations only.
▶ SYNONYM (2): **to be like** *exp.* • *I said hello to her yesterday and she's like, 'Leave me alone!';* I said hello to her yesterday and she said, 'Leave me alone!'
⇨ NOTE (1): This is extremely popular among the younger generations only.
⇨ NOTE (2): These two expressions *"to be all"* and *"to be like,"* are commonly combined: *I walked up to her and she's all like, 'Get outta here!"* • *I walked up to her and she's like all, 'Get outta here!"*

go for it (to) *exp.* to be courageous and do something • *Don't worry and just go for it!;* Be courageous and just do it!

go under the knife (to) *exp.* to undergo surgery • *What time are you going under the knife?;* What time are you having surgery?

goings on *exp.* that which is happening • *Have you heard about the goings on between Michelle and Eric?;* Have you heard about that which is happening between Michelle and Eric?

grab a bite (to) *exp.* to get something to eat quickly • *Let's grab a bite before the movie;* Let's get something to eat quickly before the movie.
▶ SYNONYM: **to eat on the run** *exp.* to eat while en route • *We don't have time to stop and eat. Let's just eat on the run;* We don't have time to stop and eat. Let's just eat en route.
▶ NOTE: There is a slight difference between these two expressions: *"to grab a bite"* indicates that the subject

has just enough time to stop and eat, whereas the expression *"to eat on the run"* depicts someone who does not have the time to stop and therefore must eat while proceeding to his/her destination. Both expressions are extremely popular.

gross (to be) *adj.* to be disgusting • *I'm not eating that! It looks gross!;* I'm not eating that! It looks disgusting!
 ♦ NOTE: This was created from the adjective "grotesque."

"Guy!" *exclam.* exclamation denoting surprise or disbelief • *Guy! I can't believe he did that to you!*
 ♦ NOTE: Although *"Guy!"* is literally a slang term for "Man!" it may be used in a conversation when speaking with women as well. *"Man!"* may also be used as an exclamation, a common synonym for *"Guy!"*

guy *n.* man (in general) • *Do you know that guy?;* Do you know that man?
 ♦ NOTE: This is extremely popular and used by everyone.
 ♦ SYNONYM: **fellow** *n.* [commonly pronounced: *fella*] • *We just hired that fellow over there;* We just hired that man over there.
 ⇨ NOTE: This is popular among the older generations only.

-H-

hand someone something (to) *exp.* to give someone something • *He handed me his car keys;* He gave me his car keys.
 ♦ ALSO: **to hand over** *exp.* to give or relinquish • *He handed over his car keys to me;* He relinquished his car keys to me.

handle someone or something (to be unable to) *exp.* to be unable to tolerate someone or

something • *I can't handle babysitting my little brother;* I can't tolerate babysitting my little brother.
 ♦ ALSO: **to handle someone or something** *exp.* to be capable of managing someone or something • *I just got a new big job. I'll have a lot of responsibilities but I know I can handle it;* I just got a new job. I'll have a lot of responsibilities but I know I'm capable of managing it.
 ♦ SYNONYM: **to be unable to take someone or something** *exp.* • *I can't take this anymore!;* I can't tolerate this anymore!

haul (to) *v.* to hurry • (lit); to drag or carry • *We only have five minutes to get there. Let's haul!;* We only have five minutes to get there. Let's hurry!
 ♦ NOTE: Another variation of *"to haul"* is *"to haul butt."* In this expression, the noun *butt* can certainly be replaced with any number of slang synonyms, i.e. *buns, ass (vulgar),* etc.

have a clue (not to) *exp.* not to have the slightest idea • *I haven't got a clue why he's so angry at me;* I haven't the slightest idea why he's so angry at me.
 ♦ SYNONYM: **to be clueless** *exp.* • *I'm clueless!;* I haven't got the slightest idea!
 ♦ ANTONYM: **to get a clue** *exp.* to become aware and enlightened • *Oh, get a clue! He's lying to you!;* Oh, become aware and enlightened! He's lying to you!

have a cow (to) *exp.* to become angry and upset • *Don't have a cow, man!;* Don't get so angry and upset, friend!
 ♦ NOTE: This expression has always been popular but has become even more so in the early 1990's due to a popular television cartoon in which the younger son is known for always using this phrase. It is very common

to see T-shirts, bumper stickers, etc. bearing this expression.

have one's name on something

(to) *exp.* to be perfectly suited to someone • *That shirt has my name on it;* That shirt is perfectly suited to me.
‣ SYNONYM: **to fit to a T** *exp.* • *That dress fits me to a T;* That dress fits me perfectly.

heave (to) *v.* to vomit profusely.
‣ SYNONYM: **to throw one's guts up** *exp.* • *I'm gonna throw my guts up if I eat that;* I'm going to vomit profusely if I eat that.
‣ ANTONYM: **to dry heave** *exp.* to go through the motions of vomiting without regurgitating.

hell in a handbasket/handbag

(to go to) *exp.* to deteriorate severely • *She's really gone to hell in a handbasket/handbag;* She's really deteriorated severely.

hey • 1. *exp.* hello, hi • *Hey, Steve!;* Hi, Steve! • 2. *exclam.* used to indicate a sudden thought or idea • *Hey, I've got an idea! I know how we can do this!* • 3. *exclam.* used to attract someone's attention • *Hey, Kirk! Wait for me!* • *Hey, be careful! You almost went through the red light!*

history (to be) *exp.* to leave, to no longer exist (in a location, in one's estimation, in life) • 1. (in a location) *It's already 1:00? I'm history!;* It's already 1:00? I'm gone! • 2. (in one's estimation) *He cheated me again! I swear, that friend's history!;* He cheated me again! I swear, he's no longer my friend! • 3. (in life) *You wrecked your dad's car? You're history!;* You wrecked your dad's car? You're going to get killed!
‣ SYNONYM: **to be outta here** *exp.* • *I'm outta here!;* I'm leaving!

hit the road (to) *exp.* to leave • *It's getting late. I'd better hit the road;* It's getting late. I'd better leave. • *Hit the road!;* Leave!
‣ SYNONYM (1): **to beat it** *exp.* • *Beat it!;* Leave!
‣ SYNONYM (2): **to scram** *exp.* • *Scram!;* Leave!

hit the showers (to) *exp.* to go to the shower facility of a gymnasium • *Time to hit the showers!;* Time to go to the showers!
‣ NOTE: The verb *"to hit"* is popularly used in gyms when referring to taking a shower. However, it is also commonly used when going to other locations as well, i.e. bar, town, beach, etc. • *Let's go hit the bars tonight;* Let's go to the bars tonight.

hit the stores (to) *exp.* to enter the stores • *Let's go hit the stores;* Let's go to the stores.

hold (to) *exp.* to omit • *I'd like a hamburger but hold the mustard;* I'd like a hamburger but omit the mustard.
‣ NOTE: This is extremely popular slang when placing a food order.

hold it down (to) *exp.* to be quiet • *Hold it down when you go to the library;* Be quiet when you go to the library.
‣ SYNONYM: **to pipe down** *exp.* • *Pipe down!;* Be quiet!

"Holy cow!" *exclam.* (exclamation of astonishment) • *Holy cow! That was unbelievable!*
‣ SYNONYM: **"Holy Toledo!"** *exp.* *Holy Toledo! That was unbelievable!*

honker *n.* large nose • *Jimmy Durante was known for his huge honker;* Jimmy Durante was known for his huge nose.
‣ NOTE: This term originated because early cars had horns which were

activated by squeezing a large
bulbous rubber balloon called a
honker.

hop in (to) *exp.* (very popular) to enter
• (lit); to enter by jumping on one foot
• *If you want a ride to school, hop in!;*
If you want a ride to school, enter!
♦ VARIATION: **to hop on in** *exp.* • *If
you want a ride to school, hop on in!*
⇨ NOTE: If the preposition *"in"* is
omitted from this expression (*"to hop
on"*), it takes on the meaning of *"to
mount"* • *Want to ride my bike? Hop
on!;* Want to ride my bike? Climb up!

horn *n.* telephone (since the shape of a
horn resembles that of the receiver of
a telephone) • *Get on the horn and
call the restaurant for reservations;*
Get on the phone and call the
restaurant for reservations.
♦ NOTE: *"phone"* is a commonly used
abbreviation of "telephone."

hot *adj.* sexy • *He's really hot!;* He's
really sexy!

hots for someone (to have the)
exp. to be interested sexually in
someone.
♦ SYNONYM: **to be turned on by
someone** *exp.*
⇨ NOTE: It is rare to hear this
expression used as *"I'm turned on by
her."* It is much more common to
hear *"She turns me on."*
⇨ ALSO (1): *Math really turns me
on;* I really like math. • *Math is a real
turn on/off!;* Math is really
exciting/unappealing!
⇨ ALSO (2): *She's a real turn
on/off!;* She's very sexy/unappealing!
♦ ALSO: **to be hot** *exp.* to be good
looking and sexy • *He's hot!;* He's
sexy!

-I-

"I hear ya" *exp.* "I agree with you."
♦ NOTE: In this expression, it is
common to use *"ya"* which is the
common pronunciation of "you."

in a big way *exp.* severely • *She
cheated on her test in a big way;* She
cheated extensively on her test.
♦ SYNONYM: **big-time** *exp.* extensive
• *She had big-time surgery;* [or] *She
had surgery big-time;* She had
extensive surgery.

in no time flat *exp.* immediately •
The police arrived in no time flat; The
police arrived immediately.
♦ SYNONYM: **in a jiffy** *exp.* • *I'll be
there in a jiffy;* I'll be there
immediately.

in the raw *exp.* naked • *He walks
around his house in the raw;* He
walks around his house naked.
♦ SYNONYM: **in the buff** *exp. There's
a man standing outside in the buff!;*
There's a man standing outside naked!
⇨ ALSO **buffo** *adj.* • *She walks
around her house buffo;* She walks
around her house naked.

into (to be) *adj.* **1.** to enjoy
(something) • *I'm really into golf;* I
enjoy golf • **2.** to be infatuated with
(someone) • *You're really into him,
aren't you?;* You're really infatuated
with him, aren't you?
♦ SYNONYM: **to dig** *v.* • *I dig
football;* I enjoy football • *I really
don't dig him;* I really don't like him.
⇨ NOTE: The verb *"to dig"* was
especially popular in the 1960's and is
occasionally heard today particularly
in movies and television shows of the
period.

-J-

Jeez! *exclam.* (or **Geez!**) This exclamation of surprise is actually a euphemism for *"Jesus Christ!"* • *Jeez! I can't believe he did that!*
‣ SYNONYM: **Man!** *exclam.* • *Man! I can't believe he did that!*

jinx someone or something (to)
• **1.** *v.* to curse someone or something• *If you talk about it too much, you may jinx it;* If you talk about it too much, you may curse it. • **2.** *n.* that which causes bad luck • *Every time I'm with her, something terrible happens. I think she's a curse;* Every time I'm with her, something terrible happens. I think she causes bad luck.
‣ SYNONYM: **to put a whammy on something or someone** *exp.* • *The witch put a whammy on him;* The witch put a curse on him.

john *n.* toilet • *I have to run to the john;* I have to go to the toilet.
‣ NOTE: Here is some interesting trivia that most Americans are not even aware of. Many years ago, John Crapper invented the first flush toilet. His design was referred to as a *"John Crapper"* which was later shortened to *"John"* or *"Crapper."* Oddly enough, the term *"john"* is extremely popular and simply casual slang yet the term *"crapper"* is considered vulgar. This was taken one step further in the expression *"to take a crap"* meaning "to defecate" and is also extremely popular yet vulgar.

joint *n.* **1.** place (in general) • *This is a nice joint;* This is a nice place. • **2.** a marijuana cigarette.
‣ SYNONYM: **spot** *n.* • *This is a nice spot;* This is a nice place.

-K-

keep someone (to) *exp.* to detain someone •*What's keeping him?;* What's detaining him? • *She kept him after school;* She detained him after school.
‣ SYNONYM: **to hold someone up** *exp.* **1.** to detain someone • *What's holding her up?;* What's detaining her? • *She held me up for an hour;* She detained me for an hour. • **2.** to rob someone • *There's the man who held up that old woman!;* There's the man who robbed that old woman!

kick someone out (to) *exp.* to eject someone • *The manager kicked the children out of the theater for being noisy;* The manager ejected the children from the theater for being noisy.
‣ SYNONYM: **to boot someone out** *exp.*
‣ NOTE: These two expressions are used figuratively although they are occasionally seen depicted literally in cartoons and comic strips.

kick *n.* **1.** fad or craze • *How long has he been on this exercise kick?;* How long has he been into this exercise fad? • **2.** enjoyment • *I got a kick out of that film;* I really enjoyed that film. • **3.** *pl.* fun • *We sneaked into the theatre just for kicks;* We snuck into the theatre just for fun.

kid gloves (to use/wear) *exp.* to be delicate and tactful • *She's very sensitive about this issue. You have to handle her with kid gloves;* She's very sensitive about this issue. You have to be delicate and tactful with her.

killer *adj.* **1.** that which is very difficult • *What a killer assignment!;* What a difficult assignment! • **2.** exceptional, extraordinary • *That's a killer dress!;* That's a beautiful dress!

kiss up to someone (to) *exp.* to flatter someone in order to obtain something.
  ♦ SYNONYM: **to butter someone up** *exp.* • *Stop trying to butter him up!;* Stop trying to flatter him!
  ♦ ANTONYM: **to put someone down** *exp.* to criticize someone • *Why do you always put me down?;* Why do you always criticize me?

knock it off (to) *exp.* to stop • *Could you please knock it off? Your drums are driving me crazy!;* Could you please stop it? Your drums are driving me crazy!
  ♦ SYNONYM: **to hold it** *exp.* • *Could you hold it for a moment?;* Could you stop that for a moment?
  ⇨ ALSO: **to hold it down** *exp.* to be quieter • *Hold it down in there!;* Be quieter in there!

-L-

laid back *exp.* calm.
  ♦ SYNONYM: **easygoing** *adj.* • *She's very easygoing;* She's very calm about everything.
  ♦ ALSO: **to take it easy** *exp.* **1.** to relax • *I'm going to take it easy all day at the beach;* I'm going to relax all day at the beach • **2.** to calm down • *Don't get so upset! Take it easy!;* Don't get so upset! Calm down! • **3.** to be gentle or careful • *Take it easy driving around those curves!;* Be careful driving around those curves!
  ♦ ANTONYM: **uptight** *adj.* tense • *She's always so uptight;* She's always so tense.

lardo *n.* (derogatory) fat person • *If you don't stop eating all that chocolate, you're gonna turn into a lardo;* If you don't stop eating all that chocolate, you're going to become a fat person.
  ♦ SYNONYM (1): **oinker** *n.* (humorous yet derogatory) one who eats like a pig.

  ⇨ NOTE: This slang term comes from the sound a pig makes, *"oink!"*
  ♦ SYNONYM (2): **fatso / fatty** *n.* (humorous yet derogatory) • *What a fatso! / What a fatty!*

last straw *exp.* the final act that one can tolerate • *He used my car again without asking me?! That's the last straw!;* He used my car again without asking me?! That's the final incident that I can tolerate!
  ♦ ALSO: **the straw that broke the camel's back** *exp.* This expression conjures up an image of pieces of straw, being placed on a camel's back until it can support no more • *When I found out that she didn't invite me to the party, that was the straw that broke the camel's back;* When I found out that she didn't invite me to the party, that was all I could tolerate.
  ♦ SYNONYM: **"That did it!"** *exp.* • *That did it! I'm leaving!;* That's all I can tolerate! I'm leaving!

lead foot (to have a) *exp.* to have a tendency to drive fast • *I hate driving with him. He has such a lead foot;* I hate driving with him. He has such a tendency to drive fast.
  ♦ NOTE: This conjures up an image of someone with such a heavy foot, that the accelerator is always pressed down to the floor.

lie like a rug (to) *exp.* to tell enormous lies.
  ♦ NOTE: This expression is a play-on-words since the verb *"to lie"* means "to tell untruths" as well as "to span, cover, or stretch out" as does a rug.

lift a finger (not to) *exp.* not to be helpful, to be lazy • *I do all the work and he doesn't ever lift a finger!;* I do all the work and he is never helpful!
  ♦ NOTE: It would be incorrect to use this expression in the positive sense: *to lift a finger.*

♦ SYNONYM: **not to do dirt** *exp.* • *He doesn't do dirt around here!;* He doesn't offer any help around here!

like *exp.* This is an extremely popular expression used by younger people. It could best be translated as, "how should I put this…" or "uh…" • *He's like really weird;* He's, uh… really weird.

line *n.* **1.** an excuse • *You actually believed that line?;* You actually believed that excuse? • **2.** an overused statement used to allure • *While I was sitting at the bar, this guy comes up to me and says, 'Hi. Didn't we meet somewhere before?' I can't believe he used that old line on me!;* While I was sitting at the bar, this guy comes up to me and says, 'Hi. Didn't we meet somewhere before?' I can't believe he used that old overused statement on me!

living soul *exp.* a person • *There wasn't a living soul in that city;* There was absolutely no one in that city.

load (to get a) *exp.* to observe • *Get a load of that beautiful house!;* Observe that beautiful house!
♦ SYNONYM: **to check out** *exp.* • *Check out that car!;* Observe that car!

loaded (to be) *adj.* **1.** to be rich • *I didn't know he was loaded;* I didn't know he was rich • **2.** to be drunk (or on drugs) • *That guy's really loaded;* That man is really drunk.
♦ NOTE: The difference between connotations simply depends on the context.

"Look what the cat dragged in!" *exclam.* "Look what annoying person walked in!"
♦ NOTE: This expression is commonly used in two ways: **1.** when referring to an unpopular person • When this is the case, the expression would not be said loudly enough for the targeted person to hear • **2.** upon the entrance of someone who is well-liked • When this is the case, the expression would be said directly to the person, signifying affection and friendly teasing.

"Lookit" *exp.* "Observe" • *Lookit! A rainbow!;* Observe! A rainbow!
♦ NOTE: *"Lookit"* is a popular contraction of "Look at it."

lose it (to) *exp.* **1.** to throw up • **2.** to go crazy • *If he doesn't stop it, I'm gonna lose it;* If he doesn't stop it, I'm going to go crazy.

lose it (to) *exp.* **1.** to vomit • *I almost lost it at the restaurant when they served snails!;* I almost vomited at the restaurant when they served snails!
♦ NOTE: As learned in lesson one, the expression *"to lose it"* has other slang meanings as well: **2.** to let go suddenly of one's mental faculties • *In the middle of the test, I just lost it;* In the middle of the test, I just forgot every- thing • **3.** to become very angry • *If he doesn't stop bothering me, I'm gonna lose it;* If he doesn't stop bothering me, I'm going to get very angry.

lose one's cool (to) *exp.* to lose one's temper • *I know I shouldn't have yelled at her but I just lost my cool;* I know I shouldn't have yelled at her but I just lost my temper.
♦ SYNONYM (1): **to blow up** *exp. She blew up when I told her I lost her book;* She lost her temper when I told her I lost her book.
♦ SYNONYM (2): **to fly off the handle** *exp.* • *I know I shouldn't have flown off the handle like that;* I know I shouldn't have lost my temper like that.
♦ ALSO: **to lose it** *exp.* to lose one's temper • *I know I shouldn't have yelled at her but I just lost it;* I know I

shouldn't have yelled at her but I just lost my temper.
> ⇨ NOTE: Used in this connotation, it is understood that *"it"* replaces "one's temper."

lowdown *exp.* the whole story • *Give me the lowdown. How did everything go?;* Tell me the whole story. How did everything go?
> ♦ SYNONYM: **to give someone the dirt** *exp.* • *What happened? Give me the dirt!;* What happened? Bring me up-to-date!
> ⇨ ALSO: **to dish the dirt** *exp.* to gossip • *There they go dishing the dirt again;* There they go gossiping again.

-M-

made in the shade (to have it) *exp.* to have an easy time of something • *This test isn't long! Once I answer the questions in this difficult section, I should have it made in the shade;* This test isn't long! Once I answer the questions in this difficult section, I should have an easy time of it.
> ♦ NOTE: For an extensive list of more rhyming slang, see *Street Talk II*.

make it in (to) *exp.* to arrive to a particular destination (usually at home or work) • *What time did you make it in last night?;* What time did you arrive home last night?
> ♦ SYNONYM: **to roll in** *exp.* to arrive (usually late yet unhurried) • *She finally rolled in about 9:00;* She finally arrived to work about 9:00.

"Man!" *exclam.* "Wow!"
> ♦ NOTE: The exclamation *"Man!"* can certainly be used among girls since it is only a term of surprise and does not indicate any of the persons involved in the conversation.
> ♦ SYNONYM: **"Boy!"** *exclam.*

moonlight (to) *v.* to work a second job (traditionally in the evenings • *She has to moonlight because she doesn't make enough money for rent;* She has to work a second job because she doesn't make enough money for rent.

mouth off (to) *exp.* to speak rudely • *Can you believe how her children mouth off to her?;* Can you believe how her children speak so rudely to her?
> ♦ SYNONYM: **to shoot off one's mouth** *exp.* to speak rudely and somewhat irrationally • *Stop shooting off your mouth. You don't know what you're talking about!;* Stop speaking rudely and irrationally. You don't know what you're talking about!

-N-

nail the brakes *exp.* to apply the brakes suddenly • *If I hadn't nailed the brakes at that very moment, I would have been in a fender-bender;* If I hadn't applied the brakes at that very moment, I would have been in an accident.
> ♦ NOTE: The term *"fender-bender"* is popularly used to mean a "minor accident."

"No pain no gain" *exp.* "Without suffering, there is no (physical) growth."
> ♦ NOTE: This expression was originally developed by bodybuilders and is still very popular at any gym. It is also occasionally heard when referring to emotional growth: *I know it hurts to tell him, but 'no pain no gain.';* I know it hurts to tell him, but 'without suffering, there is no (emotional) growth.'

"No way!" *exclam.* "Absolutely not!"
> ♦ ALSO: **No way, José!** *exp.* • SEE: *Street Talk II - Rhyming Slang.*

noise *n.* nonsense • *Don't gimme that noise!;* Don't give me that nonsense!
◗ SYNONYM: **baloney** *n.* • *What he told you was nothing but baloney;* What he told you was nothing but nonsense.

"Now you're talkin' " *exp.* "Now you're being sensible."
◗ NOTE: In this expression, the verb *"talking"* is usually heard in its abbreviated form *"talkin'."*
◗ SYNONYM: **"I'm with you"** *exp.*

number *exp.* **1.** outfit • *What do you think of the new number I just bought?;* What do you think of the new outfit I just bought? • **2.** a very attractive person • *She's quite a number!;* She's very pretty!

nuts *adj.* to be crazy • *Don't walk outside in the snow dressed in those shorts! What are you, nuts?;* Don't walk outside in the snow dressed in those shorts! Are you crazy?
◗ SYNONYM: **wacked out** *exp.* • *That guy keeps talking to himself. I think he's really wacked out;* That guy keeps talking to himself. I think he's really crazy.

-O-

odds and ends *exp.* various insignificant items • *What kind of odds and ends did you buy at the store?;* What kind of various insignificant items did you buy at the store?

old man *exp.* (disrespectful) **1.** father • **2.** boyfriend • **3.** husband.
◗ ANTONYM: **old lady** *exp.* (derogatory) **1.** mother • **2.** girlfriend • **3.** wife.

on someone *exp.* **1.** paid for by someone • *Order anything you want from the menu. It's on my father;* Order anything you want from the

menu. My father is paying. • **2.** to harass someone • *You're always on me about something!;* You're always harassing me about something!
◗ SYNONYM: **to pick up the check/tab** *exp.* • *Let me pick up the check/tab this time;* Let me pay the bill this time.

one-track mind (to have a) *exp.* to have one's thoughts permanently focused on one topic • *All she ever does is talk about eating. She sure does have a one-track mind;* All she ever does is talk about eating. She sure does have all her thoughts permanently focused on one topic.

out of it (to be) *exp.* to be in a daze.
◗ SYNONYM: **to be spaced out** *exp.* • *You look really spaced out;* You look really dazed.
◗ ANTONYM: **to have it together** *exp.* to have control of one's emotions • *I think I've got it together now;* I think I'm in control of my emotions now.
◗ ALSO: **to pull it together** *exp.* **1.** to regain control of one's emotions • *After her scare, she needs some time to pull together before she can go back on stage;* After her scare, she needs some time to regain control of her emotions before she can go back on stage. • **2.** to get ready • *I was just asked to make a presentation at work tomorrow, but I don't don't think I'll have time to pull it together;* I was just asked to make a presentation at work tomorrow, but I don't think I'll have time to get ready.

-P-

pan (to) *v.* to criticize brutally an element of the arts (such as a play, a movie, an actor, etc.) • *The critics panned the play;* The critics brutally criticized the play.
◗ SYNONYM: **to rake over the coals** *exp.* • *The critics really raked them*

over the coals; The critics really criticized them unmercifully.
▶ NOTE: This expression may be used in reference to that which is outside the arts as well.

pick up (to) *exp.* **1.** to purchase • *Did you pick up some bread at the store for me?;* Did you purchase some bread at the store for me? • **2.** to contract (a sickness) • *I think I picked up a cold from one of the other students;* I think I caught a cold from one of the other students. • **3.** to find someone for a sexual encounter • *He goes to bars just to pick up women;* He goes to bars just to meet women for sexual encounters.

pile (a) *n.* a lot • *He gave me a pile of excuses;* He gave me a lot of excuses.
▶ SYNONYM: **a mess** *n.* • (lit); disorder • *The teacher gave us a mess of homework;* The teacher gave us a lot of homework.

pissed off (to be) *exp.* (extremely popular) to be angry.
▶ NOTE (1): Although having absolutely nothing to do with urinating, some people consider this expression to be vulgar since it comes from the slang verb *"to piss"* meaning "to urinate," a most definitely vulgar expression. A mild yet equally widely used synonym for this expression is *"to be ticked off"* • *I'm really ticked off at her!;* I'm really angry at her.
▶ NOTE (2): The expression *"to be pissed off"* is commonly heard in an abbreviated form: *"to be P.O.'d"* • *She looks really P.O.'d about something!;* She looks really angry about something!
▶ SEE: A Closer Look (2): *Commonly Used Initials,* p. 24.

place *n.* home • *Welcome to our place!;* Welcome to our home?
▶ SYNONYM: **pad** *n.* Although no

longer used, this word became extremely popular in the 60's when it was introduced by musicians. You may still hear it used in old movies, television shows, or in jest.

polish off something (to) *exp.* to eat something completely • *He polished off that hamburger in a few minutes;* He ate that complete hamburger in a few minutes.
▶ SYNONYM: **to eat up a storm** *exp.* • *We ate up a storm at the restaurant;* We ate a lot at the restaurant.

porker *n.* **1.** one who eats like a pig • *Did you see him eat? What a porker!;* Did you see him eat? What a pig! • **2.** one who is fat • *She's a real porker!;* She's a real fat pig!
▶ SYNONYM: **oinker** *n.* (humorous yet derogatory) one who eats like a pig.
⇨ NOTE: This slang term comes from the sound a pig makes, *oink!*

pot belly *exp.* a fat stomach (which is round like a pot) • *If I ever get a pot belly, I'm gonna kill myself!;* If I ever get a fat stomach, I'm going to kill myself!
▶ ALSO: **pot** *n.* a common abbreviation of *"pot belly"* • *Did you notice that Jeff is starting to get a pot?;* Did you notice that Jeff is starting to get a fat stomach?

pull something (to) *exp.* to succeed at doing something dishonest • *What's he trying to pull this time?;* What dishonest thing is he trying to do this time?
▶ SYNONYM: **to get away with something** *exp.* • *What's he trying to get away with this time?;* What dishonest thing is he trying to do this time?

punch it (to) *exp.* to accelerate quickly, to push the accelerator down to the floor in one quick motion • *If*

she sees us, we're gonna be in trouble! Punch it!; If she sees us, we're going to be in trouble! Push the accelerator down to the floor!
♦ SYNONYM: **to put the pedal to the metal** *exp.* • (lit); to put the pedal (accelerator) to the floor.

put it away (to) *exp.* • (lit); to put something in its place • to eat voraciously • *He can really put it away!;* He can really eat voraciously!
♦ NOTE: In this expression, *"it"* refers to "food.".
♦ SYNONYM: **to scarf it up** *exp.* • *Did you see how he can scarf it up?;* Did you see how he can eat voraciously?

put one's finger on something (to) *exp.* to determine the problem or cause of something • *I think you just put your finger on it. The reason for his depression is boredom;* I think you just determined the problem. The reason for his depression is boredom.
♦ SYNONYM: **to hit the nail on the head** *exp.* • *You hit the nail on the head. You should be a detective!;* You determined the cause of it. You should be a detective!

put someone up (to) *exp.* to lodge someone • *Can you put me up for the night?;* Can you lodge me for the night?
♦ NOTE: **to put someone up to something** *exp.* to convince someone to do something • *He put me up to it!;* He convinced me to do it!

put something on the back burner (to) *exp.* to postpone something • *You'll have to put your project on the back burner for now. There just isn't enough time to do it;* You'll have to postpone your project for now. There just isn't enough time to do it.
♦ NOTE: This expression comes from the culinary world where the less

crucial items to be cooked are placed on the back burner of the stove.

put up with (to) *exp.* to tolerate (someone or something) • *I'm not putting up with this anymore;* I'm not tolerating this anymore.
♦ SYNONYM (1): **to stick it out** *exp.* *Our house guest will be leaving in just two days. Try and stick it out a little longer;* Our house guest will be leaving in just two days. Try and tolerate it a little longer.
♦ SYNONYM (2): **to take something** *exp.* • *I'm not taking this anymore;* I'm not tolerating this anymore.
⇨ NOTE: **I'm mad as hell and I'm not going to take it anymore!** *exp.* This expression became extremely popular in the 1980's when it was heard in the movie called "Network."

-R-

rag on someone (to) *exp.* to harass someone • *Stop ragging on him!;* Stop harassing him!
♦ SYNONYM: **to pick on someone** *exp.* • *Stop picking on me!;* Stop harassing me!

rag *n.* magazine or newspaper containing absurd articles and commentaries • *You actually buy those rags?;* You actually buy those ridiculous magazines?

raid the fridge (to) *exp.* to attack the food in the refrigerator • *Last night, I got so hungry in the middle of the night that I raided the fridge;* Last night, I got so hungry in the middle of the night that I ate everything out of the refrigerator.
♦ NOTE: The noun *"fridge"* is a popular abbreviation of "refrigerator."

rarin' to go *exp.* invigorated and ready for action • *After that long nap, I'm rarin' to go!;* After that long nap, I'm

invigorated and ready for action!
▶ NOTE: In this expression, *"rarin'"*, the contracted form of *"raring"* is always used. Otherwise, this expression would actually sound unnatural.

read someone the riot act (to)
exp. to reprimand someone • *She really read me the riot act;* She really reprimanded me.
▶ SYNONYM: **to lay into someone** *exp.* • *I heard your mother really laid into you!;* I heard your mother really reprimanded you!

reek (to) *exp.* to stink • *That cheese reeks!;* That cheese stinks!
▶ ALSO: **to reek to high heaven** *exp.* to stink intensely • *That rotten egg reeks to high heaven!;* That rotten egg stinks unbelievably!

revved *adj.* primed and ready • *After that workout, I'm revved!;* After that workout, I'm primed and ready!
▶ ALSO: **revved up** *exp.* • *After that lecture, I'm really revved up;* After that lecture, I'm really primed and ready.
⇨ NOTE: This adjective is traditionally used to refer to a car that has been warmed up and ready to drive.
▶ SYNONYM: **charged up** *exp.* • *If you're all charged up, let's go on a hike;* If you're all primed and ready, let's go on a hike.
⇨ NOTE: Traditionally, this expression is used when referring to a battery.

right off the bat *exp.* right from the beginning • *I liked her right off the bat;* I liked her right from the beginning.
▶ SYNONYM: **from the get go** *exp.* • *They didn't like each other from the get go;* They didn't like each other right from the beginning.

rip-off *n.* thievery • *You were charged $400 for a pair of pants? What a rip-off!;* You were charged $400 for a pair of pants? What thievery!
▶ ALSO: **rip-off** *v.* to cheat someone of money • *You were charged $400 for a pair of pants? You were ripped off!;* You were charged $400 for a pair of pants? You were cheated!
▶ SYNONYM: **highway robbery** *exp.* • *I'm not paying that much money for that! That's highway robbery!;* I'm not paying that much money for that! That's thievery!

ripped *adj.* extremely drunk • *Don't let him drive home! He's ripped!;* Don't let him drive home! He's totally drunk!
▶ SYNONYM: **plastered** *adj.* • *If I drink just one glass of wine, I get plastered;* If I drink just one glass of wine, I get extremely drunk.
▶ NOTE: **tipsy** *adj.* slightly drunk • *I'm starting to feel tipsy;* I'm starting to feel drunk.

ritzy *adj.* expensive and lavish • *This is some ritzy hotel here!;* This is an extremely expensive and lavish hotel here!
▶ NOTE: The term *"some"* is commonly used in two ways: **1.** *adv.* extremely • Note that when this expression is used, the article which precedes the adjective is simply replaced by *"some"*: *This is a ritzy hotel = This is some ritzy hotel!* • *This is a nice house = This is some nice house!* • **2.** *adj.* impressive • (only when *some* precedes the noun directly) • *This is a very nice house = This is some house!* • *She is a very good student = She is some student!*

rolling in it *exp.* rich • *You have a beautiful house! You must be rolling in it!;* You have a beautiful house! You must be rich!
▶ NOTE: In this expression, *"it"*

represents "money."

♦ SYNONYM: **to have money to burn**
exp. • *She has money to burn;* She's
rich.

rub the wrong way (to) *exp.* to
irritate.
♦ SYNONYM: **to get on someone's
nerves** *exp.* • *She gets on my nerves;*
She irritates me.
♦ ANTONYM: **to sweep off one's feet**
exp. to charm someone • *He swept us
all off our feet;* He charmed us all.
♦ NOTE: This expression comes from
rubbing an animal in the opposite
direction of his coat causing him to
bristle.

run a [red] light (to) *exp.* to go
through a red light • *I got a ticket for
running a [red] light;* I got a ticket for
going through a [red] light.

run into someone (to) *exp.* to
encounter someone unintentionally •
*Can you believe it? I ran into him in
Paris!;* Can you believe it? I
encountered him unintentionally in
Paris!
♦ SYNONYM: **to bump into someone**
exp. • *You'll never guess who I
bumped into today!;* You'll never
guess who I encountered
inadvertently today!

-S-

scarf out (to) *exp.* to eat a lot.
♦ NOTE: On the West Coast, the
expression *"to scarf"* or *"to scarf
out"* is extremely popular. If you visit
any young people in California, for
example, you'll probably hear it
within the first few hours. Although
this expression has great popularity
on the West Coast, in the East it is not
well known at all. Therefore, when
visiting New York, for example, the
expressions you are more likely to
hear are *"to pig out"* or *"to pork*

out." These expressions are equally
popular on the West Coast.
♦ SYNONYM (1): **to pig out** *exp.* • *I
feel sick because I pigged out on pie
today;* I feel sick because I ate a lot of
pie today.
♦ SYNONYM (2): **to pork out** *exp.* to
eat a lot • *We're really gonna pork
out tonight!;* We're really going to eat
a lot tonight!

scream (to be a) *exp.* to be hilarious •
That movie was a scream!; That
movie was hilarious!
♦ SYNONYM: **to be a hoot** *exp.* • *Your
mother's a real hoot;* Your mother's
really funny.

screw loose (to have a) *exp.* to be
eccentric, to be slightly crazy • *That
woman is screaming at an imaginary
person. I think she has a screw loose;*
That woman is screaming at an
imaginary person. I think she's
slightly crazy.
♦ NOTE: On occasion, you may hear
this expression slightly transposed:
"to have a loose screw," although
this is not as common as *"to have a
screw loose."*
♦ SYNONYM (1): **not to be playing
with a full deck** *exp.* • *That woman is
talking to her purse. I don't think
she's playing with a full deck;* That
woman is talking to her purse. I don't
think she's totally rational.
⇨ NOTE: This humorous expression
is taken from the game world of cards
where if the participants are not
playing with a full deck, the game
will be irregular and unbalanced.
When this expression is used in
regards to a crazy person, it implies
that the individual is not functioning
with a full set of brains.
♦ SYNONYM (2): **"The lights are on
but nobody's home"** *exp.*
(humorous) "The person seems to be
awake yet completely lacking in
awareness."

screw up (to) *exp.* to make a mistake, to blunder • *I really screwed up when I forgot to pick up my mom from the airport;* I really blundered when I forgot to pick up my mom from the airport.
♦ ALSO: **screw-up** *n.* one who makes a lot of blunders • *He's such a screw-up!;* He makes so many blunders!
♦ SYNONYM: **to goof up** *exp.* • *I think I goofed up my test;* I think I made a big mistake on my test.

set foot in (to) *exp.* **1.** to enter willingly • *I wouldn't set foot in there if you paid me;* I wouldn't enter there willingly if you paid me • **2.** to enter a room by only one footstep • *As soon as I set foot in the room, she started insulting me;* As soon as I entered the room by only one footstep, she started insulting me.

set of skins *exp.* set of tires • *My first set of skins only lasted six months;* My first set of tires only lasted six months.

set of wheels *exp.* car • *Nice set of wheels!;* Nice car!
♦ ALSO: **wheels** *n.* • Nice wheels!; Nice car!

shop till one drops (to) *exp.* to shop until one has no more energy left • *Let's shop till we drop!;* Let's shop till we don't have any more energy!

show up (to) *exp.* to arrive • *He finally showed up at 10:00;* He finally arrived at 10:00.
♦ NOTE: **no-show** *n.* one who fails to arrive • *Where's Tom? It looks like he's a no-show;* Where's Tom? It looks like he's not coming.
♦ SYNONYM: **to turn up** *exp.* • *He finally turned up about 8:00;* He finally arrived at 8:00.

slammer (to throw someone in the) *n.* to put someone in jail • *They threw him in the slammer for robbery;* They threw him in jail for robbery.
♦ NOTE: Although the noun *"slammer"* was considered jive talk in the 1930's, it is still used in jest and occasionally heard in old movies.
♦ SYNONYM (1): **to put someone away** *exp.* • *They put him away for five years;* They put him in jail for five years.
♦ SYNONYM (2): **to lock someone up (and throw away the key)** *exp.* • *They should have locked him up (and thrown away the key) years ago;* They should have put him (permanently) in jail years ago.
♦ SYNONYM (3): **to send someone up the river** *exp. They sent him up the river;* They put him in jail.
⇨ NOTE: Although this expression was created in the mid 1800's, it is still occasionally heard used in jest as well as in old movies.

sleep in (to) *exp.* to sleep past a usual wake-up time • *He slept in till 9:00;* He slept past his usual wake-up time till 9:00.
♦ SYNONYM: **to sleep the morning away** *exp.* to waste an entire morning by sleeping • *Wake up! You don't want to sleep the morning away!;* Wake up! You don't want to waste an entire morning by sleeping!

slop *n.* inferior food • *How can you expect me to eat this slop?;* How can you expect me to eat this inferior food?
♦ NOTE: The term *"slop"* is traditionally used in reference to "pig feed."
♦ ANTONYM: **goodies** *exp.* food that is pleasing to the eye and the palate • *If I start eating these goodies, I won't be able to stop!;* If I start eating this good food, I won't be able to stop!

smash hit *exp.* a tremendous success •
The movie was a smash hit; The
movie was a tremendous success.
♦ ANTONYM: See - **bomb.**
♦ ALSO: *The movie was a smash;* The
movie was a huge success • *The
movie was a hit;* The movie was a
success.
♦ NOTE: *hit* = success; *smash* = big
success; *smash hit* = huge success.

sneaking suspicion *exp.* (growing)
feeling (about something or someone)
• *I have a sneaking suspicion that he
was the one who stole the bracelet;* I
have a growing feeling that he was
the one who stole the bracelet.

"So help me..." *exp.* "I swear" • *So
help me, if he bothers me again, I'll
kill him!;* I swear, if he bothers me
again, I'll kill him!

"So what!" *exclam.* This is an
exclamation of indifference • *He
didn't like the gift I gave him? So
what!;* He didn't like the gift I gave
him? I don't care!
♦ SYNONYM: **"Big deal!"** *exclam.* •
Big deal if she's always late!; I don't
care if she's always late!

soak (to) *v.* to overcharge • *They really
soak you at that restaurant;* They
really overcharge at that restaurant.
♦ SYNONYM: **to take someone** *exp.* •
1. to overcharge • *How much did they
take you for?;* How much did they
cheat you out of? • **2.** to con • *The
swindler took him for all his money;*
The swindler conned him out of all
his money.

sponge off someone (to) *exp.* to
borrow money from someone • *He
always sponges off me;* He always
borrows money from me.
♦ SYNONYM: **to hit someone up** *exp.*
to ask to borrow money from
someone • *He hit me up for $200;* He
asked me if he could borrow $200.

**stay up till all hours of the
night (to)** *exp.* to remain awake
until early in the morning • *I'm
exhausted! Last night, I stayed up till
all hours of the night;* I'm exhausted!
Last night, I stayed awake until early
in the morning.
♦ NOTE: The term *"till"* is a popular
abbreviation of "until."
♦ SYNONYM: **to pull an all-nighter**
exp. to stay awake all night
(extremely popular among students) •
*I pulled an all-nighter in order to
study for the test today;* I stayed
awake all night in order to study for
the test today.

stiff a waiter (to) *exp.* not to leave a
tip for a waiter • *That waiter is so
unpleasant, I bet he always gets
stiffed;* That waiter is so unpleasant, I
bet he never gets a tip.

stink (to) *v.* to be extremely
unsatisfactory • (lit); to smell badly •
This whole situation stinks!; This
whole situation is extremely
unsatisfactory!
♦ SYNONYM (1): **to suck** *v.* • *The
service here sucks!;* The service here
is extremely unsatisfactory!
♦ SYNONYM (2): **to bite** *v.* • *This
situation bites!;* This situation is
terrible!
♦ NOTE: When used to mean *"to be
extremely unsatisfactory,"* the verbs
"to suck" and *"to bite"* take on
vulgar connotations and should,
therefore, be used with discretion.
The verb *"to stink,"* however, is not
vulgar.

stone sober *exp.* completely sober •
*Of course I can drive. I'm stone
sober!;* Of course I can drive. I'm
thoroughly sober!
♦ SYNONYM: **to be cold sober** *exp.*

stop in (to) *exp.* to enter for a brief
stay • *He stopped in to say hello and
lingered for three hours!;* He entered

for a brief stay and lingered for three hours!

stop on a dime (to) *exp.* to stop suddenly • *It's a good thing I was able to stop on a dime when the little girl jumped in front of my car;* It's a good thing I was able to stop suddenly when the little girl jumped in front of my car.

strip down (to) *exp.* to undress • *She stripped down to nothing!;* She undressed until she was wearing nothing!
♦ ALSO (1): **to strip** *v.* • *When I got my physical examination, the doctor made me strip;* When I got my physical examination, the doctor made me undress.
♦ ALSO (2): **stripper** *n.* man or woman who performs in a nightclub while undressing and dancing • *She's a stripper?!;* She's a performer who undresses in a nightclub?
♦ ALSO (3): **striptease** *n.* sexually provocative performance of one or more people who undress while dancing • *She does striptease at night;* She does sexually provocative performances of undressing and dancing at night.
♦ ALSO (4): **strip joint** *n.* night club that features striptease acts.

strut one's stuff (to) *exp.* to show off one's body.
♦ SYNONYM: **to let it all hang out** *exp.* to wear skimpy clothing in order to show off one's body • *She lets it all hang out;* She shows off her body.

stuff one's face (to) *exp.* to eat heartily • *We really stuffed our faces at the party;* We really overate at the party.
♦ SYNONYM: **to chow down** *exp.* • *I'm getting hungry. Wanna go chow down?;* I'm getting hungry. Do you want to go eat?

stuff *n.* **1.** junk • *How can you expect me to eat this stuff?;* How can you expect me to eat this junk? • **2.** merchandise in general • *Look at all this great stuff!;* Look at all this great merchandise! • **3.** possessions • *Don't touch that! That's my stuff!;* Don't touch that! Those are my possessions! • **4.** actions (of a person) • *Can you believe the stuff he did to me?;* Can you believe the things he did to me? • **5.** nonsense • *She actually believed that stuff he told her;* She actually believed that nonsense he told her.

stuff *n.* **1.** merchandise in general • *Look at all this great stuff!;* Look at all this great merchandise! • **2.** possessions • *Don't touch that! That's my stuff!;* Don't touch that! Those are my possessions! • **3.** junk • *How can you expect me to eat this stuff?;* How can you expect me to eat this junk? • **4.** actions (of a person) • *Can you believe the stuff he did to me?;* Can you believe the actions he did to me? • **5.** nonsense • *She actually believed that stuff he told her;* She actually believed that nonsense he told her.
♦ NOTE: You may have noticed that you've already encountered this word in lesson two where it was used to mean "junk." It is important to use it here as well since its definition of "merchandise in general" is also extremely popular.

sucker *n.* **1.** a general term for any object or person • *What a beautiful necklace! This sucker must have cost a fortune!* • *He's been training for years. That sucker can really box!* • **2. an extremely gullible person** • *You believed everything she told you? What a sucker!;* You believed everything she told you? What a gullible person you are!
♦ SYNONYM: **baby** *n.* • *This baby must have cost a fortune!*

sweat like a pig (to) *exp.* to perspire profusely • *I sweat like a pig when I work out;* • I perspire profusely when I work out.

-T-

take a spin (to) *exp.* to take a short excursion in a car • (lit); to take a twirl (around the block, the neighborhood, etc.) • *Want to take a spin in my new car? Hop in!;* Want to take a quick excursion in my car? Come in!
❱ NOTE: It is extremely common to use the verbs *"to hop"* and *"to jump"* literally meaning "to leap or bound," when referring to entering a car.

take off (to) *exp.* to leave • *We'd better take off now if we don't want to be late;* We'd better leave now if we don't want to be late.
❱ NOTE: This expression literally refers to the departure of an aircraft but is commonly used colloquially when referring to the departure of a person.
❱ SYNONYM: **to split** *v.* • *We'd better split if we don't want to be late;* We'd better leave if we don't want to be late.

take off *exp.* to leave (said of airplanes) • *We'd better take off or we're gonna be late;* We'd better leave or we're going to be late.
❱ SYNONYM: **to beat it** *exp.* • *You'd better beat it before she comes back!;* You'd better leave before she comes back.

take one's mind off something (to) *exp.* to remove one's thoughts from a certain subject • *Let's go to the movies. It'll take your mind off your troubles;* Let's go to the movies. It'll remove your thoughts from your troubles.

"Talk about a(n)…" *exclam.* "That was a real…" • *Talk about a funny movie!;* That was a real funny movie! • *Talk about an idiot!;* That person is a real idiot!

teacher's pet *exp.* the teacher's favorite student • *She never gets in trouble for not doing her homework because she's the teacher's pet;* She never gets in trouble for not doing her homework because she's the teacher's favorite.

thanks *exp.* a very common abbreviation of *"thank you."*
❱ NOTE: This abbreviation should only be used in an informal setting since it implies familiarity and comfort between the speakers.

ticked off *exp.* angry • *That really ticks me off;* That really makes me angry.
❱ ALSO: **to be ticked** *exp.* to be angry • *I'm really ticked;* I'm really angry.

tip someone off (to) *exp.* to inform someone • *"How did you discover that she was the burglar?" "One of the neighbors tipped me off";* "How did you discover that she was the burglar?" "One of the neighbors informed me."

too rich for my blood *exp.* expensive • *This restaurant is too rich for my blood;* This restaurant is too expensive for me.
❱ SYNONYM: **pricey** *adj.* • *That's very pricey;* That's very expensive.

total (to) *v.* to destroy completely • *His car was totalled in the accident;* His car was completely destroyed in the accident.
❱ SYNONYM: **to trash** *v.* **1.** to destroy completely • (lit); to reduce something to a state ready for the trash • *She trashed her new bicycle;* She ruined her new bicycle • **2.** to

criticize unmercifully • *I can't believe how she trashed him!;* I can't believe how she criticized him so severely!

totally sure *exclam.* incredulous • *She got elected president of the school? I'm totally sure!;* She got elected president of the school? I don't believe it!

trash someone (to) *exp.* **1.** to criticize someone unmercifully • *I didn't come here to have you trash me!;* I didn't come here to have you criticize me so unmercifully! • **2.** to destroy something • *My brother borrowed my car and trashed it;* My brother borrowed my car and destroyed it.
♦ SYNONYM: **to rake someone over the coals** *exp.* • *His mother raked him over the coals;* His mother criticized him unmercifully.

tube *n.* television • *All he does is sit watching the tube all day;* All he does is sit watching the television all day.
♦ NOTE: The noun *"tube"* actually refers to the "picture tube" but is popularly used to refer to the television set itself.
♦ SYNONYM: **boob tube** *exp.*
⇨ NOTE: The noun *"boob"* is a slang term for "idiot" since it is said that those who sit endlessly in front of the television set will become mindless.

turn in (to) *exp.* to go to bed • *It's getting late. I think I'll turn in;* It's getting late. I think I'll go to bed.
♦ SYNONYM: **to hit the hay** *exp.* • *It's time to hit the hay!;* It's time to go to bed!

turn on (to be a) *exp.* (said of someone or something) to be sexually exciting.
♦ ALSO: **to turn on** *exp.* to excite sexually • *He turns me on;* He excites me.

-U-

"Uh, oh!" *exclam.* expression signifying sudden displeasure or panic • *Uh, oh! What did I do with my car keys?*
♦ SYNONYM: **"Yike!"** *exclam.* • *Yike! What was that?!*
⇨ ALSO: **"Yikes!"**

unable to stand someone or something (to be) *exp.* to be unable to tolerate someone or something • *I just can't stand it anymore!;* I just can't tolerate it anymore!
♦ SYNONYM: **to be unable to handle someone or something** *exp.* • *I can't handle doing homework anymore;* I can't tolerate doing homework anymore.
♦ ANTONYM: **to take someone or something** *exp. I can usually only take her for an hour;* I can usually only tolerate her for an hour.

-W-

what's-her-face *exp.* [pronounced: *what's-'er-face*] This expression is commonly used as a replacement for a woman's name when the speaker can not remember it.
♦ SYNONYM: **what's-her-name** *exp.* [pronounced: *what's-'er-name*]
♦ NOTE: The common replacement for a man's name is *"what's-his-face"* [pronounced: *what's-'is-face*] or *"what's-his-name"* [pronounced: *what's-'is-name*] whereas for an object, it would be *"what-cha-macallit"* ("what you may call it") i.e. *Give me that what-cha-macallit;* Give me that thing.

up to something *exp.* **1.** in the process of doing something • *What are you up to?;* What are you in the process of doing? • **2.** in the process

of doing something suspicious • *Hey! What are you up to?!;* Hey! What kind of sneaky thing are you doing? • **3.** to be in the mood • *Are you up to going to the movies?;* Are you in the mood to go to the movies? • **4.** to be healthy enough to do something • *Are you up to walking to the store after your surgery?;* Are you healthy enough to walk to the store after your surgery?
♦ NOTE: The difference in connotation between **1.** and **2.** depends on the inflection and intent of the speaker.

wash it down (to) *exp.* **1.** to drink in order to make something unpalatable go down easier • *I need some water to wash this hamburger down;* I need some water to make this hamburger go down easier. • **2.** to follow up a meal with either more food or drink • *Let's order dessert to wash it all down;* Let's order dessert to follow up the meal.

"We're talkin'..." *exp.* "I mean…"
♦ NOTE: This expression is used to add emphasis to a statement by modifying the adjective or phrase that follows: *She's weird! We're talkin', from another planet!;* She's weird! I mean, from another planet! Since this expression must begin a sentence, it would be incorrect to say, *"She's we're talkin' weird!"* Also, notice that in this expression, the abbreviated form of *"talking"* is always used.

"What do you say..." *exp.* "What do you think about the idea of …" • *What do you say we go to the movies tonight?;* What do you think about the idea of going to the movies tonight?

"What's eating you?" *exp.* "What's the matter with you?"
♦ SYNONYM: **"What's with you?"** *exp.*

"What's going on?" *exp.* "What's happening?"
♦ SYNONYM: **"What's up?"** *exp.*

"What's up?" *exp.* "What's happening?"
♦ SYNONYM: **"What's new?"** *exp.*
♦ NOTE: The expression *"What's up?"* is very casual and is therefore only used with good friends. It would not be considered good form to use this expression when speaking with someone with whom you have strictly a business relationship. Of course, if he/she has become a friend through your dealings, it would certainly be acceptable. Although the expression *"What's new?"* is also very casual, it does not have the same degree of familiarity as does, *"What's up?"* and may be used when addressing just about anyone except perhaps dignitaries, royalty, etc. In this case, it is usually a good idea to avoid using slang entirely, being an informal style of communication. Once again, *you* must be the judge in determining whether or not using slang is appropriate in a given situation.

"What's up?" *exp.* "What's happening?"
♦ SYNONYM (1): **"What's going down?"** *exp.*
♦ SYNONYM (2): **"What's shakin'?"** *exp.*
⇨ NOTE: The contracted form of the verb "shaking" is commonly used in this popular expression.

"What's with you?" *exp.* (very popular) "What's bothering you?"
♦ SYNONYM: **"What's eating you?"** *exp.*

"When hell freezes over" *exp.* "Absolutely never" • *"When do you suppose he'll graduate from college?" "When hell freezes over";* "When do you suppose he'll graduate from college?" "Absolutely never!"

white lie *exp.* harmless untruth used to avoid confrontation • *I didn't feel like going into work today, so I told the boss I was sick. It was just a little white lie;* I didn't feel like going into work today so I told the boss I was sick. It was just a little harmless untruth.

"Whoa!" *exclam.* exclamation of surprise and amazement • *You passed the test? Whoa!*

wimp *n.* weakling • *He'll never take control. He's such a wimp;* He'll never take control. He's such a weakling.

window-shop (to) *exp.* to look in store windows without making any purchases • *Since I don't have any money, I can only window-shop;* Since I don't have any money, I can only look in the store windows without making any purchases.

wiped out *exp.* exhausted • *I need to rest. I'm wiped out;* I need to rest. I'm exhausted.
  ♦ VARIATION: **wiped** *adj.* • *I'm going to bed. I'm wiped;* I'm going to bed. I'm exhausted.
  ♦ SYNONYM: **to be pooped** *exp.* • *I'm pooped!;* I'm exhausted.
    ⇨ NOTE: Occasionally, you may hear the outdated expression *"to be too pooped to pop"* used *only* in jest.
  ♦ NOTE: **to wipe out** *v.* (surfer slang) to fall off one's surfboard.

"Wow!" *exclam.* exclamation denoting surprise or disbelief • *Wow! That's a beautiful car!*
  ♦ SYNONYM: **"Geez! (or "Jeez!")** *exclam.* • *Geez! What an idiot!*
    ⇨ NOTE: *"Geez!"* is a euphemism for *"Jesus Christ!"*

wuss *n.* weakling • *Don't be such a wuss. Just ask him for a raise!;* Don't be such a coward. Just ask him for a raise!
  ♦ ALSO: **wussy** *adj.* cowardly, spineless • *I've never seen anyone so wussy before;* I've never seen anyone so spineless before.

-Y-

yeah *adv.* (informal and extremely popular) yes • *Yeah, I know her;* Yes, I know her.
  ♦ SYNONYMS: **yep/yup/uh,huh** *adv.* (informal) • *"Are you coming right back?" "Yep/Yup/Uh,huh";* "Are you coming right back?" "Yes."

"You can say *that* again!" *exclam.* "That's very true!"
  ♦ NOTE: In this expression, it is important to stress the word *"that."*
  ♦ SYNONYM: **"I'll say!"** *exp.*
    ⇨ NOTE: In this expression, it is important to stress the contraction *"I'll."*

"You said it!" *exclam.* "I agree!"
  ♦ SYNONYM: **"You got it!"** *exclam.*

"Yuck!" *exclam.* used to signify great displeasure.
  ♦ SYNONYM: **Ew!** *exclam.* • *Ew! What is this stuff?*
  ♦ NOTE: **Pew!** *exclam.* used to signify displeasure upon smelling a foul odor.

-Z-

zoned *adj.* dazed and senseless, oblivious • *I'm zoned today because I only got two hours of sleep last night;* I'm oblivious today because I only got two hours of sleep last night.
  ♦ SYNONYM: **out of it** *exp.* • *I feel out of it today;* I feel oblivious today.

Current Titles from OPTIMA BOOKS

Check our web page for more information, or write for catalog
www.optimabooks.com

American English	Book	Cassette
STREET TALK-1	$16.95	$12.50
How to Speak and Understand American Slang		
STREET TALK-2	$16.95	$12.50
Slang Used in Popular American Television Shows		
STREET TALK-3	$18.95	$12.50
The Best of American Idioms		
BIZ TALK-1	$16.95	$12.50
American Business Slang & Jargon		
(general office • finance • meetings & negotiations •		
business travel • "computerese" • marketing & advertising)		
BIZ TALK-2	$16.95	$12.50
More American Business Slang & Jargon		
(general business slang and jargon • international trade •		
more computer slang • management • "bureaucratese" • politics)		
Robert Takes Over	$18.95	
An Interactive Intermediate Reading and Grammar Text		
THE DICTIONARY OF ESSENTIAL AMERICAN SLANG	$12.95	
A Dictionary of Only the Most Important Words		
and Phrases for Students of American English		
Ya Gotta Know It!	$21.95	$12.50
A Conversational Approach to American Slang		
for the ESL Classroom		
STREET TALK DICTIONARY	$21.95	
Popular American Slang Terms, Jargon, Idioms, and Expressions		
BLEEP! (Second Edition)	$18.95	$12.50
A Guide to Popular American Obscenities		

German		
STREET GERMAN-1	$16.95	$12.50
The Best of German Idioms		

OPTIMA BOOKS
2820 Eighth Street
Berkeley, CA 94710
order on-line at www.optimabooks.com
email: esl@optimabooks.com

Toll Free: Phone 1-877-710-2196
FAX 1-800-515-8737

Outside US: Phone 1-510-848-8708
FAX 1-510-848-8737

SAN 299-7460

Name _____

Shipping Address _____

City _____ State/Province _____ Postal Code _____

Country _____ Phone _____

Quantity	Title	Book or Audio?	Price Each	Total Price

Total for Merchandise
Sales Tax (California Residents Only)
Shipping (See Below)
ORDER TOTAL

METHOD OF PAYMENT (check one)

☐ Check or Money Order   ☐ VISA   ☐ Master Card   ☐ American Express   ☐ Discover
(Money orders and personal checks must be in US funds and drawn on a US bank.)

Credit Card Number: Card Expires:

Name on card (please print)

SHIPPING

Domestic orders shipped ground UPS or USPS Priority Mail (delivery 5-7 days) Add $5 for the first item, $1 for each additional item. (For UPS rush service or shipment by FEDEX or DHL, please call, FAX or email for rates)

Overseas Surface (not recommended, delivery time 6-8 weeks) Add $6 for the first item, $2 for each additional.

Overseas Airmail (delivery 4-7 days) Shipping charges based on weight, see below.
(1 book ~ 1.2 lb, 1 cassette ~ 0.2 lb.)

ST1

package weight in pounds (round up to nearest pound)	1 lb.	2	3	4	5	6	7	8
Mexico, Cental/South America	$6	8	11	14	17	20	23	28
Canada	$6	7	8	9	12	14	15	16
Great Britain/Europe	$8	13	18	23	28	33	36	42
Pacific Rim (Japan, Korea, Taiwan, Australia, etc)	$10	18	25	32	40	47	54	62